THE GARDEN

OF

HOPES

AND

DREAMS

Barbara Hannay writes women's fiction, with over twelve million books sold worldwide. Her novels set in Australia have been translated into twenty-six languages, and she has won the Romance Writers of America's RITA award and been shortlisted five times. Two of Barbara's novels have also won the Romance Writers of Australia's Romantic Book of the Year award.

Barbara lives in Townsville with her writer husband and enjoys being close to the Coral Sea, the stunning tropical scenery and colourful characters, all of which find their way into her popular stories.

barbarahannay.com

ALSO BY BARBARA HANNAY

BARBARA HANNAY

THE GARDEN OF HOPES AND DREAMS

MICHAEL JOSEPH
an imprint of
PENGUIN BOOKS

MICHAEL JOSEPH

UK | USA | Canada | Ireland | Australia
India | New Zealand | South Africa | China

Michael Joseph is part of the Penguin Random House group of companies
whose addresses can be found at global.penguinrandomhouse.com

Penguin
Random House
Australia

First published by Michael Joseph in 2021

Cover images: bees © In Art/Shutterstock.com; watering can © Sky vectors/
Shutterstock.com; plant on left © momo sama/Shutterstock.com;
other plants © Giuseppe_R/Shutterstock.com
Cover design by Louisa Maggio © Penguin Random House Australia Pty Ltd
Typeset in Sabon by Midland Typesetters, Australia

Printed and bound in Australia by Griffin Press, part of Ovato, an accredited
ISO AS/NZS 14001 Environmental Management Systems printer

A catalogue record for this
book is available from the
National Library of Australia

ISBN 978 1 76089 941 7

penguin.com.au

For the generations of gardeners in my family

No white nor red was ever seen
So am'rous as this lovely green.
'The Garden' by Andrew Marvell

What is a weed? A plant whose virtues
have not yet been discovered.
Ralph Waldo Emerson

PROLOGUE

She is coming, my dove, my dear;
She is coming, my life, my fate;
'Come into the Garden, Maud'
by Alfred, Lord Tennyson

Kent, England, 1969

The ominous question came out of the blue.

'So, no one's told you about the farm?'

Vera frowned as she turned from the oval mirror where she'd been checking her wedding gown before adding a final touch of lipstick. 'Told me what?'

Now Pandora, the youngest and prettiest of Vera's five bridesmaids, looked worried, as if she realised that she might have made a huge gaffe.

'What are you talking about?' Vera demanded, unnerved and more than a little annoyed. She'd only invited the fifteen-year-old to be her bridesmaid after everyone insisted it was de rigueur to include the bridegroom's young sister in the wedding party.

'Oh . . .' Pandora gave an awkward shrug accompanied by a flap of her hands and an embarrassed giggle. 'It's nothing. Silly slip. Sorry.'

Vera wanted to insist that the girl answer. If there was a problem with Felix's farm, she needed to know, but her mother rushed in at that moment, her mushroom pink satin gown rustling as she leaned forward to drop an air kiss in the vicinity of Vera's cheek.

'I'm heading off to the church now, darling. Michael's coming with me, of course, and your father is ready and waiting with Benson and the Rolls.' Straightening, Vera's mother gave a brief nod to Pandora. 'Hello, dear, you look lovely. I assume all the bridesmaids are ready?'

'Oh, yes, Lady Glenbrook. I just popped in to let Vera know we're all ready and waiting.'

'Wonderful. Everything's in order then. Now, Vera, let me look at you.' Taking a step back, Vera's mother narrowed her gaze as she ran a practised eye over the dress, the train, the heirloom diamond and pearl necklace. At last, she smiled. 'Claude has done very well with your hair, hasn't he? How's that tiara sitting with your veil? Are you quite comfortable?'

'Yes, thanks, Mother.'

'You look beautiful, darling.'

'You do too.'

'Nonsense. I look old and matronly. Thank heavens I can wear these long gloves to cover my arms.'

Like Vera, who had preferred to manage this day without the assistance of a maid, Lady Glenbrook cherished an independent streak and loved to spend hours in her extensive gardens, getting herself sunburned and dirty and scratched, despite having an army of groundsmen. Now, she gently touched a gloved hand to Vera's cheek. 'I'm enormously proud of you today.'

Vera smiled. She did feel quite beautiful, which was a relief, given how important it was for a bride to look her best on her big day. And it helped to know how pleased and relieved her parents were that she'd found herself a suitable husband.

Felix Challinor might have been the second son of an earl, rather than the heir, but at least he wasn't a starving artist or an actor like

Vera's previous boyfriends. Felix was tall and handsome, was indisputably charming and he actually had a chin, which, in aristocratic circles, was always a bonus. He was perhaps a little too fond of betting at the racetrack, but he could afford this indulgence, and at least he didn't drink too much or take drugs.

Vera's father seemed happy enough with Felix's prospects. Her parents had certainly gone to no end of effort and expense when it came to the lavish wedding banquet to be held right here at Glenbrook House.

Vera's smile wavered now, however, when she realised that Pandora had slipped out of the room, which meant she wouldn't be able to quiz the girl further about her cryptic question.

So, no one's told you about the farm?

Surely, a bride's wedding day was the very worst time to suddenly pose a disturbing question about the bridegroom's property?

Trying not to worry, Vera frantically backtracked through her seemingly innocuous conversation with Pandora. They'd agreed that this day was lovely: warm and sunny and simply perfect for a spring wedding. Pandora had offered polite compliments about the beautiful gardens and grounds of Glenbrook House, and Vera had agreed that she'd never seen her family estate looking prettier, with the lawns so smooth and green and the huge urns on the terraces overflowing with colour, the roses on the arches in full bloom, and the clematis and honeysuckle flowering over the ancient walls.

Just thinking about the home that she'd loved and was about to leave, Vera had felt a little nostalgic and she had cheered herself by remarking that she was very much looking forward to the lovely garden at Felix's farm in Devon. At which point, Pandora had stared back at her in blank dismay.

So, no one's told you about the farm?

'All right then.' Vera's mother was back at the doorway now, and she flashed another smile as she prepared to leave. 'I'll let your father know that he can come and collect you, shall I?'

Vera almost called, *No, wait for a moment, please.*

She was desperate to know if her mother had heard any news about Felix's property, but how could she voice such an awkward question at the eleventh hour? Already, the wedding guests would be filing into the church, the organist would be playing 'Sheep May Safely Graze', and Vera's grandmother, having been escorted to the front pew, would be sitting stiff-backed, gazing stoically at the rose window above the altar, and no doubt remembering all the funerals she'd attended in that very same church.

And Felix would be waiting.

Perplexing as Pandora's question had been, it couldn't be anything serious, surely? Felix would have told Vera if it was. Most likely, it was a simple case of Pandora enjoying a small tease. The girl had giggled, after all.

Perhaps Pandora had simply meant that the garden was a bit of a mess, but that wouldn't bother Vera. With a little advice from her mother she would enjoy knocking it into shape.

Telling herself she was overreacting, she bit back the questions tingling on her tongue, and she nodded instead. 'Yes,' she told her mother. 'I'm ready.'

She would have to trust Felix. As brides had done throughout history, she had to have faith that all would be well.

Really, what choice did she have?

CHAPTER ONE

New feet within my garden go –
New fingers stir the sod –
'New Feet Within My Garden Go'
by Emily Dickinson

Just five minutes before Maddie learned that her boyfriend was two-timing her, she bought a pot plant. It had been sitting in a shop window, rather like the dog in the famous song, but instead of a waggly tail, the plant had eye-catching, healthy green leaves splashed with showy bright splotches of pink.

Maddie had been wandering through an arcade during her lunch break and when she passed the florist, she knew immediately that this plant in its trendy grey stone pot would be perfect for her apartment, lending a touch of glamour to the rather quiet decor. She was always on the lookout for ways to enhance her living space. Mainly to impress Simon, of course.

Mind you, most of Simon's visits happened late at night, after they'd been to a party or to dinner somewhere, and by then the lights in Maddie's apartment were mostly out and Simon's attention was focused entirely between the sheets. Not that she was ever going to mind about that.

'Set this philodendron near a window if you can,' the florist told Maddie. 'Some place where it will get natural light.'

Maddie suggested that the big window in her living room should be fine.

The woman frowned as she considered this. 'Morning or afternoon sun?'

'Morning.'

'Sounds perfect then.' Now she offered Maddie a beaming smile that gave her a pleasing boost of confidence. 'And with our premium potting mix you should only need to water this once a week.'

That sounded pretty foolproof. Maddie had little firsthand experience with plants, even though her parents were keen gardeners. Actually, slightly obsessed gardeners would be a more accurate label for her mum and dad, but to Maddie, gardening was a hobby for oldies. She'd been trying to make her own mark since she'd moved away from the family cane farm to the city.

But indoor plants were clearly trendy, and maybe a few of those green-thumb genes had passed down to her. As Maddie headed back to the office, with the show-off plant in her arms, she was feeling rather upbeat. Until she passed a café and saw a sight that almost felled her.

Later, she couldn't quite remember how the couple sitting in the farthest corner had caught her attention. After all, the café was crowded and they were quite a distance away, but Simon's hair was a very particular shade of gold and when it came to her boyfriend, Maddie's internal radar was very finely tuned.

At work, she always seemed to know when Simon had entered the office, even before she actually saw him or heard his voice. She supposed that tingle of awareness was a natural extension of being deeply in love. Simon was the most devastatingly handsome man Maddie had ever met, *and* he was a partner in the same law firm where she was a humble paralegal. Becoming his girlfriend had caused something of a scandal in the office, especially as he was quite a bit older than Maddie, but for her, it had been living proof that Cinderella fairytales could happen in real life.

Of course, Maddie was aware that Simon sometimes lunched with clients, so she wouldn't have come to a lurching halt if he'd been dining with a woman who needed his professional help. Reflecting on the situation later, Maddie liked to think she would have remained admirably calm if Simon had been reaching across the table and clasping the hand of an anonymous client.

The source of Simon's obvious enchantment, however, was Ruby Reid, the ridiculously pretty lawyer who had joined their firm just a month ago. Ruby had long auburn hair and the kind of fine boned and lissom delicacy that made any normal girl feel enormous. And now, as Ruby and Simon shared soppy smiles, the glow on their faces was blinding.

It was the worst moment for Maddie to remember the lame excuse Simon had texted last night to cancel their plans to see a movie. Now, flinching at that memory, Maddie made a catastrophic situation ten times worse by dropping the pot plant!

Stupid of her, but the sight of Simon flashing Ruby the adoring smile that was supposed to be hers alone had, quite literally, made her lose her grip. Her hands simply let go and her knees almost gave way as well.

The lovely pot made a loud cracking sound as it hit the arcade's floor, spilling premium potting mix all over the classic terrazzo, and leaving shoppers to glare sulkily at Maddie, or send her pitying smiles as they skirted around the mess she'd made.

So embarrassing. A disaster.

'Sorry,' she said to no one in particular. 'I'm so sorry.' But she had no idea how she was going to clean the mess up. There were no dustpans and brooms in sight. Would she have to kneel down and use her bare hands?

Unfortunately, she was also painfully aware, out of the corner of her eye, that customers inside the café were looking her way. Including Simon.

She didn't imagine it. She knew Simon had seen her, although he instantly snatched his gaze away and paid her absolutely no attention whatsoever. Which made it painfully clear that he didn't want to acknowledge her presence and he certainly had no plans to leap into hero mode and rush to her aid.

More shattered than she could have believed possible, Maddie stared again at her mess. Should she ask at the shoe shop on the other side of the arcade for an empty box? And a broom? She was wondering if she could somehow piece together the broken pot when she heard a warm voice coming from behind her.

'Don't worry too much, love.'

It was a woman with a pop-up stall selling incense candles, patchwork tablecloths and cushion covers made from Indian saris. She had a round smiling face topped by a mop of silvery curls and was wearing a colourful embroidered kaftan that stood out among the rather conservative clothes of the city shoppers. 'The cleaners will see to that,' the woman told Maddie as she waved a dismissive hand towards the spilled soil. 'Here's a plastic bag for your poor pot plant.'

'Thank you.' Maddie accepted the bag gratefully. 'This is lovely of you,' she remembered to add as she stooped to rescue the broken pot and the battered, drooping plant. 'But are you sure about the mess?' She'd scooped as much dirt as she could manage into the bag, but there was still quite a lot on the floor. 'Won't we need to put a sign there or something?' Working in a legal office, Maddie was well aware of the danger of leaving such a hazard unmarked.

'Actually,' the woman said, as she registered Maddie's worried expression, 'if you could mind my stall for a tick, I'll fetch Reggie, the cleaner, and make sure he gets straight onto it. Don't panic, I'll be quick. You won't have to sell anything, just make sure none of my stuff walks.'

'Oh, that would be wonderful. Thank you.'

Maddie didn't like to mention that she was due back at work in five minutes. As the woman hurried away, she tried to keep simultaneous watch on both the stall and the dirt-strewn floor. It was quite a responsibility to make sure that no incense sticks or cushion covers were stolen, while also checking that no shoppers came to mishap. But this task also meant that Maddie had no chance to check out what was happening inside the café.

She was shocked to discover, on the stallholder's return, that Simon and Ruby had vanished, that they'd somehow managed to slip past her. The implications of this were gut-wrenchingly obvious. Simon couldn't care two hoots about her. Her boyfriend didn't even want to admit he knew her.

She was past tense. They were over.

Maddie knew it as clearly as if Simon had actually said the words. The fact that the guy was obviously a total prick was of no consolation whatsoever. Her heart was too busy breaking. She needed to run away and hide, to cry her eyes out. To stay away for a week if necessary.

What an idiot she was. She'd been obsessed with Simon Marten. And no, he wasn't her first boyfriend or anything lame like that. Of course, there had been other guys – her first teenage crush at high school and a range of different blokes at uni, some of them dreadful, others really quite nice. But when it came to looks, not one of them could have held a candle to Simon.

For five months he had been Maddie's. Five glorious months. And now she had to go back to work to face total humiliation.

Arrgh. Gossip ran like wildfire through the office, especially after a few drinks on Friday afternoons. Maddie was remembering the glee several staff members had taken in sharing every gory detail when Melissa on the third floor was dumped by her fiancé. Clients were treated with the utmost discretion, but it was a different matter for the staff.

Through tear-blurred eyes, she looked down at the pot plant she was nursing, saw the pink and green leaves poking from the bag and recalled how naïvely happy she'd been just a short time earlier when she'd bought it. Now she was tempted to dump the bloody thing in the nearest rubbish bin.

Why hadn't she known this would happen? How could she have hoped, even believed – foolishly, obviously – that the magic with Simon would last, that his flattery was genuine?

And why in hell's name had she blabbed to her parents about Simon when she'd gone home last Christmas? Her mum and dad had been quietly excited and although they were too careful to say as much, Maddie knew they'd been hugging the secret hope that they'd score a successful lawyer as their son-in-law. Now she couldn't bear to think of them struggling to cover their disappointment or sending her messages of caring sympathy when she confessed this news.

'Are you okay, love?' The stallholder had returned and was looking at her with genuine concern. 'Don't feel too bad. I'm sure you'll be able to save that lovely plant.'

Maddie blinked. 'Yes, of course. I'm okay, thanks. I'm fine.' She forced a smile, which felt very shaky, but she found herself saying, 'And before I go, I'd like to buy a couple of your lovely cushion covers.' At least, buying the covers provided a momentary distraction and was better than bawling. Maddie pointed to the brightest fabrics she could see with lovely beaded embroidery in coral and turquoise and mauve.

'Great choice,' the woman said, smiling broadly as Maddie tapped her card to the EFTPOS machine and her purchase was approved. 'I'm sure these will look perfect with your pretty plant.'

Maddie didn't really care how her apartment looked now that Simon wouldn't be there to see it, but she gave a small nod. 'Thanks again for your help.'

'No worries,' the woman said.

Offering her a scant wave, Maddie hurried away. She was going to be late back to work, but although she was normally conscientious, she couldn't bring herself to care. She hadn't known it was possible to feel so gutted. She would have liked to head straight for home, to the anonymity of an apartment block where conversation between residents was limited to the weather, or a grumble about the slow speed of the lift.

When she spied a rubbish bin, she lifted the bag to its gaping mouth, but then, at the last moment, she couldn't quite bring herself to throw the plant away. It was a living thing, after all, not quite at the level of a kitten or a puppy, but still . . .

Problem was, she had been planning to take it back to the office and let it grace her desk for the rest of the afternoon, but that was out of the question now. Apart from the inevitable questions and awkward explanations, the very thought of Simon or Ruby seeing it in its sad current state was just too embarrassing to bear.

As she hurried back to work, aware that she was late and would draw even more attention, she decided to stash the plant and her cushion covers with one of the mailroom guys. They were always friendly and not nearly as gossipy as the rest of the staff.

But by the time Maddie reached the office, she had a horrible suspicion that the sorry news was already out. There was no sign of Simon or Ruby, but that wasn't unusual. Lawyers spent most of their days behind closed doors. Maddie only had to see the cautious smile from the receptionist though to fear that everyone already knew about the dropped pot plant and the dropped girlfriend.

When, Lisa, a fellow paralegal came in, her studied avoidance of eye contact with Maddie was especially unsettling, and then, just before five, Lisa came back and stopped at Maddie's desk.

'Are you okay?' she asked gently.

Maddie could feel her face burning and she didn't dare look up. 'Sure,' she managed to say, while staring hard at her screen.

'I heard what happened.' Lisa leaned close, her voice just above a whisper. 'If you need to talk, or anything . . .'

Go away, Maddie wanted to scream. She was only just holding herself together and was desperate to get out of the office and home. Sympathy from a fellow worker would tear her apart. Lisa probably assumed that she and Simon were finished, but Maddie had decided she couldn't accept that finality until Simon actually told her so.

'Thanks,' she told Lisa as firmly as she could manage. 'But I'm fine.'

And then, as Lisa left, after offering another sickeningly sympathetic smile, a text pinged on Maddie's phone. A message from Simon.

Her heart banged in her chest. When they'd first started dating, he'd texted her all the time with cheeky little messages or plans for the evening. Lately, his communications had been sparse to say the least. Now, she felt a flurry of hope. It was all a silly mistake. Simon still wanted her. She tapped her screen.

Sorry.

Her heart sank to her stomach, but she was frowning too. Just one freaking word? Was that all he could offer? What a cop-out.

Quickly she texted back. *What exactly are you apologising for?* Simon was a lawyer. He should know better than to dodge the crucial heart of the matter.

The reply, when it came, was at least prompt. *I was planning to talk to you first.*

A flare of hurt and anger flamed inside Maddie now. Not good enough, Simon. If he was dumping her, he bloody well needed to be man enough to spit it out.

It took all of her remaining courage to text back. *Talk about??*

His answer was brutally quick. *About us breaking up.*

A chill seeped through Maddie then, freezing the blood flow in her veins, shrivelling her foolishly hopeful heart.

CHAPTER TWO

A weed is any plant that is out of place.

Anonymous

Vera told herself she was trying to make the best of it. She knew she probably hadn't really tried to meet people, but on the whole, she thought she'd made a fair fist of adjusting to city life, and if her decision to move to inner Brisbane had been completely voluntary, she might have been quite contented.

For the most part, she'd accepted her fate. As a widow, she had already been used to whole days of not talking to anyone and eating meals on her own, and now she quite enjoyed the busyness of the city. Not the blaring of sirens at midnight, mind you, but the abundance of public transport was a blessing, especially for someone who'd lived in the bush for so long that the very thought of driving in city traffic was traumatising. But she was at least game enough, thank heavens, to drive her little Hyundai via back streets to her nearest suburban shopping centre.

Vera couldn't deny that having a multi-storey complex nearby was a bonus, and she had gallantly taken herself off to theatres and art galleries, drinking fancy coffee in any number of trendy little cafés. Also, as her son Archie had pointed out, Brisbane offered excellent medical facilities, a reminder Vera hadn't particularly enjoyed, but old age was a looming reality that couldn't be ignored.

Even so, the move from Jinda Station to Brisbane had been far harder than Vera had expected. After spending almost all of her married life in loose cotton blouses and faded denim jeans, with her hair left to grow long and piled into an untidy topknot, she'd actually found it a chore to shop for dresses and skirts and stylish trousers. She'd made the effort, however, along with regular trips to the hairdresser where her snow-white locks were now styled and blow dried.

It was during a trip to the hairdresser, actually, that Vera had read in a magazine about nail polish options for ageing hands. The suggestion of a nude tone with a hint of mauve had appealed. She couldn't remember the last time she'd worn nail polish – back in the sixties, perhaps? These days her poor old nails had unattractive ridges, but she'd decided to give it a try. And yes, she had known there were salons in her neighbourhood's shopping centre, where expert nail stylists were ready to offer a long list of services, but her independent spirit had deemed that as going a step too far.

Which was how Vera found herself, on a Saturday morning in late April, perched on a stool at her kitchen bench and attempting to paint her nails. It was exactly the wrong moment for her phone to ring, but she received so very few calls these days, and she'd never been comfortable with ignoring her phone's summons.

What a bother it was, though, trying to skewer the little brush back into the bottle before picking up her small mobile phone, without any time to read on the display who was calling, while simultaneously trying not to spoil the still damp polish.

'Hello?' She probably sounded a little snappier than she'd intended.

'Hello. How are you? It's Brooke here.'

'Oh?' This was a surprise. A huge one. 'How are you, Brooke?' Vera so rarely heard from her daughter-in-law that she couldn't help a sudden stab of worry that something had happened to Archie. Not an accident, surely? Was he ill? 'Is everything all right?'

'All good,' came Brooke's breezy response. 'I'm downstairs, actually. In Brisbane for the day. The girls have a netball carnival and I've just dropped them off. I have Henry with me. I thought we might pop up to see you.'

'Are you here? Downstairs at Riverview Place?'

'Yes,' came the surprising reply.

Vera slumped a little with shock. She'd left Jinda under a cloud of tension, and since then she and Brooke hadn't really been speaking. There'd never been a face-to-face row – Archie had worked hard as mediator – but there'd been a definite stand-off.

Certainly, there'd been very little correspondence from Brooke. No real bridge building. The odd email or text with a photo of the children, and then a card and a carefully selected gift at Christmas – Vera had been terribly hurt when she hadn't been invited back to Jinda for any Christmas or birthday celebrations. Any important communication had come via Archie.

Now, Vera sent a quick glance around her apartment. Everything was in order. Well, it would be, wouldn't it? She was the only occupant and she didn't like to mess things up. And anyway, she shouldn't be worrying about tidiness. It would be wonderful to see Henry.

Just the same, she would have appreciated advance warning of visitors, especially her daughter-in-law. She might have chosen her clothes more carefully and put on a little lipstick, and she would have made scones, or a date loaf. Actually, no, she was a city woman now, so she most likely would have bought something fancy from the little cake shop in the Toowong Village shopping centre.

'Is that okay?' she heard Brooke ask. 'Are you free?'

'Yes, of course.' And then, with more enthusiasm. 'Lovely!'

Vera hurried to the small panel on the wall by the front door and as she pressed the switch that would open the doorway below, she noticed she'd botched the polish on her forefinger. Darn it. 'There,' she said into the intercom. 'I've let you in.'

Blowing on her nails, in case others were still damp, she opened her apartment's front door and experienced an unexpected prickling of excitement as she stood waiting for the lift to arrive on her floor. She wondered how tall Henry had grown. He was sure to have changed in subtle ways.

'Gran!' The boy came bursting out of the lift as soon as the doors opened, his skinny arms wide, his dear face split by a grin of such obvious delight, as he ran down the hallway, that Vera felt a prickling of tears. And then Henry was clasping her around the middle and burying his face into her chest as he hugged her tight, and although she was overjoyed, she also wondered how on earth she had earned such exuberant affection.

'Hey, there.' Her voice was a little shaky and breathless as Henry released her. 'My goodness, how lovely to see you. And you've grown, haven't you? Look, you're almost up to my shoulder.'

Henry was a thin boy of eight with his mother's straight black hair, his father's clear light-blue eyes and a dimple in his chin. Vera's breathing stopped for a split second as she remembered the exact same dint in her husband Felix's chin.

'Hello.' Brooke's smile, as she kissed Vera's cheek, was unexpected.

'This is a nice surprise,' Vera responded. 'How is everyone?'

'Oh, we're all fine, thanks.'

'Did you drive down?' Jinda was five hours away. Surely, they hadn't been driving all night.

'Yes, we came down yesterday. We're staying in a hotel at South Bank.'

This was a small kick in the teeth. Vera couldn't help herself. 'You know I have two spare bedrooms?'

'I know,' Brooke said, and she *did* look apologetic. 'But it's a lot of trouble for you for just a couple of nights, and the rest of the team are staying at the hotel.'

The others didn't have relatives in Brisbane, Vera supposed, but then, to cover any possible awkwardness, she manufactured a smile. 'Come on in. I'll put the kettle on.'

Morning sunlight was streaming through the big picture windows in the living room, catching the colours in Vera's carefully chosen accessories and paintings.

'Oh, you've made yourself very at home, haven't you?' Brooke said, letting her gaze traverse the lovingly selected antiques in the lounge room, then settle on the silver-framed photo of her own three children, positioned in pride of place on the sideboard.

'I suppose I have.' Vera shrugged. Despite being on the top floor, with three bedrooms, two bathrooms and a generous living area, she was still trying to adjust to this apartment. She'd spent almost four decades in a classic, rambling Queenslander homestead with tongue-and-groove timber walls and an iron roof surrounded by wrap-around verandahs four metres deep. And even later, in the cottage on Jinda, she'd always had a garden.

'I like your pot plants.'

Brooke was trying. Vera would give her that.

'Well, yes,' she said. 'I needed a little greenery.'

'They look good.'

'Thanks. How's the garden at Jinda?'

'Oh.' Brooke's shrug was accompanied by an exasperated eye-roll. 'I'm so busy. You wouldn't believe all the netball training the girls have now. I hardly have time for anything else.'

Vera hoped her smile was sufficiently sympathetic. Quickly she turned her attention to her grandson. 'What about you, Henry? You play soccer, don't you?'

Henry shook his head and his mouth twisted into an awkward

grimace that might have been an attempt at an apologetic smile. Vera thought he looked a little worried.

'He's given soccer away. He never really tried.' His mother spoke so dismissively that Vera felt her hackles rise.

If Henry hadn't tried at soccer, it probably meant he wasn't interested, or perhaps he'd been intimidated by all the fuss over his older sisters' prowess at netball. She couldn't help feeling sorry for the boy. He'd moved away from them to the window and was peering down into the street, no doubt trying to ignore the current conversation.

Perhaps it was just as well that the kettle came to the boil at that moment. Vera might have felt compelled to make a comment that would sink her even lower in her daughter-in-law's estimation.

'Tea or coffee?' she asked as she set mugs on the bench.

Instead of answering, Brooke pulled out her phone and frowned. She was still frowning when she looked up. 'Just checking the time,' she said. 'Keeping an eye on the meter. I had to park a block away, but that's the city for you.'

'Yes, I'm afraid it's always busy around here.' Vera decided she would make tea. 'I do have a visitor spot in our car park,' she said as she swilled scalding water from the kettle into the pot. 'I would have offered it if I'd known you were coming.'

'No, it's okay, I can't stay long. The girls' first game will start soon.' Brooke glanced at her phone again. 'Actually —' She paused and had the grace to look apologetic. 'I was wondering if you'd mind – if I could leave Henry here. With you.'

Vera wasn't quick enough to cover her gasp of surprise. But at least she now understood the real reason for this visit. It wasn't so Brooke could complain about Archie, thank heavens. Vera was exceedingly grateful for that. But it was a mere matter of convenience. She was required as a babysitter.

'I hope that's okay,' Brooke said, eyeing Vera cautiously. 'I suppose I should have checked if you're busy. Did you have anything planned?'

Vera would have liked to play the martyr at this point and suggest she'd had a string of engagements lined up – a hairdressing appointment, a meeting with her book club friends for lunch and a late afternoon game of bridge – but of course she would be prepared to cancel them for Brooke at the drop of a hat. Actually, the sad truth was she still hadn't joined a book club or any other kind of club since she'd arrived in the city, but she might have invented such a list, if Henry hadn't been listening.

'No,' she said instead, with just a teensy touch of ice. 'Nothing important.' She looked to Henry, who was still at the window and apparently fascinated by something in the street below, but no doubt also listening very carefully to his mother's and grandmother's every word.

Her heart swelled with love for the boy. She'd missed him so much – much more than she'd expected to. She'd missed his sisters, Sienna and Emily, too, but they'd been born just eleven months apart and they'd always had each other for company, while Henry, whose birth Vera knew had been unplanned, had always been like a little shadow trailing after his sisters. *Wait for me . . .*

Such a vulnerable, earnest, sweet little boy.

'I'd love it if Henry stayed here for the day,' Vera said and she meant it, even though she was sadly conscious of the limited entertainment options that a seventy-year-old woman could offer an eight-year-old boy.

'It's just that he gets so bored at netball.'

Vera could well imagine. She'd seen Brooke on the sidelines of the netball courts in Jindabilla, totally absorbed in her daughters' every move, cheering madly and yelling instructions or advice, ready with water bottles and orange quarters and even more advice at half-time.

Remembering this, Vera decided she would take Henry to Toowong Village. Henry could have a special treat at her favourite café and he could ride the escalator, as well as the lift with walls of see-through glass. A tame enough pastime, perhaps, but it would be something quite different for a boy from the bush.

Vera remembered when she was a child, living in Kent, and how she'd loved visiting her relatives in London. She'd found taking the Underground quite thrilling.

'I'd better go then,' said Brooke. She was already heading for the door as she called back to her son, 'Bye, Henry. Have a lovely day with Gran.'

CHAPTER THREE

Maddie would have liked to spend Saturday morning in bed, nursing her hangover and feeling desperately sorry for herself. She had been so sure she'd never have to go through this kind of pain again – a pain so deep she feared she might never climb out of it.

It didn't help that yesterday had been a sickening replay of the Very Worst Night of her life – at the high school formal, when her partner had been Jackson Evans, football star, brainiac, house captain and generally recognised hottest guy in Year 12.

Maddie's girlfriends had been emerald with envy when Jackson had chosen her as his date for the formal. When she and Jackson had pulled up at the steps of the Bundaberg School of Arts in a silver Audi that Jackson's parents had hired, Maddie had felt like a movie star arriving at the Oscars.

Everything had gone swiftly downhill, though, when Jackson, the total jerk, abandoned Maddie almost as soon as the official photographs were taken. Her moment of glory fizzled to a night of wallflower agony. And when her girlfriends *kindly* reported that Jackson was pashing Kristin Gable in the shrubbery behind the hall,

Maddie was reduced to making an excruciating, tearful phone call to her poor dad to come and rescue her.

Afterwards, Jackson had made absolutely no attempt to explain or apologise for his behaviour and, in time, Maddie had consoled herself that most high-school kids had to go through that kind of crap.

But it cut much deeper now, in her mid-twenties, to know that history could so cruelly and heartlessly repeat its bloody self.

Maddie had adored Simon. Last night she'd dragged herself through the misery of endlessly tracking back through the past months, digging up the signs she should surely have recognised as obvious clues that their relationship was on shaky ground.

Simon had probably lost interest weeks ago, she realised now. She should have twigged as soon as he'd stopped sending her those sweet and cheeky texts that he'd wowed her with in their early weeks of dating. And lately, there'd been those times when he'd left her guessing until the weekend was almost upon them before he'd asked her out. He'd even made fun of her a few times, and she'd felt quite foolish. But not as bloody foolish as she felt right now.

God, she was an idiot.

And last night, to make everything a thousand times worse, she'd found a whole host of messages from her workmates on her phone. Not just from the girls in the office, but also a couple of pseudo-sympathetic texts from male lawyers! Of course, she'd known they were all secretly enjoying a juicy gossip fest and she'd simply deleted them without bothering to respond.

Unfortunately, she also hadn't bothered to pull her curtains closed, and now a clear and sunny autumn morning blazed outside, searing her eyeballs and seeming to mock her.

Everyone else in Brisbane would be out there in that sunshine, doing all manner of fun things, but all Maddie wanted to do was to haul the sheets over her head and hide.

Annoyingly, she remembered the plant she'd bought, now wilting rather sadly in her cupboard-sized laundry. Too bad. She would let it die, along with her relationship, a fitting symbol of her failures. To keep it would be too painful, a constant reminder of the New Worst Day of her life.

But damn it . . .

Her conscience niggled.

Letting such a lovely plant just wither away and die was rather pathetic and even a bit cruel, wasn't it? Not a crime exactly. Plants didn't have faces or souls, and Maddie was fairly sure they didn't have feelings. But still . . .

Rolling onto her back, she reluctantly inched the sheet back away from her face and squinted at the bright morning light. She contemplated dragging herself out of bed and buying a new pot to replace the broken one. Given how depressed she felt, the simple task would be a monumental act of heroism.

Maddie sat up, wincing as a sharp pain shot through her skull, but at the same time, she was also conscious of a tiny flicker of fighting spirit. Fuck Simon. Why should she let him ruin a perfectly good weekend?

Of course, she would buy a new pot and rescue her plant. She would be the Florence Nightingale of pot plants, or Joan of Arc, or Greta Thunberg – someone heroic at any rate. And she wouldn't just opt for the limited pot choices that the local supermarket offered. Why not try somewhere that specialised in gardening gear?

Maddie had no idea where the nearest nursery might be, but after taking aspirin and showering and washing her hair, she felt slightly more normal, and a check of her phone showed that The Happy Garden Centre was located in a nearby suburb. The round trip shouldn't take her more than an hour, tops, and then she could retreat back to the relative safety of her apartment.

'Okay, little guy,' she told the wilting plant in her laundry tub. 'Let's see what we can do for you.'

Entering via a lush green courtyard that opened into the garden centre's massive display was a totally new experience for Maddie. And the wealth of variety on offer was jaw-dropping.

She'd come to replace a simple grey ceramic pot, but now she faced shelves and shelves ranging metres high and carrying a massive array of pots in every shape, size and colour and in every material from terracotta, ceramic and plastic to corrugated iron and timber. And plants absolutely everywhere! Rows and rows of them lining tiered wire racks or suspended overhead in hanging baskets. Ferns and palms, flowers and herbs, fruit trees and vegetables. It was all quite amazing.

As a book lover, Maddie had always been conscious of a special thrill whenever she'd walked into a library and found herself surrounded by shelves and walls lined with books. Now, she supposed gardeners must feel a similar lift to their spirits when they came here. She actually felt a little that way herself, even though she was nursing a broken heart and only owned one sad and slightly damaged plant.

'Well, hello!' boomed a cheery voice from behind her.

Maddie froze. She didn't recognise the male voice, but she was terrified it belonged to someone from her work. *Damn.* She'd been hoping for at least one entire weekend to nurse her wounds in private.

'It's our neighbour, isn't it?' the voice said next.

Okay, so it wasn't a workmate, and when Maddie cautiously turned, she discovered two guys she recognised as living in her apartment block.

She offered them a careful smile. They were probably in their late thirties, and they had moved in about six months earlier. She knew extraordinarily little about them, though. The residents

in their building weren't given to socialising with each other. Given
Maddie's obsession with Simon, she'd never really minded.

This pair had introduced themselves on arrival and she remembered they were called Joe and Dennis. She was pretty sure they were
a couple, but that was the sum total of her knowledge. And, unfortunately, despite emerging this morning on her pot-buying mission,
she still wasn't in the mood to be sociable.

'So, you're a gardener too?' asked Joe, who was tall, ginger
headed and wore glasses.

'Oh, no.' Maddie was compelled to be honest. 'I only own one
poor little plant and I managed to break its pot before I even got it
home.'

As she made this confession, she noticed Joe and Dennis's loaded
trolley. Goodness, they were buying three different kinds of ferns, a
collection of gorgeous white ceramic pots and a massive bag of potting mix – platinum grade, no less. 'Looks like you guys know what
you're doing.'

'Oh, we love our greenery.' It was Dennis who spoke now. He
was a good deal shorter and rounder than Joe and he was beaming
broadly at Maddie. He might have resembled a garden gnome if he
hadn't kept his balding sandy hair and beard so closely trimmed.
'We love this garden centre,' he enthused. 'We seem to end up here
almost every weekend.'

'Really?' Despite her current desire for solitude, Maddie couldn't
help but be intrigued. 'But don't you have trouble growing plants in
an apartment?'

'Not really,' said Dennis. 'Not when we have those big windows
offering so much natural light. We have plants everywhere.'

'Mind you,' added Joe, 'neither of us minds living in a jungle.'

'A jungle in an apartment? Wow.' Maddie, fretting over her soli-
tary, partly crushed plant, couldn't begin to imagine having greenery
everywhere.

'Joe even bought me a compost bin for my birthday,' Dennis said next, and Maddie thought he couldn't have looked more excited if Joe had gifted him a Ferrari or a holiday to Europe.

'Where do you keep your compost bin?' she couldn't help asking, while trying not to look amused. 'Does it fit on your balcony?'

Dennis seemed appalled by the very thought. 'There's space up on the roof. We've got permission from Body Corporate to use it. And, actually, I'm going to put a sign up in the mail room inviting all the residents to put their food scraps up there.'

Their enthusiasm was so infectious, Maddie found that she was smiling, something she hadn't thought possible when she'd left home. 'Sounds like a great idea. I've never been up to the roof, but I guess we can all do our little bit to help save the planet.'

'Exactly,' said Joe.

'And you should pop in sometime to see our plants,' added Dennis. 'We're forever rearranging, so we're still setting things up, of course, but we'd be happy to show you what we've done.'

'Oh, well, thanks,' Maddie said with slightly less enthusiasm, aware that it was time to retreat.

'Are you free later today?' Dennis asked next, after exchanging a quick glance with Joe. 'Say, around five?'

'Ah . . .' This was unexpected. Maddie had planned to spend another evening alone, starting quite early, drinking far too much wine, eating way too many slices of pizza, and bawling her eyes out over soppy chick flicks.

Of course, she would have preferred to spend the evening pouring her heart out to a girlfriend bearing cake and vino, but since she'd started dating Simon she'd pretty much lost touch with her uni mates, and workmates weren't an option this evening.

She wasn't sure what to say, but these guys were so friendly and she never liked to be impolite. Bonus, they knew nothing about her private life. 'Thanks,' she said quickly, before she had time for doubts. 'That would be lovely.'

After all, while she'd been tempted to spend another night moping, that would amount to a win for Simon, wouldn't it? He'd be having fun with beautiful Ruby, after all, and if nothing else, this invitation from her neighbours offered another useful distraction.

'Come and have a drink with us,' chipped in Joe. 'Bring a friend if you like.'

'That's exceedingly kind of you.' Maddie couldn't believe she'd weakened so quickly. 'I probably won't bring a friend, but I could bring a bottle of wine.'

'Perfect.' They were both grinning. 'See you later then.'

And before she had time for second thoughts, or to come up with a last-minute excuse, they were off, pushing their trolley to the checkout.

CHAPTER FOUR

Henry wasn't quite as overjoyed about riding up the shopping centre's elevator or down the glass-walled lift as Vera had hoped he might be. He was growing up, of course. She could remember, back when he was three, he'd been thrilled by anything mechanical, and almost hysterical with excitement whenever his father allowed him to ride along on the tractor or the quad bike. Even as a seven-year-old, just before Vera had left for the city, Henry had been over the moon whenever the massive road trains had arrived at Jinda to transport their cattle.

Now the boy was eight and his interest in moving parts lingered, but he had no desire to make endless repeat trips on the escalator, as Vera had anticipated. He was happy enough to ride up and down sedately like any seasoned city shopper. However, he *was* seriously impressed by the sheer size of the three-storeyed shopping centre and quite excited to dine on toasted ham and cheese sandwiches and a strawberry milkshake in a cleverly designed café that hung suspended over the shoppers below.

Vera supposed she shouldn't have been surprised that what most excited Henry today was a toy store. Not a conventional toy store, mind you – there wasn't a cuddly toy in sight – but one with a host of different kinds of puzzles and what Vera tended to think of as 'instructional' toys. Then again, Henry was growing into a rather serious boy. She might have worried about this, if he hadn't reminded her so much of her brother, Michael. Goodness, she hated to think how many years it had been since she'd seen Michael. She missed him terribly.

'Let me buy you something,' she said, her heart melting as she watched Henry's eyes widen with excitement as they entered the toy store.

'Really?' It was obvious that the boy couldn't quite believe her.

'Yes. Why not?' After all, Vera decided, his sisters had always scored the lion's share of their mother's attention and if he was being dumped on her for the day, she was quite within her rights to spoil him as she saw fit.

Selecting the perfect gift took a little time, but that was fine. They had all day and Vera could forego her siesta for once. Henry hovered for some time over a microscope, but in the end, he settled for some sort of boxed set with tracks that he could construct to roll marbles up and down and around.

After this was paid for and placed in a large brown paper bag with strong string handles for an overjoyed Henry to carry, Vera went to the supermarket and bought a packet of little jam tarts for afternoon tea. Sienna and Emily were bound to be ravenous when they finished their netball games. She almost threw a leg of lamb in the trolley, thinking how much fun it would be to have a proper roast dinner with all the trimmings when Brooke and the girls finished their big day.

But would Brooke see that as going a little overboard? It could be hard trying to second-guess her daughter-in-law's reaction.

Playing it safe, Vera swapped the lamb leg for the ingredients for a shepherd's pie, which she knew was a family favourite. The children had always called it Gran's pie, and Archie had confided that their mother never made it quite the way she did.

Vera bought Granny Smith apples and cream as well. She would make a crumble for dessert and they could all have a lovely evening meal together.

Back at the apartment, she was eager to get on with the cooking, but Henry, of course, wanted to unpack his new game.

Oh, dear. Vera was expecting his mother and sisters back soon and she could imagine Brooke's frown and possible scolding if the living room was littered with scattered marbles and pieces of Henry's track. She supposed she could send him off to a spare bed-room, but that seemed antisocial.

'Don't you think you should save that game till you get home?' she suggested. 'That big verandah off your bedroom will be the per-fect place to set it up.'

The boy's lower lip drooped, and Vera frantically tried to think of something else to keep him entertained while she was busy in the kitchen. The jam tarts helped. Vera set two of these on a plate for Henry with a glass of lemonade.

They were downed in no time, however, and she wondered if she should put the television on. But she could picture another of his mother's exaggerated eye-rolls if she returned and found the boy sprawled on the carpet in front of the telly.

'Would you like to take the lift down to the mail room?' Vera asked, reaching for the little key that dangled from a row of hooks on her kitchen wall. 'I forgot to check my mailbox this morning. Here you are. Take the key and my box is number 12. Do you think you can remember that?'

'Of course,' said Henry. 'It's the same as the number on your front door.'

'That's right. Good boy. Just go down and come straight back again, mind. Don't go out on the street.'

'No, Gran.'

Henry went off happily and Vera was warmed by a cheering inner buzz as she busied herself with chopping onions and carrots. She was looking forward to dishing up shepherd's pie and apple crumble, just as she had countless times at Jinda, and for once she wouldn't be dining alone. For the first time in ages, she felt needed.

CHAPTER FIVE

When Maddie knocked on Joe and Dennis's door late in the afternoon, she was feeling several degrees better. Not happier, perhaps, but definitely stronger in spirit. She'd bought a bag of potting mix at The Happy Garden Centre and had chosen a lovely round watermelon-pink pot for her plant. The colour enhanced the pink splashes on the plant's leaves, and after watching a short how-to video on YouTube, she had carefully transferred it to its new home, before setting it in a corner of her living room next to the sofa.

Thanks to this small touch and the colourful new cushion covers made from gorgeous Indian saris, her living space now looked much brighter, even a little exotic. The atmosphere was improved even further when Maddie removed a photo of Simon from the bookcase and replaced it with a vase that she would fill with bright flowers just as soon as she had a chance.

On her way up to Joe and Dennis's apartment, which was two floors above hers, she shared the lift with a small boy she'd never seen before. He had an appealing face with bright, intelligent blue eyes, framed by straight black hair, and he seemed particularly interested in the nicely chilled bottle of white wine that she carried, along with a box of crackers and a beetroot dip – a homemade dip, no less, the making of which had provided Maddie with another useful distraction.

'Are you going to a party?' the boy asked her.

'Well, yes, sort of,' she said, wondering if inspecting your neighbours' greenery counted as a party.

'It must be fun living in an apartment block with a lift and everything.' The boy sounded a little wistful as he said this, and it occurred to Maddie that if they'd met earlier that morning, she might have felt compelled to warn him that living in an apartment block wasn't any more fun than living anywhere else. Life could be shitty wherever you lived.

Now, at least, she was feeling much less cruddy – thanks to neighbours who knew nothing about her heartache and had innocently extended an unexpected hand of friendship. In return, she was able to offer the boy a warm smile that would have been impossible when she'd woken that morning. 'It's pretty cool living here,' she agreed.

'I'm staying with my gran. Just for the day.'

'Lovely.' Maddie wondered if his grandmother was the rather snobby woman on the top floor who spoke with a posh English accent.

'I'm Henry,' he said next.

'Hello, Henry. I'm Maddie.' She might have offered her hand, except that her arms were full. The lift pinged then, and the doors opened. 'Gotta go,' she said.

'Bye.' Before the doors closed again, Henry waved to her and his smile was so sweet she could almost feel a small corner of her embittered heart actually melt.

A moment later, Dennis was opening his front door. He was dressed in an amazing combo of purple shirt and mustard trousers that might have looked scary on anyone else, but somehow seemed perfect on him, and he was all beaming smiles, as if he too was delighted, even excited, to see Maddie.

Joe, dressed much more quietly in jeans and a loose grey T-shirt, appeared behind Dennis, waving to her over his shoulder.

'Come in,' they chorused in cheerful unison.

Dennis stepped back with an elaborate sweep of his arm to make way for Maddie. 'Oh, you shouldn't have gone to any trouble,' he added when he saw the goodies she carried. 'But how lovely of you.'

Maddie followed the guys down a hallway that was pretty much a mirror of her own, but when she entered the main living area, the difference was huge. They truly had created a green oasis.

Most of the furnishings were in neutral tones, but they had set up a clever shelf system across the big main living-room windows and these were home to all kinds of plants – some spiky and upright, others dainty and trailing, while feathery ferns sat happily next to plants with round shiny leaves.

The kitchen was exactly like Maddie's, with the same white cupboards and pale terracotta floor tiles, the same faux timber benchtops where she set down her wine and dip, but that was where the similarity ended. Here, pots of herbs lined the windowsill, and again near a tall window, baskets of herbs and other greenery hung at varying heights. Then, leaning against the wall beside the pantry cupboard, a stepladder held yet more plants, while beyond, on the small balcony, shrubs filled tubs and there was even a lemon tree in a shiny metal bin.

'And these are my favourite little guys,' said Dennis, as he showed Maddie into an immaculate bathroom where a small shelf over the window held a row of various tiny cacti in little pots shaped like owls.

'They're adorable,' Maddie told him, and she meant it. 'The whole place is absolutely amazing.' In fact, she'd been oohing and aahing from the moment she'd walked in, and she wasn't even a proper plant lover.

They returned to the kitchen where Joe had set out wine glasses and a platter of lovely cheeses. Maddie took the lid off her dip. 'It's beetroot hummus,' she said, hoping this was acceptable.

'Ooh, lovely.' Joe clapped his hands. 'How did you know we're vegetarian?'

'Um . . .' Maddie hadn't had a clue. She'd simply chosen vegetarian as a safer option, given that she hardly knew them. But now she smiled and gave a little shrug. 'Feminine intuition?'

As she said this, she realised that in certain circles, such a coy response might be interpreted as flirting, which for her, usually involved a certain amount of tension, not always pleasurable. Today, though, she could relax.

It was a relief to know that she didn't have to worry about fancying Dennis or Joe, or competing with them, or even wondering what they might think about her looks. She felt totally comfortable, safe in the knowledge that they weren't judging her sex appeal or sizing up her dating potential. That she could just be herself, without trying to be clever or sexy or witty.

'Should we sit outside on the balcony?' asked Joe. Somehow, despite the pots and plants, they'd managed to fit a round wrought-iron table out there, with comfy canvas director's chairs for seating.

'Why not?' The balcony would be a novelty for Maddie. Her apartment was on the first floor, just above the garages, and she hardly used her little front patio.

Outside, it was pleasantly cool, almost nippy, and they could look down into the area of parkland on the other side of the street.

Dennis poured wine. 'Take a seat,' he said. 'Make yourself comfortable.'

They sat, clinked glasses. 'Here's to greenery!' As Maddie made this toast, she marvelled at the way her day had transformed. From the deepest pit of despair to —

'Plants cheer us up,' Dennis was saying as he lifted his glass to his lips.

'And calm us down,' added Joe with a wink.

Maddie nodded. 'I suspect there might be some truth in that.' She was feeling rather smug about the way her one small planting expedition had helped her today.

Dennis sampled a cracker piled with a rosy dollop of dip. 'This is divine,' he said with his mouth half full.

'You're looking a bit better,' Joe said next.

'Better?' Maddie supposed this was possible. She'd been battling that hangover when she'd seen them this morning.

'Sorry. Wrong word choice,' said Joe. 'I meant you're looking happier.'

'Oh.' So, they'd known, even though she'd been trying so hard to keep her smile in place at the garden centre.

Now she nodded. Joe was dead right. It was a lovely evening, she was feeling heaps better and she was incredibly grateful to both of them for being so damn nice to her. But without warning, and to her absolute horror, her mouth pulled out of shape and her eyes filled with tears.

'Oh, sweetheart,' said Dennis.

Maddie gave a fierce shake of her head. 'No, no. It's okay. I'm okay. Truly.' Except that she wasn't.

The pain of losing Simon was still there, deep and raw and bleeding, and she knew she'd been fooling herself if she'd thought, for a moment, that she might get off lightly after such a hurtful shock.

A moment later, an embarrassing, gulping sob broke from her. 'I'm sorry,' she wailed, and she just managed to set her glass on the table before she was overtaken by an explosion of messy tears.

CHAPTER SIX

It was only as Vera turned the heat down on the simmering pot of mince, vegetables and herbs that she realised Henry had been gone rather longer than was necessary for a simple trip to the mailbox and back. She hadn't checked the time before he left, but surely he should have returned by now.

She tried not to panic as she made another quick check of the simmering pot, then snatched up her door key and hurried out to wait for the lift. But although she tried to stay calm, she found herself praying hard as the lift slowly ascended to her floor.

Please let the doors open to reveal Henry. He couldn't have wandered off, surely? He was such a sensible little fellow.

But when the lift reached her level and the doors sighed open, there was no one inside. And now Vera was drenched by real panic. Where on earth could Henry be? She'd told him not to go outside the building.

She'd been confident that the boy could be trusted, but now she chastised herself for letting him go anywhere on his own. He was only eight, for heaven's sake, an innocent country lad whose mother had entrusted him into her care.

Vera's imagination went into overdrive as she took the lift downwards. By the time it reached the ground floor, she'd come up with all manner of horrors – kidnapping, child molestation, murder.

Now she prayed that she would find her grandson lingering in the mail room, chatting with one of the residents perhaps, or checking out the numbers on all the letterboxes, or reading every single message on the noticeboard. Despite these hopes, she felt quite sick as she stepped out into the empty blue-tiled foyer. Her stomach was churning, her heart flapping like a trapped bird in a cage.

The mail room was through a door to the right, and Vera was feeling so faint, she had only just enough strength to push the heavy door open and peer timidly but hopefully inside. Just as she'd feared, the room was empty.

Vera's letterbox was closed and the key was gone, but that didn't really tell her anything. In despair, she rushed back into the foyer and out through the automatic sliding glass doors to the street. Frantically, she scanned up and down the footpaths on both sides, but there was no sign anywhere of a small, dark-haired boy.

Oh, God. Poor little Henry. Vera hated the thought of calling the police, but what choice did she have? She hadn't brought her phone, though, so she would have to go back up to her apartment first.

She was shaking as she re-entered the lift, and she wouldn't have minded if there'd been other people in there who saw how upset she was. At least she could have shared her terror and there was always a chance that someone else might have seen Henry.

But sadly, the lift was empty again. Most of the residents were probably busy getting ready to spend Saturday night out on the town, having fun. As the lift climbed upwards once more, Vera caught a glimpse of her face in the mirror. White cheeks, red eyed, ancient and haggard. None of which mattered if Henry was lost.

Closing her eyes, she tried to pray, but no words would come to her now. Her mind was too numb with fear.

Once again, the doors slid open and, on shaky legs, Vera stepped out and turned. And nearly fell over when she saw Henry standing outside her door.

'Gran!'

'H–henry.' She could scarcely hear her voice above her hammering heart. 'Where —' She had to pause and lean against the wall in the hallway while she caught her breath. 'Where have you been?'

'Where have *you* been?' Henry demanded, looking quite put out. 'I've been knocking and knocking.'

'But I've been downstairs looking for you.'

'Oh.' Now he looked a little shamefaced.

'Where were you, Henry?'

'I went up those stairs.' He was pointing to the short flight of stairs that led up to the roof, a disused space that Vera had only ever visited once and then ignored.

'But you must have been up there for such a long time,' she said, trying not to imagine how close the boy might have come to leaning over the edge, in danger of falling, or coming to some other misfortune.

'I was talking to Ned,' Henry said, as if the reason for his delay was perfectly excusable.

Vera was vaguely aware of Ned Marlowe, another resident on the top floor. He was a youngish chap, probably in his mid-to-late thirties, although she could never really tell young people's ages these days.

A tall man, Ned had rather shaggy dark hair and intense grey eyes. A university person, of some sort. Dr Marlowe, according to an item of his mail that had been mistakenly put in Vera's letterbox.

'Was Ned up on the roof?' Vera asked in surprise.

'Yes, he showed me his worms. They're huge.'

'His what?' Vera gasped as fresh horror gripped her now.

'His worms. They're in a box. It's so cool, Gran. It's a worm farm.'

'Ah.' Vera breathed a little more easily at the thought of an entire worm farm, but she still wasn't quite sure what to make of this. 'Perhaps you'd better show them to me too,' she said. 'Just so I'm in the know.'

'Sure.' Henry's eyes were shining as he took Vera's hand and gave it a tug. 'It's great. Come on, it's just up these stairs.'

There were only about four or five stairs to a door, and an autumn wind greeted them as Vera pushed the door open and stepped out onto the concrete roof. The wind was so brisk she wished she'd thrown on a cardigan, but the walls around the edge of the roof were higher than she'd remembered, so that was reassuring.

In the gathering dusk, the flat rooftop was bare apart from air conditioning units and a couple of waste bins, plus a few gardening tools leaning against a concrete walled storage room, presumably used by the maintenance men. Ned Marlowe was no longer to be seen.

'The worms are over here,' called Henry, running ahead towards a small tier of rectangular black plastic bins on legs that had been positioned against another of the storage room walls.

And of course, the boy had been absolutely right. This was indeed a worm farm with layers of composting food and, in the dark earth beneath damp sheets of newspaper, a myriad of wriggling, healthy worms. A sight a small boy would almost certainly adore.

'Well, well,' said Vera, breathing a deep sigh of relief. 'That's very clever of Ned to set up something like that here, isn't it?'

Henry nodded, his eyes huge and shining with delight. 'The worms are stupendous.'

'But a worm farm is a strange thing to have in an apartment block when there's no garden,' Vera mused.

'Ned said a couple of people here want to make a garden too.' Henry waved his arms to indicate the empty rooftop. 'Up here.'

'Really?' Vera looked about her. She supposed there was a fair amount of unused space, and when she looked more closely, there were a few empty rectangles edged by low concrete block walls that might have been designed as raised garden beds at some time in the past, but had obviously been neglected. It might be interesting to see if Ned Marlowe or others went ahead with this plan, but right now she remembered the dinner she'd left simmering on the stove.

She shivered. 'Let's get back inside,' she said as she helped Henry to replace the lid on the worms. 'It's getting late and cold, and your mother and sisters will be here at any minute.'

The shepherd's pie was in the oven and smelling rather delicious, and Vera and Henry were sitting on stools at the kitchen bench, rather companionably peeling apples, when the intercom unit on the wall buzzed, signalling Brooke and the girls' return.

'Would you like to press the button to let your sisters in?' Vera asked.

To her surprise Henry shook his head. He was concentrating on carefully peeling his apple. 'I want to see how long I can make this curl.'

Vera laughed. 'Oh, all right then.' And she was smiling as she went to the door. From there, she looked back into the apartment. She'd lit the lamps and drawn the curtains in the living room so that it had a welcoming glow.

The open plan design also allowed a view of the kitchen where an overhead light caught the gleam of Henry's dark hair as he bent, with all seriousness, over his task. She'd enjoyed his company so much today, the little worry over his disappearance only serving to deepen her love for him.

She knew she hadn't felt this happy or contented for a very long time, and tonight she would have the extra pleasure of Brooke,

Sienna and Emily all gathered around her dining table, enjoying their favourite 'Gran tucker', as Archie liked to call her cooking.

The lift arrived, spilling Brooke and the girls. The sisters were so close in age they were almost the same height and build, which also meant they could play in the same team, a lucky fluke that saved their mother too many extra trips into Jindabilla for training sessions. Sienna had inherited her mother's straight black hair, while Emily had Archie's blonde curls and now, still in their netball gear, with their hair tied back in bouncing ponytails, they looked flushed and excited, as they hurried down the hall to Vera.

'Hello,' she called, holding her arms out to greet them. 'Have you had a good day?'

'The best,' said Sienna, hugging her warmly. 'Our team almost won the tournament.'

'We were beaten in the very last match,' moaned Emily as she took her turn to give Vera a hug. 'By the Gold Coast. Twenty-five to thirty.'

'Ooh, close game. Must have been exciting. I'm sure you girls both played well.'

'They were stars,' claimed their beaming mother.

'Hello, there, Brooke.' Vera's smile was warm. 'Sounds like you've had a wonderful day too. Come on in.'

'Ooh, something smells great!' Emily exclaimed as soon as she was inside.

Sienna looked excited. 'Is it Gran's pie?'

'Yes, it is!' Vera was still smiling, delighted that they hadn't forgotten.

The girls clapped their hands, and she looked towards Henry who was still on the kitchen stool and proudly holding up his apple peel, but the others barely paid him any attention.

'Are you going to tell Gran your big news?' Brooke asked her daughters.

'We were selected to go to Melbourne.' Sienna's announcement was accompanied by a squeal of excitement.

'For a national camp,' joined in Emily.

'Both of them,' their mother added proudly.

'My goodness, isn't that wonderful?' Perhaps these girls would end up playing for the Australian Diamonds, after all, and fulfil their mother's fondest dream. Vera hoped she looked suitably impressed.

She gestured towards the kitchen. 'Well, we've had a lovely day too, haven't we, Henry?'

At last the newcomers turned their attention to the boy who was still smiling proudly and holding his lengthy apple peeling aloft.

'Has Gran got you working?' was all his mother said.

Vera saw Henry's smile fade and she felt her spine stiffen with annoyance. 'Henry's been a great help,' she replied defensively. 'And I think he might have just broken a world record for peeling an apple without breaking the curl.'

Finally, Brooke went over and kissed her son, commenting that he was a good boy, while Sienna and Emily discovered the brown paper carry bag from the shopping centre and demanded to know what it contained.

'You've been spoiling him,' Brooke commented as the girls exclaimed over the box of tracks.

Vera decided to shrug this off, continuing instead with her best hostess smile. 'Now, make yourself comfortable, Brooke. I'm sure you must be exhausted after such a big day. What would you like? A cup of tea? A glass of wine before dinner?'

Brooke frowned. 'Dinner? Were you expecting us to eat with you?'

'Of course. That's why there's a shepherd's pie in the oven.'

Brooke looked pained. 'Did you make that for us, Vera? Oh, that's sweet of you, but I'm afraid we've already arranged to have dinner at South Bank with the rest of the team.'

'Oh.' Vera wondered why on earth she hadn't expected this.

'Burgers at Grill'd,' said Brooke. 'The girls are so looking forward to it, aren't you girls?'

To their credit, Sienna and Emily looked torn, and Vera was sorely tempted to mention the apple crumble and cream.

'I'm sure you realise they hardly ever get to socialise with their friends or to eat out,' their mother added, as if to settle the matter.

'Yes, of course.' Vera knew it was ridiculous to feel so disappointed. After living through five decades littered with disillusionment, she liked to think she had toughened by now. She was certainly far too proud to bother reminding Brooke about the popular hamburger café in Jindabilla where young people loved to hang out.

'I don't even have time for a cuppa, really,' Brooke said next. 'These girls need to get back to the hotel for showers before dinner. I'm afraid we're going to have to love you and leave you.'

Vera was rather proud of the way she suppressed the biting comment that sprang to mind.

'You'll have to come too, Henry,' Brooke was calling. 'Come on now. Time to say goodbye to Gran.'

The boy looked as disappointed as Vera felt, a minor consolation. He even launched a small protest. 'But Gran's making her special pie.'

Bless you, sweetheart.

His mother merely frowned at him and flapped her hand in an impatient, beckoning gesture.

'You'll have to come and see me again,' Vera told him hopefully. 'And maybe you'll be able to stay a bit longer next time.' She shot a hopeful, questioning glance to Brooke. 'Perhaps I might help by minding Henry when Sienna and Emily go to Melbourne?'

'Oh, they'll be away for at least a week. You wouldn't want him *here* for that amount of time.'

'I wouldn't mind,' Vera said, surprising herself. She wasn't sure she could keep Henry happily entertained for a whole week, but she would have a darned good try.

But Brooke had obviously dismissed this as an impossible option. Almost certainly, if Archie was too busy, Brooke would leave Henry with her own mother, who lived in Jindabilla. And now, already, she was busily gathering her children and ushering them to the door.

A ghastly desolation swamped Vera, but she hoped it didn't show. 'Don't forget your new game, Henry,' she cried, hurrying to pick up his carrier bag.

'Thanks, Gran.' He gave her a lovely, extra tight hug that brought tears to her eyes.

Now, terrified that she might give her feelings away, Vera chose not to accompany the little family in the lift to the ground floor. After quick hugs and kisses, she closed her front door rather abruptly and drew several deep breaths. Looking over to the kitchen, she saw the apples awaiting her attention and let out a heavy sigh. She'd been so looking forward to having her grandchildren at her dining table, reliving old times, and enjoying what had been one of their favourite meals. Once upon a time . . .

Now, she supposed she would have to divide the pie into plastic containers and pile them into the freezer. Such an unappealing prospect.

Out of seemingly nowhere, Vera found herself remembering a story from her long-ago childhood, from the days when she'd been marched off to church each Sunday by her nanny. A Bible story about a fellow who'd prepared a great feast that no one wanted to attend.

Vera had always felt so sorry for the chap. In the end, he'd ordered his servant to go out into the highways and hedges to find people, anyone, really, to come and dine with him, so that his effort and generosity hadn't been wasted.

A bitter little laugh escaped her now, as she crossed to her living room, opened the sliding doors, and stepped out onto her balcony to survey the city street below. There was no sign of Brooke or the children.

Still, the view was nice. One of the reasons she and Archie had settled on this apartment was the outlook over the trees in the park across the road. So much better than staring into other buildings. Apparently, when Riverview Place had first been built, there'd been actual views of the Brisbane River, which was only a block away. Now the trees had grown, along with a forest of tower blocks, so there was no chance of seeing the water from here, but having the river close by was still a bonus.

If Henry ever visited her again, she would take him for a ride downriver on the CityCat ferry. He would love it.

Unfortunately, Vera knew there was little chance that Henry would be back in the near future. If his mother had her way, Henry would probably be old enough to take himself on the CityCat by the time he visited her again. And with that thought, a fresh wave of loneliness swept back, sinking into Vera with the bite of a winter westerly.

It didn't help that laughter drifted up to her from a balcony below. She almost didn't bother to lean out to see who was being so jovial, but curiosity got the better of her. And, as she did so, she saw a girl she recognised as a resident, sitting with the two chaps who shared an apartment on the third floor.

The trio were relaxed in white canvas director's chairs set amid a thriving collection of potted shrubbery. They were drinking wine and chatting happily, while the glow from the setting sun made their wine glasses sparkle and warmed the girl's shoulder-length chestnut hair to a burnished honey.

Vera told herself she was genuinely happy to see them enjoy-ing each other's company, and it was pathetic of her to even think of calling out to them and inviting them up to her place for supper.

Heavens, what a foolish idea. She would not only embarrass her neighbours but embarrass herself.

Why on earth would lively young people want to dine with an ancient old stick they didn't know, when her own family wasn't even interested?

CHAPTER SEVEN

Maddie was dreadfully embarrassed by her flood of tears. She couldn't imagine what poor Joe and Dennis must think of her, falling to pieces almost as soon as she'd walked through their doorway.

The annoying thing was, she'd thought she'd been managing pretty well today. She'd been immensely proud of the way she'd given Simon a mental 'up yours' and then distracted herself with commendable endeavours like shopping, gardening and cooking.

She'd felt quite composed and on top of things, until Joe had kindly enquired if she was all right. One minute she'd been relishing the comfortable sense of ease these new friends offered, the next she'd found herself reliving the soul-sickening scene from yesterday, with Simon in the café reaching out to lovingly caress Ruby Reid's hand.

The memory had been like falling off a cliff.

Maddie had been helpless. And of course, she'd wept buckets.

At first, her tears had come from the sheer pain of her loss, but then all the other horrors rolled in, crashing over her like dumping breakers, and she'd cried because she was such a hopeless bloody failure, and everyone in the office knew she wasn't pretty enough, or slim enough or, most importantly, *sexy* enough to hold onto such an impressively hot guy as Simon.

And on top of the despair over her own hopelessness, Maddie also wept because the man she'd loved with all of her being was so selfish and uncaring. A turd who couldn't even take the trouble to let her down gently.

Of course, at some point during this storm burst, while Maddie used up almost an entire box of Dennis and Joe's double strength tissues, she did realise that she was incredibly lucky to be offloading her woes onto such absolute darlings. She couldn't imagine any of her girlfriends being quite so patient or understanding.

Incredibly, she'd found herself telling these two guys, whom she'd barely spoken to until this morning, all about her disaster. The thrill of being Simon's 'chosen one', the glamour of the parties and dinners they'd attended. She'd even confessed about the warning signs of Simon's waning interest that she'd stubbornly refused to see, and the embarrassing detail that, okay, maybe she *had* been a little too needy at times.

Eventually, as her sob story finally finished, and her tears had reduced to an occasional sniffle, she offered profuse apologies.

'Don't worry,' Dennis said kindly. 'Both Joe and I have been through those darkest depths of misery.'

'Really?' Maddie knew it was totally self-absorbed of her, but could anyone else really have suffered her level of pain?

'Absolutely,' Joe agreed. 'We've both been deeply, deeply wounded by lovers we absolutely adored.'

'And we've lived to tell the tale,' added Dennis as he topped up their wine glasses.

'That's good to hear, I guess.' Although right now, despite the pleasant setting on their balcony, Maddie couldn't imagine ever feeling happy again.

'Dare I say it,' Joe said next, 'there's some merit in the old saying about getting straight back on the horse after a fall.'

Maddie gave an exaggerated shudder to express her distaste. 'God, no. Sorry, but I couldn't bear to even think about dating again.'

'Well, no, not this weekend.'

'Not for ages,' she insisted. Really, she couldn't bring herself to contemplate *ever* having another boyfriend. And while she knew deep down that she should be hating Simon the scumbag for the way he'd dumped her, she didn't *want* another boyfriend. The pathetic truth was, if she couldn't have Simon, she didn't want anyone.

Dennis was smiling as he watched her. 'Fair enough,' he said with an easy shrug. 'That's perfectly understandable, but I hope you're not going to hide away like a widow in sackcloth and ashes for ten years before venturing out again.'

Maddie gave a tired shrug. 'Maybe I am. Who knows?'

No one spoke for a bit after that, and she felt bad about putting such a dampener on what should have been a perfectly pleasant social occasion – her very first with this lovely pair. Gosh, she'd come here to talk about their pot plants and instead she'd just blubbered about herself. In an attempt to make amends, she passed the platter with the dip around.

Overhead, a small flock of birds swooped low before settling in treetops in the park across the road. Quite possibly the birds would spend the night there. Maddie realised it was getting dark. She should go soon.

'Anyway,' Dennis said as he scooped another helping of rosy hummus onto a cracker, 'for what it's worth, Joe and I are living proof of the "other fish in the sea" scenario.' His smile took on a wry tilt. 'Although in our case, I guess it was more like "other queers on the internet".'

'The internet?' Maddie repeated, frowning. 'Did you guys meet on a dating app?'

'Ah-huh,' said Dennis as Joe nodded.

'Wow.'

'Best move we ever made,' said Joe and they both shared a smile that was so dazzlingly happy, Maddie could do little but smile back at them. And wonder.

'Just putting the idea out there,' Joe said next, watching her.

Which was nice of them, but no thank you. Online dating was something Maddie had never considered. She hadn't even downloaded any of the apps. She'd heard too many horror stories from her girlfriends of dates with awful men and had steered clear. Call her old-fashioned, but she was much more comfortable with face-to-face, in the flesh, real-time meetings.

Then again . . . look where a face-to-face meeting had left her.

A chill wind rushed towards them. Joe drained his glass. 'Time to head indoors,' he said. 'How about I throw together a mushroom bolognese? You'll join us, won't you, Maddie?'

'Oh, no,' she cried, jumping to her feet. 'Thanks, guys, but I can't take up any more of your time. I've stayed far too long, belly-aching about my woes.'

'Don't be silly,' said Dennis. 'You can't go back to your flat tonight, all on your own.'

It was awfully sweet of them, but she was already feeling better for having shared her burden. That said, once alone again, she would probably sink back into moping and eating packet noodles in front of the telly.

'Come on,' said Joe, gathering plates and glasses as he rose from his seat. 'You can help. What are you like at chopping veggies?'

How could she reject such a kind offer? In no time, they were all inside the cosy, plant-filled apartment, with a huge pot of water simmering on the stove, Noah Cyrus singing on the sound system, while Maddie, seated on a kitchen stool, sliced mushrooms, Joe sautéed onions and garlic and Dennis turned on lamps and set the table.

The subject of Simon was dropped, thankfully. Another bottle of wine was opened, and the guys happily chatted about their plants and their compost bin, about their favourite books and the latest Netflix shows worth watching. Online dating, or any kind of dating for that matter, wasn't mentioned again.

But at some point, as Maddie tucked into delicious pasta smothered in a sauce rich with homegrown herbs, it did occur to her that if she *were* to meet someone online – in the far distant future – no one at work would ever need to know about it. And that had to be a major bonus, surely?

CHAPTER EIGHT

*Twilight drops her curtain down, and pins
it with a star.*
Lucy Maud Montgomery

Jinda Station, 2017

Dusk was stretching soft fingers over the western Queensland plains as Vera finished watering her veggie patch. It was a time of day she had always loved, when the sun lost its sting, the birds winged their way homewards and the sky turned a gentle mix of mauves and greys. Vera had always thought there were lessons to be learned from the peace that came with the day gently letting go.

This evening, as she turned off the hose, she noticed that the tap had a small leak and the nasturtiums at its base were reaping the benefit. The humble blossoms were a riot of colour glowing even brighter gold and orange than usual in the last of the day's light. Such a cheerful sight.

At least, these days, the water was coming from the farm dam and not from precious house tanks, as it had for many years after she and Felix had first moved to Jinda. No doubt the tap needed a new washer. At least she had learned to tackle small jobs like that for herself.

She picked a handful of cherry tomatoes before heading inside, and then a few garlic chives to toss into the simple omelette she would make for her supper. But as she walked back through the garden to the cottage, a bleak sense of loneliness sank over her. Annoyed with herself, she made a determined effort to shrug this shadow aside.

After all, she should be used to this feeling by now. She'd spent most of her adult life feeling isolated in one way or another. How could she not, when she'd been an outcast from the very start of her marriage, sent off to the colonies in shame after Felix had gambled away his farm in Devonshire?

Like the nineteenth-century remittance men, who had been sent by their aristocratic British families to Australia and paid to stay there, Vera had returned from her honeymoon in the West Indies to find that her husband was penniless and homeless, and had been banished to the bottom of the world. They were to manage Jinda Station, far away from family and friends, all alone in a stark and alien landscape.

Somehow – in retrospect, Vera was never quite sure how she'd managed in those early years – she had soldiered on. She'd promised for better or for worse and, despite her husband's faults, she'd been foolishly fond of him.

Besides, to walk away would have felt like turning her back on a significant challenge. And perhaps she'd also been just angry enough with Felix's family to refuse them the satisfaction of seeing her give up on their son and come running home.

Archie's birth a year later had helped. Vera wouldn't have minded a brood of children to keep her company, but that hadn't eventuated. Meanwhile, Felix had tried quite hard to learn about raising cattle, and Vera had thrown herself into motherhood and to tending her outback garden.

Fortunately, Felix had found a wonderful stockman with a brilliant instinct for handling cattle. Roddy McGowan, who knew the country like the back of his hand, had worked on Jinda for decades and was as loyal to Felix as any butler. And his wife, Maggie, helped Vera with the housework and taught her how to cook.

In time Vera had made friends with the women on nearby properties, and after Archie had been packed off to boarding school, she'd learned to master the gears on Felix's truck, and had driven into Jindabilla to play tennis with these women and to attend their CWA meetings.

In other words, she'd settled into a very tame and quiet, but not unhappy life. There'd been parties and barbecues and even balls from time to time, although keeping Felix away from the racetrack had been an ongoing struggle. The poor man had tried to resist, but every so often the demon inside him had grown too strong. So, along with droughts that came every few years, they'd never really had enough money.

Vera's own parents had been rather aghast by the way things turned out, but they would have been even more mortified if she'd left Felix. Her father had made private arrangements to send her funds and these had kept the wolf from the door on more than one occasion. They hadn't come to Australia to visit her though, and in a way she was relieved, although she missed them. It would have been too complicated and difficult trying to cope with their dismay at her primitive lifestyle, or to explain that she really didn't mind her new life, that she'd adjusted. And when they'd died, there'd been a modest inheritance, but her brother was the primary heir.

Somehow, she and Felix had managed, however, and Vera had learned to shrug aside the lingering cloud of disappointment that had hovered over her for decades. She knew that life was always about the choices one made, and regret was a useless exercise.

These days, Vera lived in the small cottage that had been the McGowans' home for so many years and, this evening, she had almost reached her front steps when she heard the sound of a vehicle coming down the track. She recognised its particular rumble; it was Archie's ute.

This was a pleasant surprise. She waited on the steps, hoping that her son had brought one or more of the children with him. His little family now lived in the main Jinda homestead, which was less than a kilometre away, but Vera hadn't seen nearly enough of them in recent weeks.

Henry had started at Prep, so she was no longer needed for babysitting, and Brooke had stopped dropping the children off at the cottage for afternoon tea. Brooke's excuses about homework and netball practice were valid enough, Vera supposed, but she couldn't help feeling snubbed.

As the ute came to a stop, she watched, but she couldn't see any little heads inside the cabin and only one door opened and slammed, which meant Archie was on his own.

Ah, well. Vera hoped her son at least had time to sit down for a proper chat while he filled her in on all the family's doings. As Archie came towards her, though, the grim set of his mouth sparked a flurry of disquiet in her chest.

She knew her son well and something was definitely troubling him. He had the rounded jaw and thickset build of Vera's own father rather than Felix's rangy leanness, and now she could read the obvious tension in his face and in the tight hunch of his broad shoulders.

'Hello, there,' she called, carefully. 'Nice to see you.'

'Hi, Mum.'

'How are you? How's the family?'

'Fine, thanks.'

This was a relief at least. Vera's brain had been foolishly racing through all kinds of worst-case scenarios.

'Do you have time to come inside?'

'Sure.'

A niggling concern lingered as Archie followed Vera across the porch and waited while she hung her sunhat on a peg by the front door, swapping her outdoor shoes for comfy flats.

'Well,' she said, keeping her voice deliberately light as he opened the flyscreen door for her. 'You'll have time for a cuppa, won't you? Or perhaps a glass of wine?'

'Sure,' Archie said again and they continued down the short hallway into the kitchen. 'Whatever you're having.'

He still looked worried, but Vera was determined not to panic. 'I'm sure it's wine o'clock.' She had the dregs of a chardonnay in the fridge, but this was as close to a special occasion as she'd experienced in recent weeks and Archie preferred red. 'Let's open a fresh bottle.'

Setting the tomatoes and chives beside the sink, she took a bottle of shiraz from the modest rack on the old kitchen dresser, found glasses and set them on the table.

'You'll pour, won't you, dear? I'll see if I can find some cheese.'

Archie frowned, as if wanting to suggest she needn't bother with cheese, but then must have thought better of it.

Having arranged a narrow wedge of brie with a knife and crackers on an old Royal Albert plate, Vera set it on the kitchen's scrubbed pine table and took a seat. Archie had unscrewed the cap and now placed a generous glass of wine in front of her. In the last of the sunlight streaming through the kitchen window, it glowed red as rubies.

'Thanks. Here's cheers,' she said, before taking a sip.

'Cheers.' Archie actually managed to smile as he said this, or at least, his mouth turned up at the corners, but the expression in his eyes was anything but cheerful.

Vera was determined not to worry unless it was absolutely necessary and she tried her best to kickstart a normal conversation. She asked Archie about the condition of the cattle that had arrived last week from the Roma saleyards, and she enquired if Henry was still enjoying Prep. But while both subjects were dear to her son's heart, he only answered politely, without going into any of his usual chatty detail.

Eventually, Vera felt compelled to be blunt. 'You're not actually here to talk about any of these things, are you?'

Archie drew a sharp breath. 'Not really.'

'What is it?' She resisted the temptation to reach out to him and kept her hands tightly clasped in her lap. 'You've got me worried, Archie. You're not ill, are you?'

'No, nothing like that.'

So that was one hurdle cleared, but it only afforded Vera momentary relief.

Archie took a deep sip of his wine, then set the glass down. 'It's just . . .' He shifted awkwardly in his seat, looked away, then let out a sigh.

Vera was almost screaming with tension.

Archie swallowed. 'I was wondering – that is, Brooke and I were wondering – if you'd ever thought about moving. Now that Dad's gone and you're on your own, it must be pretty damn lonely for you here.'

Vera almost laughed. She'd been lonely for most of her marriage. Was this really why Archie was so nervous?

She and Felix had moved to this cottage after Felix's first stroke, Felix having surrendered his official status as owner and manager of Jinda, while Archie, Brooke and their family had taken up residence in the homestead. Vera had thought this was an ideal solution, and she'd expected to see out her days here.

Nevertheless, she had also been troubled by niggling concerns that had been growing stronger lately.

'It's Brooke, isn't it?' she said now. 'She doesn't want me here.'

Archie's throat rippled as he swallowed. 'I reckon there are times when she doesn't even want me here.'

This was a shock. Surely her son's marriage wasn't in trouble? Archie was a wonderful husband. Vera knew she was biased, but Archie was like her own father both in his appearance and his nature. While Felix had been elegant and charming, Archie was grounded and practical. Salt of the earth, and a good manager. More importantly, he loved Jinda and loved caring for the cattle.

Best of all, Archie adored Brooke. Vera was quite sure about that. And he was absolutely crazy about his children.

She didn't know what to say.

'Let's face it, Mum,' Archie said, as he twisted the stem of his wine glass. 'You and Theo —'

Theo. Oh, dear heaven. 'Is Brooke still upset about that?'

Archie nodded. 'It was pretty much the last straw after all the earlier trouble between Dad and Brooke's family.'

Vera knew that her romance with their neighbour had been a source of friction at the time, but she and dear Theo had behaved themselves, backed off. And for heaven's sake, they'd both been widowed, so she could never bring herself to feel guilty.

She'd assumed the younger generation were more broad-minded, but clearly not, at least where their parents were concerned. Such a nuisance, really. Perhaps, if she were to be banished, she should ask Theo if he'd like to come with her.

For a moment, that cheeky thought cheered Vera immensely, but she knew it wasn't realistic. Theo had lived in this district for his entire life. He wouldn't want to leave. But as she pondered the situation, she also found herself wondering if Brooke had been hoping for a liaison between her own mother and Theo. After all, Carolyn Tucker was also widowed and on the loose. And Theo Blaine was a damn fine catch.

'But there are other things to consider,' Archie was saying, as if he'd fulfilled his duty in regard to the awkward topic of Theo and could now move on to more comfortable matters. 'You need to think about your health too, Mum.'

'I'm perfectly healthy, thank you.'

'But you're not getting any younger.'

Vera was sixty-eight, sound in wind and limb, and she refused to think of herself as elderly. She realised, however, that the clues to this problem had been smouldering for some time now.

There had been Brooke's lukewarm reception on the last occasion Vera called in to the homestead with a blueberry lattice pie. The children had been excited, of course, and it was a Sunday, so Vera had been invited to join them for lunch. But she could sense that Brooke had only *just* tolerated her presence. Shortly after that, Brooke had flat out rejected Vera's offer to help with the girls' reading homework.

I reckon there are times when she doesn't even want me here.

Vera couldn't bear to think that her friendship with Theo or her continued presence at Jinda might actually be threatening her son's marriage.

'You really should think about living closer to medical facilities,' Archie said next.

'I could move into Jindabilla, I suppose.' At least she would know people there.

Archie frowned. 'But there's no hospital for miles, and you have to remember what a saga it was getting Dad to hospital and to specialists. And Dad had the luxury of you to drive him wherever he needed. Both Brooke and I are pretty busy these days.'

Was this really the issue, Vera wondered, or was Jindabilla still too close? Brooke's own mother lived in the town, of course. Perhaps that was part of the problem? Her relationship with the Tuckers had never been an easy one.

And then Vera was remembering another time – another evening, more than a decade earlier, when she'd been woken by a phone call.

A friend in her mah-jong group, who was married to a publican, had sounded quite frantic.

'I think you should come into town, Vera. There's been a row at the pub. You should get here as quickly as you can. Before the police.'

Such a dreadful business that had been. Archie had been away on holidays at the Gold Coast with Brooke. He'd proposed marriage to her during those holidays, in fact, but Vera had only found out later that Brooke turned him down that first time. Meanwhile, on this particular evening, Felix had taken the truck to town, so Vera had been obliged to borrow Roddy McGowan's ute.

By the time Vera had arrived at The Crown, Felix was on the floor, with his long legs stretched in front of him and his back propped against the bar, while blood dripped from a wound on his head, making ghastly bright splashes on his white shirt.

Vera could see no sign of whoever had done this. The publican, Jim Chambers, looked grim, even agitated, but he wasn't about to dob. The mood among the regular patrons seemed to be a mix of concern and amusement, but no one was keen to tell Vera what had happened.

It was only later that she'd learned the full story. At the time she'd been too busy helping Felix to his feet, shepherding him, with Jim Chambers' help, out to the ute and then driving him home. It seemed, however, that Brooke's father, Fred Tucker, had stormed into the pub demanding money that Felix owed him. Fred was a stockman and fencing contractor. He and his family lived in a very modest and rather shabby cottage on the edge of town and he'd done a great deal of work on Jinda six months earlier.

Apparently, Felix still hadn't paid the man.

The debt had been paid soon afterwards. Vera had made sure of it, even though this had meant yet another grim discussion with their bank manager and a humiliating begging letter home to England.

But it wasn't until Fred had died of a heart attack about a year later that Brooke had finally agreed to marry Archie.

Brooke had been 'marrying up'. A fortunate, social climbing match as far as most of the locals were concerned. But it seemed Brooke would never have dared to marry the son of Felix Challinor while her father was still alive.

Just the same, Vera had hoped that the stigma of Felix's gambling problems was behind them now. Everyone, especially Brooke, must know that Archie was nothing like his father. But seeing the tightness in her son's face as he sat opposite her this evening, Vera had to accept that, after all these years, she was still being punished.

Archie had finished his wine and now he helped himself to another while the cheese remained untouched. 'I reckon we could find you a very nice apartment in Brisbane,' he said after a bit. 'You'd have the absolute best facilities right at hand, and you know you've always enjoyed visiting the city.'

This was true, actually. Vera had very much enjoyed her trips to Brisbane with Felix, finding somewhere to stay close to the river and the city, dining out and going to the theatre and, yes, unfortunately, to the Eagle Farm racetrack.

Now, she looked out through the window again to the dusk-dark sky where the evening star was shimmering brightly, and to the trees and the garden and the plains she'd come to think of as her home. It seemed she was expected to leave this place, where she'd spent her adult years in exile, and she was to face yet another banishment. This time, instead of becoming her family's distant daughter, she would be forever the 'other' grandmother, the distant Gran.

She shivered. 'I'm not sure I can afford to buy an apartment.'

'Yes, you can, Mum. We've had a good season.'

This was true, and now that Archie was solely in charge of the Jinda accounts, the bank balances were looking surprisingly healthy.

'I could think about Brisbane, I suppose,' Vera said slowly.

Archie was almost smiling now. At any rate, there was a gleam in his eyes that might have been relief. He reached across and gave her hand a reassuring squeeze. 'You're good at making new friends, Mum. And I'll make sure we visit you.'

CHAPTER NINE

It was around midnight when Maddie travelled home via Uber after her first experimental online date. She'd waited a mournful month after her breakup with Simon before she'd plucked up the courage to try out Tinder, and now she didn't quite know what to make of her evening's experience.

As dates went, she couldn't really complain. Jacob was two years older than her and worked in IT. He had taken her to dinner at a nice Thai place at South Bank and then to an art-house movie that was rather touching and clever, and afterwards for a drink at a rooftop bar that offered panoramic views of city lights reflected on the river.

Maddie had gone to the trouble of buying a new little grey dress, rather than the standard black: square necked and slim fitting and quite short. Jacob had told her she looked lovely. Throughout the evening, he had been pleasant, and he hadn't prattled on about himself the whole time.

At the right moment towards the end of the evening, he'd kissed her. He wasn't a sloppy kisser, and he didn't try to push his luck by suggesting they should take things further. He'd even waited with her till her Uber arrived, had opened the door for her and said that he'd really enjoyed the evening and would love to see her again.

Pleasant was an appropriate word to describe the evening's experience, Maddie supposed, although she was sure Jacob deserved higher praise than that. Unfortunately, she hadn't felt even the teensiest spark of romantic interest, but perhaps it was natural to still feel numb, as if her emotions and hormones had been anaesthetised or deep frozen to protect her from her post-Simon pain.

She wasn't sure that she should see Jacob again, though. After all, she didn't want to lead him on. It would probably be kinder to decline another pleasant invitation and try someone else. Or perhaps she should simply give up on dating and look for a hobby.

Like an old maid?

On that downbeat note, the Uber pulled up outside Maddie's apartment block, and the dark and handsome driver gave her a charming smile as he bade her goodnight. The smile was enough to lift her mood, and as she climbed out onto the footpath, she decided to think positively. At least she had learned that an online date could be a harmless diversion. And in time, when she thawed, she might actually enjoy herself.

Drawing a deep breath of cool night air, she looked upwards. In all the four storeys of the apartment block, lights shone from only two windows. Most of the sensible residents were sound asleep, and as she crossed the footpath and keyed in the code that opened the big sliding glass doors to the foyer, she found herself yawning and looking forward to bed.

Great. There were advantages to a pleasant but boring date. She might actually get a good night's sleep.

She wasn't expecting to see anyone else at this hour, so she was a little startled when a trolley loaded with heavy wooden boxes burst into the foyer through a side door from the garages.

'Goodness!' she exclaimed, taking a quick step sideways to avoid a collision.

'Hell. Sorry.' A man in dark clothing was pushing the trolley. He had a deep voice that seemed to go with his height and his rather longish dark hair, not to mention the heavy stubble that lined his jaw. In contrast to all the darkness, his eyes were a clear light grey.

Maddie recognised him as a resident, although she'd never actually met him. She fancied he lived on the top floor, near the English woman with the grandson called Henry. This man seemed quite different tonight, though, dressed in old and worn jeans and a navy sweater, and wearing leather gloves that were rather like gardening gloves. And the wooden boxes loaded onto his trolley were very solid and seemed to be tied tightly together with some kind of ratcheting strap. They looked very much like they belonged in the outdoors, not in an apartment.

She wondered why on earth he was bringing such boxes inside.

'I didn't hit you, did I?' he asked.

'No, I'm fine.'

Reassured, he now had the cheek to cast a quick but appreciative glance over Maddie, surveying her from head to toe.

In response, she found she was stupidly glad she was wearing her new dress.

Idiot.

Annoyed with herself, she couldn't help snapping at him. 'Have you been robbing a bank?' After all, what could he be transporting in those heavy boxes at midnight?

His response was a slow smile. 'More like robbing a hive.'

'A hive?' Maddie frowned. She had to admit he didn't really look like a bank robber. Apart from the dark clothing, there was nothing furtive about him. In fact, he was smiling quite openly, now that he knew he hadn't hurt her.

Perhaps it would be safer not to know what he was up to, and she made a determined show of avoiding any further eye contact as she turned her attention to the lift buttons.

An awkward silence lay between them then – or at least, Maddie felt awkward – as they waited for the lift to descend.

When it did, the guy said, 'You should go first. I'll wait.'

Maddie couldn't help frowning again. There was plenty of room in the lift for both of them, even with his bulky trolley. 'I'll hold the door for you,' she said, feeling somewhat magnanimous.

'No, I'll wait. I'm taking these bees up to the roof,' he said.

'Bees?' Oh, yes, he had mentioned a hive, hadn't he?

'It's best to move them at night, you see. That's when they're quiet, and there's no risk of leaving any foragers behind.' With a shrugging smile, he added, 'I've made sure there are no leaks in these boxes, but it's probably best if you're not stuck in a lift with me.'

'Oh, I see.' Maddie supposed she was grateful that he was so considerate, and it was silly to feel as if she was missing out on something interesting, but she was intrigued now. Bees on their apartment block's roof? Here, in the middle of the city?

She seemed to remember catching a brief glimpse on television about a similar project and she felt suddenly wide awake and would have liked to ask this guy more questions. But she couldn't stand here, holding the lift door forever. The damn thing would start beeping. 'Good luck with them,' she found herself saying.

'Thanks.'

Then she stepped inside, and the last thing she saw as the doors slid closed was the amusement dancing in the beekeeper's eyes.

Before she knew it, she had reached the first floor, so it was time to find her key and stop thinking about her midnight encounter with a potential bank robber. As she let herself into her apartment, however, she felt strangely keyed up. From experience, she knew it was the kind of feeling that signalled a sleepless night.

Damn. Five minutes ago, she'd been yawning and ready to hit the hay.

At least Maddie was wide enough awake to take her makeup off properly for once, but by the time this was achieved and she'd changed into a T-shirt and cotton pyjama pants, she still didn't feel anywhere near sleepy.

What she probably needed was a mug of warm milk and honey. This had always been her mother's remedy for sleeplessness and Maddie hadn't tried it for ages, but after a close encounter with a beehive, a honey drink seemed appropriate.

As the microwave circled, warming her milk, she found herself thinking about the beekeeper up on the roof. At midnight, the witching hour. How dark was it up there? Did he have a torch? A head-torch perhaps?

She'd never even been on the roof and had no idea what it was like. Now she almost wished she'd kept going in the lift to take a peek. What was involved in getting the bees set up?

As Maddie stirred honey into the hot milk, her brain kept firing questions. Did the beekeeper have permission from the Body Corporate? Would the bees mind being taken all the way up there? How far would they have to travel to find pollen?

Carrying the mug and her phone through to her bedroom, she turned on a lamp, climbed into bed and made herself comfortable with pillows. And with the first sip of her drink's soothing, sweet warmth, she found herself wondering what the beekeeper would do with his bees' honey. Sell it to the residents?

Who cares? she thought grumpily. It was time to forget about bees. She'd be better off going back on Tinder to check out potential future boyfriends.

Maybe just a quick google about bees wouldn't hurt, though?

Already, Maddie was typing *bees on rooftops* into the search bar, and soon she discovered that such projects really were a *thing* and growing in popularity worldwide. Masses of rooftops in London were now home to bees. And on YouTube she discovered a rooftop beekeeper in New York City who was quite anxious to boost declining bee populations.

Also, it seemed the bees didn't mind being taken up high. Apparently, they actually preferred to nest above ground level, which made sense, she decided. Left to their own devices, bees nested in trees, didn't they?

They shouldn't be taken too high, though. Anything above ten storeys was dangerous, but this apartment block was only five floors, if you included the garages, so it should be fine. And then there was the whole message about how important bees were. The ultimate pollinators. Experts had estimated that one in three mouthfuls that we eat comes to us thanks to bees. Maddie supposed the guy on the rooftop already knew all of this.

No doubt he also knew about the importance of positioning the frames correctly, and about hive tools that were, apparently, special gadgets used for prising the frames from boxes.

Okay, enough. The last thing she needed was to go down a rabbit hole of crazy bee research. It wasn't as if she had any real interest in bees.

Very deliberately, Maddie switched off her phone and set it on the bedside table. She drained her drink and turned out the light, rearranged her pillows and settled down. Closed her eyes.

Right. Good. It was very late and she was sleepy. She took several deep breaths and consciously relaxed. The drink would work its magic and any minute now she would drift off.

She was feeling quite settled when out of nowhere came the thought that the guy with the trolley had probably finished on the roof and was already in his bed, sound asleep.

And damn it, she was wide awake again.

CHAPTER TEN

RESIDENTS' MEETING Thurs June 6th at 7.30 pm
All residents of Riverview Place are invited to the above meeting
in Unit 13 to discuss the establishment of a community garden
on our building's rooftop.

Successful rooftop gardens are gaining wide popularity both
in Australia and overseas and Dr Ned Marlowe has researched
this subject in depth. The aim of the initial meeting is to gauge
the level of support from residents before presenting a submis-
sion to the Body Corporate.

We look forward to seeing you there.

When Vera found this notice in her letterbox, she almost tossed it
straight into the bin. The idea of a community garden for this apartment block was laughable. Good grief, even if enough people were
keen, they'd never get it past the Body Corporate.

When Vera had first moved into Riverview Place, she'd been to
one or two Body Corporate meetings, but they'd been so unpleasant
she could never bring herself to continue.

Such painfully boring discussions there'd been about dishwasher leaks and the time settings of security lights. These were, admittedly, practical considerations and the discussions might have been bearable if there hadn't also been hideous arguments between the committee treasurer, Godfrey Raines, a small ex-army fellow with a red face and a bristling moustache, and the secretary, Nancy Jenkins, an extremely bolshy woman in her fifties, who worked in compliance for some huge construction company and regarded herself as an expert on everything.

The pair of them had waged dreadful wars over who was responsible for the insurance after a leak, or whether the committee had the right to change the building's exterior colour scheme. It seemed to Vera that they hadn't been able to agree on anything, and although neither Godfrey nor Nancy lived in Unit 13 where this garden meeting was to be held – that was Ned Marlowe's apartment – they were both sure to be there, shooting firebombs through every suggestion.

A rooftop garden was a nice enough idea, though, Vera had to admit. When she'd had her own garden at Jinda, she'd always had something to look forward to each day – flowers to be admired or picked for vases, bulbs waiting to be divided, beds that needed mulching or weeding.

With a dog at her heels and a spade or secateurs in hand, she'd spent many happy hours outdoors. She'd even learned to appreciate the company of bees and bugs and spiders, not to mention the clever little birds singing their hearts out or building their nests.

Mind you, there'd been challenges to gardening in western Queensland, including dreadful droughts and floods and plagues of locusts. But Vera's garden had taught her patience, and it had given her a sense of purpose. In many ways, it had kept her sane.

And apart from her family, the garden was what she missed most now that she lived in the city. Nevertheless, she was quite sure this new project would never get past the idea stage. As for the prospect of creating a *community* garden here at Riverview Place. Hah!

Good luck with that. She'd seen little sense of community spirit in this building.

She was crossing the floor to drop the notice in the mail room's wastepaper bin when Nancy Jenkins came rushing through the doorway. The woman always reminded Vera of a very fussy hen. She wore her hair piled on top of her head in a messy knot and had one of those matronly figures that was all bosom. By contrast, her feet were quite tiny, and she liked to wear high heels, so she always looked unbalanced and in danger of toppling forward.

'Ah, Vera,' Nancy announced now, while waggling her mailbox key in the air, as if to signal that she had something incredibly important to say and that Vera mustn't leave. Which was par for the course with Nancy. The woman always carried on as if she were a spokesperson for the Prime Minister with news of national importance. 'I do hope you're coming to that meeting,' she said, eyeing the notice in Vera's hand. 'We're going to need all the votes we can get.'

'Really?' Vera responded with mild surprise. 'So, you're in favour of this rooftop garden, are you?'

'Good God, no. Not at all. It's a ridiculous idea. A disaster.' Nancy shuddered, then added a dramatic roll of her eyes for good measure. 'We need you to help vote *against* it. You're a sensible woman. I'm sure you can see it couldn't possibly work. Imagine the drainage problems, for starters.'

'Well, yes.' Vera had actually wondered about the drainage.

'Besides, most of our residents are far too busy to be bothered with a hobby project like rooftop gardening.' Nancy delivered this observation with an air of martyrdom. 'It's so impractical. Pie in the sky. If people wanted gardens, they would stay in the suburbs. They certainly wouldn't move into an apartment block.'

'Well —' Vera began in defensive mode.

But Nancy was too focused on her own message to listen. 'Why would any of the sensible people who live in this building want to grow bok choy on the roof? Such a waste of time when the super-market is so close, and they can buy it for next to nothing.'

'Is that what they're planning to grow? Bok choy?' Vera glanced again at the notice, which she had partly crumpled, wondering if she'd missed important details.

'They're calling it a community garden and those types only ever grow weird foreign vegetables.'

'Do they?' Vera was rather fond of bok choy and she was begin-ning to feel extremely sorry for 'those types'. She rather liked what she'd seen of Ned Marlowe.

'I'm assuming you'll back me and vote against this.' Nancy looked annoyingly smug.

Sidestepping the woman's assumption, Vera asked, 'Who else is involved besides Ned Marlowe?'

'Oh, that artist woman on the first floor – Carmen Cassidy, or whatever she calls herself – but you know how impractical artists are.'

Vera had met Carmen Cassidy briefly, and they'd exchanged nods or smiles if they passed in the foyer. Probably late-forties, Carmen was rather plump and attractive with wild blonde curls and given to wearing kaftans and striking jewellery – dangly earrings and chunky bracelets that were probably her own creations.

'Have you seen her apartment?' Nancy asked, in a more conspir-atorial tone.

Vera shook her head and Nancy gave another, even more elab-orate eye-roll. 'Every room is a different colour.'

So what? Vera wanted to ask. If Carmen Cassidy had an artistic eye, her colour choices were probably highly effective.

Lowering her voice to a stage whisper, Nancy added, 'I hear her bedroom walls are black. Can you imagine?'

She sounded so scandalised Vera almost laughed.

'And I've heard Ned discussing this garden idea with our care-taker,' Nancy went on with a downward curl of her lower lip.

The building's caretaker was a friendly chap. He rented a small bottom-floor unit, was rather skilled when it came to maintenance, and was always ready with a smile if Vera greeted him. But although he had fixed a problem with a stiff window for her cheerfully and efficiently, he was another person she hadn't really tried to get to know.

'And those gay fellows are bound to be involved,' Nancy went on, shaking her head. 'I can never remember their names.'

Vera knew the couple by sight, and now she regretted that she couldn't supply their names. Several times she'd been on the brink of speaking to them, as they also gave her friendly smiles.

'Those fellows seem to know quite a bit about gardening,' she suggested. 'They have wonderful plants on their balcony.'

Nancy merely sniffed. 'They've also put that ridiculous compost bin up on the roof.'

Vera was about to comment that a compost bin was a terrific idea, but Nancy continued, barely pausing for breath.

'They seem to think the rest of us should be cracking our necks to traipse all the way up to the roof just to drop off our kitchen scraps. It's pathetic.'

Privately, Vera had always felt guilty about throwing her vegetable peelings into the rubbish. For her, such wastage was a major downside to living in an apartment, and she'd been secretly delighted to start using the compost bin. She decided not to mention Ned Marlowe's worm farm. If Nancy didn't know about it, Vera would let sleeping worms lie.

'Anyway, you can see why we're going to need you at the meeting,' Nancy said with an air of finality.

'Mmmm.' Vera looked down at the notice she was still holding. Her doubts about the garden's prospects of success were now stronger than ever, but she couldn't help feeling sorry for Ned and any of the others who were initiating this project. 'Well, I suppose I *should* go to the meeting,' she said carefully.

But she certainly wouldn't make any promises about which way she was going to vote.

Back in her apartment, Vera did her best to flatten the crumpled notice, which she then fixed to her fridge with a magnet. The magnet had been a gift from her granddaughter Emily, last Christmas, and it was styled in the shape of a watering can, one of the old-fashioned types made of weathered metal.

It made me think of the old watering can you always used, Emily had written on the card.

Vera had been touched. These days in the apartment, she used a neat pink plastic affair to water her few pot plants, but now she fingered the magnet, remembering the heavy metal can at Jinda with its sturdy spout and spray head. So vivid was the memory, she could almost feel the sun on her back as she watered seedlings by the back steps at Jinda homestead.

This had been happening rather often lately – memories of Jinda taking over, pushing Vera's earlier nostalgic memories of England further and further away, till they were almost like photos out of focus. For so many years, Vera had mourned the loss of her family and home on the other side of the globe, but these days it was Jinda she thought of as her rightful home.

Now, picturing that old watering can, she could almost smell the dust in the air as she'd tended her plants. She could hear the rasping cry of distant crows and she pictured Felix, relaxed in a squatter's chair on the verandah, his riding books kicked off as he enjoyed an icy gin and tonic after a long, hot day of helping Roddy in the stockyards.

Felix would have been waiting for Vera to join him and, when she came up the steps, removing her hat and peeling off her gardening gloves, he would rise and fix a drink for her, complete with ice and a slice of lime. As he offered her the glass, he would smile that warm, crinkly-eyed smile of his. And in that moment, she would forgive him.

Again. For everything.

Lost in the mists of the past, alone in her apartment, Vera felt her throat tighten and sting, and she might have given in to a wretchedly sentimental tear or two if the phone hadn't suddenly broken the silence.

Her hand trembled a little as she lifted the receiver. 'Hello?' She sounded a bit shaky as she answered.

'Hello, Mum.'

'Archie? How lovely. How are you, dear? How's everyone?'

'We're fine, thanks. And you?'

'I'm well.' The possibility of tears was forgotten now. Vera didn't want to waste a moment talking about herself. She was impatient for news of the family.

'That's great,' Archie said warmly. 'We were wondering if you might be free over the June–July school holidays?'

Vera's heart thumped hard in her chest. Could this be an invitation to Jinda? Instantly, foolishly, she was picturing herself arriving out there and being greeted by the children. She could see the three of them rushing down the steps as her car pulled up. Could imagine their excited chatter, could picture the family enjoying afternoon tea on the verandah, a camp fire and barbecue down by the river.

But then, almost as quickly, reality dawned and her excitement faded. Sienna and Emily were heading off to their netball camp in the school holidays.

But wait – did this mean —?

Vera didn't dare give in to a second foolish hope. 'I certainly don't have anything planned,' she said cautiously.

'That's great. We were wondering if you could possibly mind Henry while Brooke takes the girls to Melbourne.'

Good heavens. Vera couldn't hold back her gasp of surprise. 'Are you sure about that, Archie? I thought Brooke's mother was going to look after Henry.'

'Carolyn's in line for knee replacement surgery. She's been on a waiting list and a chance has suddenly popped up that she can't afford to miss. The surgery's scheduled for next week, but then she'll need a few more weeks to recover. And I'll be busy with the mustering.'

'Yes, of course.' Vera hoped she sounded suitably sympathetic about Carolyn Tucker's plight and not too excited about her own good fortune. 'I'd love to mind Henry,' she said and then, as she remembered the dire lack of children in this apartment block, she asked more cautiously, 'Do you think he'd be happy to come here?'

'He'll be over the moon, Mum. He hasn't stopped talking about that day he spent with you. He's nuts about that worm farm. Reckons he's going to learn all about the worms, so he can start his own farm here.'

Vera laughed. Henry was coming to stay. How wonderful. She didn't mind in the least that the worms were the main attraction.

CHAPTER ELEVEN

Before Maddie finally met Adam Grainger, she tried two more Tinder dates, both with different guys, and they were both disasters. The first date was with a guy called Sandy, and she came to think of him as Sandy the drunken sailor. From the start, it was clear he had a problem with alcohol and expected Maddie to keep up with him.

She'd tried to restrict herself to just one drink to his every two or three, but she was still pretty pissed by the end of the evening. And then, somewhat predictably, Sandy had expected a round of rough and clumsy sex.

When Maddie made it clear she wasn't interested, Sandy wasn't aggressive, thank God, but he became morose, almost weepy. Turned out he'd been in the navy and had PTSD. So yes, Maddie did feel badly about rejecting him, but it was all way too heavy for a first date.

Her next date, Ethan, spent the entire night talking about himself. Maddie was worldly enough to know that many men shared this habit, but Ethan was truly tedious as he rabbited on and on about his troubles with his ex-wife and the custody battle they were having over their kids, and Maddie lost count of the number of times he moaned, 'And now there's another bloke calling my girls Dad.'

In retrospect, both Sandy and Ethan had made Jacob, Maddie's first pleasant date, seem like her Dream Man.

She was beginning to think her search was an impossible one, of needle-in-haystack proportions. It was so frustrating. She wasn't asking for a fairytale prince. She simply wanted to meet a nice, ordinary guy – well, perhaps not *quite* as nice and ordinary as Jacob, but she was sure there had to be someone out there who ticked at least a few boxes. She wasn't asking for a ten. A seven would do. But she was almost ready to give up on the app.

It probably would have helped if she'd been able to talk to her friends about this. But after the Simon fiasco had spread through the entire office, Maddie still wasn't prepared to discuss her private life with her workmates. She had also avoided going into personal details about these dating experiments when she invited Joe and Dennis over for coffee and cake.

Luckily, they hadn't noticed anything was amiss with her. They'd been too busy admiring her pot plants – Maddie had three of them now and none had died yet. And then, while wolfing down generous helpings of the blueberry and almond cake that Maddie had made using her grandmother's 'secret' recipe, Joe and Dennis had enthused about the meeting that was coming up soon to discuss plans for a garden on the apartment block's roof.

'You should have found a notice in your mailbox,' Dennis had gushed. 'You'll come, won't you, Maddie? The meeting's in Unit 13, Ned Marlowe's apartment.'

Which was how Maddie discovered that Ned Marlowe was, in fact, the beekeeper. And, remembering the strange impact of her midnight encounter with this man, she almost agreed to attend the meeting. Just out of sheer curiosity.

But a rooftop garden was the kind of project that best suited people who already had their private lives sorted. Maddie was sure she didn't have the time or the energy for such a distraction when she was still on a mission to find a new boyfriend.

She'd quickly searched for an excuse. 'I'm only a renter.'

'That doesn't matter,' Joe insisted. 'The garden will be for anyone who lives here, owners and renters alike. It's such a great project.'

She told them she would think about it. Then she promptly put it out of her mind. And in the end, she offloaded her woes about her dating onto her mum during their regular Sunday morning phone call.

By this point her parents had valiantly accepted that Simon was past history, with no chance of ever becoming their son-in-law. And while Maddie had mentioned that she'd been seeing other guys, she'd omitted the minor detail that she'd met her dates on an app. She did point out, however, that they'd been unsatisfactory.

Her mum made sympathetic noises, but it wasn't long before she asked, 'You're not being too picky for your own good, are you, dear?'

Maddie assured her this wasn't the case.

'You know you don't really need to rush to find Mr Right, Maddie.'

Yes, Maddie knew this, too, and she was also well aware of the other fact that her mother took pains to point out – that young women left it quite late these days before they worried about finding their perfect match.

It was all very well for her mum to fling these statistics about when she and Maddie's dad had known each other since primary school. In fact, her parents had actually dated straight out of high school and had never been out with anyone else.

Not that they seemed to regret this in the least. All these years later, they were still quite devoted to each other, which was sweet.

But Maddie was worldly-wise enough to know that sort of Anne-with-an-E and Gilbert Blythe romance belonged to innocent bygone eras. It never happened these days.

Sigh.

Just the same, Maddie was conscious that she shouldn't rush. She had even tried to question her motives, to ask herself why it was so damned important that she find herself a boyfriend anyway. Was it a need to fill the Simon-sized dent in her heart? In her ego? Or was she merely a victim of her own expectations?

She even wondered if she would have been quite so desperate if she hadn't moved away from Bundaberg to Brisbane. Was there something about big cities and all that ambition and competition that made a girl a little desperate?

She wasn't much good at self-analysis, however, and she had no idea if the answer lay in one of these possibilities, in a mixture of them or in none of them at all. In the meantime, she gave herself a lecture about being patient. App dating was a numbers game. If she kept trying, she'd eventually get lucky.

And indeed, she did get lucky.

On the very next date, she met Adam.

Adam worked in real estate, which Maddie had to admit, *did* send up a tiny red flag, with brief visions of crafty salesmen aka con artists. But that was stereotyping the poor guy, surely? There had to be hundreds, if not thousands of reputable salesmen in Greater Brisbane, and Adam Grainger deserved the benefit of the doubt.

For their first date, they were to meet at a bar on the Eagle Street Pier, and as a ferry stop was a mere five-minute walk from Maddie's apartment, she decided to travel by CityCat.

Right from the start, it was a magical evening, charged with a romantic air, as she glided down the river, watching the city lights come to glowing life while the dusk deepened through purple to velvety black. For a fanciful moment, she even allowed herself to think about royal barges and queens floating down the Thames to Hampton Court.

Even before the ferry docked, Adam texted her.

I'm waiting on the wharf and I think I can see you. In blue?

Maddie was indeed wearing her newish blue dress with a matching blue jacket and, despite the June evening, she found herself glowing and quite warm with anticipation.

She had learned not to take too much notice of the photos men posted on their profile page. But as the ferry docked and she came up the ramp, she could see Adam waiting and his pic had been quite accurate. He was of medium height with close cropped mid-brown hair and beard and pale blue eyes. His face was a little too round to be handsome, but Maddie had already decided that the roundness gave him a jovial air, and anyway, she didn't want to be shallow. Looks weren't everything.

What was possibly more important – Adam sure knew how to pick a perfect setting for a first date. The Black Bird Bar was like a scene from *The Great Gatsby*, with amazing one-hundred-and-eighty-degree views of the majestic curve of the Brisbane River, and it offered the most divine range of cocktails and share platters. Maddie had never been there with Simon, either, which was a definite bonus.

She settled down to enjoy herself while Adam managed to balance his salesman charm with a vibe that seemed genuine and straightforward. He told her he'd grown up in Toowoomba and his parents and sister still lived there. Understandably, he liked to invest in real estate. He had a city apartment, as well as an acreage out Boonah way on Brisbane's 'scenic rim', and Maddie, as a country girl born and bred, thought this sounded like a perfect combo.

All night she found herself smiling – over the lovely view, the drinks, the food, the stories Adam told – funny stories about clients who would remain nameless, even a story about a solicitor who'd completely messed up a conveyance.

The mere mention of the solicitor did give Maddie an uncomfortable moment. She'd told a white lie when she'd filled in her Tinder profile, claiming to work for a firm of merchant bankers, rather than lawyers.

She'd been anxious to keep her work and play separate, so the ploy had made perfect sense at the time. But in the midst of Adam's storytelling, he hinted that Maddie should share a few hot investment tips and she found herself dithering with a flustered answer about keeping such confidential matters 'in house'.

Adam looked a little put out, but then he gallantly let her off the hook by asking about her childhood on the cane farm. He didn't know the Wide Bay area very well, so Maddie talked it up, raving about the beautiful beaches.

The conversation drifted to pets. Mostly cats for Maddie – her mother collected strays – while Adam's father bred basset hounds, and he told her about a pet penny turtle that he'd lost when he was a kid, after he'd let it out for a walk in his backyard.

'I put stickers all over its back, so I was sure I could find it again,' he protested as Maddie laughed. 'And I went around the whole block, asking the neighbours if I could check their backyards.'

'But you never found it?'

His rueful smile was boyish and somehow endearing. 'Never.'

'How old were you?'

'Five. Maybe six.'

She tried to picture him at that age – round face, coppery brown hair, no beard, but she couldn't quite see him.

Once or twice during the evening he attempted to push more questions about her work, but she managed to deflect him from

wealth management strategies by telling him how uptight investment bankers were.

'Highly stressed, highly intelligent and often arrogant,' she
added, quoting an old uni mate who now worked in that industry.

'Banker tantrums are a thing,' she assured Adam. 'They get
worked up over stupid things. Where's my pen? My iPad won't
work. Why isn't my meeting room booked? My job mostly involves
staying calm and jumping in to fix their problems.'

She could apply those same observations to several lawyers she
knew, of course. At any rate, Adam seemed to accept this small
fabrication and he didn't keep pushing for investment advice. At
the end of the evening, which had been truly delightful, he scored
even more points by insisting that he accompany Maddie home in
a taxi.

By then, she'd decided she was pretty damn keen on this guy,
and she was sure the interest was mutual. As they drove through
the city, Adam talked about restaurants they should try in the future
and the possibility of a glamping weekend out on his property.

There were no clumsy attempts to grope her on the back seat,
for which she was grateful, but she was definitely planning to ask
Adam up to her apartment. She was quite restless and tingly with
anticipation by the time the cab pulled up outside Riverview Place.

Adam got out and walked with her to the front door. Maddie
gave him her best smile. 'Thanks for a wonderful night.'

'It's been great, hasn't it?'

'Lovely.' Then, quickly, 'Would you like to come up? For
coffee?'

Adam's answering smile was cute, but apologetic. 'I haven't paid
the cabbie.'

'I'll wait.' Jeez, she could have tried for a little more sophistica-
tion, couldn't she?

Still smiling with that same faint air of apology, Adam touched her lightly on the wrist, just the gentlest brush of his fingers, striking fire against her cool skin. 'Maybe next time?'

He turned then and walked back to the waiting cab, and Maddie felt slightly foolish, but even more breathless, as she typed the entry code into the keypad and the doors slid open, welcoming her inside.

CHAPTER TWELVE

'You want all of it off?' Jess, the hairdresser, asked as she cautiously fingered Vera's silvery tresses.

Vera had been watching Jess's reflection in the mirror, had seen the flare of shock in her eyes when she'd made her brave request, and now she almost weakened. Was she being too reckless in trying for a brand-new look?

When she'd first moved to the city, she'd had her long hair shortened to a bob that finished just below her jawline. Smart, serviceable, conservative, this style was also easy to care for. But it was the conservative image that accompanied this look that bothered Vera now.

She had never thought of herself as a particularly careful or conventional person. Heavens, she'd thrown her lot in with Felix, hadn't she? And until she'd been forced to do so by her family, she'd never really cared what other people thought of her. But she *had* been bothered by the conversation in the mail room with Nancy Jenkins.

Ever since then, Vera had been uneasily conscious that Nancy saw her as a traditionalist. No doubt other people shared this view of her. They probably judged her by her accent, her age and her appearance and assumed she was an old stick-in-the-mud, a fuddy-duddy, automatically opposed to new ideas.

This realisation miffed Vera greatly. She'd stewed over it for several days, but had finally reached the point where she needed to do something about it.

Just yesterday she'd picked up her new eyeglasses from the optometrist – fabulous, oversized round affairs, with snazzy black and white frames. Vera loved them. From the moment she'd popped them on she'd felt more vibrant and energetic. More interesting. More hopeful.

'Wow! Check out those fabulous frames,' Carmen Cassidy had commented in the lift. 'Love them!'

The lift's doors had opened to her floor before the conversation could go any further, but Vera had been chuffed.

Okay, so it was probably a mere trick of the mind that new glasses could lift her spirits, but she was happy to go along with it. And, while Henry would be arriving in a couple of weeks' time, she was confident he'd adapt to her new look, no matter what his mother might say.

So, Vera had headed straight to a clothing store that she'd been eyeing off for a while and she'd bought herself a swinging, cape-style knitted black top and white jeans, and she'd decided right there and then that she was also going to do something about her hair.

So here she was, staring at the scissors in Jess's hand and hovering in a moment between hopeful daring and scary doubt. Had she been getting too carried away? A new hairdo was a very different prospect from a new pair of jeans. If she hated the cut, she would have to wear a head scarf and it would take ages for her hair to grow back.

Vera stared back at her reflection. As was her habit when her hair was being cut, she had taken off her glasses and set them on the little shelf under the mirror. Without them, her reflection was a little fuzzy, blurring her sagging jawline and the bags under her eyes. But she could still see the glasses' cheeky black and white frames quite clearly and they gave her a fresh burst of courage. She mustn't back down now.

'Yes,' she told Jess decisively. 'All of it off. I want to go really short. And trendy. If that's possible at my age.'

Jess's response was a thoughtful frown as she lifted strands of Vera's hair with the comb. 'So, we'll go short around the ears, but maybe we'll keep a little on the top?'

'I think so.' Vera wished the girl looked happier. 'Is there some sort of gel I can use to give it a bit of shape?' She was actually thinking she'd like a spiky look.

'Oh, yes,' Jess assured her. 'We have a wonderful range of products.'

'And I'd like to go pink.'

Now, at last, Jess grinned. 'I can hardly wait to get started.'

On the evening of the community garden meeting, Vera knocked on Ned Marlowe's door and was greeted by one of the young men from the apartment below. She wasn't at all surprised to see him, given Nancy's prior warning as well as the lush plants that thrived on his balcony, but she was a little taken aback when he frowned at her, as if he had no idea who she was.

But before she could panic, there was a flash of recognition, and his eyes nearly popped out of his head. In the next breath, he pressed a hand to his mouth, almost like a child trying to hold back a guilty secret. A beat later, he was grinning. 'It's you, isn't it? Our neighbour, from the apartment above us.'

'That's right,' she said. 'I'm Vera.'

'And don't you look beautiful, Vera! Your hair! Your glasses! I love it.'

For a moment, Vera thought he was actually going to hug her, but then he seemed to calm down a little, as if he remembered the reason for her visit. 'Come in, come in,' he said warmly as he stepped back to make room for her. 'I'm Dennis, by the way. Come and meet Joe. You probably know Ned. And Carmen Cassidy's here too.'

As Vera followed Dennis into Ned's living room, where lounge and dining chairs had been arranged in a circle, she was met by more puzzled looks from the others.

'This is Vera,' Dennis announced, in the somewhat dramatic tones of a game show host announcing a mystery guest. 'From Unit 12.'

Now there were more gasps of surprise, a comment of 'Wow' from Joe, followed by a huge smile from Carmen, who was resplendent in a typically bright patchwork sweater. Ned Marlowe, however, accepted Vera's new look with a mere lift of one dark eyebrow and a faintly amused glimmer in his grey eyes. For which Vera was grateful. The agenda for this evening's meeting was way more important than her change of hairstyle.

Besides, she had vowed to give up worrying about other people's opinions, and she'd already decided that she liked her new image, no matter what anyone else thought. Just the same, the enthusiastic smiles were heartening.

It had been a long time since Vera had sensed a small personal victory like this, and she couldn't help feeling pleased and a little more confident as she took a seat. When she'd first come to Brisbane, she really had planned to join a few groups and to get out and meet people. But somehow, she'd allowed herself to wallow in being lonely and disconnected, and she'd never followed through on these intentions.

With luck, that was about to change. Her new glasses and new hairstyle were just the start. Now at this meeting, she could sense an air of shared excitement.

Soon others arrived. A smiling, mousey, middle-aged woman from the second floor introduced herself as Ros Grant, and then their caretaker came in. Ned welcomed him warmly and introduced him as Jock McFee.

'I'm really grateful Jock could join us at this meeting,' said Ned. 'After all, he keeps most of his equipment in the shed on the roof and it makes sense to keep him informed about our plans.'

'Thank you.' Jock smiled and gave them a cheery wave. He was an interesting-looking fellow, lean and rangy, with piercing green eyes and a longish face edged by a tawny beard. His slightly greying hair was also long and pulled back into a ponytail. 'Great to be here,' he said, and he took a seat next to Vera.

Vera happily returned his smile. She hadn't quite expected the building's caretaker to be involved in this project, but now she realised it made perfect sense and, not for the first time, she wondered if her lingering class snobbery was still getting in the way.

A moment later, Vera was very pleased to have Jock at her side as Nancy Jenkins and Godfrey Raines marched in, bristling with umbrage and self-importance. She'd been afraid she might have Nancy sitting beside her, elbowing her in the ribs to vote this way or that, and bossing her about in noisy stage whispers. Instead, Nancy now sat on the other side of the circle, which was almost as bad, as she sat staring hard at both Vera and Jock.

'I thought this meeting was only for owners,' she said loudly, while fixing Jock with a steely glare.

Ned quickly intervened. 'No, renters are more than welcome to be involved in this project.' And he explained again, patiently but firmly, about all the maintenance gear Jock kept stored on the roof, as well as the man's interest in gardening. Nancy seemed to accept this, grudgingly but without further protests, thank heavens. Then she turned her scowling attention to Vera and was clearly puzzled – until light dawned.

'Good grief, is that you, Vera? What on earth have you let them do to your hair?'

A totally predictable reaction, Vera decided with secret delight. And at that point, the meeting began.

CHAPTER THIRTEEN

Can't stop thinking about that kiss. Think I need to see you tonight.

This text from Adam arrived on Maddie's phone while she was still at work, bringing with it a sudden heatwave. Heat and a savage thrill. She was sure she was blushing bright red and she had to shrink behind her computer screen, hoping no one in the office would notice.

She hadn't stopped thinking about their kiss either. It had come at the end of her second date with Adam, and if the measure of a man was in the quality of his kissing, then Maddie was sure she was on a winner with this guy. He was an absolute champion and, once again, she'd been dead keen for him to take things further. Adam had politely retreated again, however, leaving Maddie on a knife edge of wanting, and ever since that date she'd been in a prolonged and distracted kind of daze.

But now, he wanted to see her. Tonight. Midweek.

Yes, please!

Excitedly, Maddie texted her reply. *Come to my place? For dinner?* She could throw together something quick and easy – baked salmon, perhaps – and luckily, her apartment wasn't in too much of a mess.

'Maddie?'

Maddie jumped when Lisa's voice sounded close behind her.

'Have you finished that contract for the Carruthers?'

Oops. 'Almost.' As she turned back to the document on her screen, her phone pinged. She was sure it must be a reply from Adam and she couldn't resist taking a quick peek.

Would love to come to dinner. See you at seven?

Yay! After that, trying to concentrate on her work was a tough call, but somehow Maddie finished the day's allotted tasks and managed to get away on time. She stopped off at Toowong Village on the way home and bought salmon and vegetables for a tray bake. Then at the deli, she chose a chunk of posh goat's cheese coated in ash and a packet of lavosh crackers. In the bottle shop she selected two kinds of wine – a sparkling and a shiraz, both far more expensive than her usual choices. With luck, she'd also have time to wash her hair.

She was super excited about seeing Adam again. Her hopes about him had been growing in confidence every day, whispering that he might, at last, be The One. The very fact that he'd taken his time to get to know her before making a move was a promising sign, Maddie was sure.

Ever since last weekend's kiss, her world had seemed to acquire an extra sparkle and she was almost skipping as she carried her purchases out of the lift and down the hallway to her apartment. Once inside, she set everything on the kitchen bench, eager to start prepping the vegetables, when a sudden knock sounded on her door.

Adam?

Hot flashes zapped through Maddie. Surely he wasn't here already? Wow. Maybe he was even keener than she'd realised. Now she was all aflutter, imagining an instant flaming passion fest, as she hurried to open her front door.

A young boy stood there, a rather worried-looking boy.

'Oh,' Maddie said. 'Hello.'

'Hello,' the boy responded shyly. He was vaguely familiar, although Maddie, whose focus was still entirely absorbed by her hot date, couldn't immediately place him. She certainly couldn't imagine why he'd knocked.

'Can I help you?' she asked.

'I hope so,' he said. 'My grandmother asked me to find you. She asked if you could come up to her apartment?'

Really? Struggling to hold back an irritated sigh, Maddie remembered where she'd met this boy. It was in the lift on the day she'd first visited Joe and Dennis. She'd realised then that his grandmother was the Englishwoman on the top floor. But did she really have to go up to the woman's apartment right at this very moment?

'You're Henry, aren't you?'

'Yeah.' He smiled shyly.

'So, what —' Maddie stopped, took a steadying breath and tried again. 'Has something happened? Your grandmother hasn't had a fall, has she?'

Henry shook his head and Maddie found it even harder to hang on to her patience. This was all rather weird. But the poor kid was still looking worried.

'Gran's been to the doctor,' he said. 'And she'd like to talk to you.'

Gulp. Maddie's imagination immediately fired up a host of unpleasant possibilities. But this situation was none of her business, really.

On the other hand, she could hardly turn her back on the boy, and with luck it would just be a simple matter, sorted in a moment. She certainly wasn't going to jeopardise her evening with Adam.

'Okay,' she said. 'Of course, I'll come up. Just wait while I grab my keys.'

She decided not to pester the poor kid with questions, as she headed back to the lift. All would be revealed shortly.

Sure enough, mere moments later, Henry's grandmother was opening her door to them.

'Oh, wow!' Maddie couldn't quite hold back her gasp of surprise. The woman looked so different. Her hair had been cut quite short and dyed a pretty, soft pink and she now wore oversized glasses with snazzy black and white frames. The trendy new appearance really suited her, except that it was somewhat spoiled by her worried expression.

'Thank you so much for coming,' she said. 'I know it must seem strange when we haven't even properly met. I'm Vera, by the way.'

'Hello, Vera. I'm Maddie.'

'This is so good of you, Maddie. Would you come inside?'

Maddie hesitated. Under normal circumstances, she would quite happily give up a little time for a neighbourly chat. But now? On the brink of her big chance to impress Adam with her culinary skills, and then, later, with her allures in the bedroom?

Unfortunately, though, this didn't seem to be a normal situation and Maddie supposed Vera wouldn't want to discuss it standing in the corridor.

'I know this is rather out of the blue and awkward,' Vera said, as if she could read Maddie's mind. 'It's just that I'm in a bit of a spot – and I need someone to look after Henry for me.'

Oh, no! Just in time, Maddie managed to bite back her groan of dismay.

'Henry's told me how he met you.' Vera's mouth tilted in an embarrassed smile. 'I do apologise, but it really would be best if you could come inside – just for a moment, while I explain.'

Maddie could hardly turn on her heel and leave, but she wondered where Henry's parents were. She was battling a deepening sense of apprehension as she followed Vera and Henry down the hallway.

Vera's apartment was much bigger than her own – almost of penthouse proportions – and decorated with elegant antique furniture and beautiful Oriental carpets that seemed to suit her posh English accent. Vera indicated that Maddie should sit in an elaborately upholstered armchair, while she sat opposite, and Henry lowered himself to the carpet by the coffee table where he had some kind of elaborate Lego masterpiece in mid-construction.

'I'm hoping this is a storm in a teacup,' Vera said. 'But the thing is, I've had a bit of a turn.' With a helpless flap of her hands, she added, 'I'm sure it's nothing serious, and such a nuisance thing to happen just when Henry's come to stay with me. But I had to go to the doctor this afternoon – just to the GP. Fortunately, she had a cancellation and she slotted me straight in when she heard I'd had chest pains. I guess they can't ignore those symptoms, not at my age. I had to take poor Henry with me, but he was very good.'

Vera smiled fondly at the boy, who gave an awkward little smile as he fiddled with pieces of Lego.

'It's all such a nuisance,' Vera said again. 'Henry and I had so many lovely things planned. And I've been so keen to get involved in the roof garden and everything. But the doctor gave me an ECG and took some blood tests, and she's told me I have to go to the hospital for more tests. She was quite insistent. Says it's important to have these tests as soon as possible. She would have sent me straight off to the Wesley in an ambulance, if I hadn't had Henry with me.'

'Gosh.' Maddie was instantly sympathetic. Vera had always seemed so aloof, and Maddie had assumed she was a snob. But now she seemed quite nice, really. 'What a worry for you. So, you need to go to the hospital now?'

'Yes. And I'm sorry to land this on you, Maddie. The only people I've met were the ones at the rooftop garden meeting. I would have asked Joe or Dennis from the apartment below me, but they're always out on Wednesday nights. And Ned Marlowe seems to get home quite late. I could try Carmen Cassidy, I suppose, but I don't know her at all, really. It was Henry who asked about you. He remembered meeting you when he was here with me last time.'

Henry still looked worried as he watched Maddie now. Peeping up at her with bright blue eyes from beneath his fringe of dark hair, he looked rather sweet and vulnerable, and Maddie hadn't the heart to ask where on earth his parents were. It was pretty obvious Vera would have called on them if they'd been available.

The situation was quite black and white, really. Vera had suffered some kind of turn that worried her GP. She might even have had an actual heart attack and she needed to get to hospital quickly for further tests. Clearly, her plight was a game changer, no question, and Maddie couldn't waste a moment on regrets about dinner with a sexy new boyfriend.

Of course, there would always be other times with Adam – and he would understand that Vera's situation was an emergency.

'Of course, I'll look after Henry,' she said. 'Would you like me to call for an ambulance?'

Vera pulled a face. 'I'd rather you didn't. I hate those things.'

'Well, let me drop you at the Wesley, then.' Maddie realised this was probably a more sensible option, anyway, given that the hospital was only a few blocks away.

'Oh, thank you.' Now, for the first time, tears glistened in Vera's eyes. Tears of relief, no doubt.

Everything happened quite quickly after that. Vera was already quite organised and had packed a small bag, in case she needed to stay in hospital overnight, along with another for Henry as well.

'But I haven't even checked if you have a spare bed.' She sent Maddie an apologetic smile. 'If I do have to stay overnight, perhaps it would be easier if you stayed here, in my apartment?'

'My apartment's only a one-bedder, so I think that might be better, actually.'

'Of course. Stay here then. I have two spare rooms.'

Looking about her at the lovely decor and the spacious layout, Maddie toyed, for a foolish moment, with the possibility of inviting Adam to join her here for dinner. Being a real estate agent, he was mildly obsessed with details like floor space and elevation. He was bound to be impressed by Vera's apartment.

But she dismissed the idea almost as soon as it arrived. Henry was now her responsibility for the evening and while she had zilch experience of childminding, she knew that including a brand-new boyfriend in the mix was not an option.

'Okay,' she said, accepting Vera's offer. 'That sounds like the best plan.'

She looked again to the boy. He didn't seem quite so worried now, but he must feel rather helpless, being handed about like a parcel. 'We'll be fine, won't we, Henry?'

He nodded and the corner of his mouth twisted in a shy quarter-smile. Maddie was tempted to lean down and give him a hug, but she resisted, given that they barely knew each other.

'We'd better exchange phone numbers,' she said to Vera and then, with that settled, the trio headed back to the lift where they descended to the car park, and were soon on their way to the Wesley Hospital.

'You mentioned the rooftop garden meeting,' Maddie said in an attempt to make light conversation with Vera, while they waited for the lights at the first intersection to change. 'Is the project going ahead?'

'Oh, yes,' said Vera. 'It's all systems go.'

'That's great.'

'Yes, it was a minor miracle, really.'

'Were there problems?'

Vera nodded. 'Oh, heavens, yes. I was sure we'd never get it past a couple of the old sticklers on the Body Corporate Committee. It was still a challenge, but Ned Marlowe was very well prepared and the vote from everyone else was unanimous.'

'Ned Marlowe. He's the beekeeper?'

Vera laughed. 'Beekeeper. Worm farmer. Botanist. Oh, and a jolly useful researcher.'

'Mmmm.' Maddie was remembering the sleepless night she'd spent after meeting the guy.

'Ned was wonderful,' Vera said warmly, as if this Ned Marlowe had cast a spell on her as well. 'He had an answer to every objection.'

'I suppose he'd done his homework,' Maddie couldn't help adding.

'Absolutely. He'd even gone into the history of our building and discovered there'd been faulty work in the ceiling systems years ago, when it was first constructed. Apparently, water intruded into the units on the top level during heavy rain, so the contractors were recalled and made to do the job properly. And ever since then, the roof's been inspected and maintained regularly, so it's actually in tip-top shape. We'll be able to use hoses and sprinklers up there without having to worry.'

'That's great.' Maddie frowned as she considered this. 'But how will you fund it? Are you all going to chip in?'

'No, that's the real victory. The Body Corporate will cough up a lump sum from the sinking fund. That way it's all fair and above board, and there'll be audits et cetera. Oh, and they'll set up a water meter on the garden. Apparently, they're not hard to do. That way, the people who are directly involved can cover the costs, without imposing it on the others.'

'Sounds brilliant.'

'I know. It's quite exciting. Mind you, Nancy Jenkins isn't too happy.' Vera actually chuckled. 'But she'll have to cop it sweet. I think it's going to be wonderful, with the very latest in organic and environmentally green processes.'

Maddie smiled. 'That's highly commendable.'

'Sorry if I sound smug,' said Vera. 'But I do like that everything's being done with compost. And no herbicides.'

'Sounds like you're a keen gardener.'

'Yes, or at least, I used to be,' the woman admitted and then she gave a rather heavy sigh. 'Despite the battles with the climate here in Australia, I've always thought of plants as reliable. They inevitably do their best.'

This was a strange comment and Maddie might have quizzed her further, but they had already reached the hospital.

'Don't worry about trying to find a park,' Vera said now. 'Just drop me off as close to the entrance as you can. I'll be fine to find my way.'

'Are you sure?'

'Yes, my GP has already phoned ahead.' She took a piece of paper from a zipped pocket in the shoulder bag that held her overnight things. 'I've instructions here about where to go.'

'Well —' It was quite dark now and Maddie felt uncomfortable about just abandoning an elderly woman with a possible heart condition on the footpath.

'Honestly,' Vera said. 'It'll take you ages to find a park. It's not worth the hassle. I'm just so grateful you're taking care of Henry for me.' She had already unbuckled her seatbelt and opened her door so that the interior light came on.

Now, she turned to her grandson sitting quietly in the back. 'Thank you for being such a good, brave boy, my darling. But I'll be home again in no time. And we'll do all those fun things we had planned.'

Henry nodded and Vera, with a loving smile, reached back and gave his hand a squeeze.

'See you soon, sweetheart.'

'Bye, Gran.'

The sight of the elderly, wrinkled hand tightly clasping the boy's small smooth one caused a painful lump in Maddie's throat.

'I'll ring your father when I get a chance,' Vera told Henry next. 'Just so he knows what's going on.'

'Okay, Gran.'

With a brave smile, Vera added, 'And thanks again, Maddie.'

'No problem.' Maddie hoped her smile was encouraging. 'Good luck. I hope we see you soon.'

Vera climbed out and closed the passenger door, gave them a final wave, then shouldered her bag and began to march, resolutely, along the footpath towards the big glass hospital doors. Watching her straight back and her pink-coiffed head held high, Maddie was gripped by an unsettling sense that this woman wasn't aloof and snobbish after all, but was rather like a veteran who'd faced more than her share of life's battles.

I've always thought of plants as reliable.

Remembering this unusual comment, Maddie found herself wondering if Vera had faced most of her life's battles, if not all of them, on her own.

CHAPTER FOURTEEN

Indeed, those beds and bowers
Be overgrown with bitter weeds and rue,
And wait thy weeding;
'Sonnets from the Portuguese'
by Elizabeth Barrett Browning

Jinda, 1978

'How can you bear this, Vera?'

Pandora posed her question as she leaned on the railing of the back verandah at Jinda, waving a cigarette as she gestured to the vast stretch of dusty brown paddocks. Vera's young sister-in-law had arrived that morning, dressed straight out of London's Carnaby Street, in a fringed lime-green top and tan leather jeans that left her midriff bare.

Now, still staring at the view, Pandora shuddered, rippling her shining black locks that almost reached her waist. 'Far out, Vera. I thought it was bad enough that you were stuck down here in Australia, but I had no idea you were living in a desert, literally in the middle of nowhere.'

Vera smiled tiredly. 'I think I might have mentioned the distances and the drought in one or two of my letters.'

'I was sure you had to be exaggerating.'

Pandora's distress was bordering on anger now and, for Vera, this reaction was almost amusing. From her own point of view, Jinda's landscape didn't look too bad on this early spring evening, bathed in the golden glow of the setting sun. After all, the district had actually enjoyed an above average rainfall earlier in the year, so at least there was grass.

Then again, Vera had been living on Jinda for almost a decade now, and no doubt her expectations had lowered with each passing year. Pandora, on the other hand, was a mere visitor, freshly arrived from England's green fields and forests, luxuriant hedgerows and flowing brooks. Not to mention its splendid stately homes.

Don't dwell on any of that or you'll only get angry too.

'Come and have a gin and tonic and stop fretting,' Vera soothed, pointing to the jug and glasses she'd set on a cane table.

With a dramatic sigh, Pandora flopped into a cushion-lined cane chair, stubbed out her cigarette in the ashtray Vera had remembered to provide, and accepted the proffered glass, complete with ice and a slice of lime. Now in her mid-twenties, Felix's pretty little sister had grown into a very attractive young woman. Of course, like other girls in her social circles, Pandora had been to a finishing school in Switzerland, but she'd also managed to land a job as some sort of journalist, working for a newspaper in Charing Cross Road, which was, apparently, run entirely by women.

No doubt this explained how Pandora had also been caught up in the fervour of the Women's Liberation Movement. Now, although she downed a hefty slug of the gin and tonic in one gulp, she couldn't, or wouldn't, let go of her fury.

'I could murder my bloody brother,' she declared, thumping her glass down so heavily Vera feared it might crack. 'How could he do this to you, Vera? Forcing you to live at the bottom of the world, in this dump.'

It was on the tip of Vera's tongue to remind the young woman that Pandora's own father had done the forcing. Felix had made a foolish mistake, but it was his father who had punished him by sending him here.

Vera was also tempted to mention that Pandora had known about Felix's terrible gambling mishap before their actual wedding day. If she'd really wanted to save Vera from this exile, she shouldn't have waited till it was too late before she'd mentioned the loss of his farm. Then again, Vera still mightn't have got to the actual truth.

But this was all water under the bridge, and what could be gained now by pointing the finger?

'This house is hardly a dump,' Vera defended, although she knew the homestead wasn't impressive, certainly not by Pandora's standards, or for that matter, by the standards Vera had been brought up to expect. Unlike her family holding, Glenbrook House, Jinda homestead was, indeed, a humble affair. A single-storeyed building set off the ground on fat timber stumps, its walls and floors were built of timber, while the roof was unpainted iron. Little more than a shack, if she was brutally honest.

The floorplan was incredibly simple, with a hallway leading down the centre to a kitchen and bathroom at the back, while the lounge, dining and bedrooms opened off on either side. And instead of the intricate mouldings, polished marble floors and hand-painted wallpaper of English stately homes, these rooms had plain tongue-and-groove walls and were modestly decorated with furniture from second-hand stores.

Nevertheless, the pieces of furniture were all rather lovely antiques that Vera had painstakingly selected from stores in Brisbane. And Vera had come to appreciate the deep verandahs that surrounded the homestead on all sides and kept the place shaded and relatively cool, even in the height of summer. She was also rather proud of the garden she'd managed to keep alive, but the plants were mostly Australian natives – wattles and grevillea, or hardy creepers like trumpet vine or bougainvillea – and she feared that Pandora was unlikely to be impressed.

For this reason, Vera also didn't bother to mention the certain pride she'd taken in learning how to grow vegetables in this unforgiving soil, or to 'man' the gates in the stockyards, or to bottle-feed orphaned calves. Nor had she suggested that the town of Jindabilla was really quite close, only half an hour's drive away. She knew that neither the house nor the cattle property, or even the isolation, were the real sources of Pandora's distress. It was Felix.

'How can you put up with him?' Pandora asked now as she lifted a silver lighter to another cigarette. 'I'm so ashamed of my brother. How can you bear staying here, Vera, knowing what he did?'

Vexing as this question was, it was also a question Vera had asked herself. She had felt terribly betrayed, especially in the early months of her marriage, when she'd first realised that she was about to be exiled. But by then she was already very fond of Felix, having enjoyed a glamorous honeymoon in Jamaica where her bridegroom had been totally charming and attentive and sexy.

Even so . . . if she'd been privy to the whole truth . . .

'You know you should divorce him.'

Vera flinched. 'I couldn't.'

'Of course, you can. Divorce isn't something to be ashamed of. Not anymore.' Pandora blew an emphatic cloud of smoke. 'Everyone's getting divorced these days. Even Princess Margaret.'

'Really?' This was a shock.

'And about bloody time,' Pandora added. 'Margaret's setting a great example for women everywhere. Throughout history, we've been trapped into unfair or unhappy marriages. Thank God we're finally waking up to our rights.'

Vera supposed that Pandora's Women's Libbers would see her choice to stay with Felix as foolish, as being far too passive and compliant. Were they right?

Back in the days before she'd married a supposedly suitable man, she'd been quite caught up in the swinging sixties in London. There had even been a memorable few weeks when she'd almost run away to Hollywood with her Scottish actor boyfriend. It was only at the last minute that she'd chickened out.

Standing on the dock, as she'd waved Jamie off at Southampton, Vera had been dismayed to realise that she'd caved beneath the pressures of her upbringing. But to break free of that mould had felt impossible when she was nineteen, and a year later, she'd fallen in line with her family's expectations and found herself married.

Of course, there had been times over the years that followed when she'd asked herself why she'd put up with Felix's failings, why she had simply accepted her fate and settled for so much less than she might have enjoyed. Inevitably, during these musings, it was her grandmother Edith's voice that seemed to come through.

Never expect too much from life, Vera, and then you won't be disappointed.

A grim message, it was one Vera might have dismissed, except that her grandmother's own sad experiences seemed to have justified her warnings. Grandmother Edith had lost her true love, her beloved fiancé, Gerald, in France during World War I, and the story had lingered within the family that after this bad luck, she'd been considered very fortunate to have married at all, let alone to have won Lord Glenbrook.

Edith's bad luck had continued, however. Ten years later, Lord Glenbrook, her husband, was killed in a railway accident and then her eldest son, Rupert, who'd trained as a fighter pilot as soon as World War II broke out, had died in the skies above Berlin.

Grief-stricken Edith had taken refuge in religion and gardening, along with a kind of fatalist acceptance that life was an inevitable series of tragic disappointments.

Vera could remember many times during her childhood spent in the garden with her grandmother. Tasked with carrying a large wicker basket, Vera had trailed behind while Edith wielded secateurs, dead-heading roses, plucking ripe plums or cutting gorgeous bunches of sweet-smelling lilacs.

'At least, in a garden, plants stick to the rules of Nature,' Edith had told her. 'Plants follow the rhythm of the seasons, Vera. And, unlike mankind, they won't let you down.'

Vera had never been bold enough to suggest to her grandmother that plants in a garden still depended on the people who cared for them. Only much later had she come to realise there was a good chance that plants would manage quite nicely if they were left to their own devices.

All these thoughts resurfaced again now, though, as Vera faced Pandora's challenge. But if she was totally honest with herself, she knew she couldn't really accuse her poor grandmother of influencing her decision to remain here with Felix, so far from her family and home.

The answer was really much simpler.

'Felix has always been kind to me,' she told Pandora. 'It's easy to underestimate kindness. And I have another very good reason, above all others, for staying with him, but as you're not a parent yet, I wouldn't really expect you to understand.'

'Good God,' Pandora scoffed, frowning. 'Don't tell me you're going to blame poor little Archie? You're not staying here for his sake?'

'He's not the only reason, but he's an important part of it.' Noticing her sister-in-law's obvious puzzlement, Vera couldn't help smiling. She was remembering Archie's birth in a hospital in Toowoomba and Felix's horror when he'd discovered that, as the baby's father, he was expected to be present for the delivery.

Vera had warned him about this new fad in the maternity wards, but Felix had been hoping to escape. The midwife had been rather bossy, however, and Vera had been far too busy coping with the labour pains to care who was there in the delivery room. In the end, Felix had stayed, and he'd been incredibly moved by the experience.

When the doctor handed their newborn son straight into Felix's arms, he'd fallen in love with the boy at first sight.

The affection had been mutual. Archie had always adored his father and Vera knew they'd both be heartbroken if they were separated.

As if to confirm this, Felix and Archie now appeared in the distance, walking back across the paddocks from the stockyards, with their blue heeler, Milo, faithfully following. Dressed alike in denim jeans, long-sleeved cotton shirts and broad-brimmed felt hats, the man and boy looked the epitome of outback Australian cattle folk. And even at a distance, it was clear they were engrossed in an animated conversation.

Archie was waving his arms as he told his father some story, and Felix, who'd been grinning throughout, suddenly dropped his head back and let out a loud guffaw.

See what I mean? Vera wanted to say, but she was silenced when Pandora, who'd been watching her brother and her nephew rather intently, merely gave a heavy sigh and rolled her eyes, before lighting another cigarette.

'Him,' Pandora declared the next day as she looked back through the rear-vision mirror.

Vera and Pandora were driving away from Lansdowne, their neighbours' homestead, and Pandora was at the steering wheel.

'Vera, let me please drive,' Pandora had begged. 'I'm in desperate need of a little fun.'

The girl was already going too fast, of course, so that dust rose behind them, obscuring their view of the figures on the verandah, but Vera knew Pandora was talking about Theo.

'If you really must live out here, Vera, you need a man like *that* in your life,' she declared as she crunched through a gear change. 'He's divine and his house is gorgeous.'

Theo's house was in fact built on similar lines to Vera and Felix's, in a style that was generally referred to as a Queenslander. But the proportions of the Blaines' home were much grander, and the building materials were most definitely superior. Brick walls rather than timber, gleaming honeyed parquetry flooring, extra high, moulded ceilings and elegantly carved archways, not to mention pretty stained-glass panels in the windows and doors.

'And they have help to cook and wait and clean,' Pandora continued. 'So, he obviously has plenty of money.'

'And he's married,' Vera added tiredly.

'Tosh,' Pandora scoffed. 'Why should that stop you? His wife is deadly boring. For God's sake, all she can talk about is horses. She even looks like a horse.'

'Pandora, stop it. Don't be cruel.' Vera had been uncertain about accepting the Blaines' invitation to lunch, especially when Felix had declined, pleading a headache.

'You women should go, though,' Felix had urged. 'You deserve an outing.' He'd been well aware, of course, that his sister was totally bored after only a few days at Jinda.

Vera had known this too, and she'd also been aware that Felix hadn't been on good terms with Theo Blaine in recent years. There'd been tension between them and she feared that money and some kind of debt were involved. She'd also suspected that Pandora might make a song and dance about Theo. And now those fears had been realised.

'I saw the way he looked at you,' Pandora said next. 'That flash of desire in his eyes.'

'Don't talk nonsense,' Vera snapped perhaps a little too quickly. But she knew exactly what Pandora meant by the 'look'. The lightning glance across the dinner table as Theo passed her a basket of bread rolls. The shimmering smile. And she was all too familiar with the effects on her – the warmth rippling under her skin, the tug deep inside. Foolish reactions that she couldn't seem to stop.

Vera was grateful that the truck rattled over a cattle grid just then, distracting Pandora, and when they eased onto bitumen, she made a very deliberate point of changing the subject. With this achieved, she could at last breathe more easily.

CHAPTER FIFTEEN

It was only as Maddie drove back to the apartment that she remembered she still hadn't rung Adam. She needed to tell him about her change of plans, but she didn't like the idea of a phone conversation in the car park, so she waited until she and Henry had collected her groceries and a few overnight things from her unit and were back in Vera's apartment.

Here, she turned on lamps in the living room and drew the curtains, making the room look safe and cosy. 'I just need to phone a friend to explain that I'm staying here tonight,' she told Henry. 'Can I get you anything first?'

'No. I'll finish my Lego.' He was already kneeling by the coffee table. 'I'm building a Space Rover.'

Maddie hadn't paid much attention to his Lego until he said this, but now she could see a rather futuristic machine with big tractor wheels and a satellite dish on its roof. 'You're quite an engineer, aren't you?'

Henry smiled, looking pleased, and Maddie, leaving him to it, went through to the kitchen to make her call.

Adam answered immediately. 'Hey, gorgeous.' His deep voice held a honeyed note that sent a wave of wanting coiling through her. *Damn.*

'Hey,' said Maddie. 'Look, I'm really sorry, Adam, but I'm afraid I've had to change our plans for this evening.'

This was met by silence from the other end of the phone.

'I'm so sorry,' Maddie said again. 'But one of my neighbours has had to go to hospital and I'm minding her grandson.'

With Henry just a room away, she didn't like to add how disappointed she was about cancelling their date.

There was still no response from Adam, however, which was disconcerting.

'Adam? Are you there?'

'Yeah, I'm here.' His voice held a distinct chill now. He might have been disappointed – or merely uninterested – it was hard to tell.

Maddie tried again. 'I'm sorry.'

'Yeah, so you said.'

'It's an emergency, Adam. My neighbour had chest pains, probably a problem with her heart. And she doesn't seem to know many people here. I'm sure you understand. Maybe we can have dinner tomorrow night?'

'Whatever.'

He disconnected without saying goodbye.

Dismayed, Maddie stood in the middle of the kitchen, staring at her phone, sure that Adam would realise his mistake, and call back to apologise for being so curt. Any minute now, he'd be telling her how truly sorry he was, but that he'd been so disappointed he hadn't been thinking straight.

She waited a ridiculous number of minutes, however, and no call came. Eventually, she had to accept that Adam wouldn't be ringing back, but she felt sick and incredibly confused as she set about preparing dinner for herself and Henry, lining a tray with baking paper, then arranging salmon pieces on it with sliced shallots and whole cherry tomatoes.

'Henry, I hope you like salmon?' she called as she popped the tray into the heated oven.

'Yep,' came the cheerful response.

'And broccolini?' she added, remembering her own aversion to green vegetables when she'd been Henry's age. But it seemed this boy had an obliging appetite and, after another response of 'yep', Maddie set a pot on the stove. Once the salmon was partly cooked, she would add the par-boiled broccolini to the tray, along with a drizzle of soy sauce mixed with sesame oil. With luck, she would also find sesame seeds in Vera's pantry and she would sprinkle these on as well.

This meal was one of Maddie's favourite quick and easy dinner recipes and she'd been looking forward to sharing it with Adam. But now, she should probably find a different recipe for tomorrow night – that is, if Adam had forgiven her by then.

'Can we feed those to the worms?'

'What?' Maddie hadn't noticed Henry coming into the kitchen, but he was standing by the chopping board, eyeing off the little bundle of broccolini stems that she hadn't yet cleared away. 'What worms?' she asked, mildly horrified.

'There's a worm farm up on the roof.' Henry's eyes flashed with excitement as he related this news.

'Oh?' Maddie had been feeling rather exhausted after her roller-coaster afternoon, and she'd been thinking of pouring herself a glass of wine and relaxing in the lounge room, while perhaps asking Henry polite questions about his Lego. 'How about we leave the worm feeding till after we've had dinner?' she suggested. 'It won't take long to cook.'

Luckily, the boy was happy with this.

*

It was cold up on the roof. A strong breeze was blowing up from the river and Maddie was pleased she'd told Henry to pull on an extra sweater.

'Is there a light switch?' she asked as she pushed open the door at the top of the short flight of stairs. But Henry was one step ahead of her and he was already standing on tiptoes to reach a switch on the wall.

Light flooded the area, revealing a space quite a deal larger than Maddie had imagined. Chest-high walls around the edges of the roof made it quite safe and rather like a courtyard, and Maddie could see straight away that the roof gardeners hadn't wasted any time in getting started on their project. Already, they'd planted trees into several enormous terracotta pots, and they'd stacked bags of potting mix against a wall, ready for the next project.

For a moment, her imagination was captured by possibilities. She'd been quite surprised by how well her own pot plants were growing. She'd decided there must be something miraculous in the premium potting mix, as all she'd done was add water every so often and they were galloping along.

But now she was picturing a romantic rendezvous up here – a small table and chairs, set among pot plants and a garden, with vine-covered trellises and fairy lights. Dinner for two.

Adam was bound to be impressed.

'The worms are over here.' Henry had already crossed to a far corner where a small tower of plastic boxes stood beside the compost bin. He beckoned to Maddie impatiently. 'Come and see them. They're ginormous.'

She was glad she'd found a box of disposable gloves under Vera's sink and had insisted that Henry wear a pair of these. Now she watched the excitement on the boy's face as he lifted first a lid and then a damp layer of newspaper and added the broccolini pieces to a layer of lettuce leaves and vegetable peelings.

'The worms are under here,' he told her in a thrilled voice.

Leaning closer, as Henry gently pushed the compost aside, Maddie first caught the not unpleasant scent of the dark, dank earth and then she saw the shimmering, wriggling pink worms.

'Awesome!' She wasn't quite as enraptured by the sight of the worms as Henry seemed to be, but she couldn't help but be caught up in the boy's enthusiasm.

'They're wonderful, aren't they?' he said.

'Sure are. Quite amazing.'

'And they eat this lettuce and stuff and then they make wee and poo and that's really good for growing things in the garden.'

'Yes.' Maddie had been meaning to start contributing to the community compost bin ever since Joe and Dennis had mentioned it. But now the worms needed food too. Broccoli stems, apple cores, banana skins. She vowed to tackle both immediately. And – who knew? – she might even help with a bit of gardening.

She was still coming to terms with this impulsive idea when she heard the door opening behind them. As she turned, a tall, dark figure stepped out onto the roof.

'Ned!' Henry cried gleefully, his face lighting with a fresh burst of excitement.

Maddie wasn't sure why she felt a strange thud in her chest.

She was quite annoyed with herself, and as Ned Marlowe approached them, she paid studious attention to Henry's worms. Or at least she'd intended to study the worms, but her plan was foiled when Henry quickly closed the lid on the worm farm and turned his attention completely to Ned.

'I've been showing the worms to Maddie,' Henry told him.

'Yes, so I see.' Ned gave Maddie a nod and a polite smile. 'Evening,' he said.

'Good evening.'

He was carrying a couple of potted shrubs and he set these down now next to the stacked bags of potting mix. Maddie, meanwhile, seemed to be having hot flushes, which made absolutely no sense. She couldn't believe she felt so stupidly flustered.

Perhaps it was because she only ever seemed to encounter Ned Marlowe unexpectedly at night. But that was no reason to feel nervous. He was hardly the boogieman. Vera and Henry clearly loved him, and he was actually good looking in a tall, dark and serious sort of way.

'I see your garden group has started work already,' she said as her brain re-engaged and she recalled the rudiments of polite conversation. 'Vera tells me it's all systems go.'

'Yes, there's a keen group, so that's great.' Ned stood with his hands resting lightly on his lean hips. 'Is Vera coming up tonight?' he asked Henry.

The boy shook his head. 'Gran's in hospital.'

'Oh, no.'

'She's having a few tests,' Maddie intervened quickly, as she noted Ned's understandable concern. 'We're hoping the tests won't take long, actually, and we might hear from her soon.'

'Right.' Ned's steady grey gaze met hers. 'So, you're looking after Henry?'

'Yes.'

'That's great.'

This time Ned offered Maddie a full-on smile and, to her absolute horror, she blushed. Thankfully the lighting up here on the roof was fairly subdued. She felt so stupid to be flustered. And then her phone rang, and she was so damn tense she gave a startled jump.

Hoping it was Vera, she snatched the phone from her jacket pocket. But it wasn't Vera's name that appeared on her screen. It was Adam's.

Whack. For the second time in mere moments, Maddie felt her face flame.

'Excuse me,' she said to Ned and Henry. 'I need to take this call.'

Ned nodded. 'Of course.'

'I won't be a moment.' With that, she hurried away to the far side of the roof, into the shadows.

Here, she felt quite nervous and breathless and she needed to inhale deeply before she spoke. 'Hello, Adam.'

'Where are you?' he yelled.

Maddie gasped, shocked anew by the unwarranted fury in his voice.

'Maddie?' Adam was still shouting, and she wondered if he'd been drinking.

She was tempted to hang up, but if Adam was in a crazily bad mood, he might ring straight back and make a nuisance of himself, and she didn't want to turn off her phone completely in case Vera tried to get through. 'I told you,' she said, trying not to raise her voice and dredging up way more patience than she actually felt. 'I'm minding a neighbour's grandson.'

'Like hell you are. I've been knocking on your door.'

Really? This time Maddie's shock was physical, almost as if Adam had hit her. Now she regretted that she'd told him her address and apartment number, along with the pass code for getting into the building, but she'd never expected him to just turn up after she'd cancelled their date.

'Where are you?' he demanded again, still yelling, and there was the sound of banging, as if he was thumping on the door to her apartment.

Bloody hell. Was this really the same guy who'd sent her into orbit with his glorious kissing? Maddie certainly wasn't prepared to tell him her current whereabouts. It should have been flattering to know he was so keen to see her, but this rude behaviour was totally unacceptable. She couldn't bear to think of Adam bursting up here onto the roof and letting out his anger in front of Henry.

'I'm really sorry,' she said – but then she paused, grimacing as she realised that she was apologising yet again.

She was determined to reply firmly and coolly, but she was blinking tears as she spoke. 'Look, Adam, you'll just have to accept that I'm telling you the truth. I'm looking after my neighbour's small grandson. She's in hospital, and we're quite worried about her. For all we know she might have had a heart attack.'

This time she didn't mention the possibility of rescheduling their date for another night. Right now, she was too disappointed in Adam to want to see him again. And she quickly hung up before he could snap back at her.

She needed a moment then to get her head together. To just stand and stare out into the dark night, to the black space of trees and parkland across the road, and to the buildings beyond, with their shining yellow rectangles of light, geometrically precise. Desperate to calm herself, she took long, deep breaths.

What a truly weird night this had been. Quite nerve-racking. First the drama with Vera, now this. She wasn't in the habit of hanging up on people, but Adam had asked for it, hadn't he?

Maddie hoped Henry and Ned couldn't guess how unsettling this phone call had been for her. With luck, he and Ned would have been far too busy talking about worms or compost or some other gardening matter to take any notice of her.

When she turned back, though, she saw that Henry and Ned weren't gardening at all, but sitting cross-legged on the floor and looking up at the sky.

'Maddie!' Henry called to her as she walked slowly back to them. 'Come and look, quick! Ned's found a satellite!'

'Really?' Despite her distress, she couldn't hold back a wry smile. Seemed there was no end to the ways Ned Marlowe could impress this kid.

'Look!' Henry cried excitedly as he pointed above. 'Can you see that satellite blinking?'

Obligingly, Maddie peered up at the heavens.

'Straight up between those clouds,' said Henry. 'Quick. It's going to disappear soon.'

'Oh, yes!' Just in time, Maddie did catch a blinking light moving across the inky sky way above them. And, to her surprise, she did feel a small thrill.

'That was a lucky sighting,' she said as she came closer.

Henry's eyes were shining. 'Ned has an app on his phone for tracking satellites.'

Of course he does.

Ned, however, was watching her carefully and she had the feeling that those intelligent eyes of his missed very little. 'Is everything okay?'

'Oh, sure,' she said, perhaps too quickly. 'That wasn't Vera on the phone, though. I still haven't heard from her. It was just a – a friend.' Although Adam Grainger didn't feel like a friend tonight. He was more like someone Maddie needed to disown.

She was grateful that Ned didn't push for more information.

'I've been telling Ned we have way more stars at home at Jinda,' said Henry, blithely unaware that anything might be amiss.

'And I've been trying to explain to Henry that the stars are still up here,' Ned responded tolerantly. 'We just can't see them as well, because of the haze of city lights.'

'But he's got a book that can show me all the stars in the sky and I want to learn all their names,' Henry added.

Maddie smiled. It was pretty damn clear these two were kindred spirits. 'So, you're not gardening tonight?' she couldn't help asking Ned.

'No.' As he said this, he rose lightly to his feet. 'Several folk are dropping plants off up here during the week, and I'll keep them watered, but we'll leave the official planting till Saturday morning when we have our first working bee.'

'Right.' Maddie quite liked the sound of a rooftop working bee. She wondered if it was too late to get involved. 'Speaking of bees,' she said. 'What have you done with your hive?'

Ned nodded towards a dark distant corner. 'Over there, behind the screen, away from the main garden area.'

'Good thinking.' Maddie didn't need to ask further questions. She'd already learned enough during her Great Night of Bee Research to know that bees and green rooftops were a dynamic duo, growing in popularity, and if properly managed, no more dangerous than bees in any normal garden.

'Well,' she said now. 'This is all very exciting.' But she cringed as the words left her lips. Yikes, she sounded so patronising, like an awkward aunt. But there was something about this guy that turned her into Miss Prim.

Oh, well. Too bad. She wasn't here to impress Ned Marlowe. Henry was her focus tonight and it was probably past his bedtime.

CHAPTER SIXTEEN

Having been blessed with a lifetime of good health, Vera had rarely been in hospital as a patient. On the other hand, she'd been in and out of plenty of hospitals with Felix after his stroke, so she was used to the long corridors with lingering hints of disinfectant, and to the uniformed staff buzzing about, the glimpses through doorways to patients looking distressed or ill, the tedious questions to be answered.

The waiting.

This evening, she'd had her blood pressure taken by an impossibly young and earnest male nurse, who had politely asked if she would prefer to be called Vera or Mrs Challinor. Of course, she'd told him to call her Vera, and when she'd quizzed him about her blood pressure reading, he'd hinted that it was rather high. But that was to be expected, surely, given the scare she'd had.

Then he'd taken her temperature and she'd answered his questions about the pain – the same questions the GP had asked her earlier – and someone else had come and taken a sample of her blood.

After that, Vera had been given another ECG. There'd been no hint about what this had shown, but she decided it couldn't have been too bad, for no white coats had come rushing. And since then, she'd spent ages propped on a narrow trolley in a hallway.

She wasn't sure how long she'd been there exactly, as her phone was in her shoulder bag, which was on a chair out of reach. Meanwhile, people in caps and gowns with stethoscopes hurried about attending to other people whose problems were obviously far more serious than her own.

The lack of interest in her was probably a good sign, Vera supposed, but it left her with far too much time to think about gruesome realities – like the possibility of dying, not in the dim distant future, but soonish. Too often she found herself reliving that scary pain in her chest, the tightening, and the explosion of fear when she'd realised this wasn't something she could simply ignore.

It was hard to believe, as she lay there being ignored and totally pain free, that there could be anything seriously the matter with her. Until Felix's stroke and subsequent passing, Vera had always thought of death as a far-off event. It was unnerving to feel it hovering close now, like a black-winged malevolence.

Would she mind so terribly if she learned that her days were numbered?

Goodness, yes.

In a flash of startling clarity, Vera knew for sure that she cared a great deal. She wasn't ready to die.

And as she came to terms with this answer, other questions quickly followed. Questions so basic, so universal, Vera couldn't quite believe she was seriously asking them. But it seemed suddenly, vitally important to understand what being alive actually meant. Why were we put on this earth? Really? Why, out of the entire endless universe, were billions of Homo sapiens gathered on this one tiny planet? Living and dying?

Now, lying in a hospital hallway, her entire existence felt like one big question mark. Or perhaps she had just left it too late to ask herself these all-important questions. They had never seemed so significant at Jinda.

Out there, she'd always felt so very close to Nature, and along with everyone else whose livelihood depended on the land, she'd been incredibly focused on external things – the weather, the condition of their cattle and the availability of feed.

But she'd also been more conscious of other aspects of Nature – the cycles of the moon, the nightly trek of the stars across the velvety black heavens, the rhythm of the seasons which, while less defined than the seasons in England, had been quite distinct, nevertheless.

None of these things had seemed to matter so much since she'd come to the city. Here, life was all about traffic and shopping centres, movie theatres and restaurants. But then, Vera knew she'd fallen into a bit of a slump here.

She was aware that she hadn't really tried to settle in properly. She hadn't done any of the things she'd known she should do, like joining a book club, or some kind of seniors' group, and she still hadn't signed up for the local granny gym. She'd only been living a kind of half-life, really.

I've been wasting what's left of my precious life, feeling sorry for myself, instead of getting out and meeting folk, making new friends.

It was ironic, though, that this health issue should happen now when she'd actually been trying to perk up a little, and when Henry had come to stay. At least she'd put up her hand to join in Ned's roof gardening project and she'd been looking forward to getting involved. After Ned's meeting, she'd stayed on for a cuppa and she'd really enjoyed getting to know Carmen and Jock, as well as Joe and Dennis. Even quiet Ros Grant had proved interesting when you really talked to her, and it seemed she had a contact at the City Council, which might prove helpful.

If you give me another chance, I'll try harder.

It wasn't much of a prayer. Vera was out of practice. Perhaps she should —

'Vera?' A voice sounded beside her.

A man approached. He was in his forties, perhaps, and wasn't dressed in scrubs, but in a white shirt and a blue tartan tie and grey trousers. 'Good evening, Vera,' he said. 'I'm Dr Gregory.'

Vera gave a small nod, which was all she could manage. She was suddenly too nervous to speak. Was this it? The bad news? Was she going to be kept in hospital overnight because she needed further tests? Even surgery?

'We have the results back from both of your blood tests,' the doctor said next. 'There was one from your GP and another test that we've done here.'

'Yes.' Vera wished he hadn't paused and would just get on with telling her his news.

'We're fairly certain that you haven't had a heart attack,' the doctor said next. 'In fact, we suspect that the pain you've experienced was caused by an oesophageal spasm.'

'Oh.' Vera let out her breath on a huff of relief. Or at least, relief was her immediate reaction, until she realised that she had no idea what an oesophageal spasm was. 'I – I'm hoping that's good news?' she said.

At last the doctor smiled.

Thank heavens.

'Yes, it's definitely good news,' he said. 'If you haven't had this pain before now, it could be just a one-off experience. Perhaps caused by something you ate or drank.'

'I did have a rather spicy tomato soup for lunch,' she said, remembering.

'That may have been the cause.'

'Goodness.' So much fuss over such a simple thing? She felt almost giddy with relief now.

'But I'd like you to come back next week,' the doctor went on. 'You need to book in for a stress test with one of our cardiologists, just to make doubly sure that this diagnosis is correct.'

'Oh, I see. All right.' She wouldn't enjoy a return trip to the hospital, but it seemed she'd got off lightly, so she couldn't complain. 'But I don't need to stay here overnight? I can go home now?'

The doctor smiled again. 'Absolutely.'

All good. Coming home by taxi and will see you soon. Vera x

Vera sent this text to Maddie as she waited on the footpath for her taxi. Even though it was after ten now, the hospital behind her was ablaze with bright lights and busyness, but here, outside in the street, it was quiet. Streetlights cast scant pools of yellow and a stiff wind whipped along the footpath.

Looking up to the sky, she saw clouds scudding, at first hiding the stars and then, briefly, revealing their faint glimmer.

'Thank you,' Vera whispered to the heavens. She was inordinately grateful for this reprieve. She felt as if she'd been given another chance.

Enough with pining away like a lonely old biddy. She was alive, which was a huge bonus. Not only that, but she was also apparently healthy and still had her wits about her, so she should damn well get on now and enjoy herself.

She touched a hand to her hair, newly shortened and pink, and smiled. 'I'm going to try harder. I really am.'

In a short time, she would be home. She would relieve Maddie of her babysitting duties and then resume her plans for Henry's stay. She felt quite light-hearted as a taxi pulled up and its cabin light came on.

'Vera?' the driver called.

'Yes, that's me.' She got into the back seat and gave her address. 'I'm afraid it's only a few blocks away.'

'No worries,' came his cheerful reply.

Goodness, the apartment's location really was incredibly convenient. Vera thought of the kerfuffle there would have been if she'd experienced these chest pains out at Jinda. Either Archie or Brooke would have been required to drive her into Jindabilla, and then there would have been a wait for an ambulance to take her to a hospital – probably to Roma, which was well over an hour away.

Now, with a rueful smile, she accepted the possibility that Archie might well have been right when he'd urged her to move to the city. Even so, she'd been worried tonight that he might need to interrupt his mustering and come down here to collect Henry. Thank heavens she didn't have to phone him now with that kind of news.

'Here you are, then,' the taxi driver said as he pulled up in front of the apartments.

'Thank you.' Paying with a tap of her card, and marvelling at such convenience, Vera said goodnight and climbed out. As the foyer doors slid open and she waited for the lift, she found it hard to believe that it was only a few hours since she'd left here with Maddie, trying not to worry, but in reality, feeling very scared indeed.

When she reached her apartment, she opened the door as quietly as she could, but Maddie wasn't asleep. She was in the lounge room and smiling broadly as she rose from the sofa to greet Vera.

A pretty girl in a quiet, understated kind of way, Maddie had fine, shoulder-length, shiny brown hair and clear hazel eyes fringed by lovely long lashes. 'I'm so glad you're okay,' she said as she greeted Vera and they shared a celebratory hug.

'Thank you so much for minding Henry,' Vera told her. 'It was so last minute. I hope you weren't too put out.'

'No.'

'I suppose he's asleep?'

Maddie nodded. 'Yes. I read him a story and then he was out like a light.'

'Oh, that's wonderful, Maddie. I'm so, so grateful.'

'He's such a great kid,' Maddie assured her. 'We've had a lovely time.' She smiled. 'He even showed me the worm farm on the roof.'

'Oh, dear heavens, the worm farm.' Vera rolled her eyes. 'I should have warned you about that.'

'No, it was interesting. Henry's reminded me that I should be composting. It's the least I can do.'

At this, Vera gave a small chuckle. 'Good for Henry.'

'And I'm so pleased you've had good news from the hospital,' Maddie said next. 'It must be such a relief.'

'Oh, it certainly is.' Happily, Vera told her about the oesophageal spasm. 'I'd never heard of such a thing. But I'll take it any day over a heart attack, thank you.' She was grinning, but then, studying Maddie more closely, she realised that the girl looked rather strained. As soon as she'd stopped talking about Henry, she'd seemed to droop and look worried, almost sad.

'Are you all right?' Vera couldn't help asking. 'You look a bit down.'

'Oh.' Maddie immediately brightened, but Vera was sure the effort was forced. 'I'm absolutely fine,' Maddie said, a little too emphatically. 'But I should probably hit the hay and let you get settled.' Already she was gathering up her things. 'I have to be up for work bright and early in the morning, of course.'

'Of course.' Vera didn't like to push the question of Maddie's 'absolute fineness' too far, so she accompanied her to the door and thanked her again, profusely.

It was only after the girl had gone, and Vera had taken a reassuring peek into Henry's bedroom, that she realised she was actually quite exhausted. No doubt, all the tension of the past few hours had taken its toll. She hadn't eaten any dinner at the hospital, but toast and a mug of hot chocolate would suffice this evening.

A slice of raisin bread was heating in the toaster and a mug of milk circling in the microwave when she heard Henry's voice.

'Gran, is that you?'

'Yes, darling.' Vera hurried to his room.

In the soft glow of the night light, she could see him, half sitting up now, and peering towards the doorway. 'Are you okay?' he asked.

'I am,' she assured him, and she came to sit on the edge of his bed. 'My heart seems to be fine, after all.'

His face brightened with a happy smile. 'I was scared.'

'I know you were, but you were very brave, darling, and I'm proud of you.' Tears stung Vera's eyes as she kissed his cheek. 'And Maddie tells me you were very good for her. She really enjoyed your company.'

'She's really nice,' he said. 'We went up to the roof and we talked to Ned. He told me all about the stars and then later Maddie read me a story. She downloaded the book onto her phone.'

'Goodness.' Vera was way behind when it came to the e-book scenario.

Henry was sitting upright now and seemed somewhat animated. 'The story's called *Tom's Midnight Garden*. Maddie only read me the first few chapters, but it's about a boy who goes to stay with his aunt and uncle – and there's a clock that strikes thirteen in the middle of the night and something magic happens and there's this garden and —'

'Hey,' Vera interrupted gently. 'The story sounds wonderful, but you're going to have trouble getting back to sleep if you talk too much now. You can tell me all about it in the morning.'

Henry pulled a face, looked disappointed for a moment, but then he wriggled his nose and sniffed the air. 'Are you making raisin toast?'

Vera laughed, remembering Archie, years ago, giving her that same beguiling smile. It seemed a late-night supper was in order.

CHAPTER SEVENTEEN

Maddie went for a run the next morning, after a night spent mostly awake and worrying. She was quite exhausted and stressed from all the anxious tossing and turning, and she hoped the run might wake her up, or settle her down, or at least help her to shake off the disappointment over Adam's upsetting phone call.

At any rate, she was glad to be out at dawn in the fresh, crisp morning air. She ran along the broad pathway that lined the Brisbane River's banks, heading in the opposite direction from her workplace in the CBD, past the historic Regatta Hotel and on towards the university in St Lucia.

At this early hour, there weren't too many cyclists and walkers, and the river was quiet and still, its surface broken only by the splash of a rowing eight's oars as they skilfully skimmed downstream. Maddie pushed herself to run hard and then harder still, desperate for the flood of endorphins that were supposed to arrive to lift her mood. Her heart was pumping, her breathing noisy, so she almost missed the vibration of her phone against her thigh.

She couldn't think who might be calling at this hour and she hoped it wasn't Vera, having another turn. She was panting as she came to a halt and pulled her phone from the slim pocket in her leggings. To her surprise and dismay, she saw Adam's name on the screen.

She almost didn't answer. She couldn't bear to have him rant at her at this early hour. At the last minute she relented. 'Hello?' she said breathlessly.

'Maddie?'

Thud.

'Is that you, Maddie?'

'Yes.'

'You're panting.' He sounded suspicious.

'I've been running,' she said, but bloody hell, did she really have to explain herself? Yet again?

Annoyed, she hung up. Damn the man. What had she got herself into with this guy? Was he one of those scary, crazy types who needed to keep track of their girlfriend's every move?

She was fighting tears as she slipped the phone back into her pocket. She knew she wasn't exactly hard-headed or pragmatic when it came to boyfriends, but she definitely had limits, and when her phone rang again, almost straight away, she refused to answer it.

Tears slid down her cheeks, though, as she began to run again. It was painful to accept that she'd probably chosen another dud for a boyfriend. She'd really fancied Adam. She'd thought he was fun and charming and they'd really hit it off, and she'd been looking forward to spending lots more time with him, and getting intimate . . .

When she heard the ping of a text message, she kept running. *Be strong. Ignore it.*

She had turned and was almost back at the intersection near the apartment block when she stopped again and finally checked her screen. Of course, the text was from Adam.

I'm so sorry Maddie. Please let me apologise for last night. xx A

This wasn't quite the message she'd expected and now she had to wonder if she'd been too hasty. While she waited on the footpath for the lights to change, the traffic on Coronation Drive was getting busier by the minute. She asked herself if Adam deserved a chance to apologise.

She couldn't help remembering how much she'd enjoyed his company – the happy chats, the laughs, the building, bubbling, lustful tension. The kiss. Perhaps it couldn't hurt to at least hear his apology.

She texted back. *OK.*

This time when her phone rang, she answered, cautiously. 'Hello, Adam.'

'Maddie,' he said. 'Listen, I'm so very sorry. I know it's early, but I wanted to catch you before you left for work. I wanted to apologise for last night. I don't know what came over me. I'm afraid I lost it, but I'm so sorry. I should never have carried on like that.'

Maddie swallowed. The lights on the pedestrian crossing changed to green. Several lanes of traffic were waiting, but she didn't cross. She turned away from the busy street and walked back towards the river.

'I wouldn't blame you if you wanted to dump me,' Adam said next.

She was breathing more easily now, but she felt seriously confused. She most certainly *had* been on the brink of dumping Adam. She'd never experienced anything like last night's angry phone call, and she never wanted it to happen again.

'I guess I hadn't realised just how much I cared about you,' Adam was saying now. 'I was disappointed. But my behaviour was unforgivable.'

He paused and Maddie drew a long breath while she stared out across the river, watching a white crane take off, its thin black legs extended straight behind it while its snowy wings lifted in graceful arcs. In a shaft of morning sunlight, it almost looked like an angel.

'I'm hoping you *will* forgive me, Maddie.' Adam did sound truly penitent. 'I know it's a big ask, but I want to make it up to you.'

She frowned now, wondering what on earth he might have planned.

'I was hoping you'd come out with me on Saturday,' he said. 'We could go sailing.'

'Sailing?' This was a total surprise.

'Yes. I have a yacht moored at the Cleveland Yacht Club. I thought maybe on Saturday we could sail over to North Stradbroke. Actually, we could make it a sunset sail.'

Gulp. A sunset sail did sound incredibly appealing. Maddie hadn't been sailing since her schooldays and, even then, she and her mates had only mucked about in little dinghies in the Burnett River. Normally, she would relish the offer of such a fun, new experience. But with Adam?

Maddie's BS radar was now on high alert. Did she really want to become further involved with this guy? He was sounding very much like the mega nice bloke she'd first met, but if she weakened at this point, could she be making a serious mistake?

'I didn't realise you owned a yacht,' she said, carefully. Adam had certainly never mentioned any interest in sailing until now, and a sixth sense warned her that Adam did *not* own this boat. When he didn't respond straight away, she decided that his next reply would be her litmus test.

If he claimed ownership, she would guess that he was lying, and then she would have no choice. She would have to decline the invitation and say her goodbyes, unhappily chalking Adam Grainger up as another example of the pitfalls of online dating.

After that, she should give up on guys altogether and maybe

do something sensibly boring and sedate – like join the gardening group's working bee.

Having reached this decision, Maddie realised Adam still hadn't answered. 'Are you still there?' she asked.

To her surprise, a soft chuckle now sounded in her ear. 'Yeah, I'm here,' he said. 'And no, Maddie. I don't actually own the yacht. The sloop belongs to a good mate of mine. We've sailed together for years, but he's away in the US at the moment and I'm keeping an eye on it for him. He's happy for me to use it. Actually, he rang only a few days ago to ask me to check it out, and he made a point of saying that he wants me to take it for a sail.'

'Oh, I see.'

'So . . . what do you reckon?' Adam's voice was gentle now, warm and persuasive, sounding exactly like the relaxed and pleasant guy she'd been falling in love with. After a careful pause, he asked, 'Is it a date?'

CHAPTER EIGHTEEN

'Good grief! I knew this would be a disaster.'

It was Saturday morning and the rooftop gardening group's first working bee was in full swing when Nancy Jenkins' shrill voice sliced through their cheerful buzz with the merciless cut of a guillotine blade.

Vera and Henry had been happily planting herbs in a raised garden bed that Ned had already filled with a special mix of soil, worm castings and composted matter. And now Ned was busily attending to his bees, while Joe and Dennis were hammering away, setting up a trellis to extend the far wall, so that vines could be trained to help shade the garden from the western sun. Jock was also there this morning, offering a hand to anyone who needed it, helping to support timber frames for Joe while Dennis hammered, sweeping up any mess the others made via fallen dirt, wood shavings or paint flakes.

And Henry had invited Maddie, as well, or rather he'd *pleaded* with her to join them, after she'd called in on the previous evening and delighted him with a paperback copy of *Tom's Midnight Garden*, which he'd stayed up far too late reading. Vera had found him with a torch under the sheets, for heaven's sake. But the boy seemed none the worse for the late night and now Maddie was happily helping Ros to fill a new collection of huge tubs with potting mix.

Meanwhile, Carmen Cassidy, dressed in amazingly bright multi-striped overalls and with her wild hair held back by a red bandana, was working on an old door that she had 'rescued' from a second-hand shop. Given her artistic credentials, Carmen had been designated the official designer for the rooftop gardeners. She'd outlined her plans at the latest meeting and the group had voted almost unanimously to support her vision – Nancy was the only person against the move, but she'd reluctantly agreed as long as Carmen kept them suitably informed. But it seemed her very first project had set Nancy screeching.

'You've got to be joking!' Nancy roared now as she stared at Carmen's door in wide-eyed horror.

Admittedly, the door was clearly old. It had once held two deep panes of glass, but these rectangular frames were empty now, and Carmen was stripping back a top layer of grey-blue paint, using sandpaper and steel wool, to reveal patches of ancient bare timber beneath.

'What are you trying to do?' Nancy demanded next. 'Turn our roof into a junk yard?'

Carmen merely smiled. 'This is the distressed look, Nancy,' she said in the quiet and soothing tone usually reserved for startled animals. 'It's quite trendy, you know.'

Nancy's scowl deepened. 'It looks worse than distressed. It's ghastly. Hideous.'

'But when it's set in a garden with climbing roses —'

Carmen's attempt to mollify brought a sniff of contempt from Nancy. 'As if roses would grow up here.'

'Why shouldn't they?' Carmen asked calmly. 'Roses are just like any other plant. They only need sunlight and soil and water to produce beautiful results.' She waggled her hand through one of the empty panes in the door. 'Just imagine lovely dark crimson roses peeping though this space, and climbing all over this old timber frame.'

'It will be magical,' piped up Henry, who'd been listening intently to the adults' discussion.

Vera winced. Nancy was bound to adhere to the 'children should be seen but not heard' school of thought. She took a step closer to Henry and was about to touch him on the arm and warn him to butt out of the grown-ups' conversation. But Carmen was beaming at the boy, and Nancy, while continuing to frown, stared at him, somewhat nonplussed.

'Magical?' Nancy repeated, as if the concept was beyond her comprehension. But her tone was slightly less strident, her scowl less forbidding.

Given a different audience, Vera might have explained that 'magical' was Henry's new favourite adjective. He'd already used it this morning to describe the scrambled eggs he'd had for breakfast, as well as the view through her front window of a crane delivering steel pylons to a nearby building site. The word had been inspired, she was sure, by *Tom's Midnight Garden*, which apparently had intriguing magical elements. But this detail would be wasted on Nancy.

And true to form, Nancy now gave a shrug and a 'harrumph', and marched off to inspect Joe and Dennis's trellis, leaving Vera to wish she'd bought a punnet of bok choy seedlings, just to annoy the woman.

Carmen was quite calm, though, and sent a warm smile to Henry, and a conspiratorial wink to Vera, before getting back to work with her sandpaper. And Vera and Henry got back to work too.

The boy had been tasked with tying the newly planted herbs to slim stakes with garden twine, a job he took very seriously. And Vera, who had already planted out two pots each of mint, parsley and thyme, now carefully upended a rosemary plant, loving the aromatic scent of its leaves as they brushed against her gloved hands.

She was enjoying herself immensely. It was so good to be out of doors, soaking up the winter sunshine, smelling the combined scents of earthy loam and fragrant herbs, sharing smiles and nods with the others. Good, too, to know she was living up to the vow she'd made to herself the other night outside the hospital.

Having her grandson's company helped. Yesterday, she and Henry had taken the CityCat downstream to South Bank to visit the museum, where a display of astronauts' suits and space craft involved in the first moon landings had kept Henry absolutely captivated. Then, after ferrying back upriver, the two of them had enjoyed a scrumptious afternoon tea of scones with plum jam and cream.

They'd sat on the verandah of the Regatta Hotel, looking out over the wide stretch of sun-kissed water, and Henry had declared this was 'magical' too. And now Vera was looking ahead to the next week, planning a trip to the Lone Pine Koala Sanctuary. After all, there were no koalas out at Jinda, and the boy was bound to find them enchanting.

Happily engrossed in her planting and planning, she glanced to the far corner and was rather interested to note that Maddie was now over at the beehive with Ned and Nancy. Ned seemed to be explaining something to Nancy, gesturing and pointing, while his inquisitor responded with her usual frowns and head shakes.

No doubt, Nancy was questioning the appropriateness of a beehive on the roof, but Vera noted with interest that Maddie was involved in this conversation too. And it was fairly clear that she was giving Ned her verbal support, a development Vera found rather intriguing.

Ned and Maddie made rather a charming couple, she decided, and as she gently watered the newly planted herbs, she was pleased to observe that the two of them remained chatting, even after Nancy had moved away to inspect the worm farm. And they were smiling rather a lot, which was surely a good sign.

Mind you, Vera wasn't a matchmaker – heaven forbid – but the very thought of Ned and Maddie getting together made her smile.

'Hey, folks, it's time to stop for a morning tea break.'

Vera had been so caught up in her spying, she hadn't noticed Joe and Dennis busily setting up a small folding table with a red and white gingham cloth, to which Carmen added Thermoses and a wicker basket stacked with coffee mugs. Carmen had also brought a little esky with milk, and Dennis produced a large cake tin filled with cinnamon scrolls.

'There's a sink in the tool shed if you'd like to wash your hands,' Jock announced as Joe unfolded canvas director's chairs and set them around as well.

'This is an unexpected delight,' Vera told them as she relaxed with a mug in one hand and a delicious pastry in the other.

Dennis grinned. 'You know what they say about all work and no play.'

'Indeed.'

'Are these scrolls really homemade?' Ros asked him in obvious disbelief.

'Yes, they are.' Dennis was beaming with pride, but he gave an airy, almost dismissive wave of his hand. 'They're actually quite easy to make.'

'Wow. They're amazing.' Ros was clearly in awe.

Carmen had even remembered Henry and had thoughtfully provided a small can of lemonade for the boy, and the mood was wonderfully convivial as people found chairs or perched on the raised garden edges, which proved to be just the right height for seating.

Nancy had already left by this point, which Vera thought was a pity. It might have done the woman good to witness this camaraderie, although she would probably still find some reason to vent her disapproval, no doubt calling them slackers, so they were probably better off without her.

They chatted about the garden plans, mostly – what they wanted to plant and where to position shrubs, trees or flowers – but also about ideas for dining settings, multiple seating areas, a curvy path versus broader paving, a possible barbecue, or even a little fountain or fishpond with goldfish. There was a definite buzz of excitement.

Maddie, seated on a garden edge with Jock, seemed to have discovered that he'd grown up in Far North Queensland, while Joe was quizzing Ned about the bees, about the best blossom-yielding plants to grow near the hive, and when the honey might be harvested. Dennis was telling Ros about the best websites for pastry recipes and Henry was asking Dennis if he could give any leftover scrolls to the worms.

Watching them, Vera was happy to sit quietly, enjoying the moment, while letting her imagination run ahead, picturing how their roof garden might look when the trees and plants were fully grown.

For the first time in a long time, she was looking forward to the future, but then her happy thoughts were interrupted when Maddie jumped quickly to her feet, exclaiming, 'Gosh. I've only just noticed the time. I need to get cracking. I'm supposed to be going sailing.'

'So, you sail?' Joe asked her.

'This will be my first time, actually,' Maddie replied with a smiling shrug. 'Well, my first time in a proper yacht. And I'll only be a passenger. My – um – boyfriend will be at the wheel, or manning the sail, or whatever it takes to get the yacht underway.'

Maddie had a boyfriend? A yachtsman, no less? Vera knew she shouldn't be surprised, and it was silly to be disappointed, but she couldn't help glancing Ned's way. Just a quick glance, but she was sure she caught a swift frown from Ned, a brief moment of tension betrayed by a twitch of a cheek muscle. Had Ned also been caught out by Maddie's announcement?

His reaction – if, indeed, that was what it was – vanished in a flash, however. Almost immediately, Ned was his usual relaxed self, continuing his conversation with Joe, and leaving Vera to wonder if she'd been projecting her own silly disappointment onto the man.

'Thanks so much for the morning tea,' Maddie told Dennis as she set her mug back on the table. 'Sorry I have to rush. I'll stay to do the washing up next time.'

Then, with a wave and a smile, she was gone, her shiny hair swinging as she hurried to the door that led below.

'Bye, Maddie,' Henry called after her, and then he turned back to Dennis. 'I've saved a corner of my pastry for the worms.'

CHAPTER NINETEEN

The only advice Adam had given Maddie about suitable clothing for their sailing adventure had involved slip-on shoes with soft soles, sunglasses and a hat that wasn't so big it would be at constant risk of blowing away.

'It's pretty hard to stop a sailing boat and turn back to pick anything up, so don't wear a hat you're not prepared to lose,' he'd told her during one of several phone calls he'd made over the past couple of days.

With each pleasant, good-humoured call, Maddie had felt more relaxed about Adam and increasingly excited about their proposed date. Just yesterday she'd made a special effort to shop for a new nautically themed top during her lunch break. But this morning, after staying for far too long with the gardeners, she began to worry, for a reason she couldn't quite explain, that her planned costume of jeans and a long-sleeved, square-necked, navy and white striped T-shirt, with a red scarf tied round her neck at a jaunty angle, was just a little too 'try hard'.

She stuck with this plan, however, which was just as well, as she'd been so caught up with the gardeners that she arrived downstairs to meet Adam with a bare thirty seconds to spare.

He arrived exactly on time, pulling up in front of the apartment in an impressive red Mazda sports car – with the hood down, no less – which meant Maddie's costume choice wasn't too over-the-top after all.

Bouncing out of the driver's seat with a cheerful grin, Adam greeted her with a warm kiss and then did the whole gentlemanly opening-the-door-for-her thing, and she couldn't help smiling warmly back at him. It was clear he was keen to make up for his previous tantrum and Maddie was certainly ready to forgive him. And now, a sports car and a yacht in the same afternoon! Wow!

With such a big effort from Adam, she needed to clear her head of the unexpectedly pleasant gardening group experience.

'I guess you were lucky to get the afternoon off,' she said as Adam edged the car out into the traffic.

He turned to her, frowning. 'It's Saturday.'

'Yes, I know – but I was under the impression that real estate agents are always flat out on weekends.'

She hadn't said this with any intention of catching Adam out, but she sensed a sudden tension in him. Or at least, she thought she sensed tension, but the moment was gone so quickly she might have imagined it. Almost immediately, he was smiling.

'That's the advantage of owning your own company,' he said. 'I get to roster my staff and choose my own hours.'

'Lucky you.' Maddie hadn't realised Adam actually *owned* the real estate company. Wow. She wasn't on the lookout for a super-hotshot, wealthy boyfriend, just someone who was good company and romantic, but she couldn't deny that Adam's obvious success was an attractive bonus. She decided to relax and make the most of this wonderful afternoon. And zapping up the Riverside Expressway in a low-slung, bright red sports car was a brilliant way to start.

*

An hour or so later, things weren't going so well. Which was incredibly annoying when everything should have been perfect. And this time it wasn't Adam's fault at all. He'd hadn't put a foot wrong.

The yacht was just the right size as far as Maddie was concerned – not so small that she would end up soaking wet and not so huge that it screamed ostentatious and hinted at a crew of topless girls. Adam had brought wine and a delicious-looking hamper, supplied, apparently, by his favourite deli in Fortitude Valley. And a major plus, the weather was perfect, a crystal clear winter's afternoon, with sun dancing on the small wavelets that gently broke the surface of Redland Bay.

Adam was also very good at explaining what he called 'the ship's rules'.

'If you hear me say "ready about", that means you have to keep your head down,' he told Maddie. 'And be alert for a follow-up warning of "lee ho!" That's when we're about to change direction, and the boom on the mainsail – this big pole sticking out of the mast at right angles – will suddenly swing across to the opposite side. You don't want to get in its way.'

With a cheeky grin, he added, 'And if I talk about sheets, I'm afraid it won't be a hint to head for the bunks below. They're these ropes in the cockpit. Best you don't touch them. I'll use them to set the jib – that's the sail at the front of the boat.'

Having sailed in small dinghies during high school, Maddie was actually familiar with most of these terms, but she was more than happy to be reminded of them now, especially as she was still trying to work Adam out. But after his conscientious explanations, she was relaxed and ready to enjoy herself as she took a cushioned seat in the cockpit, near the helm, while he pulled in the two ropes that had held the boat fast to the pontoon.

Moments later, he pressed a button and Maddie could sense the gentle throb and vibration of an engine somewhere below her feet.

Then with the push of a lever from Adam, the yacht moved quietly and confidently forward, out into the marina, past moored yachts, big and small, where folk onboard sent them smiling waves and thumbs up gestures.

Before long, they were out in the open bay and Adam turned the yacht directly into the light breeze before reducing its speed.

'Hey,' he called to Maddie. 'Take the wheel and just keep us facing into the wind, while I get the sails up.'

Gulp. Maddie was instantly nervous, but she was also chuffed that Adam trusted her with this responsibility. At least there were no big waves and the wind didn't seem too strong, so the wheel behaved itself in her hands. Meanwhile, Adam went to the mast and wound a winch handle, and the mainsail quickly climbed to the top.

The sudden swing of the boom startled her momentarily, but it quickly centred itself, and although the mainsail carried on with noisy flapping, it remained directly in line with the wind. So, she managed quite well for the next few minutes while the jib unrolled, and Adam secured both sets of sails.

'We can turn the motor off now,' he said, giving her shoulder a friendly squeeze as he took over the wheel.

A sudden silence fell as the throbbing motor stopped.

'That was a good, clean start.' Adam's grin warmed her insides. 'Well done, shipmate.'

Pleased and absurdly happy, Maddie drew a deep breath of clean sea air, but she had to grab a railing for balance as the yacht suddenly lurched forward when the power of the winds on the sails cut in. She heard the soft hissing sound of water rushing by, felt the whole yacht lean slightly to one side, and when she looked back, there was a wake of silver bubbles in the deep blue water.

'Yahoo!' shouted Adam. 'Name your port, shipmate. The world is ours. Next port California?'

His enjoyment and excitement were infectious. Maddie had been feeling somewhat giddy, but now, with the sea air rushing to meet her and the clear blue sky spread wide overhead, she couldn't help feeling exhilarated as well.

'Don't worry,' Adam called to her, with another engaging smile. 'You haven't been press-ganged. We can leave California for another day and just aim for a quiet sail over to Stradbroke for starters. I'll find a perfect sheltered beach for our picnic.'

It was at the mention of the picnic that Maddie felt a roiling lurch in her stomach. Oh, God, she wasn't going to be sick, was she?

Could there be anything less romantic than hanging over the side of a boat and losing your breakfast and morning tea? Unless it was curling in the cockpit in a moaning, miserable ball while the relentless nausea continued?

Maddie felt dreadful. So pathetically sick, but so annoyed with herself too. The seas weren't even rough by normal sailing standards, but there was a continuous rocking motion that wouldn't let up and she was as helpless as a landed fish. It was so unfair. Her moments of enjoyment had been so fleeting.

She lost count of the number of times she apologised to Adam, but at least he was good about it and hid his disappointment well, which was an immense relief.

'You poor thing,' he said as he brought her water to sip. 'I did my best to pick the right weather for you.'

'I know,' Maddie moaned. 'And I was sure I'd be fine. I used to sail when I was a kid, but that was only dinghies on the river. This is totally different, and I —'

Alas, she didn't get to finish that sentence.

*

Their drive home was subdued. Maddie stopped retching once she reached dry land, but she was drained and exhausted, remaining huddled in her seat with her eyes closed. Adam put the car's roof up, so she felt cosier, which she thought was a lovely gesture, and when they reached Riverview Place, he asked if she was still interested in sharing the hamper with him.

She really wanted to say yes. Adam had gone to so much trouble. He'd set up the perfect romantic date and she'd totally shattered his efforts.

She did play with the idea of taking the hamper up to her apartment. If the day had gone to plan, they would have been jumping into bed around about now, or perhaps they might have even tried out that bunk on the yacht. She desperately needed more romance with Adam and to get to experience more than his kisses.

Everything about their relationship still felt unnaturally stilted and she wondered if she could take him to the rooftop for a picnic. Perhaps they could have a pleasant, if less exciting evening – except that she knew her stomach really wasn't ready for wine and cheese or olive tapenade, or any of the other delicious treats Adam had bought.

Unfortunately, she had no choice but to offer yet another apology, and she was incredibly grateful when Adam was understanding.

'Ah, well,' he said. 'We'll have to stay on dry land and try glamping next time.'

And as he tucked a stray wing of her hair behind her ear, Maddie wondered why she'd ever had doubts about the man. In a burst of desperation, she said, 'I'm sure I'll feel fine tomorrow.'

His heavy sigh was rather flattering, as was the obvious regret that accompanied his apology. 'I'm afraid I won't be free tomorrow. I really do have to work then.'

In other words, she'd stuffed up his entire weekend.

CHAPTER TWENTY

Henry spied the cat as he and Vera were crossing the street in front of their apartment block. Vera was too busy getting across before the lights changed, so she certainly wasn't paying attention to the wee feline scrap lurking amid the rubbish bins that Jock had lined on the verge, ready for emptying by the Council truck.

As soon as Henry reached the footpath, however, he took a sideways swerve towards the bins, dived between two of them and emerged clutching a black and white ball of fur.

His eyes were shining with excitement and achievement. 'Look, Gran.'

'Goodness.' Vera's first reaction was to demand that Henry set the creature down immediately. It looked extremely thin and sickly and was probably full of fleas.

'I think it's lost,' said her grandson.

'A stray, perhaps,' Vera agreed without enthusiasm. The poor creature looked so scrawny it was easy to believe it had been abandoned.

'Can we look after it?'

'Oh, Henry.' Vera was about to tell the boy this was impossible when the pleading in his eyes silenced her. But she knew she had to be sensible. She lived in an apartment and she was sure there were Body Corporate rules about residents keeping animals. This cat was little more than a kitten, really, although past weaning age, at a guess, but it could well be somebody's pet. Its owners might be combing the streets even now, searching for it. 'It probably has a microchip,' she said doubtfully.

But as she readied herself to instruct Henry to put the kitten down, he said, 'It's a bit like Nanny Tucker's cat.'

Vera stiffened. 'Nanny Tucker has a cat?'

'Yeah. Except she's pale grey. She's called Misty and she's really fat and fluffy.'

Vera was not competitive. She was quite sure she wasn't. But Carolyn Tucker was Henry's other grandmother and she lived in Jindabilla, close to him. Carolyn saw Henry and his sisters on a regular basis, and she had her own little home in the town, complete with a garden and a circle of nearby friends. And she had a cat . . .

Vera looked again at the kitten. It wasn't struggling in Henry's arms the way a wild cat might. In fact, it looked pitiably feeble and weak, but it also looked safe, even contented, curled in the crook of Henry's arm. And it was ever so pretty with its pleading eyes, neat little pink nose and striking black and white markings.

'I don't think we're allowed to have cats in the building,' she said. 'But I suppose we could sneak this poor little thing upstairs and at least give it a feed.' Then, to make up for this weakness, she frowned. 'But we can't keep it, Henry. We should do the responsible thing and find a vet who can check it out and trace its owner.'

'Awesome, Gran.' Henry was already tucking the little mite under his jacket, ready to smuggle it into the lift.

Oh, dear. She really was a pushover where this boy was concerned.

*

Half an hour later, Henry sat cross-legged on the living room carpet, his latest Lego masterpiece abandoned and in pieces on the coffee table, while he remained very still, with his back against the upholstered sofa, gently stroking the kitten as it slept in his lap.

Vera was surprised by how tame it seemed and she was sure it must be someone's pet, but it was certainly a while since it had eaten. The small tin of tuna and saucer of milk they'd offered had been downed in a blink, and the kitten had then found a pool of sunshine in which to sit and wash itself thoroughly. Now, Vera wasn't sure who was more contented, the boy or the cat.

'We should call him Max,' Henry told her, as she relaxed in a nearby armchair, enjoying a cup of Lady Grey tea.

Vera was quite sure that naming a stray was taking things too far. 'We don't even know if it's a boy or a girl,' she hedged.

Henry's eyes sparkled with secret knowledge. 'It's a boy. I looked.'

She laughed. 'Aren't you the clever one?' But he was a country boy, of course, wise to such matters.

'Or Felix could be a good name,' Henry said next.

'Felix?' A small pang pierced Vera's heart. Henry was too young to know about the cartoon cat called Felix. It must have been back in the eighties when that had been popular. 'You can't call a cat after your grandfather,' she said quite firmly.

'I don't think Granddad would mind. I wouldn't mind if there was a cat called Henry. I think it'd be cool.'

Vera smiled and realised she was probably oversensitive where Felix was concerned. She always had been, of course. Love and loyalty were deep and delicately complicated notions, as poets and songwriters throughout the centuries had attested.

'Let's stick with Max,' she said. 'But just remember we won't be able to keep him.' She might have said more, but her phone rang at that moment. 'That might be your father.' She had left her phone on the kitchen counter, so rose now to fetch it.

But it wasn't Archie's name that showed on her screen, and this time the pang she felt was tinged by the tiniest flash of guilt.

'Hello, Theo,' she said.

'Vera, how are you?'

The fluttering in her chest was silly, but she couldn't help it. Her fling with Theo Blaine had been brief yet quite thrilling, but conscious of the tension this had caused at the time, they'd agreed to part as friends.

Over the past year, her only contact with Theo had been a very occasional email. There'd been one or two women from her old mah-jong group, though, who'd taken the trouble to call her, and in the midst of inconsequential chatter, had managed to not so subtly mention that Theo Blaine had been seen escorting quite a range of women in the district.

Given this news and the distance that separated them, Vera had thought she was well and truly over Theo, but now, the sound of his deep baritone brought heat to her skin and a flood of memories she'd tried hard to suppress.

Picnics on the riverbank at Bunyip Bend and a tartan rug spread beneath a weeping paperbark tree. Dinner in Theo's homestead, not at the dining table with a housekeeper serving, but again eaten picnic style, this time on the hearthrug, with an abundance of cushions, an open fire and champagne in elegant crystal flutes.

They'd shared a fondness for classical music too, most especially the Elgar cello concerto played by Jacqueline du Pré. And she remembered the guilty pleasure of his lips on hers, of his fingertips tracing her skin . . .

He said, 'I heard from Archie that you've been in hospital, and I wanted to check how you are.'

Vera drew a quick, calming breath. 'Oh, that's good of you,

Theo, but I'm fine. It was a false alarm. Didn't Archie tell you that?'

'Actually, he did reassure me, but it seemed like a good excuse to make contact.'

'Oh?'

'I've missed you, Vera.'

Goodness. Quite suddenly, she needed to sit down. She glanced to Henry, who was still completely absorbed by the kitten. She called to the boy, holding out the phone. 'I'm just taking this call through to the bedroom, Henry.'

At his nod, she headed down the short hallway.

'You have Henry staying with you,' Theo said, as she lowered herself to the edge of the bed.

'Yes, it's been so lovely to have him here. I'm enjoying his company enormously.'

'That's great. He's a good kid.'

'I gave him a fright when I headed off to hospital, but I was fortunate that a lovely neighbour looked after him, and I wasn't gone for long.'

'I'm glad you got off lightly.'

'Yes.' Vera decided not to mention the stress test yet to come. She had decided to put it off until after Henry was gone, which wouldn't be too long now.

'I had a similar experience last year,' Theo said.

'With chest pains?'

'Yes, although for me it was a case of blocked arteries.'

'Goodness. Not a heart attack?' Why hadn't she heard about this?

'A small one, yes.'

'Oh, Theo, that's terrible.' Vera was genuinely shocked. Theo was the archetypal outback cattleman, an outdoors man, lean and muscular and fit as a fiddle.

'It turned out fine,' he said. 'They gave me a couple of stents and now I'm as good as new.'

'Thank heavens you're all right.'

'Yeah, I was lucky, I guess.' After a short pause, he said, 'I'd really like to see you, Vera.'

'You want to come to Brisbane?'

'Yes. As I said, I've missed you.'

Her immediate reaction of joy was something of a giveaway, Vera realised. But her delight was swiftly followed by a sharp reality check. 'Forgive me, Theo, but I find that a little hard to believe, given the rumours I've been hearing.'

'You listen to rumours?'

'Oh, I take them with a grain of salt, but there've been stories that you've entertained just about every single woman in the district.' Even as Vera said this, she was sure Theo would deny it, in the same way Felix had always fiercely denied his gambling debts.

Theo's response, however, was a chuckle that merged into a groan. 'I can just imagine the stories.'

'Perhaps, but I'm sure they're not groundless.'

'Well, no,' Theo admitted. 'But the thing is, when word gets about that a man of a certain age is available and he has means, he only has to wake up in the morning, wash his face and comb his hair, and he jumps to the top of the most wanted list. Women come out of the woodwork.'

'Oh, dear, poor you,' Vera teased. 'What a terrible dilemma.' She wondered if one of those women had been Carolyn Tucker.

'I'd rather be with you.'

Theo's gentle words reached Vera with a punch that rendered her quite breathless. Her thoughts spun and it was some time before she could speak. She'd spent so many lonely months trying to adjust to life here, without her family, without Jinda, and without this man, and only recently, mainly thanks to the gardeners, she'd seen a glimmer of light at the end of that lonely tunnel.

It was ironic that Theo should reach out to her now. Nevertheless, she couldn't help feeling flattered. And pleased.

As she busily tried to summon an appropriate answer, Henry appeared in the bedroom doorway, with the kitten still curled in his arms.

'I've been checking Max all over,' he announced. 'I don't think he has a chip.'

Vera laughed. She'd been on the verge of offering Theo an impetuous invitation. Had she been saved by her grandchild from making a reckless mistake? Holding up her hand to signal Henry to wait a moment, she spoke into the phone. 'Sorry, Theo. I might have to call you back.'

'Of course,' he said, obligingly. 'Give it some thought anyway, and if you'd like me to come down, just let me know.'

'I will, and thanks for the call.'

'My pleasure. I'm so glad you're well. And give my best to Henry.'

As Vera set her phone aside, she needed a moment to collect herself. So much seemed to be happening lately. It was almost as if her stars had realigned. One thing was certain, though. She needed a much clearer head before she responded to Theo's proposal.

Meanwhile, Henry was waiting patiently in the doorway. What had he been talking about? Oh, yes, the microchip.

'I don't think you can see the chip,' she told him now. 'I'm pretty sure the vets inject them under the cat's skin.'

The boy shrugged at this news. 'Okay,' he said, and he then smiled sheepishly. 'I'm afraid Max has just done a wee on your cushion.'

CHAPTER TWENTY-ONE

An invitation waited in Maddie's mailbox. No envelope. Just a simple homemade card with *COME TO DINNER* printed in childish capitals and coloured in with a thick red felt pen. The message inside had been written by Vera and illustrated by Henry with drawings of a helicopter, a sailing boat, a spaceship and a cat.

Dear Maddie,

Henry and I would like to thank you for helping us out at such short notice last week. We're hoping you might like to join us for dinner one evening. We're free any night this week, and happy to fit in with whatever suits you.

Hope to see you soon. We send our very best wishes,

Henry and Vera

Maddie smiled. Scant months ago, when she was still caught up in her Simon obsession, she mightn't have been too thrilled about a dinner invitation from an elderly woman and a small boy. This evening, she knew it was the perfect midweek pick-me-up.

Of course, she would enjoy sharing an evening with Vera and Henry. The fact that she hadn't heard anything from Adam since they'd parted on Saturday was not a factor. Maddie assured herself that Adam's silence was fine. No doubt he was extra busy with his business after he'd given up a large chunk of the weekend for her.

She planned to text a quick response, but this became unnecessary when she stepped out of the mail room and found both Vera and Henry waiting in the foyer for the lift.

Henry's eyes were sparkling even more brightly than usual, as if he was privy to an exciting secret. Turning to his grandmother, he asked in an excited stage whisper, 'Can I tell Maddie about Max?'

Vera laughed. 'I think you may have just done that, don't you?'

The boy looked stricken until Vera added, 'I'm teasing. Go ahead, Henry. Maddie will be wondering what on earth we're talking about.'

'Yes, I'm dead curious,' said Maddie. 'Who's Max?'

'He's a kitten,' the boy whispered, coming closer and standing on tiptoes to reach her ear. 'He's a stray and he's staying in Gran's apartment.'

'Wow!' Maddie said. 'That's an awesome secret.'

'Don't worry,' Vera added, with a roll of her eyes. 'We've taken it to the vet to be checked out. It's not sick, just undernourished. But it didn't have a chip and there's no registered owner, unfortunately.'

'Well, I'm sure Max is very lucky to have found the two of you.' Maddie was remembering her own childhood and the series of stray cats that her soft-hearted mother had adopted. So many happy hours she'd spent curled in a cane hanging chair on the back deck at home, with a book in her hand and always a kitten or cat slumbering in her lap.

'By the way.' She held up the card. 'Look what I just found in my mailbox.'

Henry beamed at her. 'Gran was going to phone you, but I said we should make it a proper invitation.'

'Well done, you. It was a lovely surprise.'

'You'll come, won't you?' the boy asked eagerly.

'Henry,' intervened Vera. 'Give Maddie a chance to catch her breath.'

Maddie smiled at them both. 'I'd love to come. And I'm free any weeknight, actually.'

They settled on dinner for the very next evening and it proved to be as pleasant and diverting as Maddie had anticipated. Henry was given the honour of choosing the menu, and the roast lamb with roast vegetables, gravy and peas, followed by his Gran's apparently famous lemon meringue pie, were perfect. An old-school meal, straight out of Maddie's childhood, which made her quite nostalgic. More than once, she found herself thinking of her parents and grandparents and home. She really should take a trip back to Bundy quite soon.

She wondered if Adam would come with her. But almost immediately, she reminded herself that it was far too soon to think about taking him home. Her parents would read too much into it. And, for reasons she couldn't quite pin down, Maddie wasn't sure that her mum and dad would take to Adam.

Truth to tell, she was still trying to work out what *she* thought of him. His behaviour had been blameless on Saturday, and ever since, she'd been desperate to hear from him again. And yet tonight she'd deliberately left her phone back in her apartment, because she hadn't wanted to risk the remote possibility that he might call, discover she was busy elsewhere and flip back into angry mode.

Luckily, the scrumptious meal and diverting company sidetracked her from dwelling on this possibility, and when the meal was finished, she helped Vera to clear the table. Then, while Vera stacked the dishwasher and the kitten made himself comfy on the end of Henry's bed, Maddie read Henry another chapter of *Tom's Midnight Garden*.

He'd been reading the story to himself and was past midway, but like all children he still loved being read to. As Maddie closed the book, she looked again at its familiar cover, with Tom in his blue and white striped pyjamas and Hatty in her Early Victorian white dress and pinafore, the stone south wall that separated the garden from the orchard, the silhouette of the huge leafless yew tree.

'You know,' Henry said. 'I think our rooftop garden is magic too. Like Tom's garden.'

Maddie smiled. 'You could be right.' She was quite chuffed that Henry was enjoying the story as much as she had at his age.

'Your name Maddie sounds a bit like Hatty,' Henry said next and, out of nowhere, she was hit by an urgent longing to be a mother with kids to read to and play with, to laugh with, or to comfort when they were sick or scared, and in time, to be a grandmother like Vera.

But wasn't it wrong for a woman in her twenties to be hankering for a family of her own? This was the twenty-first century, after all, not the 1950s. Maddie knew she was supposed to have far loftier ambitions than motherhood. At the very least, she should be planning to travel the world, or write poetry, or flood Instagram with stunning photography.

Ambition was pretty much a solo gig, though, and Maddie had always seen herself more as a team player.

It was only as she watched Henry settle more comfortably in his red and blue tartan pyjamas – a bit short in the arms, as if he was growing out of them – that another, more frightening thought gripped her. 'Henry, you won't go up to the roof garden at night, will you? Not on your own?'

For a moment, the boy looked wistful, as if this was exactly what he would love to do. Guilt and terror flooded Maddie, accompanied by nightmare images of the boy somehow tumbling from the roof, despite its safety wall.

Had she made a terrible mistake in sharing this book?

'Promise me, Henry,' she begged.

To her relief, he nodded. 'Okay. I promise.'

Her guilt eased a tad, but she couldn't shake it off entirely. 'I mean it, Henry. A rooftop garden at midnight is a very different thing from Tom's midnight garden on the ground. I really need you to swear you won't go up there by yourself.'

'I already promised you. I swear.' Henry looked quite earnest now, and almost put out that she doubted him. 'But I'd like to go up there with Ned again and look at the stars.'

'Yes,' Maddie agreed softly. 'That would be fun.' It was then she noticed the other book on Henry's bedside table. *The Mysteries of the Universe.* The cover was quite dazzling with illustrations of planets and galaxies, shooting comets and exploding stars. It seemed wonderfully enticing, as did the thought of joining Henry and Ned up on the roof, while they stared at the starry night sky.

Not that there was any reason why she should join them. After all, she could go up there any night she liked.

And yet, she was picturing a scene with the three of them sitting cross-legged in a row and gazing up at those immense black heavens, searching for satellites. She could even point out a few of the stars. She knew how to find Orion's Belt and the horn of Taurus the Bull.

Then again, Ned Marlowe could probably name the whole damn lot of them.

Back in the living room, Vera asked Maddie to stay for a nightcap. 'I have a bottle of Cointreau and it's rather delicious,' she said. 'And I suspect it would go perfectly with those lovely chocolates you brought.'

An invitation too good to refuse, surely? Vera poured the golden liqueur into cut-glass tumblers and, with the room bathed in soft lamplight, they relaxed in deep, comfortable armchairs. Vera even kicked off her shoes and settled her feet on a velvet pouffe – rather elegant feet for a woman of her age, Maddie noticed.

But then, Vera was enviably elegant in every respect and, given her posh English accent, Maddie couldn't help wondering about her family background and how she'd ended up on a cattle station in outback Australia. She shied away from asking such a probing question, however.

Meanwhile, the Cointreau was very delicious indeed. Rich, warming and relaxing and, as Vera had suggested, the perfect accompaniment for melt-in-the-mouth chocolate.

Through the big living room windows, which Vera had left slightly open, soft guitar music drifted from a balcony below. The player was quite expert, fingering the strings one moment, then strumming the next. Then he began to sing in a light tenor voice, keeping the right time, but veering weirdly off-key.

'Is that Dennis singing?' Maddie asked.

'Yes.' Vera looked amused. 'He often serenades us at about this time.'

'I've never heard him,' Maddie said. 'I guess I'm too far below and at the other end of the building.' She couldn't help adding, 'It's a pity he's not in tune.'

'I know.' Vera chuckled. 'But he doesn't sing loudly, and the guitar is nice. And I honestly don't mind that he's at least a semitone flat. I think it helps Henry to drift off to sleep.'

'An off-key lullaby.' Maddie was smiling now too.

'I can shut the window,' Vera offered.

'No, no, leave it. I love it, actually.' Maddie meant this. Despite the disharmony, she found something weirdly comforting in hearing Dennis's voice. Actually, she was beginning to feel an unexpected sense of connection to these people who lived in her building – those she'd met, at any rate.

Another post-Simon bonus, no doubt, as she spent less time socialising with her workmates now. And in just a short time, she'd moved from a nodding acquaintance to budding friendships with Joe and Dennis, with Vera and Henry, and even, at a pinch, with Jock . . . and the beekeeper.

In fact, for the first time since Maddie had moved to the city, she no longer felt like a total outsider, as if she had to earn her right to belong.

'So, how's the garden going?' she asked Vera. 'I haven't been up there since the weekend.'

'It's going just fine.' Vera seemed delighted to report this. 'I've been up there almost every day to check on the plants and to do a little watering. That's the joy of a garden for me. I love being able to potter about and to notice even the tiniest changes. I can get quite excited over a new leaf.' With an apologetic smile, she added, 'But I guess I'm fortunate that I don't have to go to work, so I have plenty of time to smell the roses, so to speak.'

'I suppose the Gestapo's up there most days, checking?'

'You mean Nancy?' Now Vera gave an amused snort. 'I wouldn't be surprised. She probably rushes straight up there the minute she gets home from work, but luckily I've managed to avoid her.'

'I'm sure there always has to be at least one whinger on any project.'

'Ah, well, I imagine Nancy sees her role more as quality control. I think we're probably lucky we haven't had more complaints. It's probably a good thing that Godfrey Raines seems to have lost interest.' Leaning forward, Vera reached for the box on the coffee table and helped herself to another foil-wrapped chocolate. 'These are sinfully delicious.'

After she'd happily munched and swallowed, she licked a smear of chocolate from her finger and, once again, managed to look elegant as she did so. 'I must say it's rather lovely to see Jock, our caretaker, getting involved in the garden, isn't it? That young man seems to have so much energy.'

'Yes, he's an interesting guy, isn't he?'

Vera shrugged. 'I'm afraid I don't really know much about him. I feel rather guilty that I've never really tried to get to know him.'

'I've been the same,' confessed Maddie.

'Mind you, it's only lately that I've made any kind of effort to meet any of the people here,' Vera added.

'Jock's a writer,' said Maddie.

'A writer?' Vera blinked. 'What sort of writer?'

'He's writing a novel.'

'Good heavens.'

'I know. I hope I didn't look too surprised when he told me. I'm afraid I didn't have time to find out much about it. But who would have thought – our very own caretaker – the guy who mops our corridors and takes out our garbage bins – might actually be penning a blockbuster novel?'

'That's amazing,' agreed Vera.

'But you hear of those kinds of writers, don't you?' Maddie added. 'They take on all sorts of jobs to keep a roof over their heads while they work on their masterpieces. It's kind of romantic, isn't it?'

'Yes, I suppose it is,' said Vera. And then, she sent Maddie a smile that was almost sly. 'Speaking of romance, can I ask about your young man and your sailing adventure?'

'Oh. I guess.' To cover her lack of enthusiasm, Maddie quickly added, 'I'm glad you didn't ask that while we were having dinner. I'm afraid I was disgustingly seasick on the yacht.'

'Oh, dear.'

'But Adam – that's my, ah, boyfriend – was very understanding. He was awfully good about it, really.'

'And why shouldn't he want to look after a lovely girlfriend like you?'

Good question. Maddie did feel bad that she'd doubted Adam.

'You've known him quite some time, I imagine?' Vera asked next.

Clearly, the woman was fishing, but Maddie didn't mind. It was almost a relief to talk about Adam, although she certainly wouldn't mention that she'd met him online. 'No, I haven't known him very long,' she admitted. 'I guess he's still on probation, but he's shaping up rather well.'

'Hmmm.'

Maddie stiffened. 'What's that *hmmm* supposed to mean?'

Vera gave a helpless kind of shrug. 'Sorry. I know it's none of my business, but I was thinking that the way you talked about your chap didn't sound very – enthralled. Is that what it's like these days? Do young people resist falling hopelessly in love?'

'I'm sure it pays to be careful.' Maddie wasn't sure she could ever risk falling madly in love again. Once bitten, twice shy. 'True romance seems to be way too painful.' Now she just wanted the stability of a steady boyfriend, of not having to worry about how she would spend her weekends.

Vera was still watching her, but after a bit, she leaned back in her chair, staring off towards the windows, with a faraway look in her eyes, as if she was remembering something. Or someone. 'Romance, for want of a better word, is always something of a gamble,' she said, but as she did so, her face seemed to sag, and she seemed to suddenly age several years.

When she spoke again, her voice was so quiet Maddie could only just hear her. 'Some people hide so much from us that we can never really know them. And it doesn't help if they don't really know their true selves.'

A chill crept through Maddie. Had Vera heard about Adam's outraged phone call? Or was she remembering something else entirely?

'Forgive me, Vera,' she said. 'I don't mean to pry, but you sound as if you're speaking from experience.'

CHAPTER TWENTY-TWO

The red rose cries, 'She is near, she is near;'
And the white rose weeps, 'She is late;'
'Come into the Garden, Maud'
by Alfred, Lord Tennyson

Kent, England, 1969

Vera's stomach was in knots as she sat in the back seat of the Rolls beside her father. Ahead of them, she could see the bridesmaids' cars, beribboned and shiny black, progressing sedately beneath the overarching branches of the massive ancient oaks that lined the Glenbrook driveway.

Pandora would be in the second car, pretty in pink and clutching her posy of rosebuds and carnations, while she harboured a secret that was tearing Vera apart.

'Darling.' Her father looked worried as he reached for her hand and gave her an encouraging smile. 'Chin up, Pookie,' he said gently.

Pookie was Lord Glenbrook's nickname for Vera, chosen when she was five, after a flying rabbit, a storybook favourite from Vera's childhood and in honour of those rare, but very precious, occasions when he'd come into the nursery to take over the nightly reading duties from Vera's nanny.

Right now, Vera wished she could whizz back in time to the safety of her childhood, when the only decisions she'd been required to make had involved a choice between custard or ice cream with dessert. Instead, she was now about to plight her troth to a man with a potentially life-altering secret, and her entire future happiness hung in the balance.

The fleet of Rolls-Royces was processing through the Glenbrook entrance gates now and turning onto the main road where the cars began to speed up. In less than ten minutes they would arrive at the church, and panic flapped in Vera's chest, as fierce as the wings of a trapped bird.

'Father,' she said, unable to hold back any longer. 'Have you heard anything about Felix's farm?'

Her father frowned. 'The farm in Devon?'

'Yes.'

He shook his head. 'No.' But now his face was creased with concern. 'Why do you ask, Vera? What have you heard?'

'Nothing that makes sense,' she had to confess. 'It's just something Pandora said to me – just before we left. She asked if anyone had told me about the farm.'

'What a strange thing to say.'

'I know.'

'But she offered no explanation?'

'She didn't get a chance to, really. Mother arrived and you were waiting. It was time to leave.'

'Do you think . . .' her father began, but then he paused, as if he wasn't quite sure how to present his question.

'I don't know what to think,' Vera said. 'That's the trouble, but I sensed something really bad has happened.'

Now her father reached into the inner pocket of his formal jacket and pulled out a packet of Woodbines along with his silver monogrammed lighter. Impatiently, Vera watched while he lit a cigarette and inhaled deeply before eventually letting out a thin wisp of smoke.

'Pandora's a silly little thing,' he said at last. 'I'm sure it's nothing to worry about.'

'But can you be certain?' Vera was quite desperate now.

Her father nodded. 'Of course I'm certain,' he said. 'Felix is a fine fellow. Honest and utterly respectable.' But the shadowy flicker in his eyes told a different story.

Vera groaned.

Her father was losing patience with her now. 'Don't be so dramatic, Vera.'

But already she could see the church steeple standing in the distance above the freshly ploughed fields and the panic rising inside her was suffocating. 'I have to speak to Pandora.' Even as Vera said this, she had a better idea. 'No, I need to speak to Felix.'

'Vera, that's impossible.' Her father glanced at his watch. 'Felix will already be inside the church.'

'Only in the vestry, waiting.'

'Possibly, but he could be at the chancel steps, waiting for you in full public view.'

Tears filled Vera's eyes. If she wasn't careful, she would ruin her makeup. But more to the point, if Felix had been untruthful, she could ruin her *life*.

'I'm sorry, Father. I can't go ahead with this until I've spoken to Pandora.'

A corner of his mouth lifted in a faint, flickering smile of relief. 'At least that shouldn't be too hard to organise.'

Vera felt infinitely better now this was decided.

The crowds outside the church were even bigger than Vera had expected, and a loud cheer exploded as her father got out of the car. Vera remained seated and she was grateful for the veil over her face.

'If you wouldn't mind fetching Pandora,' she said. 'I'll wait here.'

Her father gave a stiff nod. 'Very well.'

The bridesmaids were lining up, ready to process ahead of Vera just as they'd rehearsed. She watched their surprised faces as her father approached them, saw him step closer to Pandora and lean in to whisper in her ear as he delivered the message.

The sudden terror on Pandora's face was unsettling, as was the vehement shake of her head, not to mention the looks of intense curiosity from the other bridesmaids. Murmurs ran through the crowd gathered on the footpath, rising to a high buzz as Vera's father took Pandora's elbow and steered her towards the car with its waiting bride.

'I'm sorry,' Vera said, as soon as Pandora came to the window. 'But I need to know what you meant when you asked me that question about Felix's farm.'

The poor girl's face drained of all colour now, and her lipstick and rouge stood out like clown's paint.

'Pandora,' Vera persisted between tightly clenched teeth. 'Just tell me.' She nodded towards the church's grand entrance. 'I'm not going in there till I know. Has something happened? Something terrible?'

Pandora nodded. 'He's lost it.'

A bomb exploded in Vera's chest. 'Lost the farm?'

'Yes. I don't know the whole story, but it was a racing bet. At Ascot.'

Oh, dear God. Vera was so suddenly dizzy she thought she might faint, but even as the shockwaves pounded through her, she knew it wasn't so much the loss of the farm that bothered her as Felix's lack of honesty. Surely, she couldn't possibly marry a man who would hide such an important truth from her?

Leaning through the window, she called to her father who was waiting at a discreet distance. 'I have to speak to Felix.'

'For God's sake, Vera.' Lord Glenbrook looked every inch the haughty aristocrat now as he stared at her in disbelief. 'It's far too late.'

'It's supposed to be bad luck,' Pandora said faintly, but the other two ignored her.

Coming closer, Vera's father hissed, 'You can't march into the church and demand to speak to your bridegroom.'

'No,' Vera said calmly. 'But you can take a message to him. Tell him I need to speak to him. I'll stay in this car and I'll meet him at Glenbrook Bridge.'

For a long, fraught moment, Vera was sure her father was going to refuse this incredible request. But she sat very still with her head high, willing him to cooperate.

Years later, Vera wondered if her father had remembered all the fairytales they'd read together – stories in which so many fathers had tried to impose unfair demands on their daughters. Whatever the reason, Lord Glenbrook now marched off without another word, around the side of the church to the vestry door, and the waiting crowd was totally dumbstruck as Vera asked Benson to drive her back to Glenbrook Bridge.

She thought she'd just been through the worst moments of her life, but the next five minutes of waiting were torturous. Poor Benson had no idea what to say to Vera and she hadn't the strength to try to explain, so they sat in their respective seats, silent and tense as coiled springs.

At last, another car pulled up and Felix got out. Tall, trim and broad shouldered, he looked rather splendid in his black dress-coat and tails with high-waisted, striped formal trousers.

Felix also looked very worried – touchingly so – and, in that moment, Vera was sorely tempted to bury her concerns and doubts and to just go ahead with this wedding and hope for the best. After all, she was quite in love with him – not in a totally all-consuming, worshipping kind of way, perhaps, but the attraction was strong, and she'd been eagerly looking forward to their honeymoon. As Felix continued to the car, however, she knew she had to remain firm.

'Perhaps if you could leave us now, Benson?' she asked her driver.

'Yes, ma'am.'

Her heart was beating hard as Felix opened the car door and joined her on the back seat. He looked so handsome in his dark morning suit, complete with white tie and silver waistcoat, and standing wingtip collar.

'You look amazing,' he told her.

'I'm sorry,' Vera replied quickly, not wanting to waste any more time than was strictly necessary. 'I've just been so worried. I had to speak to you.'

Felix nodded. 'It's about the farm?'

'Yes.' At least he was being direct. 'Is it true that you've lost it?' Vera kept her gaze fixed on Felix's face as she asked this. If she wanted the truth, she needed to catch his every nuance.

To her relief, he didn't once flinch. He kept his gaze as steady as her own. He even smiled.

'It's all right, Vera,' he said. 'You don't have to worry.'

'You mean, you haven't lost your farm at the races?'

Now he smiled again, gently, almost pityingly, as he took her hands in his. 'My poor darling,' he said. 'I'm so sorry you've had to go through this worry.'

'It's just that I need the truth, Felix. I couldn't bear it if you weren't being honest with me.'

His gaze didn't waver as he nodded.

'So, tell me, please.'

Now his blue eyes shimmered. 'Right. I'll be absolutely honest. Technically, I did lose the farm last Wednesday.'

'Felix!'

'Shh! Let me finish.' He gave her another, slightly lopsided smile. 'As I said, the loss was only a technical detail. There's been no hand-over of property, no settlement, and I already have the money to buy the farm straight back again.'

'Really? How?'

'Friends. People in my circle.'

'You have the full amount?'

'I have enough, and I'll have the rest soon.'

'Oh, Felix.' This was hard to believe. 'Are you sure?'

'I'm absolutely sure. I'm totally confident. The farm is mine, darling. From today it will yours *and* mine. Ours.'

'Right.' Vera supposed she should accept this and stop fretting. A church filled with family and friends awaited. Her father, her mother, her grandmother and brother – everyone would be frantic.

'I didn't tell you about this because I didn't want you to worry unnecessarily,' Felix said.

'I see.'

Lifting her veil, he pressed his lips gently to hers, a tender kiss, full of promise. 'I'll look after you, Vera, I swear.'

CHAPTER TWENTY-THREE

On Saturday morning, when Maddie joined the gardeners for another working bee, there was still quite a lot of mess on the roof-top. A load of pale, creamy gravel had been delivered during the week and left in small mountains to be spread. Maddie had no idea how the gravel had arrived. By crane, perhaps? Or had there been hours of hard work with buckets and bags carted up in the lift? And now, between these piles, Ned and Jock were laying pavers, guided by lines of string stretched between tent pegs, as dictated by Carmen's landscaping plan.

Apparently, both Ned and Jock had been up since the crack of dawn, bringing trolley loads of the pavers up to the roof. But despite the piles of gravel, the stacks of pavers and bags of cement, Maddie could see glimpses of how the rooftop garden would look in the future when the heavy labour was behind them and the plants were lush and fully grown.

Vera's newly planted herbs in the raised garden beds already looked promising. And enormous pots had been wheeled into their appropriate positions and planted with well-established trees and shrubs. Vera knew them all by name and had pointed to fan palms, weeping bottlebrushes, golden pendas, lemon trees and olive trees, and easily pruned varieties of bougainvillea, which she had assured Maddie were going to be absolutely gorgeous.

Joe and Dennis's trellis was now finished, and would add shade to the western wall, and Carmen's door had been set in the middle of the trellis. The plan was to train climbing star jasmine over the trellis. The jasmine had been planted in blue pots that Carmen had 'distressed' to match the door, and the final effect was going to be quite romantic, Maddie was sure.

Meanwhile, Vera and Ros were planting up lined wire baskets, ready for hanging when the pergola was finished, and Carmen was taking photographs so they would have a record of their progress.

Young Henry had tried to keep busy, ducking and weaving his way around the workers to check the worms and bees, but with this achieved, he seemed at a loose end and was getting in everyone's way. He tried to talk to Ned, who was crouching over a paver, lining it up for careful positioning.

'Hey, Ned, have you seen —'

'Sorry, mate.' Ned spoke over his shoulder as he eased the block into place. 'Bit busy right now.'

Maddie watched Henry's mouth droop.

'Here, Henry,' she called. 'Can you give me a hand?' She'd been allocated the task of planting three different tomato varieties in a row behind the herbs, as well as making tall cane tripods to support them – one for each plant. 'Do you think you could cut twelve pieces of twine for me? I need them this long.'

Holding out her hands, she indicated the length of the plastic-coated wire she would need to bind the apexes of the tripods.

'Absolutely,' the boy responded eagerly and, as he rushed to help her, Maddie was aware of Ned glancing her way.

Such a fleeting look, but as their gazes met, Ned sent her a nod of approval, and his smile warmed his eyes and softened the line of his mouth, making her feel as if her skin was too tight for her body.

For God's sake, get a grip, girl. You don't need that man's approval.

The moment was gone in a blink. Ned went on with his work, and Maddie returned her attention to Henry. She handed him the twine and the garden scissors, and he took the task very seriously, measuring the required length and cutting the twine with the frowning concentration of a brain surgeon.

'Great job,' Maddie told him, and the boy beamed with pride.

The gardeners had decided to reward their hard work with a rooftop barbecue in the evening. Maddie wouldn't be joining them, however, as she was going out with Adam. She hadn't seen him all week. He'd been too busy, which was fair enough, but when he'd called to arrange a Saturday night date, she *had* considered inviting him to the barbecue, instead of going to the expensive, upscale restaurant he'd booked.

Problem was, when she'd tried to imagine Adam socialising with the gardening group, the picture wouldn't quite gel. She supposed she still didn't know him quite well enough. She didn't really know much about the people he mixed with. She'd never met any of his friends or workmates, but then he'd never talked about them either.

She had told him about the rooftop gardening group, but he'd merely shrugged, as if it was, at best, a quaint idea. And then he'd proceeded to quiz her again about the people she worked with, and she'd had to dive for cover, because of her lie.

It was obvious Adam was hankering to be invited to a swanky social event where he could mingle with the investment bankers who were supposedly her workmates. Eventually, Maddie would have to set the man straight about that small mistruth, but she wanted to get to know him better, to be confident he wouldn't blow up again.

As she set the last tripod in place, she was still brooding over the whole Adam scenario when she was distracted by Vera calling to Henry.

'For heaven's sake, Henry, you can't keep checking on those worms. Leave the poor things alone.'

Maddie sent her a sympathetic smile. 'He's run out of ties to cut.'

'Yes,' Vera said with a sigh. 'I'm afraid he's a little bored this morning.'

'But he's been very good, really.' Maddie didn't state the obvious, that it must be hard for the boy to entertain himself, with no other children to play with.

Vera was nodding. 'And I think he's twitchy because his family's coming to collect him. This evening will be his last night here.'

'Oh, yes, that's right.' Maddie knew Vera was going to miss her grandson terribly, but she suspected the sadness might be mutual. 'Is Henry keen to get home?' she asked carefully.

'Yes and no. He's excited about seeing everyone, of course, but . . .'

Vera's eyes held a suspicious glint, and Maddie was sure she saw tears behind those trendy glasses, but almost immediately, Vera blinked and managed a brave, if crooked, smile.

'I suspect he will miss this place,' she said. 'It's so different from anything he's ever known.'

'Yes. I reckon this will be one of those holidays he'll remember forever,' Maddie told her. 'I've never forgotten holidays I spent with my father's parents. They lived on a cane farm way up north near Tully, so I didn't see them often. And it was probably because I didn't see them very much that the visits seemed extra special.'

'That's a nice thing to say, Maddie.'

'It's true.' Maddie's family had visited these grandparents every second Christmas and she had very fond memories of hordes of relatives gathered around their Christmas tree, or at the dining table, with aunts and uncles wearing silly paper hats, and her cousins squealing as they snapped bonbons.

These images were still sparkling clear and special for her, and there were other memories too. Mornings in the garden with her grandmother, watching vivid blue Dunk Island butterflies fluttering among the hibiscus bushes. Flying a kite with her grandfather on a windy day and getting it tangled in the branches of an enormous mango tree.

When Maddie was ten, her grandmother had taught her how to make scrambled eggs – just enough milk to fill the gaps between the eggs in the bowl, a walnut-sized knob of butter melted in the pan, parsley and chives snipped fresh from the pot at the kitchen door.

'Actually, you're right,' Vera was saying in a faraway voice, as if she might also be lost in her own memories. 'I don't suppose Henry will forget this holiday.' Her smile took a droll tilt. 'He certainly won't forget you and Ned.'

Maddie smiled too, but her skin prickled, and she dropped her gaze quickly, annoyed to find herself rattled, simply because she'd been linked in a casual, inconsequential comment with Ned.

'Hoy, folks! It's morning tea time!'

Grateful for Carmen's summons, Maddie hurried off to wash her hands at the storeroom basin, before getting on with slicing and buttering the date and ginger cake she'd made.

Everyone else downed tools and came to sit on the folding chairs. Maddie, with coffee and cake in hand, found herself next to Jock again. She grinned at him. 'We're lucky that you're so willing to share your handyman skills with us.'

Jock gave an easy, smiling shrug. 'I'm happy to help. A green rooftop is such a great project.'

'It is,' she agreed. 'Our cities are getting so crowded. We're going to need more and more green spaces.' Then, as Jock helped himself to a second piece of her cake, she leaned closer and lowered her voice. 'If it's not too prying, I'm dying to hear more about this novel you're writing. I've been trying to guess what sort it might be. I decided maybe a murder mystery.'

Jock grinned. 'There's no murder. But it does involve a mystery.' He seemed quite happy to talk, settling forward, mug in hand, elbows propped on his knees. 'It's about this modern-day private investigator who's down on his luck. A wealthy old woman offers him a job tracking down the site of a crashed World War II Liberator bomber. She tells him it contained "priceless treasures" and she's committed her life to finding the wreck.'

'Sounds fab,' said Maddie. 'Wow. And I might be speaking to a future bestselling author.'

Jock's laugh held a rueful edge. 'Yeah, well . . . some days I tell myself I'm dreaming, should chuck in the writing and find myself a proper job. Then other days the words flow . . . and I know I can't give up. Not yet.'

'Of course you mustn't.' Although Maddie, who'd never had loads of self-confidence, could imagine how the doubts might plague him. With a smile, she said, 'So, I'm guessing the plane wreck might be up on Cape York somewhere?'

Jock nodded.

'And I think you said last week that you grew up in Cooktown? So you'd know that country quite well?'

'Sure do. My wife and I both come from Cooktown.'

Maddie couldn't quite cover her gasp of surprise. She hadn't realised Jock was married, had never seen any sign of his wife. Embarrassed, she tried to think of the best way to ask him about her.

But Jock must have realised that he needed to explain. 'Zoe's overseas,' he said. 'In Nepal. She's a photographer, an adventurer. Always climbing mountains, or fighting her way through jungles, or shivering in some frozen fjord.' He smiled. 'Seriously, she actually goes to those places. It's how she gets such great photographs. I've been with her on quite a few of the trips, but we both decided I should settle down this time and concentrate on my novel.'

From the back pocket of his khaki shorts, he pulled out a phone and flipped through photos, then held the phone out to show Maddie a breathtaking shot of towering, snow-capped mountains, before flicking to another pic of a silky smooth, half-moon bay, palm trees and a brilliant, orange and purple tropical sunset.

'Wow, they're beautiful photos. She's very talented.'

'Yeah, Zoe's pretty amazing.' Now, there was no missing the pride in Jock's fond smile. He flipped to another photo – a selfie of himself and a young woman – pretty, with curly fair hair, radiant smile and a glowing complexion. A rocky cliff face formed their backdrop and Zoe was dressed for adventure in a zippered fleece, slim-fitting pants and hiking boots.

'Oh, wow!' Maddie couldn't help saying. 'Zoe's lovely, Jock.' She realised now that she had seen this woman before, somewhere in their building – in the lift, a corridor, the car park or wherever – but she'd never realised the connection. 'You both look so happy,' she said, sending him a smile. 'And you said the two of you grew up in Cooktown?'

He nodded. 'Zoe's parents own a pub in the main street and my dad's a fisherman. Dad's spent his life trawling up and down the Cape. I practically know that coastline like the back of my hand.'

'That's useful. I don't think many authors set their stories in the Far North, so it should give you a unique niche for your writing.'

This brought another grin from Jock. 'I'll have publishers beating a path to my door, huh?'

'Of course.' Maddie was grinning as she thought about the possibilities of his plot. 'I'm guessing there's plenty of adventure in your treasure hunt?'

'Tons. My hero and his trusted Aboriginal sidekick set off to find the wreckage, but they're chased by greedy mining company stooges, bad guys, the whole box and dice. And when they eventually find the plane, it'll be somewhere cool like an underwater cave surrounded by crocodiles.'

'Oh, yes!' cried Maddie. 'You've got to have crocodiles. Then you'll have film-makers fighting each other to turn your book into a movie.'

He gave a rueful chuckle. 'I wish.'

Glancing to the other gardeners, Maddie saw Ned deep in conversation with Joe and Vera. She wondered if Ned knew all about Jock's writing ambitions and his adventurous wife, and realised that he probably did. There was a good chance he'd been the first person from their building to extend a hand of friendship to their caretaker.

A few moments later, Jock got to his feet and returned to his task of laying the pavers. And Ned, who was also back at work spreading sand with a trowel, acknowledged Maddie with a quick, cheeky wink that did something very peculiar to the pit of her stomach.

CHAPTER TWENTY-FOUR

Henry was bursting with pride. His father had driven down from Jinda, bringing three huge bags of cow manure in the back of his SUV, and the boy couldn't wait to show them off to Ned.

'Manure is absolutely magical for the worms and the compost bins,' the boy announced, as soon as he spied the bags, and even before he'd properly greeted his father in the car park. 'There's a trolley over there, Dad. You can take the bags straight up to the roof in the lift.'

'Hang on there, my love,' intervened Vera. 'Give your poor father a chance to catch his breath. He's been driving for five hours.' With a rueful smile for Archie, Vera stepped closer to give her son a hug. 'Hello, darling. It's so good to see you.'

Archie, however, was looking rather shocked. 'Is that really you, Mum?'

'Oh.' She touched her new short pink hair. 'I'm afraid so.'

His face creased into a broad grin. 'For a minute there, I was thinking alien invasions, body snatchers or whatever. But, hey, you look amazing.'

'Thanks.' Secretly relieved, Vera turned to Henry again. 'Now, darling, we're taking your father upstairs to the apartment and we'll give him a nice cup of tea. The manure can wait until later.'

'But Ned will —'

'Ned won't want to worry about manure right now, Henry. He's far too busy with the paving. There'll be plenty of time to show him this later.'

Vera did understand how incredibly excited the boy was about sharing the garden and all of his new discoveries with his family, but she needed to deflect him from heading to the roof right at this very moment. It would be mayhem up there. Not only were Ned and Jock still laying the pavers, but Joe and Dennis had joined them and they were all working frantically to have the job finished in time for this evening's barbecue.

'Yeah, there's no rush, mate.' Archie gave his son's hair a fatherly ruffle. 'But I will get the bags out of the car so it's not stinking of manure when I go to the airport to fetch your mum and the girls. And I need to make room for their luggage.'

So, with the bags neatly stacked against the garage wall, Vera smiled again at her son. 'How are you, anyway, Archie? Did you have a smooth trip?'

'A perfect run, thanks.'

'And how are Brooke and the girls?' Vera hoped she didn't sound tense as she asked this question, but she couldn't help feeling nervous. This evening would be the first time since she'd moved to Brisbane that she had all of Archie's family staying under her roof, and she was worried she might inadvertently do or say something to upset her daughter-in-law.

Archie didn't seem at all bothered, though, and he assured her that Brooke and the girls were fine. According to reports from Melbourne, Sienna and Emily had been champions on the netball court, and they and their mother had all had a brilliant time. He would be picking them up from the airport at four pm.

Vera was looking forward to a relaxing lunch with Archie and Henry before the others arrived and things got more hectic. With luck, it was going to be wonderful, though, with the whole family here this evening.

Every detail was planned. Brooke, Archie and the children were all going to attend the barbecue on the roof, and Vera was hoping this event would provide shining evidence that she really was settling in here. She had bought a load of sausages and lamb chops and had made two huge salads – a pasta salad and another with sweet potato, wild rice and rocket.

As for sleeping arrangements, Archie and Brooke were to sleep in the spare bedroom that held a double bed, while Henry had happily surrendered the twin room he'd used for the past ten days for his sisters' use. Henry would sleep on a sofa in the lounge, which wasn't any sort of sacrifice, as far as he was concerned, but a 'magical' novelty. Bless him.

Given the impending excitement, Vera kept their lunch simple, serving Archie's old favourite of salmon patties and salad, along with a store-bought jam roly-poly and a pot of good strong tea. And their lunch was, of course, accompanied by a running commentary from Henry, who related excited tales for his father about the CityCat ferry rides, the space display at the museum and the cuddly koalas at Lone Pine Sanctuary. Not to mention the sighting of satellites sweeping across the night sky, and keeping tabs on worms and bees. And of course, the adventure of finding a kitten.

'We can keep Max, can't we, Dad? We can take him home with us to Jinda?'

Vera, watching from across the dining table, saw the pleading hope in her grandson's eyes and the shadow of dismay in her son's.

Oh, dear.

Archie was shaking his head. 'I'm afraid we can't have a cat, Henry. You know your mum's allergic.'

'No, I didn't.' Henry was pouting.

Vera winced. She'd been conscious of Archie's lack of enthusiasm when he'd been introduced to Max almost as soon as he'd stepped through the doorway. But if she had known about Brooke's allergy, she would have left the cat with the vet days ago, and by now it would have been taken to a refuge centre. What a bother. She should have remembered that Archie and Brooke had only ever kept dogs as pets.

'What's allergic?' Henry asked.

'It means that cats can make Mum sick,' said his father. 'They give her asthma, so she has trouble breathing.'

Henry seemed to droop at this news. Then, just as quickly, he brightened. 'But Nanny Tucker has a cat. Misty doesn't make Mum sick.'

Archie gave a shrugging nod. 'I know, but Misty's a special breed. Balinese. She's safe for people with allergies.'

Meanwhile, Max, with impeccable timing, chose this very moment to emerge from behind the sofa and, although only half grown, managed to stalk with the quiet dignity exclusive to felines. On finding a pool of sunlight, he promptly settled on the carpet with an air of total possession.

Watching the cat, Henry scowled. 'I don't get it. How can a kitten like Max make somebody sick?'

'It's something they give off,' Archie said patiently. 'Tiny, invisible microbes.' He gave a helpless shrug. 'I don't really know how to explain it, but people breathe it in and if they're allergic, they get sick.'

'Henry, we knew you might not be able to keep Max,' Vera reminded the boy gently. But then, as another thought struck, she gave a gasp of dismay. 'Oh, goodness. I really should get rid of Max now, shouldn't I? Before Brooke arrives?'

She would hate to make Brooke ill, and she certainly didn't want to hand her daughter-in-law a perfect excuse to avoid staying in the apartment this evening. But this new information also meant that even if Vera found somewhere to deposit the kitten, she would have to vacuum the entire apartment again.

Thank heavens she'd kept the door closed on the spare bedroom where Brooke would sleep. She was confident Max hadn't been in there.

Archie, watching Vera now, grimaced uncomfortably. 'Sorry, Mum. This is a total hassle to land on you at short notice.'

'I should have thought to ask you about Max. I never gave asthma a thought. And I'm not sure the vet's open on a Saturday afternoon.' Vera was thinking aloud as she went through her options.

'We could ask Maddie to mind Max,' Henry suggested.

Vera shook her head. 'Maddie's going out tonight with her boyfriend.'

Henry pouted again. 'Maddie should have Ned as her boyfriend.'

'And what would you know about such things?' Vera asked, as she shared an eye-roll with Henry's father.

'Maybe Ned would take Max?' Henry tried next.

'We're certainly not going to bother Ned. Not when he's so busy.' But even as Vera said this, she smiled. 'But there is someone else I might try.'

Until Carmen opened her front door, Vera was quite sure she'd hit on the perfect solution for Brooke's allergies. She had travelled downstairs in the lift with poor Max zipped inside a striped shopping bag. The bag was roomy, with plenty of air for Max, but he did let out a couple of bewildered meows, so she was lucky there'd been no one else in the lift to hear him.

The cat gave another small meow as Carmen's door opened and she stood before Vera, smiling and looking exceptionally glamorous in one of her lovely colourful kaftans. 'Vera,' she said warmly. 'Hello.'

But Vera took one glimpse into the beautiful living room behind Carmen and was gripped by a sudden case of cold feet. The room was quite stunning, with walls painted a gorgeous deep green, and floors decorated with beautiful Oriental rugs in reds and blues. Vera could see sofas too and interesting furniture, vases of flowers, paintings on the walls, and the result was so artistic and wonderfully coordinated that the very idea of suddenly dumping a stray cat on Carmen seemed, instantly, quite insane.

'I'm sorry,' Vera said. 'I think I've made a silly mistake.'

Carmen frowned, clearly puzzled, while Max gave a small cry of protest. 'Do you have a cat in there?' Carmen asked.

'I do.' Vera's smile was more of a grimace. 'But now I feel foolish.'

At this, the other woman laughed. 'Vera, I don't think I've ever seen you in such a flap. I think you'd better come inside.'

Vera lifted the bag. 'Is it all right to bring this in?'

'Of course.'

As the door closed behind Vera, she took a deep breath. It wasn't that she hadn't been in beautiful living rooms before, but Nancy Jenkins had made such disparaging comments about Carmen's apartment that Vera had been led to expect mess and chaos rather than this beautiful and clever harmony.

Now, she needed to adjust her expectations as she admired the scene in front of her. There were two large, comfy looking sofas – more chic than shabby – one in a paler green that was a perfect echo of the walls, the other a simple pale-sand tone, while a single armchair was upholstered in green and blue stripes. Cushions abounded on the sofas in artful combinations of red, blue and green. Paintings covered the walls, vases of flowers adorned side tables, while white cloths on these tables, as well as white urns and white lampshades, provided elegant contrasts to the deeper colours. But the pièce de résistance was a cupboard against a far wall, painted letterbox red, embossed with gold and sporting wonderful green door handles.

For added impact, lush plants stood in copper pots near the big picture windows, and on the far wall Carmen had painted tall, white-framed French doors and a beautiful view of leafy green shrubbery complete with birds in the branches.

Vera was enchanted. 'This is just brilliant,' she exclaimed, looking about her in wonderment. 'It's so hard to believe it's just an ordinary apartment like all the others in our building. You've done something quite magical here, Carmen.' She smiled as she heard herself echoing Henry's favourite adjective. Quickly she added, 'It's genius.'

'Why, thank you.' Carmen probably didn't require Vera's praise, but she still looked pleased. Then with a gracious sweep of her arm she asked, 'Won't you sit down?'

'Thank you.' Vera sat on the sand-coloured sofa and opened the shopping bag's zipper a little as she set it at her feet.

Carmen took the striped armchair, crossed her legs gracefully and smiled. She was plump in a curvaceous way that was rather attractive. 'Now,' she said. 'Tell me about this cat.'

A little shamefacedly, Vera did so, although her story, including the recent discovery about Brooke's allergies, didn't take long. As she finished, she said, 'I'm pretty sure we're not supposed to keep animals in these apartments.'

Carmen waved this aside. 'Probably not. I've never asked.'

'I'd hate Nancy Jenkins to find out.'

'Yes, but don't worry. I certainly won't let on, and what Nancy doesn't know can't hurt her.'

Vera smiled.

'So,' Carmen said, her face lighting with curiosity as she indicated the striped bag. 'Let's have a look at this poor creature.'

As soon as Vera undid the zip further, Max's head popped up, his pointed ears and golden eyes alert as he peered around him.

Vera had half expected him to take a leap for freedom, and when he didn't, she lifted him onto her lap.

'Oh, he's still quite small,' said Carmen.

'Yes, not much more than a kitten, really.'

Holding out her hand to Max, Carmen beckoned with her fingers, making her silver bangles tinkle as she tried to coax him. 'Hello, Max. Aren't you a handsome boy?'

'He's a little timid,' said Vera.

'That's understandable, but he's lovely, and I'd be happy to have him stay here overnight.'

'Are you quite sure? I know not everyone likes cats.'

'I'm perfectly sure. I wouldn't have offered if I wasn't happy to have him.'

'Ohhh.' Vera made no attempt to hide her sigh of relief. 'And if Nancy does find out for any reason, I'll take the blame, of course.'

'Whatever. I always cut Nancy a little slack, actually.' Leaning forward now, Carmen lowered her voice. 'Just between you and me, our Nancy has had a rough trot.'

'Oh?'

'It's terrible really,' Carmen said, adopting a conspiratorial tone. 'She used to have a problem with alcohol. It was so bad that her husband divorced her, and also gained custody of their children.'

'Good heavens.' Vera felt her mouth sag with shock. 'Poor Nancy.'

'Exactly. Poor Nancy.'

Silenced, Vera could only sit very still as she absorbed this surprising news. She tried to imagine the shame and pain Nancy must have suffered, the heartbreak of having her children removed from her care. She thought about the way Nancy presented herself now, so bossy and critical, finding fault wherever she could.

Was it all a front? A form of armour?

'You never can tell what pain people are hiding, can you?' Carmen said. 'I'm sure most folk are carrying wounds of some form or another.'

'Yes. And putting on brave faces.' This information certainly put Vera's own perceived misfortunes into perspective. She wondered what else Carmen knew about the people in their building.

But the artist wasn't settling in for a gossip.

'I suppose you have food for him?'

'Oh, yes.' Vera reached into the bag. 'Tins of food – more food than he'll need – and the kitty litter tray.'

'Perfect.' Rising from her chair, Carmen crossed the room and lifted Max from Vera's lap. Then, with him cradled in her arms, she made soothing noises as she stroked the soft fur just below his ear.

Vera drew a deep breath, a mixture of amazement and relief that this hurdle had been so easily cleared.

Watching her, Carmen grinned. 'Don't worry,' she said. 'Over the years, I've taken in several stray men. A stray cat should be a cinch.'

Vera didn't travel with Archie to the airport, but stayed behind for another frantic clean. She was at the door to greet everyone, however, and there was great enthusiasm, with hugs and kisses and stories from the girls, their voices high pitched and bubbling with excitement, as they shared their adventures. Vera had never seen them quite so animated. They kept talking over each other.

'It was freezing cold in Melbourne, Gran.'

'But at the zoo we saw gorillas and the cutest little lemurs with black and white striped tails.'

'And in the city, we went to the most amazing restaurants.'

'And we ate gozleme.'

'It's Turkish food. And just so OMG divine!'

'And Mum let us buy new clothes.'

'I bought these tights.'

Vera hugged the girls for a second time, loving their enthusiasm and loving even more that she was able to share it.

'And we have something for you!' announced Sienna. 'Where's Gran's present, Mum?'

'A thank you present,' Emily explained, as her mother retrieved a package from one of their bags. 'For looking after Henry.'

Brooke's smile as she handed over the package seemed genuinely warm. 'Thank you, Vera. I know Henry's had a fabulous time here with you.'

So unexpected. The gift came in an expensive, tissue-lined box, tied with a very sophisticated silver satin bow.

'Oh, goodness,' Vera whispered as she lifted the lid to discover a super-fine cashmere scarf. 'Brooke, this is truly gorgeous. Thank you.'

'Put it on, Gran,' commanded Emily, and Vera did so, draping the scarf, pashmina style, around her shoulders and flipping an end over one shoulder.

'Wow! It suits you perfectly,' Sienna exclaimed, clapping her hands in enthusiastic applause.

'Yes, it looks especially lovely with your new pink hair.' This comment came from Brooke and Vera tried not to look too surprised by the compliment.

The girls insisted that Vera check her reflection in the mirror, and she had to admit the delicate fabric with soft drifts of colour in cream, rose and grey really did make her look rather glamorous.

She thanked Brooke again and she almost gave her another hug, but she didn't want to overdo the emotion.

It was a little after six thirty when they all headed up to the rooftop, still excited, and carting an esky with food and drink as well as plastic glasses and paper napkins. The night was clear and cool and

the rooftop was looking quite transformed with the paving mirac-
ulously completed and pretty solar-powered lanterns casting just
the right amount of light. Portable barbecues were being fired up,
and trestle tables were set out ready for salad bowls, cutlery and
paper plates.

Henry had barely got a word in edgeways since his sisters had
arrived, but now he let out one enormous 'Wow!' as he looked
about him in open-mouthed delight. He understood, of course, how
many changes had been achieved in a surprisingly short space of
time. Then he saw the moon.

By now the sun had almost disappeared behind the western hills,
and the giant orb of a full moon had risen, huge and magnificent,
glowing orangey-red, perhaps reflecting the last of the sun's light as
it climbed above the trees and buildings to the east.

'Oh, my!' Vera was aware of the awestruck hush that fell over
her family. Even the excited chattering of the girls was silenced as
they all stood in appreciative quiet, drinking in the moon's stunning
beauty.

Henry was tugging at Archie's hand. 'Wow, Dad! Why is the
moon so absolutely ginormous tonight?'

Archie grinned at him. 'It's big right now because it's still quite
low in the sky. It'll start to look smaller as it gets higher.'

Hearing this, Henry stared at his father in dropped-jaw aston-
ishment. 'Do you know all about the moon and stars and stuff?'

Archie chuckled. 'Not really, but you know what it's like when
you live in the bush. You can't help noticing the sky. I'm no expert.
Not like your mate who gave you that book.'

'That's Ned.' Henry tugged again at his father's hand. 'You have
to meet Ned, Dad. I don't think he's here yet, but he's done so many
things that I have to show you. The worm farm, the beehive over
there in the dark behind the screens, the compost bins. Oh, and
come and look at the tomatoes that Maddie and me planted.'

Vera, who was carefully setting her salad bowls on one of the trestle tables, smiled as she saw Henry enthusiastically dragging his father about the rooftop, pointing out the sights he deemed so awesome, and explaining about them with a great amount of animated arm waving.

Meanwhile, she introduced Brooke and the girls to Carmen and Ros, and to Joe and Dennis, as well as Nancy and Godfrey, who were no longer quite so vocal in their criticisms, but still not smiling very much. Then Ned and Jock arrived, freshly showered after their day's exertions, and Henry dragged his father towards them.

'Hey, Ned. Hey, Jock, my dad's here and guess what he brought for you?'

Ned gave a chuckling shake of his head as he extended his hand to greet Archie. 'Hello,' he said. 'It's great to meet Henry's father at last. I've heard so much about you. All good, I should add.'

'And ditto re you,' replied Archie with a grin. 'Hi, Jock,' he added as they also shook hands. 'Great to meet you too.'

Ned turned to Henry. 'So, tell me. What's this amazing thing your dad has brought for us?'

'Manure!' squealed Henry. 'Manure from our cattle at Jinda. Three whole bags of it.'

'Brilliant!' Ned responded, grinning.

Archie laughed too. 'I've never seen a kid so excited over a pile of cow shit.'

There was laughter all round, including from Dennis who was standing nearby. And Vera joined in, until she noticed Jock positioned quietly beside Ned as he observed this exchange. Their caretaker's gaze was fixed on her son and grandson, on their clasped hands and glowing, laughter-lit faces, but the expression on his own face was incredibly wistful, like a window into a secret pain.

CHAPTER TWENTY-FIVE

Maddie had to get this evening right. She couldn't stuff up another date with Adam. She needed everything to be perfect, and to this end, she'd bought yet another new dress, inspired this time by one of her favourite British TV stars. The dress was a daring bright red, a nice match with Adam's sports car, she decided, and it had a pleated chiffon skirt that fell to mid-calf. Bravely, Maddie had teamed this with high-heeled black ankle boots.

Disappointingly, she found it hard to gauge Adam's reaction. He made no comment about her appearance when he arrived in a taxi – not the sports car – but Maddie told herself she didn't mind. Of course, she didn't. Compliments about her appearance weren't important. After all, Simon had habitually flattered her to the skies and look how that had ended.

Just the same, she *did* make a point of complimenting Adam on his smart grey suit and elegant black and gold tie. And she made sure she praised his choice of restaurant, which wasn't hard to do, given the atmospheric Middle Eastern decor, and the aromatic chicken kebab she was served, followed by a delicious dessert of ginger and walnut ice cream.

Once or twice during the meal, Maddie did wonder how the rooftop barbecue was progressing and how the paving looked now that it was finished. She wondered, too, if the gardeners had decided to play music up there. Dennis's guitar, perhaps? And were Vera's grandchildren enjoying themselves?

As she pictured their gathering, she could almost smell the slightly charred steaks and chops on the barbecue. But she couldn't allow herself to dwell on that scene, especially when Adam was plying her for detailed info about companies that he was sure were hot investments and wanting to know her opinion.

Sadly, Maddie hadn't a clue. 'I can't really comment on those companies,' she hedged. 'But I do know that big-name companies can sometimes hide serious problems from their investors. People have been caught out by sudden falls.' She had seen such catastrophes happen to clients in their legal firm, but if Adam pushed her for details, she'd be floundering to supply answers.

Now, however, Adam smiled at her. 'You really are a loyal little bunny, aren't you? Circumspect to a fault. Your bosses should give you a gold star.'

It was hard not to squirm. Maddie knew that a date shouldn't be such an ordeal, but it was her own fault – she'd created the deception.

She would have to come clean with Adam soon. Very soon, in fact. But given their last two rocky dates – one where she'd cancelled at the last minute, and the other where she'd ended up seasick – she wasn't ready to reveal that she actually knew zilch about shares and investments.

'Mind you,' Adam said next. 'The market's doing terribly on the whole, so it's probably not a good time to invest.' With that, the subject was dropped and Maddie was grateful to be off the hook. For now.

*

The big moment of the night came, of course, when their taxi pulled up outside the apartment block. This time Adam paid the driver before he accompanied Maddie to the door.

'You'll come up, won't you?' she asked, smiling shyly.

His answering smile was reassuring. 'Try to keep me away.'

The taxi left, the doors slid open, and together they went inside. In the lift, Adam started kissing Maddie. Straight away and dramatically up against the wall. It wasn't quite the same thrill of their first kiss, which seemed so long ago now, but it was still exciting.

Her apartment was on the first floor, so the trip was short and Adam was still kissing her as the doors slid open. She couldn't help thinking that if this was a movie, people would be waiting in the corridor, grinning broadly when they caught them pashing, and she would be all flustered. But there was no one waiting, no one to see them. Adam continued to nuzzle her ear as they made their way down the short stretch of tiled hallway to her apartment, and she felt surprisingly unruffled.

She had left a lamp on, with the light carefully positioned to show off her lovely, exotic cushions and the showiest of her pot plants. The scene was rather welcoming, she thought. It even looked a little sexy, but Adam made no comment about the setting. He was too busy kissing her again.

'Where's your bedroom?' he muttered against her lips.

'This way.' After all, no need to put it off. This was what she wanted, wasn't it? What she'd been hanging out for, for weeks, and Adam's fingers were already finding the zipper in her dress.

Maddie had to stop him, though. He was so eager, she was worried he'd tear the horrendously expensive, delicate fabric, so she took the dress off carefully, but quickly, and draped it over a chair in the corner. Then she was left in her new lingerie and ankle boots.

'Look at you!' Adam grinned. 'So sexy I could eat you.'

At last.

The kissing continued with gratifying enthusiasm in between helping each other out of the rest of their clothing, which ended up scattered on the floor. But everything that followed was also rather hasty and rushed.

Possibly, the hurry was excusable for a first time that had been frustratingly postponed, but Maddie would have preferred a little more foreplay. In an ideal scenario, with an especially hot guy, she might have been so turned on that lingering kisses wouldn't be necessary. But this evening with Adam, she'd been hoping for teasing and tempting seduction, rather than a quick nibble here, a hurried rub there, and then straight on to deep penetration.

Talk about wham, bam, thank you, ma'am!

Okay, she told herself when this was over, there was no need to be too disappointed. Perhaps now, she could put on a little music and offer Adam a drink and, after a cosy interlude, they might enjoy a more relaxed encore.

But before she could even offer music or a drink, Adam was rolling out of bed and groping on the floor for his clothes.

Seriously?

As Maddie watched the broad stretch of his bare, freckled back, she bit back her impulse to voice her dismay. But when it came to dating disappointments, she had just about reached saturation point with this guy.

She'd been battling doubts and questions ever since his tantrum phone call on the night she'd taken Vera to hospital. Since then, as far as she was concerned, the vibe between them had never really sparked. Now, it was time to be sensible and, as Adam pulled up his jocks, Maddie suspected that a serious rethink was in order. As he stepped into his trousers and zipped the fly, she felt surer about this.

Propped against the pillows, with the sheet pulled up to her armpits, she watched in glum and broody silence as Adam found his shirt on the floor, scooped it up and slipped his arms into the sleeves. Then he turned to her and as he began to do up the buttons, she couldn't help remembering the happy days with Simon and how she'd been so sad to watch Simon's gorgeous bare chest disappear inch by inch behind each closed button.

Tonight, as Adam completed this task and looped his tie loosely around his neck without bothering to knot it, she felt indifferent, almost bored. She hadn't even noticed he was smiling, until he spoke.

'So,' he said, his smile expanding into a full-fledged, confident grin. 'Next Saturday's our big glamping weekend.'

Gulp.

Maddie had just, this moment, reached the crucial decision that she must break up with this guy, but now she felt as if she'd stepped into quicksand.

Such lousy timing! Adam hadn't once raised the subject of glamping during this evening's conversations and that plan had totally slipped her mind. But, in reality, he'd been carrying on about glamping since the very first night she'd met him.

It was actually rather annoying that he couldn't just call it camping like everyone else, and Maddie wondered what made his camp set-up so glamorous that he felt it deserved this title. An extra-large blow-up mattress? Whatever the reason, Adam was obviously very proud of his property at Boonah and he was keen to show it off to her, and after stuffing up his sailing adventure, she almost felt —

Stop it. You're not under any obligation.

Adam found his shoes and, after a little more hunting, also discovered both of his socks. Now, he sat on the edge of Maddie's bed to put these on and as he tied a shoelace, he sent her another flashing smile. 'I've been giving some thought to the menu and I reckon we should go for lamb shanks, slow cooked in a camp oven over the coals.'

His eyes were bright and he looked boyish with excitement, just as Henry had looked when he'd told Maddie about finding the kitten.

'That sounds amazing.' The automatic response popped out too quickly. She was such an idiot.

'Great,' said Adam, who had now finished dressing, and got to his feet. He stepped closer and bent low to drop a kiss on Maddie's forehead. 'I'll be in touch to let you know what time I'll pick you up.'

But I haven't said I'm coming.

The words were quite clear in Maddie's head, but as she sat there, naked and vulnerable beneath the sheet, she couldn't find the courage to speak up. And already Adam was at the bedroom doorway, waving goodbye to her. Then she heard his footsteps in the hall and the click of the front door as he closed it behind him.

A weird kind of bleakness descended and Maddie wasn't in any way ready for sleep. As she swung her legs over the edge of the bed, she decided she needed a nice hot shower.

The heat, the drumming water and the soothing scent of lavender shower gel *did* offer a measure of comfort. Feeling somewhat better, she towelled herself dry, dressed in trackies and a T-shirt and went to the kitchen to make herself a good, old-fashioned cup of tea, hot and strong, with a dash of milk and a heaped spoonful of sugar.

She told herself she wasn't going to allow herself to get in a stew over this. She had all week to pluck up the nerve to set Adam straight. Right now, she just needed to clear her head. Actually, she would put on a sweater and take her mug of tea up to the roof. The barbecue folk would have gone to bed long ago, and the empty rooftop would be the perfect place for a little clear-headed thinking.

With this decided, Maddie felt better already, and in no time the lift had taken her to the top floor, where she ascended the short flight of stairs and pushed the door to the rooftop open. A cool breeze greeted her and she knew this was exactly what she needed.

All was quiet and still, with just a few security lights left to show the newly laid paving. The tables and chairs were scattered about, and although any mess from the party had been conscientiously cleared, Maddie fancied she could smell the lingering aroma of barbecued onions.

For a moment she stood quite still, sipping from her mug of tea as she pictured the celebrations. Had there been speeches? A toast to the gardening committee, perhaps? Or had it simply been an evening of laid-back relaxation and fun – a barbecued chop, helpings of salads and a glass of wine under the stars?

Ah, yes, the stars. Maddie looked up and saw, peeping between the clouds, a fat, full moon high overhead. Wow. The garden party might have watched that moon rise. Henry would have loved it. She imagined the boy sharing his excitement with Vera, with his family. With Ned.

It was silly how her mind seemed to stumble when she thought of Ned, especially as she had come up here with the express purpose of thinking about Adam. Ah, well, she would deal with the tricky issue of Adam in a moment. For now, she just wanted to absorb a little more of the night's peace and quiet.

Searching the skies again, Maddie found the two bright pointers for the Southern Cross, and then the Cross itself, leaning a little to the right, and all around it the dusty drift of the Milky Way. No satellites tonight, as far as she could see. And she was disappointed that she couldn't find the famous saucepan shape that signalled Orion, until she remembered that this constellation was mostly visible in summer.

With her knowledge of the heavens pretty much exhausted, Maddie found a seat and settled to finish her tea. And to decide what she should do about Adam and his glamping. But before she could begin to organise her thoughts in this direction, she was distracted by the realisation that she wasn't alone.

It was the gleam of a white shirt that first caught her eye, but then, over in the shadows, she made out a male figure. He was slumped in one of the canvas director's chairs – head back, arms dangling, legs sprawled.

Oh, God. Had he collapsed? Might he be —?

Please, no. As Maddie launched to her feet, she wouldn't allow herself to think the worst and when she hurried closer, she recognised Jock.

She called his name and he stirred, thank goodness, lifting his head a little as he turned to her. Then in the faint glow of a security light, she saw the expression on his face, the look of utter despair.

'Jock!' Maddie whispered as she knelt beside him. 'Are you okay? What's happened?'

For a moment, he stared at her, almost as if he didn't recognise her, then his mouth twisted and tears glistened in his eyes. Turning away again, he shook his head, but he seemed incapable of speech.

Maddie gulped. It was pretty clear Jock wanted to be left alone, but she hated to abandon him when he looked so upset. She tried again. 'Has something happened?'

He groaned. 'Don't ask me that.'

'Jock, you're scaring me.' Was he missing his wife far more than he'd ever let on?

'There's been terrible landslides in Nepal!' he said, suddenly sitting upright. 'It was all over the late night news. It's been raining there all week. The rivers are flooding, hillside villages are collapsing, many people have been killed – washed away. I know Zoe's up there in the mountains somewhere, but I haven't heard from her for days and I can't get through to her and I —'

He didn't finish the sentence. There was no need. It was obvious the poor man was terrified.

Maddie tried to think of something comforting to say, but her mind couldn't get past the same alarming possibilities that must have been plaguing Jock.

'I should have gone with her,' he said. 'It's killing me not knowing where she is.'

Maddie was remembering the photo Jock had shown her just that morning. He and Zoe had been glowing with happiness and it was impossible to think that anything had happened to that lovely, vibrant young woman. 'Communication out of Nepal must be very difficult at the moment,' she suggested. 'Surely, there's a very good chance Zoe's safe, but she just can't let you know.'

Jock sighed heavily. 'I do tell myself that. But I can't help thinking that if she was okay, she would have found a way – contacts or whatever – someone who could send word back to me.'

Maddie had no answer for this and she remained very still, kneeling quietly on the floor beside his chair.

After a bit, Jock slumped forward, letting his elbows rest on his knees, his hands dangling limply between his legs. 'I came up here to try to feel close to her,' he said.

Maddie looked again to the heavens. The moon had shifted further to the west and was half-hidden by cloud – the same majestic, silver moon that looked down on the mountains in Nepal, the same breathtaking heavens that had inspired hope and faith in humans the world over for hundreds of thousands of years.

'I know there's very little I can do to help,' she said. 'But if there's anything at all . . .'

Already, Jock was shaking his head and she let the sentence trail off. But then, she couldn't help adding, 'Just remember, we're all here for you, Jock. The residents here all care about you – especially the gardeners.'

Now, he managed a bleak smile. 'Thanks, Maddie.'

'There's nothing worse than feeling alone.'

'I know. I'm lucky to have you and Ned and the others. And I have a few writer mates who are good friends too.'

He got to his feet stiffly and Maddie rose too. She couldn't resist giving him a hug and he didn't seem to mind.

'Thanks, Maddie,' he said again, so quietly now, she almost missed it.

She took his hand in hers and gave it a gentle squeeze. 'Take care, won't you?'

He gave a brief nod. 'Sure. I'll be okay. But I won't hang around. I'll say goodnight.'

She felt empty and miserable as she watched Jock cross the roof and disappear through the doorway into the building. She couldn't stop seeing those smiling faces in the photo he'd shown her, was too aware that his own memories of his lovely wife must be torturing him. A pall of sadness hung over her as she gathered up her mug, poured what was left of the cold tea onto a potted lemon tree, and then made her way back across the rooftop.

She didn't like the idea of heading back down to her lonely apartment. It was all very well to hide away on her own when she'd been fretting over boyfriend woes – but Jock's worry was real and devastating and yet he was so helpless. Even though Maddie had never met Zoe, she felt weighed down by the alarming possibility that the woman had been caught in this disaster. So, perhaps it wasn't surprising that she found herself paying unnecessary attention to the light gleaming beneath Unit 13's door.

This was Ned's apartment. Maddie had to pass it on the way to the lift and in that moment – even though it was probably past midnight by now – she found that her need to speak to him, to share her worrying news about their caretaker, was too overwhelming to ignore.

She didn't stop to think twice before she knocked, but it was a judicious knock. If Ned was asleep, she didn't want to wake him.

He answered quite quickly, however, and was still hauling a T-shirt over his head as he opened the door. His shaggy hair was damp as if he'd recently showered and she caught a whiff of lemony soap.

'Maddie.' There was no missing his surprise, but at least he didn't look annoyed.

'Hi,' she said. 'Sorry to disturb you so late.'

Ned frowned now, narrowing his gaze as he stared at her. 'Are you okay? You look upset.'

'I've been up on the roof, talking to Jock. He's had bad news. I don't suppose you've heard?'

Ned's frown deepened. 'Jock left the roof hours ago. What's happened?' Then, as if he realised this might be a conversation best conducted indoors, he stepped back. 'Come on in.'

'Thanks.'

'So what's happened?' Ned asked again, as he closed the door behind her.

No point in beating about the bush. 'Apparently it was on the news tonight about terrible landslides in Nepal. Jock's worried sick about his wife.'

'Of course. She's been taking photographs up in the mountains in Nepal.'

'Yes, but Jock hasn't heard from her for days and he's just so worried. I'm sorry,' Maddie added, as Ned stood in the middle of his hallway, frowning at this news. 'I probably shouldn't have bothered you at this late hour, but I thought you might want to know.'

'Yes, of course. No need to apologise. Is Jock still on the roof?'

She shook her head. 'He's gone back to his apartment. He said he was okay, but I know he's stressed to the eyeballs.'

'I should give him a quick call.'

'I'll leave you to it then.'

'No, no, you don't have to rush away.'

'I didn't want to take up too much of your time. I know it's late. It's just – I was feeling so shaken.'

'I'm not surprised. It's worrying news, and I'm glad you thought of me.' Ned smiled then, and it warmed Maddie in ways that were totally inappropriate. He nodded down his hallway. 'Come on through to the lounge room.'

She hadn't attended the initial garden meetings, so she'd never been in Ned's apartment, and she couldn't help sending a curious glance around the place. Predictably, the walls were mostly covered with bookshelves, crowded with both fiction and non-fiction books, as far as she could tell from a hasty glance. There were paintings too, originals she was pretty sure, mostly outback landscapes – red deserts, purple hills and lush olive-green lagoons.

In the far corner, an antique silky-oak desk was home to a laptop and more books, and littered with an untidy stack of papers and folders. No pot plants were on display, she noted. Perhaps Ned believed that plants belonged outdoors. Or maybe he didn't have time for fussing with indoor plants when he was also busy caring for bees and worms. Whatever the case, his apartment had an unpretentious but comfortably lived-in vibe that she found unexpectedly appealing.

'Take a seat,' he said as he shifted a pile of manila folders from the sofa and onto the dining table. Then he picked up his phone and donned a pair of black-rimmed spectacles that made him look rather scholarly, despite his untidy, jaw-length hair and dark five o'clock shadow.

'Actually —' Ned glanced from his phone to the mug Maddie had set on his coffee table and then swivelled in the direction of his kitchen. 'I reckon we need a cuppa or something.' He chanced another smile. 'A cuppa, or a nightcap. Or both?'

Maddie might have welcomed a nightcap to soothe the emotions roiling inside her, but she was supremely self-conscious about being alone with Ned Marlowe. As a susceptible young woman who already had more than her fair share of boyfriend issues, she needed to be on her guard.

'I'd love a cuppa. I took a mug of tea to the roof, but I let it go cold.'

'Right,' said Ned. 'Tea it is. I'll put the kettle on.'

'But you want to call Jock. Why don't I see to the kettle? I'm sure I can find my way around the kitchen.'

This brought another smile. 'Great, thanks.'

As with the other apartments, Ned's kitchen opened off from the living area and Maddie had no trouble locating the kettle and mugs, a pottery container that held teabags and another with loose leaf tea. She was a little surprised to see an impressive row of chef's knives and a shelf with recipe books – Asian, Mediterranean and barbeque cookbooks, yet another called *Paddock to Plate*. Also on this shelf was a green china teapot, so she decided to make tea the old-fashioned way – warming the teapot with scalding hot water and then measuring in tea leaves from the caddy.

As the kettle hummed to life, she could hear Ned speaking quietly on the phone. But although she could sense the compassion in his deep, gentle voice, the call didn't take long and he soon joined her.

'Jock hasn't any more news,' he said. 'I suspect he'll be up all night, poor guy.'

'He would have appreciated your call, though, I'm sure.'

'Well, yeah. But it's frustrating when there's nothing any of us can do but wait to hear.'

'I know. Waiting is always the worst.'

'I invited him to join us for a cuppa or a drink, but he's not feeling very sociable.'

'No.'

'Of course, there's every chance that Zoe's quite safe.'

Maddie nodded. 'I think Jock knows that, but he's almost too scared to hope.'

'Yeah,' Ned said softly, letting the word finish on a sigh. But then he chanced a small smile. 'How about a little toast to go with the tea?'

'Sure. Why not?' Maddie had always found tea and toast comforting.

'It might help you sleep,' he said next, which would have been a harmless enough comment in line with Maddie's own thoughts, if the sudden glint in his eyes hadn't set her skin burning.

She decided to make herself useful by slicing the sourdough loaf Ned produced and slipping these into the toaster. While he supplied plates, she found butter in the fridge.

'There's a whisky marmalade,' he said, nodding to the jar on the shelf beside the butter.

'Yum.' The deep-toned marmalade looked both expensive and delicious, and Maddie decided she would slather it onto their toast.

As they carried this bounty into the lounge room and set it on the coffee table, she realised she was beginning to feel a little calmer, even though the weight of worry lingered. A perfect cup of tea and scrumptious marmalade toast really did provide a strange kind of comfort, however, and it helped that this unexpected midnight snack didn't really call for the sort of small talk she might have found awkward under more normal circumstances.

Nursing her warming mug of tea, she said, 'I suppose Jock's told you about the novel he's writing?'

'The great Cape York adventure?' Ned smiled. 'I've actually had the privilege of reading the first couple of chapters.'

'Wow. What did you think of them?'

'They're great. Sucked me right in.'

Maddie grinned. 'That's fantastic. So Jock's really got talent and might find a publisher?'

'Well, I know nothing about publishing fiction, but I reckon he probably has what it takes. He has a fabulous main character, a private detective called Spud. Spud's his nickname, of course, and he's a kind of anti-hero, loser type, but he also has really likeable qualities and you can't help hoping he finally has some luck. And Jock's brilliant at bringing his Far North setting to life.'

'It sounds great. But now the poor man's beating himself up because he stayed back here to write, instead of going to Nepal with Zoe.'

'Yeah, I can imagine.' Ned gave a slow, thoughtful nod. 'But as we all know, crossing the street can be dangerous, and Zoe often goes off on her own. She's a brilliant photographer, loves the adventure, and she makes good money selling her photos, but she also understands that if Jock's ever going to get his book written, he needs to stay in one place and get those words down.'

'And in the meantime, we've been benefitting from his handyman skills.'

'No doubt about that.'

Maddie drained her mug and set it back on the coffee table. 'I reckon everyone in the gardening group would want to help him if they could.'

'Yeah. I guess we'll just have to play it by ear. With luck he'll have good news soon.' Ned paused, released a small sigh. 'I'll stay in touch with him, of course.'

'That's good to know.'

They had finished their tea and toast and Maddie was conscious it was high time she departed this scene. Hastily, she gathered up the mugs and plates and took everything through to the kitchen.

'Thanks. Just dump those on the sink,' Ned called.

'I can throw them in the dishwasher.'

'No, don't bother.'

Fair enough. She certainly didn't want to overstep the mark. Her relaxed mood was splintering as she went back into the lounge room where Ned was once again wearing his glasses and scrolling through his phone. She supposed this bespectacled academic was the image most of his students saw. Their sexy professor. For some reason, the idea was unsettling.

He looked up at her and smiled. 'I was just having a quick check to see if there's a news site that might give us an update.'

'Any luck?'

'Not really. The images of those landslides are pretty grim.' He took off the glasses and set them down next to his phone. 'Let's hope there's good news in the morning.'

Maddie gave a self-conscious nod. 'I'll say goodnight then.'

To her surprise, Ned leapt to his feet. 'Let me see you to the door.'

This wasn't necessary, but she didn't object as he accompanied her down the hallway.

'Thanks for letting me offload,' she said as they reached the front door.

'No, I should be thanking you.' Ned's demeanour had subtly changed. His smile was somewhat crooked, and his eyes shimmered with an unexpected emotion that set Maddie's heartbeats galloping. 'I'm really grateful you let me know about Jock. Keeping connected – it's important.'

His smile slid even further off kilter as he lifted a hand to her face. Maddie thought he was going to touch her cheek, but he didn't quite connect. And yet, her skin flamed anyway.

'We'll just have to keep hoping for good news,' she said, but she was so strangely breathless, she wondered if Ned heard her.

Even though they were both so worried for Jock and Zoe, the air between them seemed to jangle with a host of additional thoughts, with things they hadn't said, would probably never say.

'Goodnight, Ned.' She turned to go, but Ned caught her elbow, leaned a little closer, and pressed a warm kiss to her forehead.

Just a brief kiss. A polite kiss. A kiss of thanks. Or consolation. Or at least, that was how it started, and it might have ended that way, if Maddie had continued with her exit. But she found that she was strangely mesmerised, and before she could snap out of it, Ned was kissing her again. On the lips this time, cupping her face in his hands and kissing her slowly and thoroughly, as if he had all the time in the world.

Suddenly weak-kneed, she gripped his shoulders to steady herself and, before she knew quite what was happening, she was clutching bunches of his shirt and clinging tight, returning his kiss with desperate urgency. While she shattered into a thousand pieces.

The lift seemed to descend way faster than it should as Maddie tried to comprehend what had just happened. That kiss had been a kind of madness, surely? An overreaction to the sadness she and Ned had shared.

When they'd stepped apart, Ned had looked almost as stunned as she'd felt. He'd offered her a small smile that carried the merest hint of an apology. 'It's been a crazy kind of night.'

'Yes.'

For breathless seconds, his gaze had seemed to burn her, but then he'd abruptly turned and opened the door for her. 'Let's keep each other updated.'

That was that, then. A sensational kiss casually dismissed.

'Thanks,' she managed to say. And somehow, she even remembered – 'But you don't have my phone number.'

'I'll leave a note in your letterbox.'

'All right.'

'Goodnight, Maddie.'

'Goodnight.'

She'd left quickly and now her head was spinning. She hardly knew Ned Marlowe. She didn't even know if he had a girlfriend. But it was no surprise that he would dismiss the kiss as a mistake, as part of the weirdness of an upsetting evening. And she'd made an absolute fool of herself by being so obviously turned on, maybe more so than she'd ever been before.

Totally bewildered and embarrassed, she clung to the handrail in the lift and forced her thoughts elsewhere, to anywhere but that kiss, which was incomprehensible on way too many levels. The alternative, of course, was to revisit Jock's misery and worry.

It was only as she reached her front door that she remembered Adam and the whole reason she'd gone up to the roof in the first place.

CHAPTER TWENTY-SIX

On the morning after the barbecue, Vera worked very hard to remain upbeat. It wasn't an easy task when Archie and his family were about to leave her, but she told herself to be sensible, to be grateful for her time with Henry and for the wonderful evening she'd been able to share with the whole family.

Mind you, this morning, with the clatter and clamour of the family finishing their breakfast and packing, of parents calling instructions down hallways and kids yelling back from behind bedroom walls, Vera almost looked forward to the peace that would descend when they were gone. Except that she knew such peace would also bring the cold, empty loneliness that had haunted her for so many months.

She wouldn't dwell on that now, as she faced the task of stacking the dishwasher. She wanted to concentrate on staying positive. After all, she had entertained Henry for a lovely long stay and he'd not only enjoyed himself thoroughly, but had made a point of mentioning this fact over and over to his parents. And an added bonus for Vera was that last night's rooftop party had gone swimmingly, without a hiccup.

She couldn't deny she'd been worried about Brooke's reaction to spending a night in her home. She'd done her best to make her daughter-in-law feel welcome and she was relieved that Brooke had genuinely seemed to enjoy the barbecue. Brooke had got on particularly well with Carmen Cassidy. The two women had enjoyed quite a long and animated chat and Carmen hadn't let on once about the kitten, even though she'd snuck back to her apartment a couple of times to make sure that Max was okay.

And after the children had gone back to Vera's apartment to watch a movie on Netflix before bedtime, Dennis had produced his guitar, and Brooke, primed with several glasses of sauvignon blanc, had joined in singing with him. The songs were far too modern for Vera to recognise, but Brooke seemed to know all the words and was gleefully unaware, or perhaps simply didn't care, that Dennis was out of tune.

Another relief for Vera was that Archie had also appeared more and more relaxed as the evening wore on. It was worrying, though, that he'd seemed on tenterhooks until he realised that his wife was enjoying herself, but she sincerely hoped she'd misread her son's tension. She'd always been far too sensitive where Archie was concerned.

Now, this morning, after a restless night, Vera was standing in the middle of her kitchen, trying to decide whether she should continue with the tidying up, or wait till everyone had gone. Already, Archie and the children were down in the car park packing their luggage into the SUV, and as Vera dithered, Brooke came into the room with a couple of tumblers the girls had left in their bedroom.

'I've stripped the beds,' Brooke said, as she rinsed the tumblers at the sink and found space for them on the draining board. 'And I've tried to check that we haven't left anything behind. But I guess, if we have, you know where to find us.'

'Of course,' said Vera. 'I can always pop a stray Lego piece or sock in the post.'

Brooke frowned. 'I wouldn't expect you to send anything trivial like a sock. Not with the cost of postage these days.'

Vera couldn't help smiling. Brooke seemed to take everything so literally. She almost made a comment about only posting the diamond rings she found, but then thought better of it.

'I should help you with all this mess,' Brooke said next, looking around her at the dirty dishes, the mugs, frying pans and plates that littered the kitchen benches.

'No, there's no need, thanks,' said Vera. 'You have to leave something for me to do when you're gone.'

Brooke turned to her then, her expression concerned, almost guilty. 'You'll be okay, won't you? You have settled in here quite happily, haven't you? You like this apartment? And you're making nice friends?'

The question caught Vera by surprise. Did Brooke have a guilty conscience?

'Yes, I'm happy enough,' she said, although she couldn't help adding, 'but it's taken a while.' She wasn't going to let her daughter-in-law off the hook too lightly. And now that Brooke had introduced the subject, she couldn't resist taking it a step further. 'Brooke?'

'Yes?'

And just like that, the question that boiled in Vera tumbled out. 'Can I ask if things are better at Jinda now that I'm out of the way?'

There was no missing Brooke's shock. The colour leached from her face and her mouth fell open in a silent O. Awkward seconds ticked by before she spoke. 'What do you mean?' she asked eventually.

Vera almost faltered at that point. Surely Brooke didn't want her to spell it out? But it was too late to retreat. 'I – I had the impression from Archie —'

'Archie told you that *I* wanted you to leave Jinda?'

'Not exactly,' Vera had to admit. 'But I felt there was some kind of tension and that I wasn't helping by living so close to you.'

Brooke was staring at the kitchen floor now, with her arms tightly folded, her mouth tense and drawn down, her expression unmistakably fearful.

'I'm sorry,' Vera said quickly, realising that she'd quite possibly made everything worse. 'I didn't want to upset you. It's just that —' She stopped, swallowed as she tried to think clearly, tried again. 'All I want is for you and Archie to be happy.'

'Of course we're happy,' Brooke said firmly, and then, without smiling, she met Vera's gaze very directly. 'I love Archie.'

Recognising the courage that this had taken, Vera felt quite over-come. 'That's wonderful news indeed,' she said, wishing she didn't sound so regal and snooty.

'On the other hand,' Brooke added, sounding quite a bit braver now. 'If we're going to be honest, I've always felt that you didn't really approve of me.'

'Oh, Brooke.'

'I just felt you never thought I was good enough for Archie. I didn't go to a private boarding school. My family never had much money. My dad was a fencing contractor and your father was a Lord Whatever, and you British are so damn class conscious.'

This barb hit home and Vera couldn't help flinching. She'd always blamed Felix for the tension with Brooke's family. Now, it truly hurt to realise that her daughter-in-law saw *her* as a snob and quite possibly as a problem. For heaven's sake, Vera had lived in Australia for far longer than she'd ever lived in England, and it had been decades since she'd thought of herself as British, or aristocratic.

Unfortunately, she couldn't help her accent or her background, but she was sick and tired of being judged in this way and she was tempted to say as much. Trying to defend herself was unlikely to improve her daughter-in-law's opinion, however.

'I'm very sorry if I gave you that impression,' she said. And then because she knew she probably still sounded haughty, she added, 'I think you're perfect for Archie, Brooke. And that's the honest truth. I know he adores you and that makes me very, very happy indeed.'

To Vera's surprise, Brooke's face screwed up and tears trembled on her eyelashes. Impulsively, Vera stepped towards her, arms extended. For a moment, she thought she might be rejected, but then, with a soft little cry, Brooke stumbled closer and they hugged.

It wasn't a long or fierce hug, but both women knew it was an important step, and they were smiling shyly as they released each other.

Vera was conscious that Archie and the children would return at any moment, but she was also anxious to clear up a few more matters. 'Brooke,' she said. 'You do know that Felix never had very much money, don't you?'

Brooke nodded. 'I know that now. I didn't when I met Archie.'

Vera was tempted to elaborate on the difficulties she'd endured during her marriage – the thrift and caution required to balance her husband's recklessness – but she'd never been disloyal to Felix and she wasn't about to start now. Changing tack, she said, 'I'm thrilled that you and Archie are making such great strides towards turning Jinda into a thriving concern.'

Again, Brooke nodded.

And then, because so much air had been cleared, Vera felt compelled to ask, 'So, Theo Blaine wasn't the problem?'

Brooke reared back, as if she couldn't quite believe her ears. 'Why would I worry about Theo?'

'Oh, I thought . . .' Vera shrugged. She'd convinced herself that Theo was the reason Brooke had wanted her to leave. But clearly, she'd had a few things wrong.

'I've made a date slice for the journey,' she said quickly, and already she was at the pantry, collecting the cake tin. 'And maybe you'd like some fruit? Apples perhaps?'

'Gosh, thanks. That's kind of you.'

Vera found a spare shopping bag for the cake tin and apples. 'You'll probably need a knife and a peeler, as well,' she said, adding these to the bag. 'What about a Thermos?'

'No, no,' said Brooke. 'You've done more than enough for us. Archie and I will probably just grab takeaway coffee.'

'Of course.'

'And the kids have already filled their water bottles.'

'All right, then. Lovely.'

With this sorted, they went through to the living room where Brooke had left her ubiquitous shoulder bag, open and bulging with last-minute finds – a hairbrush, a pair of pyjama bottoms and Henry's copy of *Tom's Midnight Garden*.

'Is Archie expecting you to meet him downstairs?' Vera asked. 'Or is he coming back up?'

'I'm not sure.' Brooke turned to Vera and once again she was frowning. 'So, you really are fine? About living here and everything?'

Vera hesitated, caught between a desire to reassure, while also being honest. 'I can't pretend I haven't missed Jinda and all of you,' she said. 'These adjustments take time.' Now she offered her warmest smile. 'But as you can see, I'm getting there.'

'Last night was certainly wonderful. I'm glad we got to meet your new friends.'

'Yes, so am I.'

'And – I didn't like to ask about your heart scare in front of the children. But that's fine?'

'Yes, yes,' Vera assured her, although she still hadn't gone in for the stress test. She would have to ring the hospital later this morning to organise that appointment. Best to get it over and done with. She shouldn't keep putting it off now that she'd run out of excuses.

As Brooke gathered up her bag and hefted it onto her shoulder, the front door burst open and the children rushed in followed by their father. The car was packed and they were ready to leave.

'Oh,' cried Henry as he saw *Tom's Midnight Garden* poking out of Brooke's bag. 'I wanted to say goodbye to Maddie.' Turning to his mother, he hurried to explain. 'Maddie looked after me when Gran had to go to hospital and she's lovely and she gave me this book and it's awesome, but she wasn't at the barbecue last night and I couldn't say goodbye.'

'Sorry, mate,' answered his father. 'We don't have time for more farewells.'

'And Maddie's probably enjoying a sleep-in,' suggested Vera.

'You can always write her a thank you note when you get home,' suggested his mother.

'Really?' Henry was obviously intrigued by this novel idea. 'And take it to the post office, with a stamp and everything?'

'Yes,' said Brooke, smiling.

'But you'll have to post a letter to me as well,' warned Vera.

'I will, Gran. And maybe I'll send one to Ned too.'

And now, with that matter happily settled, it was time for goodbyes. This was a moment Vera always dreaded, but today, as hugs and kisses were exchanged with Archie and Brooke, with Emily and Sienna and, finally, with Henry, she realised that she'd actually reached a point where she could let her family go without being ravaged by her usual regrets. And that had to be a good thing, surely?

*

It was quite late in the day when Vera rang Theo. She had taken her time tidying the apartment and then collecting Max from Carmen, who had extolled the cat's virtues and then insisted that Vera stay for a cup of coffee and a leisurely chat.

This had proved very pleasant and rather entertaining, especially as Carmen had regaled Vera with stories of her men friends. It seemed she had never married, but had enjoyed quite a string of lovers, including a French film-maker, who lived in Paris and was, apparently, still desperate for Carmen to join him.

'Why don't you go?' Vera couldn't help asking.

'Oh, I don't know.' Carmen gave a shrugging little laugh. 'He's French.' As if this explained everything.

'And arrogant?'

'God, yes. Arrogant and a smoker, and . . .' She sent a wistful glance around her beautiful apartment and gave a languid sweep of her arm that set her bracelets tinkling.

'And you'd miss this lovely place,' Vera supplied.

Carmen smiled. '*Exactement*. I prefer to think of Raphael as my Sometimes Significant Other.'

They'd shared a chuckle over this.

Back in her apartment, Vera had settled Max once more. She really had to work out what she was going to do about him, but it was nice to have his company now that everyone had left. She would deal with that problem later, along with phoning to book that stress test at the hospital.

For now, she fixed herself a scratch lunch of cheese and crackers, mulling as she did so over her conversation with Carmen. She couldn't help admiring the woman's independence and she supposed that Carmen would never have stayed with a man like Felix.

But Vera quickly consoled herself with the argument that Carmen was quite a bit younger than she was. And Carmen hadn't grown up in a stuffy British stately home, locked into old-world expectations, but in suburban Australia, buoyed by a rising tide of feminism. And Carmen hadn't attended a painfully prescriptive Swiss finishing school like Vera's, but an art school, where she'd almost certainly mixed with intelligent, creative avant-garde types.

Besides, you weren't a mistake, Felix, and I do miss you terribly, you silly, dear man.

With these thoughts reconciled, she made herself comfortable on the sofa with the intention of reading a novel. But she'd barely read a page before her eyes grew heavy and she nodded off, and by the time she woke, the sun had shifted and she felt quite cold. She found a jacket and went to the roof to water her herb garden, but with this task completed, she returned to her apartment and felt a little lost, in danger of succumbing to loneliness.

Theo came instantly to mind, possibly prompted by the morning's conversation about Carmen's beaus. Whatever the reason, Vera acted on impulse. Fetching her phone, she plumped up the cushions on the sofa, settled comfortably once more and connected to Theo's number before she had time for second thoughts.

He answered straight away, but the reception wasn't great and he sounded a long way off, which, of course, he was. 'Vera, how great to hear from you. How are you?'

'A little tired after the family's visit, but otherwise fine, thanks.'

'Did you say you're tired?'

'Just a little,' she said, raising her voice. 'You know what grandkids are like.' It was only as she said this that she remembered Theo's grandchildren were in Western Australia and he didn't see them very often.

'But the visit went well?' he asked.

'It did, yes, it was lovely.'

'Hang on a minute,' he said. 'I'm still in the car, but I'm home now. Let me get up to the house where there's better reception.'

Vera heard the click of a car door closing and she pictured Theo leaving his Range Rover and crossing the gravel drive in front of his homestead, mounting the broad, rather grand concrete steps, painted white, crossing his beautifully tiled front verandah and opening the solid timber front door with stained-glass panels.

'Vera?' His voice was clear now, as if he was standing right next to her, and she fancied that he was smiling.

'Yes, I'm still here.'

'So,' he said. 'Tell me your news.'

She filled him in on the highlights of Henry's time with her and the family's overnight stay, to which he listened politely, asking all the right questions.

'And now you're quite alone again,' he said.

'Yes, alone and free.'

After a small pause, he said, 'Is that an invitation, Vera?'

Goodness, she hadn't meant to sound quite so forward. And yet, she couldn't help feeling pleased. 'Well, you did express an interest in coming to Brisbane.'

'Of course I'm interested. I'm dying to see Brisbane.' There was a definite tease in Theo's voice now.

Vera smiled. 'Good.'

'I'll give you a day or two to recover from your family's visit, but I could be there towards the end of the week. How does that sound?'

'That sounds lovely.' Vera wondered if he could tell how pleased she was. 'Oh, just one thing, Theo, you're not allergic to cats, are you?'

CHAPTER TWENTY-SEVEN

On Tuesday evening, Maddie returned home from work to find an electricity bill and a note from Ned in her letterbox. The note was handwritten in a rather spiky scrawl.

Thought you might be interested in an update on Jock. Feel free to call me.
    Cheers, Ned.

A simple enough communication, so Maddie was miffed to find herself staring at it as if Ned's handwriting was a famous celebrity's signature. For far too long she stood in the middle of the mail room, picturing Ned as he hunted for a spare scrap of paper among the untidy stacks on his desk and then wrote this message.

She was such an idiot. Since Saturday night, she'd tried not to think too much about Ned Marlowe and she'd certainly worked extra hard to block out memories of his kiss. She'd told herself that he wasn't her type. Or, more to the point, that she wasn't *his* type. His girlfriends would be brilliant and self-confident – beautiful brainiacs with PhDs and an encyclopaedic knowledge of bees and plants. No doubt they played the violin and were chess champions as well.

More to the point, Maddie knew, with absolute certainty, that allowing herself to fall for Ned Marlowe would be setting herself up for another distressing dumping, and this time the whole apartment block would know about it. In other words, history would repeat itself in the most excruciating and humiliating way possible.

Just the same, she was certainly keen to hear how Jock was faring. She'd been so worried about him. She'd tried to talk to people at work, hoping that one of the well-connected lawyers might have contacts in Nepal who could help to track down definitive answers. But although there'd been murmurs of sympathy for Zoe McFee, Maddie's efforts had pretty much drawn blanks.

Now, on Tuesday evening, Maddie let herself into her apartment, dropped her keys into a little green pottery dish on the kitchen bench and took her phone from her handbag before hooking the bag's straps over the back of a kitchen stool. Then she continued to the living room where she stood for a moment admiring how lovely her pot plants looked in the last of the afternoon's light.

She'd been quite amazed to discover how much pleasure she derived from watching a few plants thrive. Pot plants weren't quite the same company as Vera's kitten, of course, but they were living things, dependent on her care and they rewarded her with their beauty. She made a mental note to water them this evening.

With this decided, she kicked off her high heels and made herself comfortable in an armchair with one of her exotic Indian cushions at her back. Then she immediately felt uncomfortable again as she remembered that she really should ring Adam before she rang Ned.

She still hadn't contacted Adam to tell him that she wouldn't make the glamping date, and tonight was the night that this conversation really *had* to happen. She couldn't be a wimp and keep putting it off.

Later. She would most definitely ring Adam this evening, but she would leave the call until later. Finding out about Jock was more important and she keyed in the phone number Ned had added to the bottom of his note.

He answered almost straight away. 'Ned Marlowe.'

'Hi, Ned, it's Maddie.'

'Hey there, thanks for calling.'

'Any news about Zoe?'

'Not yet, I'm afraid.' A beat later, Ned asked, 'Are you at home?'

'Yes, just in.'

'Will you be around for a bit? I mean, you're not going out again?'

Maddie frowned at the unexpected nosiness of this question. 'No, I'll be here,' she said, after a slight hesitation.

'Would it be convenient for you to come up here, then? It might be easier to talk. I was hoping Jock might join us as well, but one of his writer mates has dragged him off for a drink at the Regatta, which I'm sure will do him good.'

Maddie certainly hadn't expected another face-to-face meeting with Ned and she needed a moment or two to adjust to this suggestion.

'Maddie?'

'Um – sure, I'm, um, just —'

'Perhaps you'd rather wait till after dinner? Although I've ordered Thai takeaway and I'd be happy to share.'

'Oh, I wouldn't expect —'

'Do you like seafood red curry? Pad Thai?'

She was actually quite hungry and her tastebuds tingled at the thought of a delicious Thai meal, especially a meal she hadn't had to cook. But a meal with Ned? It all seemed a little too —

'I'll behave myself,' he said. 'I promise I won't pull another stunt like the other night. I know you're seeing someone. I was inappropriate.'

Ka-thunk. He was talking about the kiss, of course, and Maddie was uncomfortably reminded yet again of her embarrassingly uninhibited response. But at least she should be able to relax tonight, knowing Ned had no intention of starting anything with her, even though on one level this news was also ridiculously disappointing.

It was handy that Ned still believed she had a boyfriend. The fact that she planned to change that status before the evening was over was irrelevant.

Refusing to respond to Ned's last comment, she said as casually as she could, 'Okay. Thanks, I'll be up in ten minutes or so.'

And then, to calm herself and redirect her attention, she quickly called Adam. Perhaps she *should* go on that glamping weekend, after all.

'Hello,' a small, childish voice, almost certainly a little girl's, answered.

'Oh, hello. Could I please speak to Adam? That is, Mr Grainger?'

'He's busy at the moment.'

'Oh,' said Maddie again. She supposed Adam might be at work, showing off a piece of real estate. It was quite likely that this child was his customers' offspring, and Adam was busy showing her parents around.

She imagined Adam leading a young couple through a doorway, gesturing grandly. 'So, this is the master bedroom.' Perhaps he had left his phone and paperwork on the kitchen bench, or the dining table. The child had picked it up.

'I won't worry Mr Grainger now, then,' Maddie said. 'I'll try again later. Thank you. Bye.'

'Bye-bye.'

After this unsatisfactory result, Maddie went through to her bedroom, changed out of her work clothes into an old pair of comfy jeans and a loose grey sweater. She slipped her feet into navy flats and in the bathroom, she removed her makeup, brushed her hair and tied it back with an elastic.

Like most women, she was conscious that the clothes she chose sent a particular message, and tonight she really wanted Ned to pick up on the fact that she'd made absolutely no attempt to look attractive. She also decided to leave her phone behind.

She knew she could simply switch it to silent, but there was a chance Adam might call back, and even if she chose not to answer him, she didn't fancy the distraction of knowing he'd called while she was in the middle of a conversation with Ned. She needed to remain cool, calm and collected with Ned, to concentrate on Jock and his very real worry. It was time to forget about her own petty niggles.

Ned was wearing his specs again when he opened the door for her. Maddie suspected he was still in the same clothes he'd worn to work at the university – jeans and an open-necked white shirt with long sleeves rolled back to the elbows. She couldn't help noticing that his skin was quite tanned and that his shoes were elastic-sided riding boots, and she wondered, as she had on previous occasions, why a guy with such an apparent love of the outdoors had chosen to live in an inner-city apartment.

She had no intention of asking him such a personal question, however. It was one of the many questions she would never ask Ned.

'How was Jock when you spoke to him?' she asked instead, as she followed him into his living room.

'Still worried sick, I'm afraid. Trying to hang onto hope, but steeling himself for bad news. I had quite a long chat with him, though.'

'Great. I'm sure he appreciated your company.'

Ned looked a little helpless as he shrugged. 'Hard to tell. He showed me his phone – he wanted me to see the history of all his contacts with Zoe. Seems like they try to talk almost every night.'

'Gosh. No wonder he's so bothered by her silence, poor guy.'

They had reached the lounge room and Ned indicated that Maddie should take a seat. When she did so, he eased his long frame into the sofa opposite her. 'That pair have an interesting relationship,' he said. 'They miss each other like crazy, but they're both so creative, they also understand each other's different needs.'

'They've reversed the traditional roles, haven't they?' said Maddie. 'The woman is off adventuring while the male stays at home.'

'At home and feeling guilty.'

'Poor Jock.' She sighed. 'He can't be getting any writing done.'

'Not a chance. He's way too distracted.'

'Of course. I've been following the news. It all looks pretty traumatic. More torrential rain. More landslides and flash flooding.'

'Yeah. And a lot of phone lines are down. I even saw a shot of some kind of communication tower toppling into a ravine.' Despite the bleakness of their conversation, Ned was looking comfortably relaxed now, seated man style, with one arm draped along the back of the sofa and an ankle propped on the opposite knee.

Maddie tried not to stare.

'Jock asked me to thank you,' he said.

'Thank me?' She blinked in surprise. 'But I haven't done anything.'

'You made a point of being friendly at our working bees and you were interested enough to find out about his writing. And the other night – you were ready to help him.'

'Yes, but —'

'He obviously appreciated that, Maddie. He made a point of mentioning it.'

'Well, thanks for passing that on, but I just wish there was something practical that I could do.'

Ned nodded, but before he could respond, a phone rang shrilly and he jumped to his feet. 'That'll be our dinner.' He crossed to the phone on the wall. 'Yep. Thanks, mate. I'll let you in. Unit 13, Level 4.'

After he replaced the receiver, he went through to the kitchen.

'Anything I can do?' Maddie called.

'No, I'm just grabbing a couple of bowls.' He was back in no time, setting cutlery and bowls on the coffee table. He sent her a quick glance. 'You don't mind eating here?'

'No, of course not.' She hardly ever ate at her dining table when she was home alone.

Now the doorbell rang and Ned disappeared to answer it. Brief greetings were exchanged and a moment later he was back with takeaway containers that released scents of tummy-tempting deliciousness as soon as he lifted the lids.

'Help yourself,' he told Maddie. 'I'll grab us a couple of drinks. Fancy a glass of wine?'

Their meeting was certainly becoming more social than Maddie had anticipated, but she found herself nodding. 'Sure.'

'White or red?'

She actually preferred white wine, but most guys liked red, and she was used to letting them make the choice. Now, she shrugged. 'Either, thanks.'

'Great.' Ned winked. 'An ambidextrous drinker. I approve.' He disappeared once more, and returned from the kitchen with two glasses of icy white wine. 'I always think this pinot gris goes really well with Thai.'

He was absolutely right, of course. The crisp cold wine, the spicy seafood and delicately flavoured rice made a fabulous combination. Maddie was tempted to simply kick back and enjoy herself, except that she needed to keep her wits about her. It would be all too easy to fall for this guy's effortless charm, and it was rather alarming that in spite of her concerns for Jock, she was also fighting an excited buzzing that had begun inside her the minute she'd stepped into Ned's apartment.

As she helped herself to the curry, she was determined to keep to their planned agenda. 'When you were talking to Jock, did you get any sense that he'll soon have the answers he needs?'

Ned shook his head. 'Not really. Zoe's a freelancer. She sells a big percentage of her photos online, all over the world, and being independent is great under normal circumstances. But if she was with one of the big news agencies like AAP or Reuters, I'm sure Jock would find it easier to get info out of Nepal.'

'Yes, no doubt.' Maddie drew a deep breath and let it out slowly. 'It's just awful, not being able to help, especially when Jock's been such wonderful help here. He put in a huge effort with those pavers.' She speared a piece of sauce-coated broccoli. 'Do you think we should let the other gardeners know what's happened?'

'I do, actually.'

'It wouldn't be gossiping, would it? We'd just make sure they understood why Jock might seem a bit down. I'd hate him to slip up on some task and cop an earful from Nancy at her ball-breaking best.'

Ned seemed to wince at the very thought.

'How do you reckon we should handle it?' Maddie asked next. 'I don't think we'd want another notice in people's letterboxes.'

'No, I reckon it'd be best to get in touch directly. Phone calls. Or face to face.'

'Good idea. We can share the calls if you like. I'd be happy to talk to Vera – and Joe and Dennis.'

'Great,' said Ned. 'I'll handle the others.'

'I guess there's not much we can tell them, though, except that things are still up in the air?'

'That's about it, I'm afraid. But at least if everyone's aware of the situation, they can be a bit sensitive. I'm sure they'll realise that Jock won't want to be smothered with love.'

'No. It's tricky, isn't it?'

Ned nodded. 'Coming from Cape York, Jock likes to think of himself as tough, and he is – but right now, the poor guy's keeping a hell of a lot bottled up.'

'Any suggestions about how we should handle things if we meet him in the lift or wherever?'

'I'm no expert, and I'm sure you'll manage just fine.' Ned's smile held a soft light that made her breath catch. 'But if others are looking for advice, I guess just keep it simple. "Thinking of you, mate. Stay strong." Anything along those lines.'

'Okay.' Maddie shivered as she recalled Jock's desolation on Saturday night and now she reminded herself that she mustn't get carried away, hoping for miracles. Just the same, surely they mustn't give up hope that Zoe was safe somewhere in those towering mountains?

Now, Ned surveyed the takeaway containers in front of them. 'Would you like any more?'

'Everything was delicious, but no, I've had plenty, thanks.'

'I'll clear these away then. Looks like I'll have leftovers for lunch tomorrow.'

She wondered how often Ned ate takeaway meals, then asked herself why she would care.

'By the way,' he said, returning from the kitchen. 'You left this here the other night.' He handed her the mug she'd totally forgotten and, just like that, she found herself reliving their last farewell when she'd more or less hurled herself into Ned's arms.

She still felt branded by that kiss. She knew that wasn't going to happen again, but she nevertheless felt suddenly nervous. Grabbing at the first safe topic she could think of, she asked, 'So – ah – how are your bees adapting in their new hives?'

Naturally, Ned was surprised by this sudden, clumsy change of subject, but although his eyes betrayed an initial flash of amusement, he answered quite smoothly. 'The bees are thriving, thank you. We should be collecting honey before Christmas.'

'That's great.' Maddie clutched the mug tightly in two hands and retreated a couple of steps. 'Okay – well – if we've covered every-thing you wanted to discuss – I – ah – should probably get going.'

'Okay.' Ned seemed perfectly relaxed, without any of the ten-sion she was experiencing. 'Maybe you'll be able to come to the gardeners' meeting on Saturday?'

'Meeting?'

His eyes held a hard-to-read glint. 'We usually hold one after the working bee.'

'Oh, yes, of course.' Maddie realised she'd been hurrying off on dates on the previous Saturdays and so had missed the meetings. She would really like to attend this one, to feel properly part of the group, but now she felt guilty as she remembered Adam. He still thought their next date was a firm booking, and while he hadn't mentioned a departure time for the trip to Boonah on Saturday, he was planning slow-cooked lamb, which probably meant he would need to get away some time mid-morning.

She would most definitely have to call him. As soon as she got back to her apartment she would tell him that she needed to cancel. Actually, she should be firm and let him know there would be no more dates of any description. Fingers crossed, he wouldn't be too angry.

Ned, meanwhile, was watching her rather closely. 'Everything okay?'

'Yes, of course. Why?'

'You just seem a little worried.' He was still watching her, and his gaze was thoughtful, but ever so slightly amused. 'To be honest you often look worried.'

Did she? Annoyed with herself, she said, haughtily, 'I can assure you I'm fine.'

'Okay.' He gave a smiling shrug. 'That's good. And if I spoke out of turn, I apologise.'

'Accepted.' Her answering smile was tight.

But now, unfortunately, persistent memories of her recent departure seemed to hover all around them. To add to Maddie's discomfort, Ned's clear grey eyes shimmered with friendly warmth, but also with an intense, indecipherable emotion that interfered with her breathing.

She wasn't going to make a second mistake, however. Straightening her shoulders, she held her head high. 'I can see myself out.'

'That's very wise of you,' Ned said quietly.

Her face was flaming now, but she turned and left with as much dignity as she could muster. She didn't dare to look back.

Safely in her own apartment once more, Maddie went straight to her phone, half expecting to find a string of missed calls from Adam. There was nothing.

Disconcerted, she pressed his number, realising as she did so that she hadn't properly thought through what she wanted to tell him. And that was Ned's fault, of course.

'Hello.' Adam's answer was curt, which didn't help to calm her.

'Adam,' she said. 'Hi, it's Maddie here. I'm just ringing about the weekend.'

'Oh, yeah,' he replied. 'Hang on a tick.'

She fancied she heard a woman's voice in the background, but now there seemed to be a door opening and closing and then, instead of voices, she heard a steady thrum of traffic.

'I was in a meeting,' Adam said. 'Just stepped outside so we could talk properly.'

'Sorry if I'm interrupting anything important.' It hadn't occurred to her that he might have meetings at this hour. He obviously worked very hard during the week. No doubt, she thought guiltily, so he could keep his Saturdays free.

'No worries.' Adam sounded far more relaxed now. 'So, are you all set for our glamping adventure? I'm thinking, now, maybe a slow-cooked shoulder of lamb, rather than the shanks.'

'Actually . . .' Maddie began, but then a nervous knot swelled in her throat and she couldn't finish the sentence.

'You're not vegetarian, are you?' Adam sounded instantly concerned. 'No, of course you're not. You had chicken kebabs last Saturday night.'

'No,' she managed as she found her voice. 'I'm not vegetarian. But I do have a slight problem. Something's come up. An important meeting next Saturday that I really can't miss.'

Maddie knew this was bound to piss Adam off, so when she heard a muffled noise that might have been swearing, she wasn't surprised. At least, if Adam was angry, the business of dropping him was going to be much less awkward.

'What's the meeting about?' he asked, now sounding unexpectedly pleasant. 'Is it that gardening group of yours?'

'Yes.' Maddie winced. She was supposed to be telling him straight out that she couldn't go away with him at all – ever. She shouldn't be trying to fob him off with weak excuses.

Forget the meeting. Just be blunt and tell him it's over.

'What time's this meeting?' he asked in the same smooth, accommodating tone.

'Oh, around eleven thirty. Possibly midday.'

'And I guess it will take at least an hour?'

'I'd say so. I'm so sorry.'

'You wouldn't be trying to wriggle out of this, would you, Maddie?'

Yes, of course she was. Why the hell couldn't she be honest and spit it out? She wasn't scared of Adam, was she?

Maybe.

'It's just that something really important has come up,' she said again. It was almost the truth. One way or the other, the gardeners would be commiserating or celebrating with Jock. But then she held her breath, as she remembered the other time she'd disappointed Adam's plans and he'd lost his cool.

Now, she braced herself for another explosion. At least it would give her the excuse she needed.

'Oh, well,' Adam said, smoothly. 'I can see why your meeting might be important. Rooftop gardens are all the rage, and yours will probably add a hefty chunk to the value of the property.' And then, before she could interrupt, he said, 'Tell you what I'll do. I'll pre-cook the lamb at home, so all we'll have to do is reheat it in the camp oven. So, that's okay, Maddie. You go to your meeting and we can leave as soon as it's over.'

Bloody hell. Not only had she dug a hole for herself. She'd fallen right into it.

CHAPTER TWENTY-EIGHT

Vera was working on a shopping list when Maddie phoned her. She was in the midst of planning for Theo's visit and going through her recipe books, searching for bright ideas and enjoying the fact that she could ignore the 'recipes for one' section. She wanted to impress Theo, of course, which also meant being really well organised, preparing ahead as much as possible, so that she could relax once he arrived.

Theo would probably want to make the most of being in the city and to go out quite a bit, so Vera aimed to build flexibility into her planning, but she was also keen to experiment. She certainly wouldn't be dishing up the old family favourites. No shepherd's pies or apple crumbles for this worldly guest, thank you.

She had her sights set on tasty soups – asparagus or French onion, perhaps – and she liked the idea of roasting a whole fish with soy and ginger. She was also intrigued by a recipe she'd come across for roasted strawberries served with Greek yoghurt. Oh, and then there was an easy chocolate mousse that sounded delicious.

Perhaps she and Theo might also try out the rooftop barbecue. Vera certainly wanted to show off the garden. She'd spent another

happy session up there during the afternoon, watering and potter-
ing, finding the first few weeds, giving liquid fertiliser to her herbs
and adding a couple of ties to the tomato plants that were already
climbing their stakes with gratifying speed.

Apart from the menu decisions, Vera had also made an appointment for the stress test with the cardiologist. She'd felt guilty about
putting this off, but at the same time she'd half hoped that she might
have to wait a few weeks for an appointment. The people at the hospital had seemed to think it was important, however, and had made
room for her the very next day.

Given this rather sobering prospect, she supposed it was rather
incongruous that she was also deliberating over the purchase of
new bed linen for Theo's visit. In actual fact, Vera had been rather
nervous pondering the whole bedroom scenario and how it might
actually play out. When it came to romantic escapades, she was certain that Theo had played around, but for her part, she was very out
of practice.

More than eighteen months had passed since her brief romance
with him. During that time, she'd moved away to the city where
everything seemed so very busy and immediate and important, so
different from the relaxed familiarity of their country lifestyle. And
now, faced with almost certain expectations on Theo's part, her
confidence as a potential lover was diminishing rather rapidly.

Vera feared that, having recently turned seventy, she was too
long in the tooth for such antics. She was certainly far too self-
conscious about her wrinkling skin and sagging bits. She wasn't
even sure Theo would like her new hairdo and she was getting herself into a bit of a state. So, when the phone rang and the caller was
Maddie, she was quite grateful to be distracted.

'Maddie, how lovely. How are you?'

'Fine, thanks. And you? Henry's gone home, hasn't he? Did he
enjoy the barbecue?'

'Oh, yes, he's back at Jinda now, with the family, but he had a wonderful time on Saturday night. You should have seen him buzzing about, showing off the wonders of the roof to his parents.'

'Especially the worms and the bees?'

'Of course.' Vera chuckled at the memory.

'And the barbecue went well?'

'It did. I think you would have loved it, Maddie. We shared the salads, but cooked our own meats – well, and Joe and Dennis had their veggie burgers and haloumi – and it was a beautiful evening. Very relaxed and friendly and such fun to be on the roof. There was a beautiful full moon. And we even had a bit of a singalong.'

'How wonderful.' After a brief pause, Maddie said, 'Jock was there, wasn't he?'

'Oh, yes, but I thought he seemed a bit subdued.'

'He was probably missing his wife,' said Maddie. 'I suspect it's been harder for him than he was prepared to let on, having her so far away. I don't know if you've heard much about his situation?'

'Well no, not really. But I know you've been talking to him at the working bees.' Vera realised now that this was probably the reason for Maddie's call. She had information about Jock she wanted to share. 'I'm all ears if you'd like to fill me in.'

'It's actually rather worrying,' Maddie said and then she went on to deliver the news that Jock's wife was a photo journalist, apparently missing in Nepal where there'd been rather terrible weather and landslides.

'Oh, my goodness, the poor man.'

'Poor Jock hasn't heard a word and he has no idea where Zoe might be.'

Vera was silenced for a moment or two. For heaven's sake, Jock's worry certainly put her own small, shallow concerns about Theo's expectations into perspective. 'I feel terrible that Jock's been working for us all this time and I knew hardly anything about him,' she said. 'Especially as that's only because I never really took the time to talk to him – not a real conversation.'

At the working bee, Vera had been a little annoyed with Maddie for spending so much time with Jock, while wasting what she'd seen as perfect opportunities for the girl to chat up Ned.

After a small pause, she said, 'I suppose Ned's aware of Jock's situation.'

'Yes, he is. He's had a long chat with Jock, trying to help him keep his chin up.'

'Why am I not surprised?'

'Yes, well . . .' Maddie sounded ever so slightly put out. 'I know you have Ned up on a pedestal, Vera, but I'm sure he was just being neighbourly. We thought the gardeners should know what's happened. Jock's probably too upset and stressed to want to talk right now, but eventually —' Maddie stopped and let out a heavy sigh. 'At any rate, it might give him a bit of boost to know that his neighbours will also be there for him when he's ready.'

'Yes.' Vera was all too aware that grief and worry could be magnified by a sense of isolation.

'I'm not sure whether Jock will be on the roof on Saturday,' Maddie said next. 'But if we have a quick meeting after the working bee, we can see if there's any way at all that we might help or support him without being too nosy. I guess I'll see you then?'

Saturday? Vera suddenly remembered Theo. 'I'll have a friend staying with me.' Then she quickly amended this. 'But I'm sure he won't mind putting his feet up and reading for an hour or so, while I duck upstairs.' And then, 'Or perhaps he might join me. If we find ourselves discussing Jock, I'm sure Theo would be discreet.'

'Yes, that'll be fine. I'll look forward to meeting your friend.' Vera could hear a definite smile in Maddie's voice. No doubt she was amused that such an old biddy might have a male friend.

After they said their goodbyes, Vera went to make a note on the calendar that she'd stuck with a magnet to the side of her fridge. The month was beginning to look quite busy with jottings for last weekend's visitors, her appointment at the cardiologist's, as well as Theo's arrival tomorrow evening. And now the gardening reminder. Just looking at all the scribbled notes, she felt a little tired. At least she couldn't complain about being bored.

She could have done with a lovely strong cup of tea, but she'd been instructed to give up caffeine for twenty-four hours before the stress test, so she made do with a mug of mint tea as she went back to her shopping list.

Hospitals these days seemed to produce an incredible amount of paperwork. When Vera turned up for her appointment, she was required to fill in the same forms she'd completed last time in Emergency, and now there was an additional consent form for the stress test.

The nurse who came to collect her was probably in her fifties, tall and slim, with short, stylish grey hair and a clipboard that gave her a noticeable air of efficiency.

'Vera?' she asked. 'I work with Dr Gregory.' The badge on her shirt pocket said that her name was Mary, but she didn't introduce herself. 'Can you come with me?' As she turned to leave, expecting Vera to follow, she looked back and flashed a quick smile, almost as if she'd just remembered that it was part of her job to appear friendly. Then she set off down a spotless, brightly lit corridor at a swift pace, so that Vera almost needed to jog to keep up. Goodness, she was already nervous. At this rate, her heart would be totally stressed before she even started the test.

The nurse turned in at a doorway. 'Here we are,' she said brightly.

In the middle of the room stood a treadmill with a cord running to a screen on a desk. Tables lined the walls holding more medical equipment. 'You can put your handbag here,' she said, pointing to a chair, and then she stepped behind Vera and closed the door to the room. 'And if you could leave your shirt on the chair too?'

Vera's hands were shaking a little as she undid the buttons on her blouse. *Don't be silly. You're fine. You had a bit of indigestion, that's all.* Draping the blouse over the back of the chair, she stood in her bra and slacks with her tummy sucked in.

'Now, you've fasted for the past two hours?' the nurse asked.

'Yes, I haven't had anything for nearly four hours, actually.'

'You'll be looking forward to a nice cup of tea then.'

'I'm desperate for a nice cup of tea.'

The nurse smiled, but then she became quite businesslike again as she attached a belt around Vera's waist with some kind of measuring device at the front. This was connected to a host of electrodes which the nurse now attached to Vera's chest. She took her time, checking and sometimes reattaching these, and Vera took steadying breaths and told herself to remain calm. Next a blood-pressure cuff was fixed firmly around her arm. The nurse pumped up the cuff and took a reading, then fiddled with knobs at the bottom of the screen, which would no doubt provide an ECG.

'Right,' she said. 'We need to get your heart pumping as strongly as we can to give us the most accurate readings. So you'll feel a bit stressed when the pace picks up, but I'll keep a close eye on things. And it would be a great help, when this is finished, if you could get from the treadmill onto the bed there as quickly as possible. That will also give us the best ultrasound images.'

'All right. I'll do my best.'

'Of course you will. Are you ready if I turn on the treadmill?'

Vera nodded.

'All you need to do is hold onto these handles and walk. After a bit, I'll turn up the pace a notch or two, but I'll be here with you the whole time, and you can let me know if you feel any pain, or you get too tired.'

'Thank you.'

'Okay then? Here we go.'

The treadmill started and Vera walked. In her peripheral vision, she was aware of the yellow line bouncing up and down on the screen beside her. It seemed to be regular, but she refused to pay it close attention. Unfortunately, when she stared straight ahead, she had to look at charts on the wall with diagrams of hearts and arteries, so they weren't any more cheering than the yellow line, but at least they weren't her own heart and arteries.

As the treadmill's pace picked up, she began to feel a bit puffed and then more so, and it was hard not to worry about the results of this test. What if they picked up a problem? Would it mean she'd have to have more tests? Then treatment? Surgery, a pacemaker, perhaps? And what would she tell Theo? She didn't want to spoil his visit.

Afterwards, having felt she'd run a marathon, she was shown to a row of seats in a waiting room and given a cup of tea and two biscuits in a cellophane packet. She enjoyed the tea immensely and was just finishing the second biscuit, an indulgence she rarely allowed herself, when a door opened and an elderly male patient emerged. He was stooped and rather grey about the gills and moved very slowly.

Vera caught a glimpse through the doorway of the doctor who had spoken to her in Emergency, but then he disappeared as the door closed again. The nurse arrived, took the male patient by the elbow and guided him back down the hallway. Vera drew another deep breath. Not long now, surely?

She had turned her phone to silent, but now she took it out of her handbag and found a text message from Theo, which he'd sent forty-five minutes earlier.

Just leaving Jindabilla now. See you this evening.

She had left a chicken in the slow cooker back at her apartment and had stocked up on good-quality wine. She'd also completed the rest of her shopping and had her menus all planned, but although she'd made a special trip to Myer, she hadn't lashed out on expensive bed linen. She still needed to be careful with her finances and it wasn't as if one hundred percent French flax linen would make her feel any more confident or seductive. And now, she didn't even know if this evening would be a cause for celebration. Was she expecting too much by still hoping to be fit and healthy?

The door opened again and the doctor appeared. 'Vera?'

Rising, she followed him into the room, wishing he would offer her a smile, a little hope. He indicated that she should sit and then he took a seat at his desk, frowned at his computer screen, and opened the manila folder in front of him. His expression was noncommittal as he read the information before him.

After what felt like an age, he looked at her and, finally, he smiled. 'Good news,' he said. 'The original diagnosis of an oesophageal spasm was correct. You passed today's stress test with flying colours and your heart is in great shape.'

CHAPTER TWENTY-NINE

'Oh, my God, Maddie, of course Joe and I will be there at the meeting.' Dennis was quite overcome when Maddie phoned to tell him about Jock. 'The poor man. I can't bear it. Just think what he must be going through. It's terrible. Jock's been so wonderful, an absolute saint, helping us in the garden. Now this! He must be so worried.'

Clearly, Dennis was very anxious to help now in any way he could. He wanted to discuss Jock's situation at great length and threw in quite a few names – people Maddie hadn't heard of, but who apparently worked in various government departments or in news networks and might be able to help discover Zoe's whereabouts.

Maddie assured him that any help would be appreciated.

'I'm so glad you rang,' Dennis said next. 'Joe and I have been planning to invite you to dinner. Now, I'm thinking it might be lovely if we invite Jock as well?'

'Oh, that's a nice thought, but I'm not sure.' Maddie had made a point of knocking on Jock's door, but he hadn't answered, so she'd left a card in his letterbox. So far, there'd been no reply. 'It might be a bit soon. He's probably feeling incredibly stressed at the moment. Not knowing is always the worst.'

'Yes, you're probably right.' After a beat, Dennis said, 'But you'll come, won't you? We could make it for Friday evening. Would that suit? Hopefully, you'll have more news from Jock and we'll keep the meal low fuss. Something simple, and a nice bottle of wine. It's the end of the working week, after all.'

The invitation felt like the exact morale boost Maddie needed, and the perfect calming antidote to the tension she'd been battling all week. What with her worry about Jock, the simmering, bewildering tension with Ned, and then her stuff-up with Adam, she'd been feeling pretty stressed. It didn't help that she'd never found the courage to ring Adam back and call off the glamping gig.

'Thanks so much, Dennis, I'd love to come, but let me bring something for the meal. I've discovered a colourful veggie noodle dish I'm keen to try.'

'You're on,' said Dennis. 'It sounds delish.'

Maddie ducked into the shops on her way home from work on Friday evening to grab the necessary ingredients. She added an excellent bottle of shiraz – excellent, according to the guy in the bottle shop at any rate – as well as a new pottery serving bowl that had caught her eye. So she ended up in the apartment block's foyer, waiting for the lift with loaded shopping bags in both hands.

She was looking forward to hitting the kitchen, kicking off her heels and tuning into her favourite music stream as she tackled the new recipe. It sounded pretty easy. The noodles would boil in a flash and while they cooled, she would slice the veggies, toast sesame seeds and whisk together a dressing. *Voila.* With luck, she would even have time for a quick shower before dinner.

Happily musing on the relaxed night ahead with two friends who were fast beginning to feel like members of her extended family, Maddie barely noticed that the door from the garage had opened.

Then Vera stepped into the foyer and, almost immediately, her companion appeared close behind her, carrying a stylish, well-worn leather overnight bag, plus an armful of beautiful flowers. Maddie instantly snapped to attention.

Wow. Tall, silver haired and extraordinarily good looking, the man wasn't young, possibly Vera's age or a touch older. And although Vera hadn't mentioned whether her visitor owned a cattle property, Maddie suspected he was a man of the land. It wasn't just the guy's outdoorsy tan, or the blue and white striped shirt with rolled-back sleeves and a discreet RM Williams logo on the pocket. While Vera's companion had the sparkling blue eyes of a movie star, he also had the lean athleticism of a man who'd spent his days being active, probably outdoors, with minimal time sitting behind a desk.

Even more telling, he carried an air of quiet confidence, and a noticeable lack of the habitual tension that seemed to haunt most of the men in Maddie's workplace. In fact, he reminded her in subtle ways of her dad, who was also a farmer, although this man was far more handsome.

Lucky Vera.

Maddie hoped she wasn't staring too hard and she swiftly switched her attention to her friend. Vera was looking a little flushed, she thought. A romantic glow, perhaps? Almost certainly Vera was excited and happily buzzing. Maddie smiled at her. 'Good evening.'

'Maddie, how lovely to catch you.' Barely concealing her delighted smile, Vera touched her companion's elbow. 'Theo, let me introduce you to my lovely new friend, Maddie Armitage.'

The lift arrived at that moment and, before Maddie or Theo could respond, its doors slid open, spilling residents dressed for a Friday night on the town. Theo stepped back to let these people pass and then gallantly held the doors ajar for the women. Close up, inside the lift, he seemed even taller and more impressive. The scent of the flowers swirled around them, casting an air of romance, and Maddie almost felt like an intruder.

But once they'd attended to the business of pressing buttons for their floors, she spoke up. 'It's lovely to meet you, Theo.' Then she gave an apologetic shrug as she held up her shopping bags. 'Sorry. Can't offer to shake hands.'

Theo's response was a charming smile and a dip of his head. 'It's a pleasure to meet you, Maddie.'

Vera, meanwhile, was eyeing Maddie's shopping bags. 'Are these supplies for your glamping adventure?'

'No,' Maddie said quickly to cover the uncomfortable lurch in her stomach. 'I'm having dinner tonight with Joe and Dennis.'

At this news, Vera looked genuinely delighted. 'How lovely.' But even if she'd wanted to say more, they had already reached Maddie's floor. 'Say hello to the boys from me,' she called as Maddie stepped out.

'I will.' She sent a cheeky smile back over her shoulder. 'And you two have a great evening.'

Before the lift's doors closed, Maddie saw the smile Vera and Theo exchanged. They looked like a pair of lovestruck teenagers.

Of course, she couldn't resist telling Joe and Dennis about Vera's beau. They were going to meet him on the roof the next morning, so there was little point in keeping him a secret. By that point, Maddie had already admired Joe and Dennis's amazing plants, which were more lush and beautiful than ever, and the three of them had talked about Jock who, sadly, had still had no news. But then Dennis produced a bottle of champagne and promptly proceeded to release the cork.

'Bubbles?' Maddie asked, surprised. 'I thought you guys were red wine drinkers.'

'Oh, we are for the most part,' Joe assured her.

'But tonight, we want to celebrate.' Dennis looked coy as he said this and the two men grinned at each other.

'Really? Are you —?' Maddie stopped herself just in time. It would be terrible to voice her thoughts out loud and find she was on the wrong track.

As Dennis handed her a slim flute of cold, fizzing wine, his eyes were shining with suppressed excitement. 'Joe's asked me to marry him.'

'Oh!' Maddie felt such an instant burst of delight, she almost spilled her drink. 'I hope you said yes?'

Both the guys laughed.

'Of course I did.' Dennis had turned a bright shade of pink, and Joe, standing quietly beside him, smiled at him with a look of such deep and honest affection that Maddie was suddenly battling tears. Happy tears, of course. And now it was necessary to set her glass down so she could hug them both.

'Congratulations!' she managed in a choked voice. 'Oh, this is just such wonderful news! I'm so happy for you.' And it was true. She truly was very, *very* happy for them, even though, in a tiny corner of her heart, she was a bit – no, maybe even more than a bit – sorry that her own love life was such a mess.

Nevertheless, she shoved those thoughts aside. 'So, is this public news?'

'Not yet,' said Joe. 'You're the first to know outside our families.'

'Wow. What an honour. I hope you'll have a party.'

'Oh, I want to make a huge fuss!' exclaimed Dennis. 'Fireworks, more champers, and all the bells and whistles.'

'But maybe not this weekend,' countered Joe. 'Not when we're all so concerned about Jock.'

'No,' agreed Dennis. 'Plenty of time for us.'

They took the champagne bottle, their glasses and a platter of cheese and crackers outside to balcony. It was quite dark by now and Joe had lit a couple of lanterns and placed them among the tubs of plants, making the small space utterly enchanting so they could almost forget they were in the middle of a big metropolis.

Taking a deep sip of her wine, Maddie told herself to relax. Tonight she would forget about her own silly worries – which were, after all, entirely of her own making – and she would immerse herself in sharing Joe and Dennis's happiness. What the heck? She might even let herself get a bit tipsy.

'What about you, Maddie?' Dennis's voice interrupted her thoughts.

'Me?' she asked. Had she missed something?

'How's your love life?'

Oh, God. *Really?* She couldn't help giving an exaggerated roll of her eyes. 'Sorry, guys. I'm afraid it's not worth discussing.'

'What about Ned?'

Bloody hell. Not these two as well. Vera had been bad enough with her little digs about Ned being such a great catch, and how well suited he and Maddie were. Now she decided to play dumb. 'What about Ned?'

'Well, you're obviously pally with him. The two of you have been getting together for rather serious discussions.'

'Kind of, but that doesn't mean . . .' Maddie hesitated over finishing the sentence, which was damn annoying. It should have been easy to declare the lack of romantic spark between herself and the beekeeper. But before she could find the right words, Dennis was off again.

'And – I don't know,' he continued, as if she hadn't even spoken, 'there's a definite vibe between the two of you. We both think so, don't we Joe?'

Joe's smile – damn him – was almost smug. 'We do.'

'Honestly!' she fumed. 'You must surely have better things to talk about. Haven't you enough to do with planning your wedding?'

'Okay, okay,' Dennis soothed. 'Sorry if we touched a sore point.'

'It's not a sore point. It's a – a non-existent point, and if you really must know, I'm still going out with Adam.'

'The real-estate chap you met on Tinder?'

'Yes.' Maddie almost added that she wouldn't be going out with him for much longer, but she feared that would only open another uncomfortable line of discussion. 'So are you two going to have engagement rings?' she asked instead, and luckily Dennis was more than happy to tell her about the endless options for men's engagement rings.

'Joe's decided that he doesn't want one, though,' Dennis said and he flashed his partner a smitten smile. 'He's such a bloke.'

'But Dennis is having a ring with diamonds,' added Joe with a grin.

'Diamonds, plural? Wow!'

'Just a few teensy ones,' amended Dennis. 'I'll show you.' Promptly, he pulled out his phone and showed Maddie a photo of a beautiful ring – a flat gold band engraved with trees and dotted with tiny diamonds like stars.

'Oh, that's truly gorgeous,' she exclaimed. 'It's perfect for you. It makes me think of the rooftop here, with all the trees and plants we've put in – and the stars.'

'Yeah, that's what we thought too.'

Fortunately, the subject of Maddie's own romantic prospects was dropped and soon after that, they went inside to eat. Her noodle salad was a huge hit and proved to be a perfect accompaniment for Joe's amazingly delicious beetroot and goat's cheese terrine. As they ate, they talked a little more about Jock, wishing there were more avenues to help him, and they chatted about their jobs – the good and bad bits – about plans for the garden and about their latest movie discoveries, about politics and climate change.

They were almost at the bottom of Maddie's bottle of shiraz when Dennis winked at her and said, 'I still reckon you should give Ned a go.'

CHAPTER THIRTY

If Vera's new glasses and hairdo were some kind of test for Theo Blaine, he passed with flying colours. He'd been surprised, of course, when he'd pulled up in front of the apartments where Vera was waiting on the footpath to greet him. For a scant second or two, he possibly didn't recognise her. His expression had been blank, but then, slowly, incredulously, he'd smiled.

'Vera.'

Choosing not to offer excuses for her transformed appearance, she responded in her best hostess voice, 'It's lovely to see you, Theo. I do hope you've had a good journey?' And she was about to point the way to the underground garage and to explain where Theo could park his Range Rover when he climbed out of his vehicle.

'Just, wow!' he said as he cast a smiling and appreciative gaze over her. 'I was expecting a country chick, and what do I find, but the ultimate city sophisticate?' And then he drew her in for a hug, right there on the footpath for anyone to see.

*

Theo had brought Vera the most beautiful bouquet, which he produced as soon as the car was safely parked. Such a lovely combination of blossoms, with two divine proteas, plus snapdragons and peonies in pastel pinks and soft yellows, all complemented by silvery foliage.

'They're just gorgeous,' Vera had said, quite touched that he'd somehow chosen her favourite colours. Not only that, but the bouquet came in an elegant glass vase, so she wouldn't have to go hunting in cupboards the minute she walked in the door.

Then there had been the coincidence of meeting Maddie in the lift and the rather gratifying experience of seeing how obviously impressed Maddie had been by Theo. But then, most women found him impressive.

'Your new home looks very comfortable and stylish,' he said once she'd shown him into the apartment.

'I still buy everything from second-hand stores,' Vera confessed.

He smiled. 'Nothing wrong with that. Especially when you have such good taste.'

A taste in line with his own, perhaps?

Vera had realised then that she should probably take him through to the bedrooms, but that prospect had left her in rather a dither, as she wasn't quite sure where he expected to sleep. She was saved from this duty, for the time being, however, by Max emerging from behind the sofa to greet them with a soft meow.

'Ah,' said Theo. 'So this is your new companion.'

'Yes, this is Max.'

'A handsome chap.' Theo looked amused. 'Are you really going to keep him?'

'I'm not sure.' She had explained over the phone about giving in to a moment of weakness, and that she'd decided the cat would help to entertain Henry. 'He's a good little fellow. Very clean. I've bought him a few toys and a scratching post and he doesn't mind living indoors. Having him here seems to be working.' She smiled as she rolled her eyes to the ceiling. 'Not that the Body Corporate knows about him.'

'Are they very strict?'

Vera tilted her hand from side to side. 'Not too bad. I haven't actually enquired about their policy on cats, but I'm pretty sure pets aren't really allowed.' She knelt down to give Max the sort of scratch behind the ears that he loved. 'I should probably try to find an animal shelter or refuge for him, but it's been rather nice to have his company.' Then she smiled up at Theo. 'Even better to have your company. Thanks for coming.'

'Thank you for inviting me.' His gaze lingered, piercing and clear, sending a shiver-sweet tremor through her.

Vera tried to ignore the reaction. She wished she knew exactly what she wanted from this man. And what he wanted or expected from her. It was lovely to see him again, but she was beginning to fear she'd been rather rash, had perhaps issued her invitation out of loneliness, or as an overreaction to the heart scare.

'I'm sure you're dying for a cup of tea,' she said, but after a quick glance to the darkness that had arrived outside, she added, 'Or perhaps you're ready for wine?'

Theo opted for wine, claiming that he'd drunk a great deal of water plus an entire Thermos of tea during his journey. Vera showed him to the bathroom – the guest bathroom, not the ensuite attached to her bedroom, and on the way, they passed the spare bedroom with a double bed.

Theo paused at this doorway, overnight bag in hand. 'Am I in here?'

'Would that suit?' In her flurry of uncertainty, Vera had prepared this room, to cover all bases, so to speak.

'It looks extremely comfortable.'

'Right you are, then,' she said and, just like that, the awkward hurdle seemed to have been cleared in a single, seamless bound. She was flooded with relief. 'And the bathroom's right next door,' she told him. 'Take your time and I'll go and open the wine.'

Breathing much more easily now, she returned to the kitchen to fetch glasses and a bottle of expensive red and to assemble a little platter with cheese and olives. The chicken in her slow cooker was smelling delicious and the salad that would accompany this was ready in the fridge. So, at last, she could actually relax, stop worrying about geriatric love affairs, and enjoy the company of a long-time friend.

Dinner was very pleasant. Theo complimented Vera's food while she plied him with questions about the many folk she knew in the Jindabilla district, and he answered these patiently, and in pleasing and sometimes amusing detail. And afterwards, she took him to the roof.

Her original plan had been to wait until the next morning to reveal this treasure in daylight, but having exhausted news from western Queensland, Theo had begun to quiz Vera about her new life in Brisbane. Whom had she met? What groups had she joined? What were her new hobbies?

She hadn't been keen to confess that she'd spent far too many months brooding and moping and being generally depressed, so she'd felt compelled to expound on the gardening group and their wonderful new project.

'Come and I'll show you,' she said. 'It's only a few steps away. Let's take the wine.' Theo had already opened a second bottle, a very fine vintage shiraz that he'd brought, which possibly wasn't wise, but this evening *was* a special occasion. 'We can sit and enjoy the stars for a bit,' she said.

The roof was in darkness, but Vera soon found the light switch that illuminated the entertaining area. As the lights came on, however, she was startled to see a figure sitting alone at one of the little wrought-iron tables. A woman dressed all in black, with her hair scraped up into a high, messy knot.

Nancy Jenkins.

'Nancy!' Vera exclaimed. 'I'm sorry. I didn't realise anyone was here.' And it was only then, as a breeze wafted towards her and she saw the glowing red tip of a cigarette, that she also realised that Nancy was smoking.

'I left the lights out so the stars would be clearer.' Nancy sounded almost apologetic.

'Yes, of course. It's a lovely night. I'm sorry we disturbed you.'

'You're not disturbing anything,' Nancy replied, switching quickly to her usual abrasive manner as she stubbed out her cigarette in an ashtray that she'd obviously brought with her, and then jumped to her feet.

'But we don't want to chase you away.' Vera turned to Theo. 'We can come back in the morning, can't we?'

'Of course.'

'Don't be silly,' snapped Nancy as she dumped the ashtray and its contents in a capacious shoulder bag.

Vera might have been unsettled by this reaction, but having been warned by Carmen about Nancy's rather tragic past, she felt sympathy now. Losing custody of her children would be enough to leave any woman bitter and twisted.

'Well, you're very welcome to stay,' she told Nancy. 'I was just bringing my friend, Theo, up to see the garden. Maybe you'd like to join us for a drink? My apartment's so close, we can easily fetch another glass.'

'I don't drink,' came Nancy's frosty retort.

Of course. Too late, Vera remembered that the whole cause of Nancy's problems had been alcohol. But before she could smooth over this tricky moment, Nancy issued an abrupt 'Goodnight' and stumped off, almost, but not quite, slamming the door behind her.

Vera glanced at Theo, who had watched this exchange with mild bemusement. 'Don't mind her,' she told him, once Nancy was safely out of earshot. 'I'll fill you in sometime, but I'm beginning to suspect that her bark might be worse than her bite.'

She pointed to the table and chairs Nancy had abandoned. 'Now, come and take a seat, and I'll tell you all about this rooftop project.'

'Absolutely. I'm all ears.'

Indeed, Theo was gratifyingly impressed and, as they made themselves comfortable, Vera pointed out the tubs of flourishing greenery, the newly laid paving, the barbecues and pergola, and further on, the trellis with Carmen's trendily distressed door as its centrepiece.

'Oh, and those herbs over there are my contribution,' she said. 'I'm so pleased with them. They're doing wonderfully well.' With a smile, she added, 'But I won't ask you to inspect the worm farm or the compost bin.'

'You have those up here, as well?'

'Oh, yes. Henry was very impressed.'

'I don't doubt it. *I'm* impressed.'

'We even have beehives.'

'Yes, I thought I saw a sign warning about bees.'

'We're quite safe here, though, unless you have an allergy.'

Theo shook his head. 'No.'

'They're way over there, in the far corner.' Vera told him then about Ned and the care he'd taken to ensure that the bees were as safe as possible. 'Ned chose that position for the hives. Bees need sunlight and apparently morning sun is best, but they also need shade in the hottest part of the day, so there's shade cloth for now until the trees we've planted grow tall enough. And he's kept them well away from this entertaining area. Apart from the fact that they might bother us, they don't like bright lights. So, it all works out rather well.'

'It sounds fantastic,' said Theo. 'Quite brilliant.' And so Vera told him about Joe and Dennis then. And about Maddie and Carmen, although she decided not to mention Jock just now. His story was rather too serious to land on her guest on the very first evening.

'Carmen's quite a character,' she said. 'Oh, my God, you should see her apartment. It's gorgeous! She's an artist and —' She was about to expand on the wonders of Carmen's apartment when she stopped herself. 'Actually, no, perhaps you shouldn't see Carmen's place. She's likely to take one look at you and start flirting madly.'

Good grief. Vera couldn't believe she'd actually said that out loud. Bugger, she'd had too much to drink.

Theo merely chuckled, however, leaving her to wonder what on earth he was thinking. But he'd always been circumspect, and whatever his thoughts were about flirtatious women, he kept them to himself. Instead, he looked about him, as if taking a mental inventory of everything the gardeners had achieved, after which, he asked Vera quietly, almost carefully, 'So I guess you don't miss your garden at Jinda now?'

'Oh, I *have* missed it,' she admitted. 'For a long time, I missed it terribly. And I still do miss hearing the birds, and being able to potter all day long if I want, to dig deep in the soil or to plan new beds. And I miss just being able to stand in the garden and drink in those wonderful views we had out there – the way they stretch forever to the distant hills. Caring for a few herbs can't really compensate.'

Quickly, she added, 'But at the same time, I can't deny that getting together to work on this garden has helped me to feel much more settled here.'

Theo absorbed this without comment and his smile was ambiguous.

'I'm not saying that gardening is the be-all and end-all,' Vera continued. 'It's more about the people, really. Before you can feel properly settled, you need to feel connected, don't you?'

'I imagine that might be the case,' said Theo. 'But I've lived in the one place all my life, so I've never experienced having to resettle somewhere.' He smiled. 'I'm a hermit from the back of beyond.'

'Nonsense. You've never been truly isolated, and you've always been a fabulous mixer.' Theo had been on wonderfully good terms with anyone he met – from cooks, fencers and truck drivers to bank managers and stock and station agents. He called them all by their first names and never forgot to enquire about their families.

Rather than a hermit, he was a man for all seasons. He and his wife had hosted many grand balls in their beautiful home, raising funds for all kinds of charities. They'd entertained top-ranking politicians and international entrepreneurs with accomplished ease, but then Theo could also, and just as happily, take off on a cattle muster and camp in a swag under the stars, exchanging yarns and blue jokes around the campfire with the ringers.

'Felix learned so much from you about how to fit in with the people in the bush,' she said. 'We both did.' With a rueful smile, she added, 'Although I have to admit we were slow learners.'

Theo gave a gentle shake of his head and reached for the wine bottle to top up her glass.

'No, thank you. I'm sure I've already had more than enough. But please, you go ahead.'

He did so and lifted his glass to take an appreciative sip. As he set it back down he said, 'When you left Jinda, I had the impression that you thought you were being sent into some kind of exile.'

'Ah, yes.' Vera drew a deep breath and let it out slowly. 'There were tensions at the time.' She had never actually spelled out her fears to Theo about Archie and Brooke's marriage, and she wouldn't start now, especially after the recent bridge-building conversation with her daughter-in-law. 'Things are much better,' she said. 'But it was probably for the best that I moved away and let the new generation have some . . . breathing room.'

Discreet as ever, Theo simply nodded. 'Archie's doing a great job. You're lucky you have a son who's keen to take over the reins.'

'So, your girls and their partners still aren't interested in Lansdowne?'

'Not in the slightest. I'm sure they can't wait till I sell the property and they can inherit their shares.'

'But you're not planning to sell, are you? Not yet?'

Theo shook his head. 'Hopefully not for quite some time.'

He drained his glass and Vera knew it was late. It was time to return to the apartment.

'Shall we go back now?' she asked, keeping her voice light.

Together they rose, picked up their glasses and the bottle and left the roof, turning out the light and descending the short flight of steps. Vera felt in the pocket of her slacks for the door key, worried for a moment that she'd left the apartment without it, but she hadn't, of course. The key was there, at the very bottom of the deep pocket. She was just tense again. Still wondering what might happen next . . .

She'd left a lamp on in the living room and the low light made the space look inviting and intimate. 'Would you like coffee?' she asked Theo as she took the glasses into the kitchen and set them in the sink.

'No, thank you.'

'Right.' It was time for bed, then. Returning to the living room, she smiled. 'I think you'll find everything you need in your bathroom. Towels, soap, shampoo. I imagine you have your shaving gear?'

He smiled. 'Of course.'

'And one of the great bonuses of being in the city is that you can use as much hot water as you like.'

Vera turned out the lamp and switched the hall light on. When they reached the doorway to his room, she paused. 'You might like to open the window.' It was a window that had received Jock's attention and opened very easily now. 'There's often a good breeze from the river.' Without waiting for his response, she crossed the room, turned on the bedside lamp, pulled the curtain aside and slid the window open. 'There.'

Her heart was thumping weirdly as she repositioned the curtain and turned back to him. 'I hope you'll be comfortable.'

'I'm sure I will be. This bed looks far more comfortable than the floor.'

The floor. He was referring to the night they had spent together, making love on the rug in front of his fireplace.

She knew she should leave, but her head was swimming with memories of that night and she hesitated a moment too long. Theo reached for her hand. He smiled again. 'I've missed you so much.'

And now Vera was no longer wondering what might happen next. Theo was asking a very clear question and she answered by taking a step closer.

CHAPTER THIRTY-ONE

On Saturday, Maddie sat at the back of the meeting. There was a chance it might take a little longer than planned and she would need to make her exit before it was finished. She still had the glamping commitment – she'd wasted her chance to get out of that – so she had her bag packed and ready on the floor beside her, and her stomach was a mass of butterflies whenever she thought about the evening ahead that she'd been too chicken to escape.

She'd learned her lesson, though. This was the absolute last time she'd date a guy she had doubts about.

At least the meeting was going well. They'd moved from the roof down to the privacy of Ned's apartment, with everyone sitting on an assortment of lounge and dining chairs. All the gardeners had turned up, including Vera and her new man. Carmen had also brought a friend, a Frenchman who was staying with her, and she'd produced a loaf of crusty bread, along with pâté and brie, in case anyone was feeling peckish. Unsurprisingly, it seemed everyone was suddenly hungry.

So the meeting had started on an upbeat note. Nancy and Godfrey also arrived, frowning as usual, but they listened politely without interference.

Maddie knew there'd been no more news from Nepal, so she was surprised when Jock also joined them, looking pale and strained.

'I just wanted to thank you all,' he said. 'I know you'd like to help if you could, so I thought you should know how things stand.'

Tears welled in Maddie's eyes and she hoped like crazy that she didn't start bawling.

'I've been working through the consular emergency helpline in Canberra,' Jock told them. 'And they've put me in email contact with the Australian Embassy in Kathmandu. Everyone's been sympathetic and they've tried to help, but so far no luck. It's still too difficult to get into the more remote areas.' His mouth tilted in a grimly brave smile. 'And unfortunately, remote areas are my Zoe's specialty.'

Maddie could see that a few others in the group were battling to hold off tears. She could only hope that just knowing these people cared might be helpful for Jock, but of course no one could offer any immediate solutions, although Dennis tried, bless him.

'I was wondering if we should make enquiries through some of the non-government aid agencies,' he said. 'I don't know – World Vision, that sort of thing.'

The group was visibly buoyed by even the tiniest possibility of hope and Ros was immediately murmuring a comment to Carmen, but before she could speak up, the moment was spoiled by a knock at the front door. Joe was closest and he hurried down the hallway to answer it.

Maddie heard Adam's voice.

Zap! An unpleasant shiver slithered down her spine.

She hadn't told Adam where this meeting was being held, and so she'd kept her phone ready, expecting a text message from him. Instead, he must have let himself into the building and somehow tracked her down. Here, to Ned's apartment.

Annoyed, she slipped her notepad and pen into the outside pocket of her bag and jumped to her feet. She was conscious of Ned watching her, but she didn't meet his gaze. She had warned the group that she had a prior engagement and might have to leave early, and she wanted to exit now as unobtrusively as possible.

As she hefted the bag's straps onto her shoulder, however, Joe came back into the room with Adam in tow.

'Hey, there!' Adam waved to the group and gave them a beaming smile, like a rock star greeting his fans. 'Don't let me interrupt you. I'm with Maddie.'

'I can leave now,' Maddie told him, wishing she didn't sound so upset.

'Heavens, no! I wouldn't want to drag you away.' Dramatically, Adam now stood with a hand over his heart, his head bowed, in a pose of abject apology. Then, as he straightened again, he gestured to the group. 'I've taken a look at the roof, folks, and I gotta say – love your work! So, please, go ahead with your discussion. I can wait.'

The mood had been ruined, though, the train of thought interrupted. Lost. Maddie could sense everyone's eyes on her – the questioning frowns, the silent disapproval. Deep down, she had always known that Adam wouldn't stand up to close scrutiny from these friends. Now, she was conscious of Ned eyeing him off. She couldn't bear it.

'Excuse me,' she said to the group. 'I'll head off now. I can catch up with any final discussion later.'

A few people nodded.

'We'll keep in touch,' Joe offered kindly.

'Thanks.' She turned to leave, indicating with a flick of her hand that Adam should precede her.

'Maddie!' It was Jock's voice.

Maddie turned.

Jock had been sitting beside her and now he reached out and gripped her hand, his green eyes brimming with emotion. 'Thanks, mate.'

A painful lump filled her throat. Never had she felt so conscious of being caught between two worlds. The world where she belonged, real and solid, here with her neighbours who were also her caring friends – and the world she thought she'd been searching for that kept shifting beneath her like sand in the wind.

She gave Jock's hand a squeeze, but she was too choked to speak, so she managed a tight-lipped smile. Then, keeping her eyes carefully averted, she turned and departed, shooing Adam ahead of her down the hall and out the door.

'What the fuck was that about?' Adam was clearly furious but he'd hung onto his question until they were in the lift.

'What do you mean?'

'Don't play dumb, Maddie. That wasn't a gardening meeting. What was it?' He was snarling as he punched the button for the ground floor. 'A room full of do-gooders? Some bleeding heart thanking you, as if you'd saved his life?'

'What's the matter with you?' Maddie would have turned and marched away if they hadn't been already descending in the lift. 'Actually, if you're going to be like that, I think you'd better go on this trip without me.'

'Maddie!' Adam looked instantly worried. 'I just didn't understand. Can't you explain?'

She glared at him. 'Jock's our caretaker and he needs our help. But, if you don't like it, I can always —'

'No need to get uptight,' he interrupted quickly.

'No need?' she scoffed. 'That's a matter of opinion.'

'Hey.' Adam softened his tone. 'Sorry if I offended you. It was just a surprise. I was expecting a discussion about fertiliser or watering systems.'

He was an expert at backing down, of course, almost too good, as if it was a habit. The pattern was clear to Maddie now. Every time Adam sensed she wanted to retreat, to walk away, he would turn on the charm again, just as he was doing right at this moment, offering her the smile of a small boy desperate to please.

But if she tried to back out now, there was bound to be another tantrum, quite possibly out on the footpath, in full view of anyone who might glance down from Ned's window.

Already, the lift had reached ground level. Adam shepherded her through the foyer to the street outside, and she saw his vehicle, not a sports car this time, but a latest model SUV with a very swish camping trailer hooked behind. The set-up required two parking spaces and it was a wonder he hadn't copped a fine.

Adam was grinning as he patted the trailer. 'I have everything we could possibly want in here, including the kitchen sink. There's also a fridge, of course. And the champagne's on ice.'

Clearly, he'd gone to a great deal of trouble and she uneasily realised she might have to overlook his crassness about Jock and their meeting. But if he was hoping for red-hot passion this evening, he would be sorely disappointed, and this was, most definitely, the very last time she'd go out with him.

Thirty minutes later, Adam was zooming down the Ipswich–Boonah Road at well over the speed limit, tailgating any cars that he deemed too slow, and then passing them recklessly.

Maddie couldn't help speaking up. 'Do you think we're going a bit too fast?'

Of course, Adam scowled at her. 'I don't need a lecture. I'm trying to make up for the time we've lost. Thanks to your meeting, we've already wasted most of the day.'

She was not going to apologise. He'd agreed that she could attend the meeting and their lateness was really no excuse for speeding. But then, she'd always been a bit nervous about driving on highways. She'd had an accident once, just after she'd started uni. Her parents had bought her a little second-hand Honda and she'd been driving home to Bundaberg, travelling too close to a car in front, when the car had propped to make a sudden turn, and she'd run right into the back of it.

The police had come, Maddie's car had been towed away and it had been rather traumatic all round – with the result that she'd been exceptionally careful ever since.

Nevertheless, Adam seemed to be quite an expert driver, despite his excessive speed, so Maddie folded her arms and kept her thoughts quiet as he rushed on. She told herself that the glamping was going to be an interesting experience – out in the bush with a camp fire. She conjured a picture of the late afternoon in a bushy setting, with the sun slipping lower and wallabies emerging from the scrub to graze as the shadows lengthened.

Her imaginings were interrupted by the wail of a siren.

'Fuck.' The expletive slipped from Adam as he stared into the rear-vision mirror.

Maddie turned to look behind them and saw a car with unmistakable blue and white checked markings and flashing blue lights. 'Do they want you to pull over?'

A stupid question, perhaps. Adam certainly didn't answer. He didn't need to. Already, the police car had pulled out to pass them and the cop in the passenger seat was glaring at them and pointing to the kerb. For a moment, Maddie was terrified that Adam would ignore this instruction and try to race away. But then, still swearing, he slowed to a reluctant stop.

Neither he nor Maddie spoke as the cop who'd been driving climbed out of his vehicle and strode towards them. The cop was middle aged and had a ruddy face and when he reached them, he stood, macho style, with his thumbs hooked over his belt.

With a heavy sigh, Adam depressed the button that lowered his window.

'You were exceeding the speed limit,' the cop said. 'Any reason for that?'

Adam glared at him. 'No comment.'

From beneath the brim of his cap, the cop scowled back. 'Could you show me your licence please, sir?'

Adam looked for a moment as if he was going to refuse. *Please don't make any trouble*, Maddie silently begged. This situation was already bad enough. All she wanted now was for Adam to cooperate and accept the fine and then the cops would leave them in peace.

To her relief, Adam must have realised he had little choice, but his jaw was hard as granite as he extracted his wallet from his hip pocket. He slipped the licence from its sleeve and Maddie caught a glimpse of a headshot of him in a white business shirt. He looked particularly grim, but then photos on licences never looked happy. You weren't allowed to smile, were you?

'Thank you,' the cop said and then he frowned as he studied the details on the licence, and he continued to frown as he studied Adam. 'You own this vehicle?'

Adam huffed an elaborate sigh. 'I've rented it for the weekend.'

Maddie might have been surprised by this news if she hadn't been so tense. The cop merely nodded. Then without another word, he headed back to his vehicle, taking Adam's licence with him.

'Bastards,' Adam snarled as he punched at the steering wheel.

Maddie's chest was so tight she could scarcely breathe. She'd never had a speeding fine and wasn't sure of the protocols, but something about this didn't feel quite right. Why should Adam be so angry? He knew he'd been way over the speed limit. 'What's the problem? What's happening?' she asked him.

Once again, he didn't bother to answer her. He merely stared straight ahead, glaring at the cop car and breathing heavily as he tapped the steering wheel in a tense tattoo. Meanwhile, the cop had handed the licence to his fellow officer in the vehicle.

Maddie knew from working with lawyers that the police would be able to log into a website and check Adam's records. Perhaps he had a history of speeding tickets. Or he might have forgotten to pay his rego – if he actually owned a vehicle.

It seemed ages before the cop came back to them. His face was grave. 'Adam Stuart Grainger?'

'Yep.' Adam's bored sigh sounded juvenile under the circumstances, like a kid who'd been sent to the principal's office and was trying to play it cool. Any sympathy Maddie might have felt now hit rock bottom.

'I'm sure you must know a domestic violence order has been issued against you?'

A what?

Maddie's head was suddenly filled with static.

'You were supposed to attend a court hearing, but you never showed up.' The cop paused, tilted his head at a slight angle as he watched Adam through narrowed eyes, obviously waiting for some kind of answer. 'You got anything to say about that?'

Adam continued to sit perfectly still, sulky and silent, not making eye contact. Maddie was so mortified she wanted to scream.

'When you failed to appear in court, the magistrate issued a warrant,' the cop said next. 'And now I'll have to take you into custody and make sure you turn up in court.'

'You can't arrest me!'

'I certainly can. Now, if you'll step out of your vehicle.'

'This is insane.' Adam sounded panicked.

'Step out of your vehicle now, please.'

To Maddie's horror, the cop produced handcuffs, and as Adam reluctantly pushed his car door open, drivers and passengers in passing vehicles stared at them, gobsmacked, mouths hanging open, desperately curious. She heard the click of the cuffs closing around Adam's wrists.

'If you'll excuse me, ma'am, I'll be back in a moment.'

A whimper broke from her as Adam was led to the police car. She couldn't help it. She'd never been so shocked, so appalled, so embarrassed.

She supposed this must be what it felt like to be mugged, to be hit by a blow you couldn't see coming, a punch that felled you, winded you, left you helpless.

She had asked for this, though, hadn't she? She only had herself to blame. She'd been foolish, as gullible as every other woman who'd been conned by a guy over the internet. People were always warning women about this danger and yet she'd stupidly let herself be sucked in, despite her suspicions.

But those suspicions had always been vague and dubious. She'd never in her wildest dreams suspected that Adam might have a history of violence, that there could be a woman – or *women* – out there who were totally scared of him and needed to be protected. That reality was too shocking to comprehend.

Even as she thought this, though, Maddie was remembering the time she'd rung Adam and a little girl had answered. And that other time, when there'd been a woman's voice in the background . . .

Was this the poor woman who needed the courts to protect her? Were there others?

When Maddie had made those calls, Adam had claimed to be at work, but had that been a lie? How many lies might he have told her? Would he have admitted to her that he didn't own this vehicle or the trailer, just as he hadn't owned the yacht? Had he owned the sports car? Now, Maddie wondered if he actually owned a real-estate business.

Probably not. He was a mirage. Nothing about him was real. Chances were, he didn't even own the land he'd been taking her to for this stupid glamping trip.

She wasn't even sure why Adam had dated her. What had he wanted from her, apart from investment information which she could never have delivered? Had that been her downfall? That tiny white lie?

A wild sound broke from her, halfway between a sob and a groan. It seemed incredible now that she'd been so desperately upset when she'd found Simon having lunch with Ruby Reid. Their crime seemed totally innocent compared with this.

'Excuse me, ma'am.' The policeman was back. 'Can you tell me your name?'

'Madeline Armitage.'

He nodded. 'May I see your licence?'

Maddie wasn't quite brave enough to ask why he needed this, but she found her purse and fished out the licence.

'Thank you, Ms Armitage. Do you still live at this address in Auchenflower?'

'Yes.'

He didn't take her licence away, as he had done with Adam's, and after a quick check, he handed it straight back to her.

'Did you know Adam Grainger had a DVO filed against him?'

'No, I had no idea.' She tightened her jaw as she struggled not to cry. She didn't want to break down, to look any weaker than she already felt.

Blinking hard, she drew a deep breath and then another. 'Adam hasn't been violent with me,' she felt compelled to explain.

'I'm very glad to hear that.'

But Maddie was sure she'd dodged a bullet. She hated to think how Adam might have reacted if she'd followed through with her plan to refuse sex with him tonight.

The cop nodded towards the other vehicle. 'My fellow officer has called for another police car. We'll make sure you get home safely.'

'Thank you.' She supposed she was grateful, but her brain was firing in a thousand directions. 'What about this vehicle? How will it get back to the rental people?' Not that she was in any fit state to drive.

'You don't have to worry about that,' she was told. 'We'll take care of it.'

Having dug in her pocket for a tissue, Maddie blew her nose, but she didn't dare to dab at her eyes for fear she might tempt the banked-up tears.

Watching her, the cop asked, 'Will you be all right when you get home? Do you have family or friends who can support you?'

'Yes, thanks. I have friends in my apartment block.' It was good to be able to tell him this, although she had no idea if any of her neighbours would be home this evening. It was, after all, a Saturday.

He seemed satisfied, however, and it wasn't long before another police car arrived. This time, the officer who approached Maddie was a woman, young, tanned and athletic, with blonde hair pulled into a neat bun, and a gun holster dangling from her hip. She introduced herself, but the name went in one ear and out the other.

Maddie just wanted to get out of here now. Home to her apartment. As far away from Adam and his bloody glamping trailer as possible.

None of the officers suggested that she might like to say goodbye to him, and she was grateful to be able to simply grab her bag and climb into the back of the waiting car, strapping on her seatbelt. As they took off, she raised a mental finger in the air. *Good riddance.*

*

For most of the return journey she sank back against the head rest with her eyes closed, not wanting to talk, or even to think. She couldn't blank her mind completely, though, so she took her thoughts back to just an hour or so before Adam's arrival, to the meeting with Jock. She saw the faces of her friends crowded into Ned's apartment. Joe and Dennis and a couple of their neighbours from Level 3. Vera, Carmen and their men. Ros had also brought a friend, and even Nancy and Godfrey had been there, frowning as sternly as ever, but not interrupting or voicing objections.

Maddie recalled the obvious sense of connection in the group, the feeling of caring, of reaching out – only to be obliterated by Adam's arrival.

Arrgh.

'This has been very traumatic for you.'

Maddie opened her eyes to find the policewoman watching her from the front seat. The woman smiled, gently, carefully. 'You know there's counselling available if you need it.'

'Oh, um, yes. Thanks.' The last thing Maddie wanted was to have to talk with someone about Adam. She just wanted to erase him from her memory bank, to forget about the many occasions she'd let slip through her fingers when she should have finished with him. But when the woman handed her a card with phone numbers, she accepted it. 'Thanks,' she said again.

It was only when the car turned into her street that she realised she now faced the humiliation of turning up at the apartment block in a police vehicle. Damn. Why hadn't she thought to give them a different address from the one on her licence? Every apartment in Riverview Place faced onto this street. People only had to glance out their front windows. People who had seen her take off a short while ago with Adam.

'Are you sure you're going to be okay now?' the policewoman asked as the driver pulled into the loading zone right in front of the foyer's sliding doors.

'Yes, thanks.' Maddie just wanted to get out of this high-visibility vehicle as quickly as possible and then scurry inside to her apartment where she would close the door and stay there. For a month, if necessary. 'Thanks so much for the lift. I really appreciate it.'

Terrified that the policewoman would want to do something hugely embarrassing like escort her into the building, she grabbed her bag and quickly closed the car door. 'Bye! Thank you.'

Her prayer that she could make it to her apartment without running into anyone she knew was granted. *Phew!* Maddie almost collapsed with relief as she closed the door behind her. She realised that she was trembling and her legs nearly gave way as she headed down the hall. The tears were falling now. Wretched tears of self-pity. Tears of anger. No, it was more than anger. Fury. Rage. Rage at Adam. Rage at herself for letting her life sink to such a low.

She reached the lounge room, but when she saw the bright cushions and the pot plants that usually gave her such a lift, her fury built even higher. She saw the show-off philodendron sitting there smugly, with its splashes of pink on deep green leaves, and suddenly she hated it.

All her troubles had started from the moment she'd first seen that damn plant in the shop window. She'd only bought the thing to impress Simon, but within five minutes of the purchase she'd discovered him lunching with Ruby Reid, and from that point, her life had fallen to pieces.

If she hadn't stopped to buy this plant, she might never have lost Simon. She might have shopped somewhere else that day and not even seen him, and he might have grown tired of Ruby and come back to her and she wouldn't have had to start searching on fricking Tinder for another bloody boyfriend and —

Crack!

Splat!

Oh, God.

It was only as the pot exploded on the ground below that Maddie realised what she'd done. In her fury, she had grabbed the philodendron, stormed onto her balcony and hurled it over the railing. *No-o-o-o-o!*

She was on the first floor, so it had only fallen a few metres, but still – she might have killed someone if it had hit them. Oh, dear God, how had this happened? What was wrong with her?

Her legs truly gave way now and she had to cling to the railing to stop herself from falling, while below, of all people, Nancy Jenkins appeared.

Nancy was staring at the broken wreckage of pot, at the plant and soil spilling over the asphalt. Then, with her hands propped on her sturdy hips, she dropped her head back to glare up at Maddie with murder in her eyes.

CHAPTER THIRTY-TWO

Vera was in the bathroom, putting the last touches to her makeup, when she heard the loud knocking on her front door.

Theo ducked his head around her bathroom doorway. He was already dressed and ready for their evening out, looking rather spiffy in pale chinos and a blue linen shirt. They had booked a table at The Boatshed restaurant at the Regatta Hotel and were looking forward to a pleasant stroll to one of Brisbane's most iconic riverside venues.

'Would you like me to answer the door?' he asked as the knocking continued.

Vera frowned. She had no idea who it could be. 'Perhaps I should go.' She slipped the lid back over her lipstick, pressed her lips together and gave a quick glance to her reflection in the mirror before hurrying past Theo and down the hallway.

Nancy Jenkins stood on her doorstep. An exceptionally distressed-looking Nancy. 'Vera!' she cried with a dramatic sense of urgency. 'I'm so glad you're in.'

Vera refrained from responding that she was about to leave. 'Has something happened?' she asked.

'Yes, it's Maddie. I'm sure she's in trouble. A few minutes ago she was delivered home in a police vehicle, and now I think she's having some kind of breakdown.'

'Good heavens.' Vera thought of the last time she'd seen Maddie, when she'd left the meeting with that rather slimy boyfriend. She'd looked quite miserable, which Vera had found disturbing, but what on earth could have happened since then?

'I think she might need help,' Nancy said next. 'And I know you're good friends with her.'

'Yes,' Vera agreed.

'She's just hurled a pot plant off her balcony.'

'Maddie has?' Vera stared at Nancy in horror. Clearly, something was terribly wrong. 'All right,' she said. 'I'll go and talk to her. Will you come with me?'

'I should probably clean up the mess downstairs. The fewer people who know what's happened, the better.'

This offer from Nancy was so very out of character, Vera found herself blinking with surprise. 'Right,' she said as she recovered. 'I'll go check on Maddie. I'll just need to grab my phone and I'll have to let my friend Theo know what's happening. We have a booking at The Boatshed. I'll see if he can change it.'

Nancy nodded. 'I hope he won't mind.'

Vera might have been more worried about Theo's reaction if she hadn't been so thrown by Nancy's rather alarming display of concern. Such sympathy from this woman could only suggest that Maddie was in a very bad way indeed.

Vera decided to ring Maddie before she knocked at her apartment. Chances were, if the girl was seriously upset, she wouldn't be prepared to answer the door. Of course, she also might not want to answer her phone.

At least Theo was being very good about the sudden change of plans, especially as Vera had already explained how Maddie had helped her out on the night of her 'heart event'. Vera's main concern now, however, was whether she had the skills or the wisdom to actually help Maddie. She supposed she would just have to play it by ear and do her best.

'Hello.' Maddie's voice sounded dreadfully teary and stuffed up.

'Maddie, sweetheart, it's Vera. I was just checking if you're okay? I understand you've had a rather dramatic afternoon.'

'I guess Nancy told you.'

'She did, and I'd like to come and see you. I'm sure you need a hug. You'll let me in, won't you?'

At first, Maddie didn't answer, but then, in a very small voice, 'All right.' And then, 'Thanks.'

She looked dreadful. Her skin was pale and mottled with bright pink splotches, her eyes red, her hair wild. Vera didn't speak when she saw her. She simply pushed the door closed behind her and opened her arms, and Maddie fell into her embrace, clinging to her and burying her face into her shoulder.

Maddie didn't cry, but Vera suspected the poor girl had already cried herself dry, and after a good and thorough hug, Maddie stepped away and offered a faint, watery smile. 'Thank you,' she said shyly. 'I suppose Nancy's ready to kick me out?'

'Heavens no,' Vera assured her. 'Nancy told me about the pot plant. But she's actually very worried about you.'

'I'm sorry. I just went a little crazy.'

'It happens to the best of us.' Vera nodded down the hallway to the living room. 'Shall we sit?'

'Oh, yes, of course. I'm still not thinking straight.'

Maddie's apartment was much smaller than Vera's, with only

one bedroom and the tiniest of dining alcoves, but the flooring and paintwork, the cupboards and kitchen appliances were of a similar good quality, and apart from a small mountain of damp tissues and a few cushions that seemed to have been tossed hither and thither, the girl kept the place neat.

Now, Maddie hastily picked up the tissues and disposed of them, then set the cushions on the sofa. 'Please, make yourself comfy,' she told Vera. 'I'll sit here,' she added, indicating the one single armchair.

They took their seats and there was an awkward moment of silence. Carefully feeling her way, Vera said, 'Nancy mentioned that a police car delivered you home. I hope you weren't involved in an accident.'

'No, not an accident.' Leaning back in her chair, Maddie closed her eyes, as if gathering strength to tell her story. Then she sent Vera a very wonky attempt at a wry smile. 'Adam – the guy I was with – was pulled over for speeding. And when the police made a closer check, they discovered he'd had a domestic violence order issued against him.'

'Goodness.'

'But there's worse. He never showed up in court when he was supposed to.' Maddie gave a helpless shrug. 'So they arrested him.'

'Arrested?'

'Yes. Handcuffed him right there on the edge of the highway.'

'Oh, Maddie, how awful.'

Again, Vera was remembering the smirking boyfriend and his overdone attempts to charm the gardening group that had fallen totally flat. 'I'm guessing you had no idea – about the violence?'

'No, not at all. Adam was never violent with me. Although he did throw a tantrum that I suppose should have warned me.' Maddie let out a heavy sigh. 'But it's not just the violence that's upsetting me now. Adam catfished me well and truly.'

'Catfished?'

'I met him on Tinder, the dating app, and he said he was in real estate. Made out he had all this money and property. Yachts and flash cars. Every so often he'd cover himself. He did admit that the yacht we took out on the bay belonged to a friend. But in reality, he didn't own any of those things. I feel so stupid. It's not as if I even really care about money and status.'

'No, I wouldn't have seen you as a gold-digger.'

Maddie reached for another tissue from a box on the coffee table and blew her nose.

'Don't be too hard on yourself, Maddie.' Then, abandoning her usual reticence, Vera added, 'Believe me, you're not the first woman to fall for a man who's not all he's cracked up to be.' And she patted her handbag. 'Look, I'm not sure if it's appropriate, but I brought a bottle of wine.'

This roused a small smile.

'And I also took the liberty of asking Theo to order a pizza for us.' Vera had been concerned that drinking wine on an empty stomach might not be wise if Maddie was already upset. She'd suggested that Theo order a pizza for himself as well and the dear man had obliged.

'Aren't you wonderful? A glass of wine, pizza and your company.' New tears shone in Maddie's lovely eyes and she pressed her fingers against her lips, as if she needed to physically hold back another outburst of crying. Then she jumped to her feet. 'I'll grab us some glasses.'

She brought wine glasses, plates, knives and paper serviettes back from her kitchen and set them on the coffee table.

Vera poured the wine. 'Cheers,' she said, raising her glass.

'Cheers,' responded Maddie. 'And good riddance to a certain no-hoper male that I can now add to my history of no-hoper males.'

'At least they're all history,' Vera suggested gently. 'Past tense.'

Maddie shrugged. 'Except that, for me, it doesn't really feel like past tense. It's more like a permanent state of being. When it comes to boyfriends, I just seem to jump from one bad choice to the next.'

While ignoring a perfectly wonderful catch right under your nose? Vera knew better than to voice this private opinion out loud.

'The really annoying thing is,' Maddie said next, 'I *did* already have doubts about Adam. That's what's really bugging me. For starters, just meeting him on Tinder was a mistake, and I'd more or less sensed that something wasn't quite right about him. I'd even been planning to break up with him, but somehow I never seemed to quite manage it. Now, looking back, I can't believe I've been so lame.'

Her mouth twisted and she had to stop again and take a deep breath, but she seemed to want to keep talking, so Vera didn't interrupt.

'Adam had been carrying on about this damn glamping weekend from practically the first time we met. I was trying to wriggle out of it and I thought the meeting today might have given me a good excuse.' She drained her glass and set it down. 'Then he insisted the meeting wouldn't be a problem. He was all for me going, said we could leave straight after. But I had no idea he would barge in like that.'

'I could see he'd upset you.'

'I was so embarrassed.' Maddie shivered. 'But I was a thousand times more embarrassed when he was arrested on the side of the bloody highway.' Wincing, she added, 'I was so upset when I hurled that pot plant. Nancy will probably want to evict me now.'

'I'm not sure she has that kind of power, but anyway, I doubt she'll want to. She actually seemed rather sympathetic.'

'Oh, God.' Maddie jumped to her feet. 'I just remembered all the mess I made downstairs. I should be cleaning it up.'

'I think you'll find Nancy's already done that for you.'

'Really?'

'I know.' Vera couldn't help smiling at Maddie's shocked expression. 'Incredible, isn't it?'

'It sure is.' Clearly finding this totally impossible to believe, Maddie rushed out to the balcony. 'Gosh, you're right. It's all gone.'

Just then Vera's phone rang. 'Oh, that'll be Theo with our pizza. If you'll excuse me for a moment.'

When Vera arrived back, pizza in hand, she could see that Maddie had washed her face and brushed her hair, although she still looked pale and exhausted.

'Thanks so much for this, Vera. And please pass on my thanks to Theo. I feel bad about dragging you away from him.'

'Oh, tosh. This is an emergency and he understands how you've helped me. Besides, there's a Wallabies game on TV. Don't worry about Theo. He's fine.'

'I'm glad one of us has great taste in men, at least.'

Vera smiled. 'Theo's on his best behaviour this weekend, but I know he's not faultless. Now, I thought I'd play it safe with the trimmings, so it's just pepperoni and olives.'

'That's great. It smells fabulous. I've just realised how hungry I am.'

As they helped themselves to crispy slices, they talked for a bit about the meeting for Jock, about how worried they were for him, but how much they both wanted to hang on to hope.

'I think he appreciated knowing that his neighbours care,' Vera added. 'I believe Ned was planning to invite him to dinner this evening.'

Maddie nodded at this news and Vera wasn't sure if it was her imagination, or whether the mention of Ned had made the girl uncomfortable. Perhaps Maddie was embarrassed, realising that

Ned would have to hear about her boyfriend's arrest. 'He won't think badly of *you*, Maddie.'

Wariness flashed in Maddie's eyes. 'Who won't?'

'Ned.'

'Why do you need to tell me that? It doesn't matter what Ned thinks.'

No? Then why are you so touchy? As Vera helped herself to another slice of pizza and set it on her plate, she decided to dive in with a touchy subject of her own. Perhaps it would help Maddie to know she wasn't the only one who'd been disappointed by a man.

'I don't know if my story will help you in any way,' she said. 'But my husband, Felix, had a gambling problem that I only found out about on my wedding day.'

'Your wedding day?' Maddie looked understandably shocked.

'Yes. I knew Felix was keen on horseracing, but I had no idea that he'd gambled away his farm in Devon.' Fortunately, after so many years, it no longer hurt Vera to admit this. 'When I found out at the very last minute, I almost called off the wedding. Instead, I challenged Felix about it, and he assured me that he already had enough money to buy the farm straight back. And,' she gave a small shrug, 'I believed him.'

'Was he lying?' Maddie whispered.

'He wasn't lying, exactly. He did have the money, but then he convinced himself that he should put all the money people had either lent him or given him on another sure win at Ascot.'

'Oh, Vera. Don't tell me he lost it?'

'Of course he lost it. Lost the lot.' Vera might not have elaborated further, but Maddie was listening so intently, she felt compelled to continue. 'This all happened while we were honeymooning in Jamaica. I had no idea, of course. I was busily enjoying a wonderful two weeks, perhaps the happiest fortnight of my life. But by the time we got back to England, Felix had lost everything. Again. So then his family packed us off to Australia.'

Maddie was staring at her now, her mouth slack, clearly too shocked to comment.

'I don't know if you've heard of the term remittance man,' Vera said next. 'It seems to be a thing of the past, thank heavens, but Felix's father had a holding in Queensland and he paid us a small allowance to move Down Under and stay there. Out of sight, out of mind.'

'Vera, how terrible. I – I don't know what to say.' But then, almost immediately, Maddie asked, 'But you stayed with Felix?'

'I did, yes. Mind you, there have been times when I've asked myself why I stayed. I think it was a matter of pride, at first, and partly my fondness for Felix.'

'Fondness? That's an interesting choice of words.'

'It is, isn't it?' Vera smiled. 'That's probably my British stuffiness showing. I tend to feel awkward talking about love, but I'm sure I loved Felix. I must have.' She gave a sly wink. 'He was marvellous in bed. But then there was also the whole business of "for better or for worse". And later, I could see how much Archie loved living on the land. And Felix *did* try to conquer the gambling. I'll give him that. He still had lapses, but nothing too disastrous.'

'I'm glad to hear that.'

'Yes. And I guess, over time, I adapted to my life in the Aussie outback.' Vera smiled. 'Besides, I'd made a garden that I'd come to love . . .'

'And now you're here, with us, starting a new garden.'

'Yes.' It was true that the rooftop garden had made a huge difference to how Vera felt about living here, but it was the 'with us' part of Maddie's sentence and the sincere smile that accompanied it that truly warmed her heart.

After taking a sip of wine, she said, 'Maddie, I suppose I'm telling you this to show that most of us have past mistakes or sorry stories that we hide from the world.'

'I guess.' Maddie pondered this for a moment or two and then sighed heavily. 'I suppose the reason I've been so hung up about my mistakes is because they feel so public. Everyone at my work knew when Simon dropped me. And now everyone here in this building will know about Adam —'

Vera couldn't help interrupting. 'But we love you, Maddie, and none of us will judge you for your boyfriend's sins.'

CHAPTER THIRTY-THREE

It was during her Monday lunch break that Maddie received a phone call from Ned. She was both surprised and a little nervous as she answered. One of the many memories that had tortured her since Saturday had been Ned's look of disdain when Adam had burst into their meeting. Over and over, she'd told herself she didn't care what Ned Marlowe thought, but the problem was she *did* care. She cared too much.

Now, as she answered her phone, she hoped she sounded far cooler and calmer than she felt. 'Hi, Ned.'

'Maddie,' he said. 'Sorry to bother you at work, but I've just had a very interesting phone call from Nancy Jenkins.'

Maddie winced. Had Nancy told him about her pot plant hurling episode? She'd left a note of apology in Nancy's letterbox, which in retrospect seemed pretty feeble. Was she about to be expelled from the gardening group?

'It seems Nancy has a daughter who works for Médecins Sans Frontieres,' Ned said next. 'She's back in Australia now, but in the past she's worked in Nepal, and in particular the border areas.

Nancy seems to think she just might have one or two useful contacts who are still working there.'

'People who might help to track Zoe?'

'Yes.'

'Wow.' Maddie couldn't believe she'd immediately assumed this phone call would be all about herself. Of course Jock would be Ned's focus. 'That's wonderful news.'

'I know. It does sound promising. There's one small catch, though.'

'Oh?'

'It seems Nancy's had very little to do with this daughter. There's been some kind of family estrangement. I'm not sure what the story is. Nancy certainly didn't offer any details, but I got the impression she was almost afraid of her daughter. Well, perhaps afraid is too strong a word, but she certainly seems rather anxious about seeing her.'

'So why doesn't Nancy just discuss it with her over the phone?'

'I know it sounds weird, but apparently that's not an option. Nancy would rather arrange a meeting, but she's asked if we can go with her.'

'We? You mean you and me?'

'Well, yeah. I suspect Nancy wants us for moral support. Although that wasn't the way she put it. She pointed out that we were the residents in closest contact with Jock. We know his story.'

'Mmmm,' said Maddie.

'You sound uncertain.'

'I'm just wondering how Jock might feel about a group of us meeting to discuss him when he's not there.'

'Yes, it is a bit off, isn't it?'

'Shouldn't he be invited? He could answer any questions Nancy's daughter might have far better than we could.'

'You're right, of course. But three of us might be overkill.' After a beat, Ned said, 'If you can make it, you'd be best.'

This was a surprise. 'You think so?'

'I do. You get on well with Jock and it makes sense logistically. The meeting will almost certainly be in the CBD and you work in the city, don't you?'

'Yes.'

'So what do you think? Would you be able to wangle an hour or so?'

Maddie thought about the work she had to get through this week, the research, the memoranda, pleadings and briefs that needed to be filed. She could always work through her lunch breaks, or stay back for a bit at the end of the day. 'I guess I'd be able to manage it, but Nancy contacted you, Ned. She'll be expecting you.'

'I'm sure she'll understand. And if she's tense with her daughter, I think your presence would be more helpful than mine. It was her suggestion to invite you as well.'

Gosh, what a turnaround. It was hard to take in. 'It's pretty amazing that Nancy wants to actively support us for once.'

'Yeah, that's why I'm keen to grab this opportunity, in case she changes her mind. It would need to be a weekday meeting and, ideally, as soon as possible.'

'Okay,' said Maddie. 'I doubt anyone at work will complain when I explain.'

'Wonderful. I'll speak to Jock,' he said next. 'And I'll ask Nancy to let both of you know as soon as she has a day and a time.'

The plans fell into place with surprising ease. Jock was very grateful for the chance to meet Nancy's daughter, and a meeting was arranged for eleven am on Wednesday at a café off the Queen Street Mall. Nancy had reserved a table in a discreet corner and Maddie barely recognised her at first. The dowdy grouch of Riverview Place was quite transformed.

Today she was dressed in an emerald-green sheath dress with three-quarter sleeves, and she had styled her hair into a neat bun at her nape, rather than her usual scruffy topknot. She had even made an effort with her makeup and, with the addition of pretty pearl earrings, she looked surprisingly attractive. And incredibly nervous.

'I'm so glad you could come,' she said as she greeted Maddie.

'I'm very happy to be here. Your daughter sounds like a wonderful contact.'

'I hope so.'

Having arrived ten minutes early, Maddie wondered if she should mention the pot-throwing incident before the others arrived. But she soon realised Nancy was far too agitated to concentrate on anything but the matter to hand. The poor woman was constantly looking over her shoulder and anxiously peering past an indoor palm to the café's main entrance.

Jock arrived next. He waved to them as he made his way between the tables and Maddie could only imagine the fear, excitement and hope eddying inside him. He took the seat opposite Nancy, leaving the chair next to her vacant for her daughter.

'Good morning,' he said. 'How are you both?'

'Fine, thanks,' answered Maddie, but Nancy remained silent, although one corner of her mouth twitched in what might have been an attempt to smile. She looked almost as if she wanted to flee.

An awkward silence fell and Maddie turned her attention to filling their water glasses from the chilled jug that a waitress supplied.

Nancy sent another nervous glance towards the doorway, then checked the time on her phone. 'I suppose we should wait for Phillipa before we order our coffee.' She sounded a little grumpy, closer to her usual MO.

'Yes, that's fine,' Maddie assured her. 'It's not quite eleven yet.'

Nancy drew a shaky breath. 'I hope she's not late.'

Maddie wondered how long it had been since Nancy had last seen her daughter. She couldn't imagine what might have happened within their family to cause a rift. But having so recently heard Vera's surprising story about her own less-than-ideal marriage, she supposed it was true that most people had secrets and private worries or hurts that they tried to hide from the rest of the world.

'She's here,' Nancy hissed.

A woman had just stepped through the doorway. Maddie guessed she was in her late thirties. Her hair was dark and thick like Nancy's, but cut into a jaw-length bob. Her face was rounder and softer than Nancy's, her eyes a paler shade of brown, but she had the same generous bosom and short straight legs. She wore a black dress and her handbag and high heels were also black. No-nonsense and businesslike. A chip off the old block.

Jock rose from his chair, looking tense as the woman reached them. Nancy remained seated and statue still.

'Hello,' Jock said with a nod of his head and a small, polite smile.

'You must be Jock.' She smiled warmly and nodded, but didn't offer her hand. 'Very pleased to meet you.'

There was still no word from Nancy, so Maddie jumped up too. 'Hi, I'm Maddie. It's so good of you to meet with us.'

'Hi Maddie. I only hope I can be of help. I'm Phillipa, by the way.'

Phillipa then turned to her mother. Her smile faded and her expression was wary. 'Hello, Nancy.'

'Hello, Phillipa.'

No kiss. No hug. Not even a touch.

Nancy's face muscles twitched, as if she might have been trying to dredge up a smile. Phillipa looked equally ill at ease, but they both seemed to recover a little as everyone took their seats and the waitress arrived, notepad and pen in hand, to take their orders.

As soon as the waitress had left, slightly disgruntled because they'd only ordered coffee without any food – Nancy had cast a wistful glance to the glass cabinet of sweet pastries but regretfully declined – Phillipa turned to Jock. 'I'm very sorry to hear that your wife is missing. So you still haven't heard anything?'

Maddie didn't mind the way Phillipa took charge, with no small talk, just getting straight down to business, but she was unsettled by the woman's total lack of warmth towards her mother. She knew she had to put these concerns aside, though, and concentrate on Jock's situation.

And she was extremely pleased that Jock was there to answer Phillipa's questions. Only he could give accurate details of the towns in Nepal where Zoe had been and where she'd been heading when she'd last made contact.

'DFAT has already been making enquiries for me,' he told Phillipa. 'But the weather is still really foul. They can't get helicopters up into the mountains. Searchers are having to make their way up there on foot.'

'I'd believe that,' Phillipa said, nodding. 'Well, I don't want to raise false hope, but MSF are always involved when there's an emergency like the current situation and they have the village level contacts that might not be accessible to DFAT.' Having scooped a spoonful of froth from her cappuccino, she set her spoon down and then reached into her handbag, extracting her phone. But then she sent a rueful smile around the table. 'Oops. I was getting carried away, about to fire off a text, but it's still a bit too early in the morning in Nepal. I might leave it a couple of hours before I try to contact Louis.'

'Of course,' said Jock.

'We're really grateful for your help,' added Maddie. 'Not knowing anything has been awful. Any kind of lead is a step forward.' She caught Jock's eye and sent him what she hoped was an encouraging smile.

To her relief, he nodded and a brief answering smile flickered.

Phillipa was fiddling with her phone again. 'Jock, it would be helpful if I could have your phone number. And if you could give me a description of Zoe, I'll make a note. Anything else you think might be helpful.'

'Yes, of course. How about I forward you a photo of Zoe?'

'Yes, do. That would be perfect.'

Maddie and Nancy sat quietly while Jock and Phillipa exchanged phone numbers and Phillipa keyed the extra info into her phone. Maddie realised there was probably little more that could be achieved right now, which meant they'd barely finished their coffees and the business discussion was pretty much over. She wondered if Phillipa might share an anecdote or two about her experiences of working for Medecins San Frontieres, but it was soon pretty clear she had no plans for chitchat.

An uncomfortable silence had fallen on the group. Nancy was once again looking anxious. Maddie supposed it was time to leave.

'Mum.'

The single word dropped into their silence like a falling marble hitting a tiled floor. Phillipa was looking directly at Nancy and, for heart-stopping seconds, the two women stared at each other while an emotion that could only be described as fear blazed in their eyes.

'Could I speak to you for a moment?' Phillipa asked her mother.

Maddie realised she was holding her breath as Nancy's mouth trembled in yet another attempt to smile. The poor woman seemed incapable of speech, but she nodded. Meanwhile, Jock had pushed back his chair, as if preparing to leave, and Maddie quickly followed his example. A hasty exit was in order.

Jock nodded again to Phillipa. 'Thank you so much for this meeting.'

'Yes, thank you,' said Maddie. 'We're so grateful for your help. And thank you, Nancy.' But she wasn't sure Nancy heard her, and she and Jock departed quickly, stopping only at the front counter where Maddie insisted on paying the bill.

Outside, the footpath was busy with shoppers and city workers rushing like ants. Maddie sent Jock a smile. 'One more step.'

'Yes,' he said. 'And such a surprise that it was Nancy who helped.' He allowed a small smile then.

'I know,' said Maddie.

'A weird relationship, though,' Jock commented.

'Yes,' Maddie agreed, and then, remembering how very worried Nancy had looked she said, 'Actually, I'm wondering if we should wait for her.'

Now it was Jock who looked a little awkward. He checked the time on his phone. 'I should probably get back to work.'

'Yes, of course.' Maddie knew that Nancy's family issues weren't really any of their business, and she didn't want to seem overly curious – a stickybeak – but Ned had hinted that Nancy might need moral support. 'Off you go,' she told Jock. 'I might hang around for a bit.'

She might need someone, she added silently.

'Bye,' she said to Jock. 'I'll be typing with my fingers crossed today, hoping for good news for you.'

With another nod, he headed off, quickly disappearing on the crowded footpath. Meanwhile, Maddie decided on a plan. She would walk up the street for a bit and wait in a spot where she'd be able to keep an eye on the café's entrance and see anyone coming out. If Nancy seemed fine, she would continue back to work.

She hadn't walked far at all, however, before she looked back over her shoulder and saw Nancy already hurrying out of the café, while Phillipa marched off in the opposite direction.

Her heart fell.

She could see immediately that Nancy was distressed.

What on earth could Phillipa have said to make her mother so upset? Without hesitation, Maddie hurried back down the footpath, dodging pedestrians. She was sure Nancy was crying and as she got closer, her fears were confirmed. Tears were streaming down the woman's face, so much so that she seemed blinded, almost lost.

'Nancy,' Maddie called to her.

'Oh.' Nancy looked around, blinking tears.

As soon as Maddie reached her, she wrapped an arm around her shoulders. 'Here,' she said, shepherding Nancy off the busy footpath and into the less crowded foyer of a department store.

By now, Nancy's expression had changed from distress to embarrassment, which was understandable. 'I'm all right,' she insisted as she snapped open her handbag and found a tissue.

'Well, that's good to hear.' Although Maddie found it hard to believe that this weeping woman, usually so tough and in control, could possibly be okay.

'It's just that it's been years and years since I've seen Phillipa.' Nancy dabbed at her face with the tissue and it seemed she was regaining composure with commendable speed. 'But just now —'

Having started with confidence, Nancy stopped abruptly, and her mouth trembled and pulled out of shape.

Impulsively, Maddie hugged her.

'No, I'm all right,' Nancy insisted again. She didn't pull away from the hug, though, and she managed a lopsided smile as Maddie gently released her. 'I don't know why I'm crying,' she said. 'It's ridiculous, really. You see, Phillipa's invited me to her home for dinner. She wants me to meet my grandsons.'

And then, having delivered this wonderful news, Nancy burst into tears again.

CHAPTER THIRTY-FOUR

Dear Gran,

*I now have a worm farm. Dad dug up worms from the
mud down near the river and we put them in a box by
the back steps. We put a sugar bag over them to keep them
nice and dark and Mum lets me have apple cores and lettuce
and peelings and stuff, and they eat and eat. If I put my ear
down close, I can hear them wriggling and eating.*

Please tell Ned.

I miss you so much.

Lots and lots of love,

Henry xx

Vera was a little misty eyed as she read this letter to Theo.

'I'm sure you must be missing Henry too,' he said.

'Oh, yes. I miss all the family, of course.' She didn't like to admit
to having an especially soft spot for Henry.

It was Wednesday. Theo had stayed beyond his original plan
of a weekend visit and they'd had the best of times, taking ferry
trips down the river, visiting art galleries and dining out at trendy

restaurants, even seeing a movie. This evening, however, was to be their last together.

Theo had quoted the famous Benjamin Franklin saying about guests, like fish, beginning to smell after three days and Vera had playfully sniffed at him. 'You smell fine to me.' But she knew he had commitments back at Lansdowne and she didn't want to be the lonely hostess delaying her guest's departure.

They dined in on this last evening. Theo insisted on helping in the kitchen and Vera handed him the vegetable peeler to deal with the sweet potatoes while she grated ginger for the sauce she would pour over her baked fish.

'Don't throw the peelings in the bin,' she warned him. 'I'll save them and take them upstairs for the worms.'

Theo chuckled. 'Those damn worms have no idea how lucky they are.'

'No, we gardeners are the lucky ones. You should see the lovely brown water we drain from them. The herbs love it. They're thriving.'

Theo lifted an eyebrow. 'No wonder Henry's obsessed. You've brainwashed the boy.'

'Nonsense. It was the other way round. Henry discovered Ned's worm farm and then worked hard at converting me.' She handed Theo a bunch of asparagus. 'If you snap the ends off these, I'll toss the spears in with the other veggies towards the end.'

The meal was simple enough to prepare and there was time for a pre-dinner drink while everything baked. As they settled on the sofa, Theo reached for Vera's hand and gave it a gentle squeeze. 'Henry's not the only one who's going to miss you.'

She smiled, but found herself also needing to sigh. 'This has been lovely, hasn't it?'

'Perfect.'

She thought of the long drive that he faced in the morning, through the Brisbane Valley and up the range, then out across the

Darling Downs, heading west to the beautiful, but empty, homestead that awaited him at the other end. Would he be lonely?

During Theo's visit Vera hadn't allowed herself to think about the rumours regarding his women 'friends', but she supposed the stories must be true. She couldn't imagine Theo living like a monk. No, he wasn't going to be lonely.

'I don't suppose you'd come back with me,' he said.

'To visit my family?'

'Well, yes, that goes without saying – but perhaps you could stay at Lansdowne?'

Vera couldn't quite hide her surprise. 'Do you think that's a good idea?'

Theo's eyes sparkled. 'I think it's one of the very best ideas I've ever had.'

'But you don't think it might be risky? Putting the cat among the pigeons, so to speak?'

'I'm not sure I catch your drift.'

Was he being deliberately obtuse? 'I'm trying to imagine how the good women of Jindabilla might react.'

'I don't give a damn what they might think.'

Vera stared at Theo now, wondering if he was joking. During the past few days, they'd had many rather personal conversations and at times these discussions had been quite deep and meaningful, especially when they'd talked about their respective marriages. But they'd skirted around any talk of the future. Their future.

Somewhat unsettled, she reached for her wine glass and downed a hefty slug.

Watching her, Theo asked, 'Would you consider coming back?'

'You mean for a short visit?'

'No, permanently.'

'To live with you?'

'Vera, you look horrified.'

'Sorry. I'm not horrified. Just rather stunned.'

Theo's slow smile was especially charming. 'I've always had – what is it the young people say? – a thing for you.'

She couldn't believe she was blushing.

'I'm putting pressure on you,' he said, watching her. 'And that's unfair.'

'This *has* come as rather a surprise.' Vera glanced towards the kitchen and remembered the asparagus. 'I should check the oven,' she said but she sent him a coy smile as she said this. 'I'm not trying to dodge your question. I'll be back in a moment.'

With the asparagus added to the vegetables, and the fish basted with its sauce, she was about to return when the phone she'd left on the kitchen bench rang. It was a call from Maddie, and Vera quickly tapped to connect.

'Hello, Maddie?'

'Vera, I just had to call you. Jock's just heard the most wonderful news. Zoe is safe and well.'

'Oh, Maddie.' Vera found herself suddenly rendered speechless with delight.

'And you won't believe this,' Maddie said next. 'It was Nancy's daughter who helped to find her.'

'Goodness. Our Nancy? Nancy Jenkins?'

'The one and only.'

This was almost a bigger surprise than the first.

'I'll explain about the daughter some other time,' said Maddie.

Vera decided this wasn't the right time to explain that she did know about Nancy and her daughter's estrangement.

'Anyway,' said Maddie. 'Nancy's daughter Phillipa has worked for Medecins San Frontieres and she still has contacts on the ground in Nepal. She sent them one of Jock's photos of Zoe and they posted it up at a makeshift medical camp in one of the remote villages, and some refugees from higher up the valley reported they'd seen her.

Alive and well. Just the day before. She was still making her way down with a slower group of women and children.'

'How wonderful.' Vera's throat was so suddenly choked she could barely speak. 'That's amazing.'

'I know. A doctor phoned Phillipa straight away and then she broke the great news to Jock. Then a few hours later Zoe turned up at the camp. She was exhausted of course, poor thing. And her mobile was useless. It hadn't been charged for a week. But the doctor let her ring Jock, as well as the embassy in Kathmandu.'

'So Jock's actually spoken to Zoe?'

'Yes! Can you imagine?'

'I feel like crying, just thinking about it.'

'I know. Jock said he bawled, but of course he's over the moon.' Maddie also sounded quite weepy with joy. But then in a slightly different tone, she said, 'Anyway, I couldn't wait to tell you, but I need to ring Joe and Dennis now.'

'Yes, all right, but thanks for letting me know. I'm so happy for Jock. It's just the most wonderful news.'

Vera disconnected and hurried back to the living room. 'You probably heard, we've had good news,' she said to Theo.

He nodded, smiling. 'About Jock?'

'Yes, they've found his wife. She's safe.'

'Wow. That's fantastic.'

'It is, isn't it? It's amazing.' Vera was remembering how distressed Jock had looked just two nights earlier, when she'd knocked on his door to drop off a casserole. He'd seemed touched by the gesture, but totally distracted with worry.

'I can see another rooftop celebration in your future,' Theo said now.

'Maybe. We'll certainly have to have one when Jock finally has Zoe safely home again.' Vera noticed that Theo had finished his drink. 'Would you like another?' she asked, pointing to his glass.

'No rush,' he said. 'Relax.'

With something of a start, she remembered their interrupted conversation and Theo's rather astonishing invitation for her to go back to Lansdowne to live with him.

'Come here,' he said now, patting the sofa beside him. 'And stop fretting.'

'I'm not fretting.' But Vera knew this wasn't true. She was totally confused.

Once upon a time – and not all that long ago, actually – she would have jumped at an offer like this from Theo. It had been her dream to stay in the countryside that she'd grown to love, to stay close enough to see her family regularly, to be free of money worries, to have a beautiful garden and, perhaps most importantly, to enjoy the company and the affection of this lovely and close-to-perfect man.

And now that she and Brooke had talked things through, she was reasonably confident there would be no barrier from her daughter-in-law.

But ever since her night in hospital, she'd been consciously working to adjust to life here in her city apartment. She'd made new friends, new connections. She'd experienced the joy of this evening's phone call, which had thrilled her far more than she could have imagined just a few short months ago.

'I truly appreciate your invitation, Theo, and in many ways it's exactly what I want.' To prove this, Vera leaned in and kissed him.

'Now you're teasing,' he said.

'Sorry, it wasn't meant as a tease. More a gesture of – of appreciation.' She couldn't talk of love. It was far too soon for anything like that.

'You don't have to answer straight away. Think about it.'

'Thank you,' she said. 'Yes, I do need time to think.'

As he drew her close for another kiss, however, she was pretty sure she already knew the answer she would give him.

CHAPTER·THIRTY-FIVE

'Are you free this weekend?'

This was the last question Maddie wanted to hear, especially from Ned Marlowe. She had lost count of the number of weekends she'd stuffed up recently, and she'd been looking forward to a blank slate for the next two days. For weekends in the foreseeable future, actually, all Maddie wanted was to be left alone, without having to worry about what anyone else might expect of her, or how they might judge her.

Besides, she couldn't imagine what Ned had in mind when he asked this question. She, Ned, Nancy and Jock had enjoyed a happy impromptu celebration last Wednesday night in Ned's apartment – with Nancy drinking iced tea, while the others enjoyed the fine Scottish single malt that Jock insisted on sharing with them. Their celebration had been tempered by the knowledge that it was still raining in Nepal and Zoe was still trekking back through the mountains. But she had almost reached Kathmandu and she was definitely on her way home. An elated Jock had even reported that after all the drama and emotional angst, he'd come up with a new idea for how to finish his novel.

So, given this success, Maddie had felt free to make her own plans. This morning, a Saturday, she'd been up at the crack of dawn and had been for a run beside the river, and afterwards she'd come up to the garden.

According to the roster, it was her turn to water the potted trees and raised garden beds, which she was more than happy to do. She loved being up here at this early hour and it was fun to check out the plants' progress.

Maddie was rather proud that she could now recognise and name most of the plants. The garden boasted both lemon and lime trees, as well as natives such as banksias and callistemons. Beneath these trees, native grasses and groundcovers like sea daisy and sedum had been planted and were slowly beginning to spread. The jasmine was starting to climb the trellis, and the roses that would one day trail over the central door were slower growing, but also looked healthy.

The plants that had made the most impressive progress, however, were the tomatoes and herbs in the raised beds. Here, there were three kinds of tomatoes – yellow pear, cherry and mini Roma truss – and these were already beginning to flower. And there was a wonderful variety of herbs – rosemary, thyme, garlic chives, parsley, oregano, sage, mint, chillies.

Everything seemed to be doing so well. Even the watering system was behaving itself and draining into the guttering just the way it was designed to do. After the mess of her personal life, Maddie was comforted by the fact that the garden project had been such a great success.

She had finished watering and was reeling in the hose before she realised that Ned had also been on the roof the whole time. He'd been working at the beehives, hidden behind the screen that kept the hives separate from the rest of the garden. But now, he came towards her, all wild, dark hair and big shoulders and slow, steady smile. 'Morning, Maddie.'

It was so annoying to feel suddenly flustered, but he'd caught her by surprise. 'Hi, Ned. How are the bees?' She knew she sounded pathetically dim. Again.

'The bees are just fine, thanks.'

'And Jock's still floating with relief?' she asked quickly, to cover her inexplicable tension.

'More like quietly excited.' Then, before Maddie could think up another unnecessary query, Ned delivered a question of his own. 'Are you free this weekend?'

Her heart took off at a ridiculous gallop and although she had already reeled in the hose, she now made a business of checking that the tap was firmly turned off. She couldn't bring herself to meet Ned's steady gaze. 'Why do you ask? Are there still things we can do for Jock?'

'No, Maddie, this has nothing to do with Jock.'

When she risked a glance in Ned's direction, his smile tugged at her cruelly.

'I'm trying to ask you out.'

'Not on a date?' *Oh, help.* Maddie knew this sounded both stupid and rude, but her battle scars from the previous weekend were still gaping wounds that hadn't even *begun* to heal.

The only reason she'd managed to behave with any semblance of normality at the little party on Wednesday night was because the focus had been entirely on Jock and she'd been able to keep thoughts of Adam strictly sidelined. But this was completely different.

Watching her now, Ned surprised her by looking shamefaced and he ploughed a hand through his hair, making it shaggier than ever, then took a step back. 'I told myself not to rush you.'

The possibility that Ned Marlowe might be impatient to go out with her sent Maddie's thoughts scattering haphazardly. Memories of their kiss resurfaced, filling her with ridiculous steam, but she quickly slammed a lid on them.

She glared at him. 'You do know what happened to me last weekend, don't you?'

'I heard what happened to the guy you were with, and I realise it must have been distressing for you.'

'Yes, I'm a mess. In pieces.'

'Very attractive pieces.' Then, almost immediately, 'Sorry. I'm being crass. I understand you've had a rough time.' Ned's smile was shyer now. She'd never seen so many smiles from him. 'I wondered if you might need cheering up. I thought, maybe, just a casual lunch somewhere?'

A casual lunch did sound harmless enough. And rather pleasant actually. But the whole Adam thing was still too raw and painful, and Maddie couldn't imagine ever risking a date again, certainly not with this man, even though he'd been more or less hand-picked for her by Vera and Joe and Dennis. Sure, her own ability to choose boyfriends was crap, but her friends had one-track minds where Ned Marlowe was concerned. They all thought he walked on water.

Oh, no. Maddie gasped as she realised what was happening. Ned probably viewed her as another good cause he should adopt. Appalled, she lifted her head and summoned all the dignity she could muster. 'I don't need you to take pity on me, Ned.'

'Pity?' A sound that might have been frustration erupted from him now. 'Hell, Maddie, I'm not inviting you to lunch out of pity.'

He looked as if he was about to expand on this, when he stopped and frowned, as if he'd read a message in her face that silenced him.

Contrarily, Maddie was desperately curious to hear what he'd been going to say. She needed to know why a man like Ned Marlowe might actually want to go out with her. But perhaps his silence was for the best. Apart from a possible boost to her ego, it would be a useless line of discussion. She had a host of reasons why she wouldn't dream of dating him.

It wasn't that she didn't like the man. He had oodles of good points, as her friends had pointed out ad nauseam. And she couldn't deny that even if she discounted his obvious intelligence and leadership qualities and his compassion for others, he was rather gorgeous in a neo-hippie, academic kind of way. And their accidental kiss had exposed a highly explosive, albeit embarrassing chemistry.

But despite these impressive qualities, Maddie knew she must never succumb to Ned's charms. She'd learned important lessons in the past months and the only social interactions she planned for the near future were a good long chat with her parents, and a handwritten reply to the sweet note Henry had sent her.

'I'm afraid I can't go out with you,' she said bravely. 'Not on a date.'

'I realise this weekend might be too soon.'

'Not next weekend, either.'

Ned swallowed and an expression that might have been dismay passed like a shadow over his face. 'Are you saying you never want to go out with me?'

Looking quickly away from his clear grey eyes to the row of cane tripods and tomato plants, she said, stiff-lipped, 'Yes, that's exactly what I'm saying.' But then she had to keep staring at the garden and forcing her focus onto two small weeds poking through the newly dampened soil.

'Maddie.' Ned's voice was so quiet now she could scarcely hear him. 'Are you quite certain about this?'

She swallowed. 'I am. Absolutely certain.'

The only problem was that with Ned standing so close to her and looking so damned disappointed, it was hard to remember the all-important reasons why she must reject him. Frantically, Maddie dredged up these reasons now, forcing her mind to run through the comprehensive list.

Ned lived right here in this building, which meant that everyone in Riverview Place would know they were seeing each other. Gossip would be rife. And she abso-bloody-lutely knew that he would tire of her as soon as a sexier or cleverer girl came along. And when Ned dumped her, which was inevitable, everyone in the building would know about that too, and there was no way in this lifetime she was setting herself up for another round of that ghastly pain and public humiliation.

It was good to have these reasons clear in her head. Obvious and unambiguous. Even so, Maddie felt weirdly brittle, as if she might snap at any moment. She needed to leave. Now. The sun was quite high and soon others would arrive on the roof, maybe with happy plans for a breakfast barbecue.

Ned spoke again. 'Can I say one thing?'

'What?'

'You're not the first person to date someone who lets you down.'

'Of course, I know that. I don't need a lecture, thanks.'

But Maddie also knew that she hadn't been nearly as snappy when Vera had suggested much the same thing to her. And only a few days ago she'd witnessed Nancy's emotional meltdown, so there were examples all around her of the sad reality that no one got through life and relationships scot free. Almost everyone was nursing some kind of hurt, or worry, or deeply buried disappointment.

Even so, she was still annoyed that Ned felt compelled to point this out to her. Righteous anger stirred. Damn it, given her history with men, she had very good reasons to sulk and feel sorry for herself.

Not waiting to hear whatever else Ned might have to say, Maddie marched off without so much as a 'see you later'.

*

Dear Maddie,

Thanks so much for 'Tom's Midnight Garden'. I have finished it and I loved it.

Now I feel a bit like Tom, except that he wrote letters to his brother and I'm writing to my friend. I wish I could go back in Time like Tom and walk through doors like he can.

Last night after I read The End I dreamed that the door in your rooftop garden was magic and the Brisbane River froze over like in the book and you, me and Ned went skating all the way down to the museum.

Tell Ned the moon here has a halo and Dad says it means it will rain soon.

Love,

Henry xx

PS. I think you and Ned might be like Hatty and Young Barty.

Henry's letter had arrived a few days ago, and the first time Maddie read it she'd merely smiled and rolled her eyes at his closing comments about her and Ned being like the characters in his book who had married and lived long, happy lives together. Today, as she read the letter again, she didn't feel in the least like smiling, and her eyes were swimming with so much unwanted moisture that she couldn't even see the page.

She hadn't been able to stop thinking about the way she'd stormed off from Ned like a self-obsessed teenager. The guy had simply asked her out, which was hardly a crime, but she'd been so bloody full of herself, so preoccupied with her own hurts and hardship, that she hadn't even given him the chance to finish whatever he'd been going to tell her.

You're not the first person to date someone who lets you down.

At the time, Maddie had assumed Ned was making a generalised claim, inferring that most people were hurt at some point or other.

But now she couldn't help wondering if he'd been speaking from personal experience. As she sat with pen and notepad in hand, trying to write a letter to Henry, new questions kept intruding. After all, Ned didn't seem to have a current girlfriend, so was he getting over some sort of unhappiness?

In the end she gave up on the letter. Henry probably wasn't expecting a response from her, certainly not straight away. She would write to him another time, when she was in a better mood.

So, she rang home instead, even though Sunday morning was her usual time slot for a chat with her folks. Her father was out playing golf at Bargara – she should have remembered he usually did this on Saturday afternoons – but her mother was at home and happy to talk. Maddie brushed over the Adam saga, mentioning only that she had broken up with him, and no, she wasn't too upset; it was one of those things.

Thankfully, her mum didn't push for details, and she was impressed to hear about the meeting with Phillipa to help Jock, and then the happy aftermath.

'This Ned fellow sounds rather admirable.'

God, no, not you too, Mum. You haven't even met him.

Too late, Maddie realised that she probably *had* mentioned Ned a tad too often. Seemed she had the guy on the brain. Hastily, she hunted for other things to talk about, but it wasn't long at all before she ran out of news. Her mum gossiped about their neighbours for a bit, the weather was discussed and then, rather sooner than usual, they were saying their goodbyes.

Maddie spent the rest of the afternoon trolling the internet for comfort-food recipes. Bright, zingy salads held no interest today. She was on the hunt for lush soups and dishes with luxurious flavour and loads of carbs.

She wasn't sure it was possible to eat herself happy, but she was going to have a darn good try.

CHAPTER THIRTY-SIX

When Vera answered the knocking on her front door and discovered Nancy Jenkins on her doorstep for the second time in a week, she was a little ashamed of the way her spirits sank. She'd been hoping the caller might be Maddie, or Carmen, or even Dennis or Joe.

Nancy looked a little nervous, which was totally out of character, and to make up for her less than friendly reaction, Vera pinned on a bright smile. 'Hello, Nancy. How are you?'

'I'm fine thanks, but I was wondering if I can pick your brains. I need some advice.'

'Oh?' This was so unexpected, Vera stood for a moment, almost certainly with her mouth gaping.

'Your grandson was staying with you,' said Nancy. 'And the two of you got on so well I figured you'd be the best person to ask about buying presents for small boys.'

Just in time, Vera stopped herself from emitting another exclamation. Even so, she was truly astonished. 'Of course,' she said, remembering her manners. 'I'd be happy to offer a few ideas.' And then, after only a slight hesitation, 'Won't you come in?'

'Thank you.' Nancy sounded genuinely grateful and Vera couldn't help remembering the woman's surprisingly sympathetic reaction to Maddie's breakdown last weekend. And during the week there'd also been that phone call from Maddie with the amazing news that Nancy had been instrumental in tracking down Zoe McFee.

Was it really possible that the leopard had changed its spots?

'Please, make yourself comfortable,' Vera said as they reached the lounge room, and her guest perched awkwardly on the edge of the sofa.

But it seemed Nancy hadn't come to relax. As Vera lowered herself into an armchair, Nancy got straight down to business.

'Thanks for seeing me,' she began nervously. 'I suppose there are people where I work I could have asked, but I didn't feel comfortable.' Her mouth twisted self-consciously. 'It's not easy to admit that I know nothing at all about my own grandsons and that I'm about to meet them for the very first time.'

Surely this was one surprise too many? Fortunately, Vera managed not to gape this time. 'How – how wonderful.'

'I suppose Maddie told you.'

'No, not a word.'

Now it was Nancy who looked surprised. 'Well, there you go. That girl's not just a pretty face, but the soul of discretion.'

Vera decided it was best not to mention that while Maddie had been discreet, Carmen *had* confided about Nancy's history with alcohol. But it seemed Nancy needed to get this off her chest anyway. 'You're bound to hear about it eventually, so you may as well get it from the horse's mouth.'

The story now came tumbling out – about Nancy's alcohol addiction and divorce, losing custody of her daughters and the subsequent long, lonely years of silence and estrangement. And now, having had so little to do with the raising of her daughters, she felt utterly clueless when it came to interacting with her grandsons.

Such a different Nancy this was. No longer the bossy, self-opinionated tyrant, but a reticent and uncertain middle-aged woman asking for help. Vera wondered if Nancy's customary high-handedness had been a front, a suit of armour to hide her pain.

'Now Phillipa's invited me to dinner.' The tremor in Nancy's voice told its own story. 'And I'll be meeting her boys – Noah and Liam.'

'That's wonderful.' Vera's throat was choked with sympathy. 'Are you sure you wouldn't like a cup of tea?'

'Thank you, but not now. I need to buy gifts for the boys. It's not their birthdays or anything, but I can't go empty-handed and I'd like to get on with the shopping as soon as I can.'

Of course. Some things wouldn't change. Nancy would always be no-nonsense, and let's get straight down to business.

Vera was happy to oblige. Noah and Liam, she soon learned, were five and three, so she told Nancy about Henry's keen interest in toys with moving parts. They discussed Lego and all sorts of vehicles, and then chatted about puzzles, books and games, the huge appeal for small boys of spaceships and dinosaurs and monsters. Vera gave a quick review of the toy stores at Toowong Village and Nancy conscientiously took notes.

Vera tried to conjure Nancy, all smiling and grandmotherly, with her purchases carefully wrapped, handing them to the two little boys. Somehow the picture wouldn't quite gel, but she hoped that was merely her inadequate imagination.

'Thank you,' Nancy said when she was happy with her list, and she immediately jumped to her feet, keen to get going.

Which would have been fine if Max hadn't chosen this very moment to make his appearance. Vera had been so taken up with Nancy's story, she hadn't given the cat a thought, but now he arrived in all his black and white glory, prowling around the corner of the sofa from his favourite sleeping spot behind a floor cushion.

Nancy stiffened when she saw him. 'Good heavens.'

Oh, help. Vera's mind seemed to freeze.

'Is this your cat?' It was a demand. Nancy at her bossiest.

'Yes. More or less.' Helplessly, Vera watched as Max pounced onto his favourite toy, a little mop-head monster, and began batting it with his paws and then chasing it over the carpet. 'I hope you're not allergic.'

'No, I'm not.' Nancy was frowning, however.

'I didn't plan to have a cat,' Vera felt compelled to explain. 'It happened when Henry was staying with me.' Was it terrible, under the circumstances, to lay the blame on her grandson? 'Henry found Max downstairs, in the street. He was a stray, and of course the boy fell in love.'

When Nancy made no comment, Vera rushed on. 'We've had him checked by the vet and he's quite healthy, and he has a micro-chip now.'

But she was also quite sure that the Body Corporate axe was about to fall. Max was going to be evicted.

Nancy remained in the middle of Vera's lounge room, no doubt noticing more details of Max's presence – the collection of plush mice and, in the corner, the scratching post. It was pretty clear he'd taken up permanent residence.

'I know I should have spoken to the Body Corporate,' Vera confessed.

Nancy nodded. 'It's always best to keep everything above board. If you want to keep a pet in your apartment, you're supposed to apply for official approval.'

'I think I was afraid of a knockback.'

'It's quite a straightforward matter, actually. There's no prob-lem if you stick to the rules. You can't let the pet roam around the building, or be a nuisance. The permission will be revoked if that happens. And if you're bringing the cat in or out of the place, you need to carry it, or have it in a container.'

'Yes, of course.' Could it really be as simple as this?

'And if it makes a mess, you have to clean it up, of course.'

'Of course.'

'But apart from that, there's no problem.'

Goodness. Vera had been making Mt Everest out of a molehill. 'That's such good news,' she said and they were both smiling as she saw Nancy to the door.

This wasn't the last of Vera's surprises for the day. An hour or so later, she had a phone call from Maddie.

'I've made a lasagne and I'd love help with eating it. Would you like to join me?'

This invitation was no sooner accepted than Carmen made a similar phone call. Her Frenchman had left and she was at a loose end. She wondered if Vera would be interested in strolling down to the Regatta for a drink and a bite to eat.

After another phone call or two, the three women came up with a new plan. Maddie would bring her lasagne to Carmen's apartment, Vera would supply nibbles, Carmen the drinks, and the trio would enjoy a small girls-only party. Fun time!

CHAPTER THIRTY-SEVEN

Carmen lifted her glass high. 'Let's drink a toast to our absent menfolk.'

'As long as one particular male *remains* absent,' countered Maddie.

Carmen's and Vera's smiles were sympathetic as they clinked their glasses with hers.

'At least there are plenty of prospective replacement guys you can look forward to,' said Carmen.

Sorry. Not interested. Maddie kept this thought to herself as she took her first sip of pink prosecco. The drink had been Carmen's choice and the light, sweet bubbles seemed perfect for a girls' night in. Maddie was particularly grateful for the other women's company and was desperately hoping that their bright and breezy chatter might distract her from the questions that had haunted her all afternoon.

It was so annoying that she couldn't stop thinking about Ned, even though she'd done her best to keep busy, cleaning her apartment from top to bottom, putting through loads of washing and assembling the lavish, multi-layered lasagne that was now being kept warm in Carmen's oven.

Now, finally, for the first time since she'd left the roof this morning, Maddie was starting to relax. And she was more than happy to let Vera and Carmen chatter away, while she sat and looked about her, taking in details of this lovely apartment – the unexpected colour combinations, the intricately patterned carpets, the elegant side table with curved spindly legs and the white lampshades that looked so pretty against a backdrop of green walls.

She was in awe of all that Carmen had achieved here in an apartment that had the same layout, flooring and fittings as everyone else's. The predictable space had been completely transformed by the artist's clever use of colour and furniture selections. The result reminded Maddie of the fabulous, fresh and exciting look that Joe and Dennis had created with all their greenery, and she wondered how many other surprises lay behind doors in this building.

Still musing on this, she realised that Vera and Carmen were now talking about Nancy. It seemed Carmen had known for some time about Nancy's estrangement from her family.

'You have amazing insider knowledge about people in this place.' Vera somehow managed to make this comment sound like a compliment rather than an accusation.

Carmen gave a shrug. 'It's just that I've been living here for so long. I bought this unit off the plan when the place was first built. So, I was here when Nancy arrived and I invited her around for drinks. At the time, I had no idea she was working so hard to stay sober.' With a sheepish smile, Carmen added, 'I'm afraid she fell off the wagon that night. Got completely plastered and ended up telling me her whole story.' After another small shrug, 'I'm not sure she's ever forgiven me.'

'You might be surprised,' said Vera. 'Nancy's definitely shown recent signs of mellowing.'

'Well, yes. I must say it's wonderful that she's been able to help Jock.'

Carmen lifted the bottle from the ice bucket and topped up their glasses, and perhaps it was the fresh burst of bubbles going to Maddie's head that prompted her to introduce a new slant to the conversation.

'I don't suppose you know Ned's story?'

Vera's eyebrows lifted, making her forehead wrinkle. 'Does Ned have a story?'

'I'm not sure. I just wondered . . .' Already, Maddie wished she hadn't spoken up. She could see that Vera was too intrigued to let the matter drop. 'It's just that I was speaking to him up on the roof this morning. He was looking after his bees. I was watering,' she felt compelled to explain. 'Ned knew I was still jumpy and sensitive about Adam and he made a comment. Nothing dramatic —'

Now she gave a flap of her hands, trying to downplay what she was telling them, even though it had plagued her all afternoon.

'He made a comment about most people getting hurt at some time or another and I assumed it was just – you know – a generalisation. Everyone has a noise in their heads. Everyone feels uncomfortable about something. But afterwards, I couldn't help wondering if he was speaking more directly from personal experience.'

Carmen was nodding. 'He might have been talking about his fiancée.'

An audible gasp broke from Vera, while Maddie felt as if she'd smashed headfirst into a glass wall. Her face exploded with heat. But her reaction made no sense. Why should it bother her if Ned had once loved a woman so deeply that he'd asked her to marry him?

Vera recovered first. 'Does Ned have a fiancée?'

'He *had* a fiancée,' corrected Carmen. 'Past tense.'

'What happened?'

Maddie, struggling and dumbstruck, was grateful that Vera was so keen to ask these questions.

'It's no secret,' Carmen said. 'At least not in university circles.'

'Don't tell me you've taught at the same university as Ned?' Vera persisted.

'Not at St Lucia. I was at QUT, but I used to go out with a fellow who worked in the Science Department with Ned. So I heard the whole story.' Carmen paused. Clearly she enjoyed keeping her audience hanging.

'And?' Vera prompted.

'And Ned was engaged to a young woman called Rose, a fellow scientist, a botanist. Ned did extensive research into a particular weed, some sort of major problem weed. I think he discovered something important about its seed dispersal patterns. Something like that. At any rate, he came up with a whole new set of guidelines for managing this weed and he was all set to publish, when he learned that Rose had stolen his thunder. Or rather, she'd stolen his entire research paper and published it as her own.'

'Good grief,' murmured Vera. 'The poor man.'

Maddie had heard of this sort of theft happening in academic circles from time to time, but that knowledge couldn't diminish the anguish she felt now for Ned. She couldn't begin to imagine how shocked and hurt he must have been, how appalled to learn that the woman he loved, the woman he'd wanted to share his life with, could do such a thing.

'Where's this woman now?' Vera asked.

'Melbourne. She scored a job at RMIT on the strength of that paper.'

'And Ned let her get away with it? He never spoke up?'

Carmen shook her head. 'He never took any official action.'

For the first time, Maddie spoke. 'I guess the legal gymnastics would have been rather messy.'

'Yes, no doubt,' Carmen agreed. 'But at the time – this was about three or four years ago – I think Ned was simply too gutted to bother.'

It was a double shock for Maddie to realise, yet again, that her own angst over Adam was rather tame by comparison with another person's terrible experience. She cringed as she remembered how offhand and dismissive she'd been with Ned this morning.

She'd been so busy protecting her own stupid ego, she'd brushed aside his offer of lunch without a single thought for his feelings.

But what if . . . ?

'Maddie, are you all right?'

'You look like you've seen a ghost.'

Her head was spinning. *What if Ned actually —*

She couldn't allow herself to finish asking this question. She was too busy being gut-wrenchingly blindsided by the most painful, sickening moment of clarity.

'I should check on that lasagne,' Carmen was saying. 'We don't want to let it dry out.'

As Carmen rose from her chair, Maddie shot to her feet too.

'It's okay,' Carmen told her. 'I'll check the oven. You finish your drink.'

'No,' Maddie said. 'If – if you'll both excuse me, I need to check on something else.'

Carmen frowned. 'You're not leaving us?'

'Yes, there's something I have to do.' Maddie gestured to the dining table already set with a lovely linen cloth and pottery dinnerware. 'Please, go ahead.'

Now Vera joined in. 'But we can't eat without you, Maddie. You've done all the cooking.'

'No, please, enjoy it! If I'm not back in a few minutes, don't wait for me.' Already Maddie was heading for the hallway, and when she looked back over her shoulder, she saw comprehension dawn, first on Vera's face and then on Carmen's. A knowing glance passed between the two women.

'All right,' Carmen called, perhaps a tad too smoothly. 'Off you go then. We'll see you when we see you.'

In the lift, heading upwards, all Maddie could think about was Ned and the time he'd kissed her. From the first touch of his lips on hers, she'd been consumed by the hottest, wildest wanting.

At the time, she'd been shocked by how completely out of control she'd felt. And in the weeks ever since that night she'd tried, unsuccessfully, to erase that kiss from her memory, while at the same time hammering home her list of reasons why Ned Marlowe must remain a no-go zone for her.

But just now, in the aftermath of Carmen's revelation, she had discovered an incredibly painful truth, a realisation that left her with no option but to find Ned.

Even so, she was absolutely terrified that she was about to make the biggest mistake of her life – and God knew, she'd already made plenty. Balanced against this danger, however, was the possibility that she'd already made her biggest mistake this morning. So maybe she now had nothing to lose. Or maybe it didn't really matter, was irrelevant. Quite simply, she no longer had a choice.

Any way she looked at this, it was time to dig deep. To be honest with herself. With Ned.

The lift reached the top floor, the doors slid open, and Maddie felt strangely calm – or was she merely numb? – as she stepped out and crossed the hallway to Ned's door. Raising her hand, she knocked quite firmly and then held her breath, listening for the sound of footsteps inside.

All she heard was silence.

Perhaps Ned's feet were bare and the first she would know was the door opening. She must remember to smile.

The door remained shut, however, and there was no whisper of a sound from within. No music, no television. Of course, she should have known that Ned would have better things to do than stay at home on his own on a Saturday night.

Damn, she was an idiot. Did she really think that just because she'd come to her senses, the universe would instantly align for her? That she could simply float from her sea of misery on a fricking silver moonbeam and sail straight into Happy Ever After?

Maddie wasn't sure how long she stayed there, slumped against the door to Ned's apartment. One thing was certain, though. She couldn't go back to Vera and Carmen.

She knew they would be kind and understanding and wouldn't press her to answer awkward questions, but their empathy would be her undoing. She would almost certainly end up blubbing and spoiling what should have been a lovely evening. They were better off without her, and she liked the idea of the two of them down there, drinking prosecco and eating lasagne, chatting about their menfolk and becoming closer friends.

It was only as the cool night air touched her skin that she realised she'd drifted up the stairs and onto the roof. But that was good. This was where she needed to be. On her own with just the stars for company.

She chose the table and chairs near the tool shed. The security lights left this spot in shadow, which suited her mood. Perhaps she would see the stars more clearly from there.

It was only as she got closer that she noticed the shadowy figure sitting in one of the chairs.

'Sorry,' she said, disappointed. 'I didn't realise anyone else was here. I didn't mean to disturb you.'

'You're not disturbing me.'

Ned's voice.

Maddie's insides tumbled.

His face was in darkness, but she could make out the shape of him, his broad shoulders and long legs in jeans. He was relaxed in a chair and a couple of beer stubbies stood on the table beside him. Her own voice came out tight and high-pitched. 'What are you doing up here?'

'I could ask you the same question.'

She shrugged. 'I thought there might be stars.'

'You're out of luck,' he said. 'It's too cloudy.'

Her resolve to be completely honest with this man felt a little shaky right at that moment. But she had too much to lose. It was time to be brave. 'Actually, I was looking for you, but you weren't home.' Then, with a nervous smile, 'Now, your turn. Why are you here?'

'I've been sitting here thinking about you.'

'Oh.'

Without haste, Ned got to his feet. 'Was there something specific you wanted to tell me?'

Her heart began to thud hard. 'Yes. I needed to let you know —' He was standing quite close now and Maddie's impulse was to fold her arms over her chest to protect herself somehow. But she'd been a wimp for too long. Bravely, she stood tall, shoulders back as she spoke. 'I wanted to tell you that I – I'm kind of – I mean I've realised – I'm – actually, quite crazy about you.'

There. She'd said it. And she had no idea what might happen next, but she'd been scared for too long. Truth to tell, she'd been deeply crazy about this guy from the first time she'd met him on that long ago midnight when he'd moved the beehives, but her feelings had been so over the top, she'd forced herself to ignore them. Bury them. Keep herself safe.

'Maddie.' Her name was barely a whisper, but he took a step closer. She felt his touch on her bare elbow and then she was stumbling into his arms. His mouth was close to her ear, when he murmured, 'I've been quietly going out of my mind.'

And now, he wrapped her close and she could feel his heart thundering, and then, at last, he was kissing her.

Much later, Maddie couldn't quite remember the journey back to Ned's apartment. It had all been a happy blur of kisses and whispered endearments, a heady mix of joy and disbelief, of wonder and overwhelming lust.

In the end the lust won out. And perhaps she shouldn't have been surprised that this sensitive guy who was attuned to Nature, who was physically strong, yet could nurture baby plants or delicately handle queen bees, might also be the amazingly attentive lover she'd always dreamed of finding.

It was only afterwards, nestled close to him in the dark and happier than she'd ever thought possible, that she saw the stars at last, shining out in a now clear sky through the window they'd forgotten to cover. And Ned told her all the reasons she was the most wonderful girl he'd ever met, how she was perfect in every way, as kind and caring as she was beautiful and sexy. She decided to accept these compliments, as they were exactly in line with the way she felt about him.

Somewhere beyond midnight, they realised they were starving and so made avocado toast. Then they went back to bed and woke late to sunlight streaming through the window where they still hadn't drawn the curtains. Ned made coffee now, which they drank in bed, propped up by pillows, while they talked and talked and talked.

Eventually, Maddie asked a question that had bothered her. She needed to know why Ned lived in an apartment when he was obviously such an outdoor type. And he explained that he *had* bought a lifestyle block out at Kenmore and that he'd planned to live there with Rose.

'I thought we'd plant tons of native trees and do the whole suburban farm thing together.'

'Chooks, bees and worm farms?'

He smiled wryly. 'All of the above.'

'Instead you've created something quite magical here,' she told him.

'Yeah, it's been a good outcome,' he said. 'A new kind of challenge that I couldn't resist.'

'And we're all immensely grateful.' And then she gave in to her urge to kiss him again.

EPILOGUE

Calm soul of all things! make it mine
To feel, amid the city's jar,
That there abides a peace of thine,
Man did not make, and cannot mar.
'Lines Written in Kensington Gardens'
by Matthew Arnold

It was a warm spring evening when Vera went up to the rooftop garden to sit alone and to enjoy the peace and quiet. The space was empty of people, but the garden still looked quite splendid in the moonlight and all the pretty lights that Joe had originally strung in the trees for his and Dennis's wedding were still in place and would come to life at the flick of a switch.

For now, Vera was happy to make her way across the roof with the help of the ground-level security lights that kept the pathways safe. When she reached her favourite garden seat, she eased herself down, took a long deep breath and caught the scent of jasmine on the light breeze.

Just twenty-four hours earlier, a joyous party had taken place right here on this roof. These days the gardeners chose any opportunity to enjoy a social gathering. There'd been a wonderful celebration after Zoe's safe return, and on that occasion Theo had made a special trip, bringing Henry with him. Such a special bonus, especially as Nancy's daughter and grandsons had also joined them and Henry had loved introducing the boys to the hidden wonders of the rooftop.

Since then, there'd been the huge excitement of Joe and Dennis's wedding, as well as birthdays for Ros and for Ned. And now Jock had finished his novel. Which was, of course, another cause for celebration, particularly as he seemed to have found a literary agent who was dead keen to present his novel to big name publishers.

Jock had excitedly shared with them the agent's glowing praise for the beautiful final chapter in which the 'priceless treasure' the hero had been searching for turned out to be letters written by soldiers to their loved ones. The result, apparently, was touching closure for the old woman who'd funded the mission – the gift of a beautiful, farewell love letter written almost eighty years earlier by her fiancé, who had died bravely on the Kokoda trail.

The gardeners had all agreed that the book sounded wonderful and now they were keeping their fingers crossed that Jock might have news of a publishing deal in the not-too-distant future. Jock McFee would soon be a household name, they were certain.

So, the mood last night had been wonderfully festive and the food delicious, with the usual barbecued specialities, shared salads and scrumptious desserts, along with laughter and happy chatter. Jock and Ned had made short but meaningful speeches. And it was just lovely to see Zoe, now happily part of their group and so obviously proud of her husband.

'I know I've said it before, but we owe so much to all of you,' Zoe had told them as she and Jock stood together, arms clasped tightly around each other's waists. 'So many times, Jock's told me how wonderful you were when I caused him all that grief and we feel incredibly lucky to live here.'

*

Now, it was Monday evening and Theo was back at Lansdowne, and as Vera watched a thin crescent moon appearing above the hills, just as it had when she'd lived out west, she was exceedingly comfortable with her decision to stay here in the city rather than scuttling back to Jindabilla.

After a lifetime of having changes forced upon her, she'd been determined to make this last choice entirely on her own. And she'd come to realise that home wasn't so much a place as a state of mind. She now enjoyed her life here very much and felt completely at home.

She loved her new friends and adored this garden. She'd also started using the nearby library and had joined a book club, which meant more new friends, and in the end, Theo had adjusted quite well to their compromise.

These days he really looked forward to his weekend breaks in the city. Even Vera's granddaughters were begging to be allowed to stay with her in the Christmas holidays – most likely because the shopping was so much better in Brisbane, but that was fine.

All in all, she felt more settled and happier than she would have believed possible twelve months ago. Her contented mood was interrupted, however, when lights suddenly burst on all over the rooftop.

In a blink, the garden was exposed in all its glory, with the pergola, the jasmine-covered trellis, and some of the trees tall enough already to give shade, while Carmen's door provided a perfect back-drop, entwined with pretty lights. Vera could even see the second generation of tomatoes coming into fruit, as well as the ground orchids she'd asked Archie to bring from Jinda, which had thrived and were looking especially purple and splendid in this bright light.

And now a woman appeared in the doorway. A stranger, middle aged and somewhat dumpy, dressed in a grey blouse with a badge on the pocket and a pleated black skirt. Her hair was limp and her shoulders seemed to sag, as if she was tired, and had perhaps arrived here straight from work.

She frowned when she saw Vera. 'Were you sitting here in the dark?'

'There are security lights,' Vera said. 'I didn't bother with the others.'

The woman shrugged, but her expression suggested she thought Vera was rather strange. Just the same, she helped herself to a seat close by.

'Have you just moved in?' Vera felt compelled to ask.

'Yes,' she said with a nod. 'Moved in on Saturday. Unit 2 on the first floor.'

'Oh, that was Maddie's apartment.'

'Maybe. I wouldn't know.'

Vera decided not to mention that Maddie had now moved into Unit 13 with Ned, even though this was close to the very best of the good news she'd heard lately. It was beyond wonderful to see how very much in love those two were. 'I'm sure you'll be very happy here,' she told the woman instead.

'Maybe.' She didn't sound too certain.

'I'm Vera, by the way.'

'Daphne.' Her handshake was rather half-hearted. 'She left a pot plant behind.'

'Maddie did? A pot plant in your apartment?'

'Yes. A rather pretty one with pink and green leaves.'

'Oh, yes. I know the one.' It was, Vera realised, the unfortunate philodendron Maddie had tossed over the balcony. After Nancy had cleared it up, she'd taken the debris to Joe and Dennis to see what they could salvage. They'd promptly divided it into many small pieces, which they'd re-planted into pots, and last month, there'd been a little jar of rooftop honey and one of these pretty plants delivered to all the gardeners.

'Maddie would have left that plant there deliberately,' Vera said now. 'A kind of welcome for the new owner. I hope you enjoy it.'

'Oh, I will, it's beautiful.' Daphne frowned as she looked about her. 'It's quiet up here, isn't it?'

'Yes, it's hard to believe we're in the middle of a big city.'

'I suppose,' Daphne said. 'Have you been here long?'

'Nearly two years now.'

This was met by a raised eyebrow. 'Did you come to that function they had here last night?'

'I did, yes. It was a wonderful evening.'

'I didn't bother. I'm not very good with people and it's hard when you don't know anyone.'

'It can be, yes.'

'I love this garden though. I hope they'll find a spot for me on the roster. It's so special to have something like this, isn't it?'

Vera smiled at the newcomer. She would fit in just fine.

ACKNOWLEDGEMENTS

I'd like to say a special thanks to Ali Watts and Nikki Lusk for their wise and helpful feedback and to Melissa Lane and Meaghan Amor, who helped me to refine and polish this story.

A big thanks also goes to family members and friends who engaged in helpful conversations as this story came to life, with special mention for my husband Elliot, my sister Marg and son Richard, as well as my writing mate Anne and friends Julie and Tony.

Perhaps I should mention here, as well, that the philodendron pink princess, which plays a role in this story and is featured on the cover, has special significance for me. Many years ago, my father, John Dow, gave me a piece of this plant that he had climbing a tree on his property west of Brisbane. Dad died in 1996, and I have moved house several times since then, but I've kept this beauty growing and still have it in both a pot and a hanging basket. I love it.

Bx